# GUN MEISTER ONLINE

## Noah Barnett

"A computer would deserve to be called intelligent if it could deceive a human into believing that it was human."
— Alan Turing

# CHAPTER ONE

## *Character Creation*

Gun Meister Online loading...
Logging into server...
New Player Detected...
Initiating Character Creation...

The game began with an embryo as it floated serenely in the blue-green amniotic fluid. The tiny sexless creature had more in common with a tadpole than an unborn child. It was suspended in a five foot tall cylindrical tube and robotic arms hung from the top with surgical tools.

Slowly a cloning laboratory became visible, which was clinically white. Tubes filled with the same amniotic fluid lined the walls, and as Charlie looked down, he was caught in a moment of vertigo. Through a thick glass floor, thousands of embryonic capsules stretched away into oblivion.

A display appeared in his view. The simple user interface was an opaque white box containing a symbol for each gender. Charlie reached forward touching [Male], and a mix of preset ethnic bodies appeared on the screen. He decided on a tall blond Eastern European, and began to customize the preset character. As he worked, the arms within the tube moved, and little injectors slid into the embryo to prepare his changes.

The generic male face narrowed with a proud chin, thin upturned lips under a hooked nose, and deep set eyes. Charlie gave the character short dirty blond hair, and changed the pupils to brown with flecks of green and gray. His avatar ended up looking like a younger version of himself, but without the imperfections of real life. Though he did add a tiny scar to his right eyebrow, which came from falling out of a tree as a young boy.

At the bottom of the display he hit accept, then confirmed his decision and waited. The body of the infant began to grow. Arms and legs lengthened as hair grew from the boy's scalp. Bubbles filled the cylinder as the child aged. Soon it was a juvenile adult and its brown eyes opened. Although its expression was blank, the boy smiled dimpling cute cheeks. More windows appeared on the console.

"Please select your character's statistics, you have five points which will never increase, so you must decide carefully on how to distribute them. Later you may reset your statistics for a heavy credit cost." Three categories appeared on his display.

The console spoke again as he touched the first word, "Strength determines carrying capacity, and helps with recoil control. Agility affects your movement speed. Endurance determines your stamina pool and adds additional health. Each stat starts with one point, and are capped at four. Spend your extra five points carefully."

He spent about a minute toying with the sliders, because it was permanent. Charlie was only allowed one character for his account, so it was important to be happy with his decision. With a finger he tapped the side of the display, and considered his options. He was going to have to sacrifice somewhere. In the end he settled with one point into strength. Next, was his agility. Moving quickly seemed important, and maxing it was an obvious choice. However, being fast wouldn't do him any good if his stamina was pathetic, so he split his remaining points between them.

[Strength - OO..]
[Agility - OOO.]
[Endurance - OOO.]

The character's stats were average, but if he didn't make a decision soon he would be stuck here all day. Charlie hit the accept button, and bubbles filled the cylinder again as his vision changed. It moved, diving forward into the maturing body. For a second, his senses were overloaded as the amniotic fluid rapidly drained from the cylinder. The case opened exposing his new naked body to the cold antiseptic air. He shivered briefly before stepping out.

The viscous fluid pooled at his bare feet as he looked around. The lab was spartan, except a white plastic table a few feet ahead of him. Heaps of

4

carefully folded towels sat atop, and he grabbed several to dry off. The white plastic surface served as an adequate mirror, so Charlie bent, inspecting his lean body in the reflection. His arms were well defined if a little thin, which was probably due to only having two strength. The distorted image flexed a bicep and grinned back at him. For certain this virtual avatar was in marginally better shape than his real world body.

He looked around for an exit. A closed door was the only entrance into the circular room. Before leaving Charlie wrapped a towel around his waist. Then he padded barefoot towards the exit, and it slid open as he neared. A dark haired young man wearing a gray military uniform stood within a room lined with lockers.

"Welcome to Gun Meister Online. I am Vitale, your guide for this part of character creation." The young man began, unphased by Charlie's near nudity.

"Is this your first time playing?"

"Yes," Charlie said, the astringent smell of a locker room infiltrating his senses.

"You must have many questions." The young man responded and Charlie nodded. He shifted his weight and just barely grabbed the towel before it fell.

"There are a plethora of virtual games, all with roughly the same type of progression. Your character struggles to gain power, skills, and abilities. Not so with Gun Meister. Here your avatar doesn't grow, you do." The young man stated magnanimously. "We strive for a realistic experience. There are no levels, no stat increases, no legendary items, in fact, there is no inventory system at all. We have eliminated the traditional user interface." The young man said with a sympathetic smile, noticing the confusion on Charlie's face.

"In order to access the system menu touch the side of your temple with two fingers." The young man added, then demonstrated by pressing an index and middle fingers to the side of his head. Charlie followed his example. A small window slid over his vision. Listed within the box was Options, Help, and Logout. When he didn't touch anything the display closed.

"How do I get dressed?" Charlie asked.

"The lockers you see contain uniforms of various sizes, and I suggest a middle one with your build." Vitale said pointing to a locker on the right. Inside was black boxers, gray slacks, and a matching military tunic. Underneath the clothes were a pair of socks and combat boots. Charlie took a minute to put them on and immediately felt better. The young man remained where he was passively smiling.

"As you just saw everything must be worn. Guns, equipment, and even ammo will be carried into battle. Winning matches, killing enemies, and surviving will earn you credits. These credits can be used to purchase most items in the game except weapons." His guide said in a rehearsed voice.

"We can't buy guns?" Charlie asked incredulously.

"Gun Meister Online uses a new dynamic NPC system. Every gun in the game is a non-player-character." Charlie's confusion must have been obvious for the young man nodded in sympathy. "It will be easier just to show you what I mean," he said turning to move down the locker room.

Charlie was guided through the next doorway into a firearms mecca. The walls were a glossy plastic, and hanging in glass frames were dozens of weapon diagrams. Several circular velvet lined tables were set up around the chamber, the middle one being the largest. Pistols nestled neatly in clear stands at the edges. So many pistols he couldn't count them all. A soft blue lighting was recessed into the tables, which set off the guns like cars at a show.

He paused upon entering. Charlie had gone directly from an empty cloning lab to a locker room, and now into what could only be described as an armory. It was like being popped out of the womb and handed running shoes. Charlie was left a little disoriented.

"These weapons have volunteered to be here, pick one pistol. Later if you are unsatisfied with the gun you may seek another." Vitale clarified.

Charlie approached the central table eying the pistols like a kid in a candy store. Black semi-autos sat next to sleek chrome revolvers. There were pistols of every description and none were set in a discernible order. He started to orbit the table feeling very overwhelmed. Not every plastic stand was filled. Several were empty and he wondered what had been there before.

California was a very liberal state. Rainbow flags were trendy, and you could buy weed at every corner store. However, the gun laws were onerous, so he knew little except the portrayal of firearms in action movies and cop shows. Finally, he stopped before a small group of pistols. The middle of the table blossomed with light, and a holo-image of a woman appeared floating above the table. She was a goddess in the truest sense, and the most beautiful thing he'd ever seen. She had long golden hair and the bluest eyes imaginable, but it was her breasts that drew his gaze. They were big, juicy, and succulent, and he couldn't help but stare.

Before Charlie, cradled in a clear plastic stand, was a semi-automatic pistol. He reached down picking up the gun. As he did a female voice squealed directly into his ear drum with sheer joy and the image hovering above the table vanished. The pistol was heavier than Charlie expected, but having never held one before, he wasn't sure if this was normal. He lifted it, turning the gun to inspect it in the blue light. Along the side it read 'Colt Government Model - 1911' followed by .45 caliber. After this, there was a stylized picture of a horse.

"Do you accept the gun?" Vitale asked.

Charlie couldn't very well put the pistol down after getting her hopes up. "Yes," he answered turning away from the table. His guide had a look in his eye, and a knowing grin. Charlie flushed in response.

"Go with the pistol into the next room, where she'll take over your instruction. There is much to learn still, so trust in your weapon." Vitale said pointing to the door. Charlie paused and looked back. The young man smiled, nodded to him, and turned to go back into the locker room.

Inside, the shag carpet was a bright cheerful creamy orange. A king sized bed took up almost the entire room and sultry jazz music played in the background.

*"What the hell?"* He thought to himself. Why was he in a bedroom strait out of a cheesy porno?

"Thank you for picking me," A female voice said next to his ear. The pistol within his grasp began to glow yellow. The light grew in intensity until there was a flash, the goddess from the projection was suddenly standing before him. The woman wore only a black bikini, and stood an inch taller than him with long supple legs. Blonde hair fell over her chest in a cascading waterfall of gold. Her brilliant blue eyes danced, as she assessed him. She was easily the most beautiful woman Charlie had ever laid eyes on.

"Wow," he said not knowing what else to say. She smiled turning around slowly for his inspection.

"What is your name?" She asked in a sweet honey and sugar voice.

"Charlie," he said before a question popped into his head. The game hadn't bothered with a name before. Was this a part of his character creation?

"It didn't ask me for one."

"The system generates a unique ID for every player, so you can call yourself anything you like. If you want to go by a specific handle that can be registered later." She replied almost expecting the question.

"What's yours?"

"I don't have one, only an object ID just like you. Unless, you would like to give me one?" She asked hopefully. His very first gun and he even got to name her too. Frankly, he was still a little flustered by her beauty.

"Can we wait on the name?" He asked feeling dizzy. She tilted her head.

"I don't mind, you can change it later."

"I want to think of a good one," he replied and she hummed a sweet note. The noise wasn't quite disapproving, but she crossed both arms over her chest.

"Are you really an NPC?"

"Worried I'm secretly human?" She asked him instead.

"It's just, you are so... life like." He replied and the girl grinned in response. She removed an arm from her chest and touched her chin considering him. Was she measuring his eagerness?

"There are currently one hundred thirty-eight databases. Some are physical responses, others spoken, more are esoteric information. I access these and pick a dozen or so things from the options. My personality causes those responses to be weighted in a particular way. There's also my unique database. All of my experiences are stored here," She said as she tapped her temple. "So that I continue to grow." She finished straightening, and his eyes were drawn back to her chest as it bounced from the movement.

"How do you pick an option, if two are equally weighted?" He asked and she put a hand to her face in surprise.

"Awww, that is so cute," she said her voice a kitten's purr. Reaching forward she caressed his face with a soft skinned hand then added, "You *are* curious about me." Despite his thirty years of age, he flushed from the contact and she smiled.

"Shall we begin?"

"Begin?" He asked swallowing hard.

"The contract needs to be fulfilled," she coo'd sweetly while moving toward the bed. The woman turned to face him, and her blonde hair fell partially over her chest again. "I'm really happy you asked about me. Please let me be your weapon."

"What do I need to do?" He asked, feeling heat rush over his face.

Instead of answering she reached behind her neck and pulled on the string. Her top fell to the floor, and he gulped as blood rushed away from his brain. Glorious gods above, never before had he seen such a perfect pair of breasts. They were like pillowed melons with perky quarter-sized areola. All the gears within his mind ground to an immediate halt as his groin leaped to attention. Charlie barely noticed as the bikini bottom slid down her legs to the carpet. She sat naked on the bed beckoning him closer, and like a man on a leash stepped toward her.

She unzipped him pushing his trousers down his legs, which was all it took. Charlie dragged his tunic over his head and tossed it to the ground next to her bikini. She laid back on the mattress, and her golden hair made a halo around her head. Charlie fought with his shoelaces before he kicked

9

his boots free, then slid his pants off, and mounted the bed. He regretted not giving her a name, but he still couldn't think of one. There was a metallic fruity smell to her skin as she pulled Charlie closer. Their mouths touched, lips pressing together, and their tongues wrestled. She tasted sweet like cotton candy.

"Make me yours," she begged pulling him between her legs. His manhood prodded open the entrance to her sex, and as he plunged fully inside, she gasped. Her insides clamped down on his erection, and they both moaned from the intense sensation. Her arms and legs wrapped around his body keeping him from withdrawing. He was too busy sucking on her incredible breasts to notice a collar circle her neck. It started off a clear plastic, but the longer he made love to her, the darker it grew until it was completely black. Numbers began to glow on the band a faint yellow, which was his unique ID. It was ten minutes later when he finished. Charlie wasn't as young as he used to be, nor as practiced. She was still smiling though as he withdrew from her.

"Please make good use of me," she said moving to the edge of the bed, so she could gather her bikini. She began to dress by first tying her bottom back on. Charlie followed her example still rather dazed by the experience.

"Just so you know. Our contract must be reaffirmed once a month," the woman said gazing at his naked rear. He had turned away to pull on his boxers but paused. "I would prefer daily, though," she continued. So that was why he'd gone through so many hoops to confirm his identity. The game had been rated mature and required his social security number before he could finalize his account. At the time he'd assumed it was because of the violence.

"I think I'd enjoy that too, but what happens if we don't?" Charlie asked with interest. There was bound to be people that stopped playing the game. Either because of money or loss of interest. She touched her neck lightly fingering the black collar, and it was only now he noticed it.

"This will start to fade, and when it becomes clear it will fall off. Afterward, a weapon may pick a new Meister to serve." She said tracing Charlie's Player ID on the collar.

"Am I your first Meister?" He asked. She smirked at him with a sly and lustful look in her eye.

"You are, Charlie. I was created two months ago." She admitted still giving him another long look. Charlie had essentially, popped her cherry. What man didn't get a rush from that?

"So you've been sitting in that room for two months?" He asked.

"No," she said with a playful smirk. "We unregistered pistols took shifts. There's an apartment complex nearby for weapons that don't have owners. We are pampered like royalty. I made many friends while I waited for a Meister. It's good for growing our personalities." She said standing and putting a hand on her hip.

"What happens now?" He asked not quite hiding the glance at the bed. The sheets were tangled and rumpled from their lovemaking.

"You have some options at this point. We could reaffirm the contract." She said stepping towards him. Her fingers brushed his face, but he caught her wrist. Even virtually, it was a little too soon for a second round. Her fine features turned momentarily sulky from disappointment, but she quickly rallied.

"Weapons training would be the next step. We'll also need to go shopping for a holster and ammunition." She said stepping away from him.

"I don't have any money."

She shook her head. "Your credit account is attached to your ID. Any money is drawn and deposited automatically."

"Whatever you think is best."

The blonde gave a last long look at the disheveled bed before turning away. Sex apparently was an intense part of her personality. Her blue eyes flashed with an inner light when she glanced back over her shoulder.

"Do you feel pleasure?" He asked following after her dangerously swaying hips.

"Of course, I receive the same sensory signals you do. The data is stored in my personal fileshare, but most is placed in short-term memory." She stated opening the door and exited the suite.

The strange bedroom opened onto a balcony overlooking the lobby, and dozens of players were moving around below. Women in skimpy black bathing suits were following men in gray military uniforms out of the glass doors. There were male guns as well which surprised him. A massive ebony-skinned Olympian strolled next to a tiny doll like girl through the lobby. His leg and back muscles rippled in the sunlight. The black speedo he wore was, in Charlie's opinion, way too revealing. The girl was a few inches over four feet tall with teal hair and a childishly flat chest. The weapon, by comparison, was over six and a half feet tall with arms like a tree trunk. Charlie stared at the two in amazement.

His companion noticed the pair and said, "Ahh, Philip found a Meister."

"You know him?" Charlie asked watching them leave the lobby.

"He's been there for six months. Not many people can handle the .500 Magnum in combat." She mused leaning over the balcony.

"Do you think that girl can do it?" He asked watching them through the large glass doors. The pair joined the crowd of pedestrians and quickly disappeared in the throng.

"They have a small body which indicates a low strength score. Either she's in it for the sex or she's planned a loadout. I hope it's an experienced player starting over with a new character."

"Loadout?" Charlie asked curiously. He followed the woman as she strode toward a set of stairs.

"Even with max strength, you can only carry so many guns. Most players go into combat with two weapons that compliment each other, along with a sidearm. That usually leaves enough weight for armor, magazines, and grenades." The girl said walking forward with those swaying hips.

"Did I screw up by only having two strength?" He asked and she glanced back at him. She eyed his thin but muscled arms. The character tutorial said he could reset his stats, but Charlie hoped he didn't have too.

"It depends on your play style. Two points will let you carry two primary weapons. They'll be light guns with limited ammo, but you can still do it." The woman said moving down the stairs. Charlie followed his guide across the lobby and out of the building. Just outside they passed another lounging player. The Meister was a muscular Asian man who was deep in conversation with a buxom oriental. If strength determined a player's size then this man was maxed out, and Charlie was starting to feel uncommonly average. Everyone was either a giant or ultra slim and short.

*"Two rifles and a sidearm,"* he thought. That would mean three women, and that... in turn meant even more sex!

"You're thinking about it, aren't you." The blonde teased and he coughed.

"No," he answered quickly and she laughed.

"You are, men always do." She said humor coloring her words. The girl didn't seem bothered by the notion of sharing as she continued to tease him. "I hope you have the stamina to keep us all registered."

"Where do we go to train?" He asked trying desperately to change the subject. Her blue eyes rolled at his evasion though she lifted a hand. With a finger she pointed to a large shopping center two blocks down, where a constant stream of people were heading. This wasn't Nigmus Online or one of the other big name MMO's, but there were enough people to fill the pedestrian sidewalk. His companion strolled along next to him completely unconcerned, or maybe she was just used to the sight.

Charlie walked up the street following other players. Many had multiple guns. A few paces ahead a good looking woman strolled lazily. A pink heavily modified AK-47 was slung over her shoulder with little adorable cell-phone dolls hanging from the rifle sling. A candy colored pistol sat in a holster at her waist. Next to her, another man walked with his arms wrapped around two beautiful women. Both were scantily clad in silk sarongs. One vixen said something to the camo-covered male and he laughed squeezing her waist.

The size of the city surprised him, especially for a simple combat shooter. It felt a bit like San Francisco. The sun was bright on his skin and the wind off the bay was pleasantly swift. This wasn't what he'd expected. The name 'Gun Meister' conjured images of dark alleys with oil and blood flowing in the gutters. Instead he was confronted with a modern paradise.

They approached the shopping mall and entered through the double glass doors. A marble tiled food court took up most of the lobby. A brightly lit central hallway led deeper within, and colorful signs indicated a multitude of wares each store sold. The amount of upgrades he could buy was mind boggling. He passed stores selling night sights, red dots, lasers, rubber grips, compensators, silencers, and upgraded triggers. Charlie had no idea what most of the items did but there were lots to choose from.

Finally, they walked into a store which sold holsters of every description. Charlie followed his companion past shelves of magazine holders and shot bandoleers. They came to a counter near the back of the store. An old grizzled man sat in front of a glass window, beyond which he could see people practicing. The shots sounded like distant firecrackers.

"I need a lane and a box of ammo. He'll need some eyes and ears too."

The old shopkeep glanced up from his tablet. A white cardboard box, a pair of ear plugs, and a set of plastic glasses were set on the counter. "Put your hand on the terminal," he rasped gesturing to the display. It was facing Charlie and he rested his palm on the flat screen. An ID number flashed on the screen followed by a thousand credit balance. The ammo and range time would cost twenty-five credits bringing him down to 975c. He pressed 'yes' to the charge.

"Lane two is open."

Charlie put the glasses on, placed the plugs in his ears, and walked into the gun range. Eight or so players fired rifles, pistols, and tight little sub-machine guns. None even glanced at him as he walked past.

"There is a lot of people here," Charlie shouted looking around.

"Not really, there's a more interactive range in the competition hall. This is just a place to test out weapon upgrades." His companion said and set the white box on the shooting bench.

"I'm going to tell you the rules for handling a gun. If you don't want to look like a dumbass I suggest you follow them. There is no such thing as friendly fire, and accidentally shooting a teammate will cost you money and reputation." She announced in a deadly serious tone.

"First, the gun is always loaded. You treat me like I'm ready to fire at all times." She said and he nodded quickly.

"Second, keep your finger off the trigger until you are ready to shoot. I will remind you gently at first, then with increasingly stronger words. Most accidents happen because people have terrible trigger discipline."

"Third, don't point the gun at anything you do not want killed. That includes that precious piece of equipment between your legs." She stated and he laughed.  Her blue eyes flashed with inner light as she glared at him, and he swallowed hard.

"Fourth, know your target, and what lies beyond it. Don't shoot at shadows, it could be a teammate. I already mentioned what will happen if you partake in unfriendly fire." She said holding up a fourth finger. "Inspect me before you start," she said and closed her eyes. Her white skin started to glow and Charlie had to look away. There was a flash and a pistol was laying on the bench. He stepped forward and picked up the gun. He was reminded again of how deadly the 1911 looked, and it's weight was reassuring in his hands.

"Your finger is on my trigger," she whispered next to his ear and he started at the sound. Just great, he'd already fucked up. It was so easy to just put it in there, like it belonged. "Keep it straight out along the side of the frame," she added after a second. When he complied she continued in a more friendly voice. "On the left side is the magazine release."

He tilted the weapon seeing a round nub next to the trigger guard. This he pushed with his thumb and an empty box slid free from the bottom of the gun. Opening the cardboard box revealed two plastic racks of ammo with a hundred rounds in total. Charlie picked up and held one in his palm admiring the size of the fat cartridge, then slid the first bullet in. He continued to load until he'd managed to squeeze in seven. That didn't seem like very many but they were big rounds. Slowly he pushed the boxy thing back into the grip. It slid home with a satisfying click.

"In order to fire you need to charge me. Remove the manual safety then rack the slide." She instructed in his ear. He followed her instruction a little awkwardly. Using his thumb he flicked the safety catch down then grabbed the slide and pulled back. There was a flash of brass before a bullet was pushed into the chamber.

"Aim at the target with the top of the sights. Keep the middle post equal with the others." She said and he pulled the trigger. The pistol jerked in his hands as the 1911 barked loudly. Three meters down range he completely missed the target.

"Squeeze my trigger gently or I might be rough with you later tonight," she admonished. He blushed despite the tone she used on him. Charlie aimed, really aimed at the target this time. When the gun fired a hole appeared in the silhouette below and to the left of center. He smiled, pleased with his effort.

"Keep at it, ammo is cheap so fire until it's all gone."

That's exactly what Charlie did, and for the next thirty minutes, he kept shooting at the target. He felt quite proud of himself for hitting it most of the time. Towards the end, he barely noticed the weight of the pistol in his hands. When the last bullet was fired the slide locked back, and he stood there smelling the gunpowder in the air. Players around him were still shooting in their own lanes.

"Done?" She asked.

"Yes," he replied and the gun began to glow. She appeared next to him and glanced down range. Her expression was suspiciously neutral when she looked back at him.

"Good job," she lied and he too glanced at the target. It was filled with holes, enough to make it look like swiss cheese. To him, it looked dead as a doornail and he mentally shrugged.

"I kinda have to pee," he admitted.

"Then you should logout. The system will let through body signals. You'll know it when you are hungry, tired, or need to answer nature's call." She stated and he quickly glanced around.

"What do I do?"

"For now let's go out to the store then find a seat and log out. Your body won't disappear when you exit. Soon you'll need to consider where to live but that's for later." She said and they left the range. Charlie returned the ear plugs and shooting glasses. They found a seat and he touched his temple with two fingers. The pop-up appeared and he quickly pressed the logout button.

# CHAPTER TWO

## *Match*

His eyes slowly focused. Charlie was sitting in an easy chair within his tiny living room. The television was on, and a news reporter was blathering about labor riots. Gingerly, he removed the virtual dive helmet and set it on the coffee table. Charlie stood stretching, then went into the bathroom to relieve himself. Afterward he returned to the chair, sat down, and pulled the dive helmet back on. The padded device fit snugly over his head. He pushed a lock of hair away from his eyes before settling back. Reaching up Charlie touched the activation button and waited while the helmet started. There was a slight humming noise as it scanned his brain. Then the world faded away.

A blonde goddess was curled in his lap purring. Her chest pressed against him as she clawed gently at his stomach with her long fingernails. Charlie's body had relaxed when he logged out, and he sat up from the awkward slouch. She looked up scanning his face with those sky blue eyes.

"What would you like to do now?" She asked batting her long lashes at him. "We could look for a place," the girl offered rather quickly.

"Let's play the game."

"That works too," she admitted sliding from his lap. Her body swiveled to face him making her breasts jiggle again.

"You mentioned a holster and ammo," he said standing awkwardly. As casually as he could, Charlie adjusted the bulge within his pants. Then followed the blonde into the first section where they sold holsters.

"What kind of holster do you prefer?" She asked.

"I have no idea. I've never owned a gun, before you." He said and she touched her chin.

"As a full-sized pistol frame, I'd suggest hip or leg carry. Really though you may just have to experiment," she offered turning away.

After searching through the hundreds of choices he found a leg holster he was satisfied with. Two straps buckled around his upper thigh, and a kydex lock secured the gun so it didn't rattle. Admittedly he was more impressed by how tactical it looked. Ammo they found near the entrance, and the person behind the counter glanced up from a tablet as he approached.

"Can I help you?" The clerk asked.

"I need point four five caliber ammunition," Charlie said proud he'd remembered the bullet type. His ego though took a dive as the clerk started to laugh. The man waved a hand apologetically.

"You must be new, but just say Forty-Five ACP."

Charlie was left feeling a bit embarrassed. "You'll just hand me ammo? People walk around with loaded guns?" He asked incredulously.

"If you'll pardon my French miss, guns aren't worth a damn without bullets." The clerk replied dipping his head towards his blonde companion. She shrugged in response but said nothing. "To answer your question yes, people do walk around with loaded guns." The clerk replied turning. On his hip was a holstered pistol of his own, and Charlie was surprised by the sight.

"Player?" He asked.

"Yep, I get paid to man the counter just like in real life. They tried an NPC but people kept getting confused and buying the wrong caliber ammunition."

"What prevents someone from killing another player in town?" Charlie asked making the clerk laugh again.

"Oh god, I love noobies. Nothing prevents you from blowing someone's brains out. Two reasons it doesn't happen often. Everyone else has a gun too. Pull it out and most people will draw on you out of habit. If you do manage to kill someone, they'll instantly respawn. You, however, will earn an immediate twenty-four-hour ban. If you don't learn your lesson it's seven days. If for some inexplicable reason you feel the need to do it a third time, the ban is permanent. They'll lock the account and blacklist the dive helmet or immersion pod you're logged in with." The shop clerk said while reorganizing the other boxes of ammo. Charlie resolved to keep his pistol holstered.

"Thanks for the help," Charlie said paying for his items. The holster cost him thirty-five credits and the ammo ten more.

"You'll need to find a corner to load your girl up." The clerk offered winking and pointing to a quiet little spot next to the entrance. Charlie thanked the man a second time and left the store. Just outside he found the bench and sat down. His weapon changed, vanishing from her human form to lay on his lap.

"After inserting the magazine, rack the slide, and engage the safety. Then push me into the holster until it locks." She instructed and he did so. Charlie had a bunch of ammo left so he stuck the box into his tunic pocket.

"Where do I go next?" He asked sliding from the bench.

"Go outside, take a left, and follow the main road to the competition center. It's in the middle of the city, you can't miss it." She replied. Charlie walked up the street following other players.

It took about ten minutes of walking, but the Competition building came into view. It was oval shaped like a stadium and festooned with streamers all over. Advertisements for real-life and in-game products liberally dotted the structure. He followed several players as they made for the main entrance.

Just inside was a huge gaming club. Hundreds of people milled about watching the battles or talking shop. A single large screen dominated the area above a reception desk. This showed a fight currently going on. There was a smoke grenade spewing its contents into a trash filled alley. Bullets were flying back and forth between several people. A man slid through the smoke with an SMG spraying rounds. He managed to kill one person before getting shot himself. It was so cool, so very bad ass.

"First day?" A girl asked and Charlie looked down. He hadn't realized he'd been staring at the screen. She was slightly built with pink hair, pink lipstick, and a pink top.

"Umm, yeah."

"That's great! Would you like the run down?" She asked in a bubbly voice and he nodded. "Put your palm on the console." The receptionist said pointing to his left. A screen rested there waiting for input, and he pressed his hand to the screen face. It quickly read his ID and displayed his statistics.

---

**Player ID - NA1339872**
**Registered Competition Name - None**
**Clan - None**
**Hours played - 1**

**Wins - 0**
**Losses - 0**

**Kills - 0**
**Deaths - 0**
**K/D Ratio - 0**

**Battle Rank - Bronze One**
**Player Score - 1000**

**Credits - 930**

Next to this was a snapshot of his face, and Charlie was glad he'd made his character look like himself. The bubbly receptionist leaned over the counter. "Do you see these two lines?" She asked pointing to his battle rank and his player score. "Everyone starts in the bronze rank. There are five levels to this class before you become silver. They begin with Bronze One then Two, Three, Four, and Master." The girl said pulling out a sheet, which was a list of ranks by metal type.

**Division Ranks are broken into five sub-ranks.**
One

**Two**
**Three (Skilled)**
**Four (Elite)**
**Master**

<u>**Division Ranks**</u>
**Bronze - New to the game. Only one pistol allowed with limited upgrades.**
**Silver - Earn one new contract. Can now use primary weapons and armor.**
**Gold - Third contract. May now buy grenades, explosives, and high tier items.**
**Platinum - Fourth contract.**
**Diamond - Six contracts.**
**Tungsten - Ten contracts.**

*"Ten contracts!"* Charlie thought to himself. That was a lot of guns to keep registered.

"To rank up you generally just play the game. I should warn you that you can only play two registered competition matches each day. The developers want people to take their score seriously. Of course you can play as many casual games as you like. It's a good way to make money and gain skill at the same time. Kills and deaths aren't held against your player statistics." She said, before pausing to see if he had any questions.

"Am I going to get destroyed my first game?" Charlie asked.

"Don't worry, the system only pits people near the same rank together. Bronze players are limited to pistols only. Think of it like a warming up period. You get used to the game without the complexity of all the weapons."

"How long does it take to rank up if you can only play twice a day?" He asked looking over the sheet. Again he saw how many contracts a Tungsten ranked player could have, and all he could imagine was a bed full of beautiful women.

"Most players rank up in a week. Ten to twenty games is normal. Skilled players have ranked up as fast as two days. Wins and losses mainly determine your battle rank. Player score measures your combat effectiveness. Every time you kill an enemy you gain some of their points, you gain more if their score is higher than yours. When you're killed some of your points go to the other player. Player score will add weight for the system to place you in the correct rank." The girl informed him. Charlie took in a long breath to focus. This was a lot to take in at once. She continued after a few seconds. "It's called BR for battle rank and P-Score respectively, but why don't we sign you up for a game?" She asked gesturing towards the console again. The girl leaned over and tapped a few menu items. Quick Death-Match and Quick Team-Battle appeared on the screen. There were more options below for custom competition games.

"Which should I pick?"

"Team battles are easier to win but a death match is more straightforward. Just kill everyone you see." She said in a cotton-candy voice. He selected 'Quick Death-Match' making the box flash several times.

"Match registered, enter game lounge 46," appeared on the screen. As the words vanished the girl clapped enthusiastically.

"Head to the elevator and good luck," she cheered pointing to the left. A set of ten tubes were set up in a ring, and people were getting in and out in waves. The first one opened and several people got out. Quickly he stepped into the tube. Instead of buttons there was a flat screen. When he touched the console, the doors closed, and the elevator started down. It opened on a private lounge with several couches and viewing screens where several players already waited.

"Please exit and wait while the other participants gather," A chibi robotic voice said, and he left the elevator. He'd barely made it ten steps into the room before a chime sounded several times. His vision began to darken then go black. Words appeared floating before his face.

### [Match Starting]

Someone had taken World War III and dropped it on a quiet Minnesotan town. A red school bus was partially covered in rubble. Brightly colored streamers were strung across the street as if everything had gone to shit right before a parade. A thick red line was bisecting an old two-door Datsun. Approaching the line he found he couldn't move past it. An invisible wall prevented him from walking out of the area. He stroked a hand across the red and his fingertips went completely numb. Charlie flexed his hand in an attempt to regain the feeling back into his fingers.

The hairs on Charlie's neck stood up on end and his heart rate began to climb. Thumbing the button on his leg holster he drew the pistol. The metal was cold against his skin but the weight was reassuring.

"What do I do?" He asked nervously.

"I can't tell you that. In this form, I have no eyes to see, nor ears to hear. You are the Gun Meister, I am the tool." His weapon said into his mind. She spoke with an easy tone but Charlie felt the reprimand. "Well, you probably should take my safety off," she added after a few seconds. Charlie awkwardly thumbed the lever off the slide. He took a breath, then another as his heart continued to thump away. He needed to get his act together. At first, he crouched next to the rusty Datsun waiting in silence, and listened to the sound of the streamers flapping in the wind. The buildings nearby were filled with bullet holes. A restaurant had been gutted by an explosion spreading glass across the street. The red line inched across the car. It wasn't noticeable at first but the boundary was slowly shrinking, and soon he'd be forced to move. He decided the bus was a better choice and he climbed up on the rubble. It shifted under his weight making something inside the vehicle crash.

"Shit!" he cried rolling down the pile. The top of the bus caved in making a huge dust cloud. He stood from the rubble and started walking away. Street stores dominated this side of the road, and businesses had put out aging displays for the parade. Windows were filled with empty and sagging balloons. He tried darting to one of the doorways but it was locked. Charlie continued from store to store before he saw the perfect place. A narrow alleyway led between two buildings, and he sprinted across the street.

As he got to the alley entrance, Charlie ran into another player already there. The man wore the same gray tunic and trousers as him, but had brown hair and an athletic build. The other player was maybe ten meters down the alley and did something unexpected. He started screaming at the top of his lungs as he charged at Charlie. A dark menacing handgun rose into view and a bullet whizzed past his head. In response, Charlie lifted his pistol and pulled the trigger as fast as he could. Again and again the gun barked. In the narrow passage the sound was deafening, like someone was boxing his ears with each pull of the trigger. A bullet missed his arm by scarcely an inch, then another hit the dumpster he stood next to.

It was pure luck that won the battle. His last bullet, by chance, struck the other man in the head right between the eyes. Blood and brains sprayed out coating the alley behind him, and the man crumpled to the ground. Charlie kept pulling the trigger even though the slide was locked back. For almost a minute he stood there looking at the corpse as adrenaline and pure terror filled his veins.

"Calm down, Charlie. The game will eject you if your heart rate doesn't drop." His gun said sharply into his ear. Charlie sagged to his knees and fell back onto his ass. The gun shook in his trembling hands. His gorge rose as he breathed in the acrid metallic tang of blood and gunpowder. Forcing his eyes closed, he turned away from the gruesome sight.

"I thought you said you couldn't see," Charlie said after conquering his urge to retch.

"My sense of touch is heightened. I can feel your pulse pounding and hear your words via the grip." She said to him. Charlie tried to calm his pounding heart by thinking of something. He needed a distraction, anything to take his mind off the bloody corpse nearby. A name for his weapon suddenly struck him.

"Elva," he said still clutching the pistol.

"What?"

"Your name will be Elva," he replied feeling his pulse slowly calm.

"I like it," she said after a few seconds. He smiled before finally noticing the pistol was empty. Clumsily he shifted the gun to drop the magazine. The white box of ammo fumbled from his grasp and fell to the ground. It broke open and bullets carelessly spilled out. Holstering the gun he started nervously slotting the large rounds into the magazine, and loaded the pistol as Elva had instructed at the shooting range. Why hadn't he bought some extra magazines? What a bone-headed thing to forget. That was something he needed to look into. After the weapon was charged, Charlie tried to put as many of the dropped bullets back into his pocket. If he was lucky he might need them later.

He was about to stand when Elva spoke, "Are you OK?"

Charlie paused looking back at the body. He hadn't expected such a visceral response to the fight, but maybe that was why the other man had started yelling. The war-cry had forced him forward. "What happens to him?" Charlie asked eying the corpse with distaste as it began to decompose.

"The person will respawn in the competition lobby," Elva reminded him. Charlie turned and left the awful stink behind.

"How many people are left?"

"I don't know exactly. There are ten players in each competition match. You killed one which leaves eight opponents left, if the others are all still alive." Charlie tried to remember if he had heard any gunshots. The fight itself was a blur in his memory, but he didn't recall hearing any before now. At the mouth of the alley, he stopped and looked both ways. The red bus was halfway down the street. The shops remained as before, ready to open for the day. From above an alarm sounded like a clipped air siren starting and stopping. It cut off after a few seconds.

"What was that buzzer?" Charlie asked.

"Half of the time remains. Each match at bronze level is only twenty minutes long. New players often 'camp' until fewer enemies remain. As the time runs out they will become more aggressive." Elva informed him. Her words heralded a short series of pops in the distance, which was followed by a loud boom.

"Twenty minutes doesn't seem like a lot of time," he whispered quietly. It worried him that the combat was only a few blocks away.

"At silver level it goes up to forty minutes. Gold matches can last an hour, at platinum it's two. Diamond is four and tungsten are eight hours." Elva whispered back into his ear.

"Is that why there are only two games a day?" Charlie asked. His mind boggled at the time investment. A top ranked player might spend sixteen hours in combat. He honestly couldn't imagine doing that.

"Yes."

His body was still coming down from the battle cocktail so he crouched in the eaves of a bookstore. The red line was over the bus, and it was creeping visibly closer forcing him down the street. More gunshots rang out followed by a longer exchange. Charlie flinched against the doorway because of a cannon-like boom nearby.

Less than a minute later he saw a new player. It was a tiny girl with long teal hair and Charlie recognized her from character creation. She was the loli with no chest. Now she was dressed in a black tank top and desert-camo shorts. The player walked along the middle of the road slowly scanning the shops, and Charlie tightened his grip on Elva. If this were real life it would be slick with his sweat. He kept telling himself he could do this. The girl was just strolling along, not even running. She was maybe twenty meters away and coming closer. About a block away several pistols exchanged fire, and the girl stopped to turn in that direction. This was his chance. Charlie rolled out of the doorway and came up crouched. The small sights entered his field of view and he started shooting. The roar deafened him but he fired again anyway. As he did the girl fell onto her face. It was over in seconds and his slide locked back. After a long pause the short girl stood up and fear tickled his heart. She was completely unhurt as she drew her pistol. He threw himself back into the doorway of the store.

"Fuck," he cursed loudly. Elva said nothing to this as he ejected the magazine. He fumbled even more clumsily to get the loose ammo out of his tunic pocket, and his fingers struggled to fill the magazine. Around the corner came the girl with the biggest revolver he'd ever seen. It was chrome silver with a bore so huge he could see the bullet.

He stared at the rifled grooves before the girl spoke in a childishly high voice, "You should take the time to aim."

"I surrender..." he said weakly lifting his hands up. The loose bullets and magazine rolled off his lap to the ground. A girlish giggle escaped her lips.

"You're silly," she said pulling the trigger. For a second he'd considered lunging the five feet and grabbing the gun. Instead, something slammed into his chest, and he was thrown backward through the glass door of the shop. It was like someone had slugged him right on the breastbone. He lay there for a few seconds struggling to breathe before everything went black. The darkness lasted only a second or two then a door slid open before him. The sound of people talking reached his ears.

"That girl is a fucking smurf," a male voice complained.

"I know right! Why the hell do people do that?" Someone else groused.

Charlie stepped out into a small private lounge. Leather couches and plush chairs circled a set of television screens. The largest of which displayed a quiet Minnesota town. The teal haired girl was loading a round into her magnum revolver.

"What's going on?" He asked and four men turned to look at him.

"Noob," a gray-clad man sneered.

"This is the match lobby. We're stuck here until the game ends." The brown haired man said. It was the person he'd killed in the alley. The man didn't seem angry at all, accepting his death with tact.

"That doesn't sound fair," Charlie said thinking about the tungsten players needing to wait upwards of eight hours, but he supposed they could just log out.

"It's so losers can't cheat and give information away. People started bringing virtual cell phones into the match to help friends when they died." The first said in that sneering tone like it would be obvious to anyone. A timer above the middle screen continued to tick down. It rolled past six minutes on its march to zero.

After his death, it didn't take long. Charlie watched the little girl kill everyone left. She did the same thing as before. Strolling along the street until something happened. Then she'd throw herself to the ground and get behind cover waiting for the other player to run out of ammo. She would then move in for the kill.

The red border forced everyone together into a single shop, and she cleaned up as each player ran inside. More people quickly filled the lounge. When she was the only one left, the match ended, and the elevator doors opened with a ding. Everyone, save the smurf, filed inside.

"At least she didn't clean sweep," the complaining man said kicking a side panel. Still, the girl did kill most of them. The elevator rose upward stopping at the main lounge. Music and conversation filled the air and the nine combatants quickly went their own ways. Charlie wasn't sure what to do next. He supposed he could play another match but his nerves said otherwise, so he started towards the exit.

"Congratulations!!!" A bubbly voice shouted from behind him. Charlie turned to see the receptionist exploding a party popper over his head. Sparkles and red confetti rained down.

"I died," he complained with a frown.

"You got a kill, that's quite impressive. It's very hard to win death matches." She complimented with a wide grin.

"If it's so hard why do people do it?" He asked and the girl giggled.

"Credits of course, deathmatches reward a lot more." She said beckoning him over to the booth. There she pulled out a small pamphlet.

---

**[Competition money and you]**
**Winning a Team Match = 2000c**
**Winning a Death Match = 10,000c**
**Killing an enemy = 100 x Battle Rank x Weapon Multiplier.**
**(Bronze 1, Silver 2, Gold 4, Platinum 6, Diamond 10, Tungsten 20)**
**(Explosives 1, Rifles 1, SMG's 1.25, Pistols 2, Melee 10)**
**Team Killing = Costs 1000c credits and reduces your player score by ten points.**
**Casual Match Kills = 100 x Weapon Multiplier (Battle Rank is not factored)**

---

"In a Team match you have an even chance of winning. If you die your team can still pull through, but in a deathmatch it's entirely up to you. There are more enemies as well which means more money." She said clapping her hands.

"For example let's take your kill. You got two hundred credits for killing that bronze player. A silver player would reward you four hundred for a pistol kill. If you ever happen to knife a diamond player it is worth ten thousand credits." She said gesturing excitedly to the console. Charlie put his palm on the display. His K/D ratio had risen to 1.0, and he now had 1130 credits. The only negative was the fact he had one loss.

"Competition matches do track your stats, but Casual matches do not. In my opinion, you shouldn't worry about it so much. Just have fun." The girl said seeing his expression.

"What's a smurf?" He asked remembering something he'd heard earlier.

"It is an experienced player in a lower ranked game. The girl who killed you was probably a gold or platinum player wishing to start over. Sometimes they do that to change their appearance or stat distribution." The receptionist said and clapped him on the shoulder. "I hope you enjoy the game," She said excitedly and he nodded his thanks. The girl had gone out of her way to welcome him, but he was done for the day. Charlie liked the game for certain. He just needed some time to cool down.

# CHAPTER THREE

## *All work...*

Real life took hold slowly, and Charlie's eyes focused on the dimly lit apartment. He licked his dry lips and took the dive helmet off. His hair was damp and matted to his head, but that was nothing compared to the swamp lake his armpits were swimming in. Even now his heart was still beating unnaturally fast in his chest. Nearby a gray house cat meowed at him before wandering into the kitchen.

He set the helmet on the coffee table and climbed on shaky legs to his feet. Before anything else happened, he was going to shower. His muddy legs carried him into the bathroom where he undressed. While the hot water ran over him, he had time to think. Time to consider what had happened in Gun Meister Online so far. He would never have thought shooting a gun could be so scary and exciting. The feel of it in his hands, the sound of the explosions, and the recoil. It was like magic. The practice had been almost cathartic.

Up until a few days ago the dive helmet had belong to his roommate whom he shared the two bedroom apartment with. Alex had sold most of his possessions, and left in a hurry saying he was planning to chase ghosts in the Caribbean Isles. After trying out Gun Meister, he understood why Alex spent so much time locked in his room. After the quick shower he dressed in new boxers and pants. The cat was still in the kitchen when he entered, and it laid lazily on the counter licking itself. As he neared Fizzgig stopped cleaning long enough to meow at him again.

"You probably need food," he said glancing toward the cat bowl. Yep, it was empty so he poured in some dry mix. Immediately Fizzgig leaped to the tile floor and started to eat.

"Sorry about that," He muttered putting the cat food away. Charlie opened the fridge and inspected his options. There was a three day old pizza that hadn't tasted right the first time, a couple of yogurt cups getting close to their expiration date, two half empty jars of pickles, and some very brown looking lettuce. It wasn't like he didn't have money. After all he managed to keep the apartment by himself. He just didn't like cooking or grocery shopping. His options were limited so he chose the least likely to cause dysentery. Grabbing the yogurt he opened one, then sniffed, fetched a spoon, and sat down in the living room.

The news was droning on as he ate. A high school was on the screen, students jubilantly fleeing their studies for more interesting activities. The reporter and cameraman moved forward.

"What do you think of the invasion of virtual online games?" The man asked a couple of teenage girls. In the background several buses were pulling away from the curb.

"Like eww, why can't dive junkies just enjoy life like normal people." She said in a California girl accent.

"I know right! It's just so ugly nerds can get off like perverts," her friend added.

Charlie winced inwardly and thought, *"Well doesn't that strike a little close to home?"* He suspected the spoiled brat would be pumping out babies before she got her diploma.

"What about the people that have anxiety disorders or medical conditions?" The reporter asked goading the girls.

"Umm... like, so what? It's like, up to them if they want to live in their own heads. Good riddance." The first girl replied and the camera panned away.

"You heard it directly from the mouth of our youth. America isn't buying the virtual hype." The reporter said as the screen changed. Those two girls had been stupid little twits but they hadn't been wrong. Having a virtual machine in the US was looked down upon. Like being gay in the 80's or 90's. It was whispered about with sneers and side-long glances. The name, 'Dive Junkies' had quickly been adopted. Alex had been a shut in for two years, and barely left his room to eat and shower. Somehow he'd always managed to pay his share of the rent though, which was all that mattered to Charlie.

The news report went on to describe the skyrocketing attention foreign nations were giving to Virtual Technology.

The first game to become ultra popular had been Nigmus Online. Even after four years the MMO boasted ten million players. From what he understood most games—including Gun Meister Online—were now based on the engine Nigmus used.

A meow caught his attention. Fizzgig looked up at him with big yellow eyes before jumping up into his lap. For a few seconds, Charlie absently scratched the cat behind the ears.

"TV off," he said as a set of long commercials started. The eighty-inch plasma screen died with a little blip.

It was still early, but Charlie felt strangely tired. In any case, tomorrow was a work day. He stood from the living room chair and wandered into the bedroom. Undressing he crawled into bed and fell asleep almost immediately.

The second hand ticked passed twenty on its slow march into infinity. Charlie told himself he wasn't watching it creep along towards the end of his suffering. The clock hung, conveniently, on the wall above the whiteboard, and it was impossible for anyone not to stare at it. Twenty-five seconds was vaulted and soon it would be thirty. Why did this meeting have to take so long? Charlie wanted to go home, drop into his living room chair, and log into Gun Meister to kill someone. It was quickly starting to consume his attention. The game was as frightening as a nightmare, but right now he'd die a hundred deaths to be away from this meeting.

"I want you all to think positively. Smile because a buyer isn't going to fork over money to a sourpuss." A man at the front of the room said, and grinned at them all. Irvin was a fifty-five year old rotund man with balding hair and a thin mustache. As always he was dressed in gray slacks buckled around a substantial paunch.

"Come on, everyone smile!" Irvin said lifting his hands up. Charlie glanced around the meeting room. Thirty or so people were showing teeth in plastic smiles. Their eyes though, like his, were glossed over. Today was the mandatory monthly meeting, and it was a ritual Charlie had slowly come to despise almost as much as the boss himself. He shifted his gaze forward and smiled as well. The job wouldn't be so bad if his boss weren't such an insipid moron. Irvin nodded and clicked the remote. The projected image changed to a picture of a map.

"You also need a plan," he said and pointed to someone in the front row. "Chad, I have a million dollars and it's yours if you can get from California to New York."

"I'll try my best."

"Of course you will, it's a million dollars cash, but all I'm going to give you is a map. A map of Chicago City, and you can only use that map." He said slapping the whiteboard. "Impossible right?" Irvin asked turning to everyone in the room. After making eye contact with the crowd he continued, "You need the right map to get where you are going."

Charlie thought they were selling cars, not fucking maps. He had no idea what the boss was trying to convey. What the hell was the point of this?

"I want you all to set a goal. Every one of you is going to sell one hundred cars this month. You're going to do it, if you think positively." Irvin said pumping his fist in the air. Charlie was positive about only one thing, that was a load of bullshit. Jennifer with her five months top employee only pulled in fifty cars a month. Most of the agents sitting in the meeting sold between fifteen and twenty. The recession—nobody would call it a depression—was still going strong. The markets were down, and Charlie hadn't had a sale in three days.

"Ok, everybody stand," he said waving his hands.

*"For fucks sake, please not this,"* Charlie thought to himself.

Everyone slowly stood from their chairs, some faster than others. "Raise your hands into the air," he said his voice growing louder with enthusiasm. "Reach way up, and keep reaching!" Charlie wasn't the only one who thought this was bullshit. Nearby, little-miss-five-months rolled her eyes.

"I want everyone to try real hard and reach just a little bit higher!"

Resisting the urge to groan Charlie stood up on tiptoes. "Come on you can do it." The GM shouted excitedly and clapped his hands. Everyone gratefully lowered their arms. "You see guys. When you thought you couldn't do any better, you managed to get just a little bit higher. If we all try just a bit more, you can each sell a hundred cars this month."

"Yeah," several people chimed in.

"Are we going to try?"

"Yeah!" The group thundered. Charlie joined them after a half-second.

The GM clapped his hands, "Alright! Sit down." As everyone took their chairs Irvin clapped again. "And now for something special," he said walking over and turned the lights off. From near the desk, he withdrew a small object. A Bic lighter flicked to life revealing a single pink cupcake with a candle atop.

"Jennifer, would you come up here please," he said smiling widely. The blonde woman stood a little awkwardly from her chair. When she got to the front of the room the GM turned her around to face the crowd. "I'd like everyone to give Jen a round of applause. She's the first employee to get Top Sales Agent, six months in a row!" He said presenting the pink cupcake like it was a gold watch. The man reverently held it out with both hands before Jennifer took it.

"Thanks," she said in a small voice.

"That's not all. This is a six-month award for your desk." He said handing her the award. Printed on the plain white paper it read, 'Employee of the Year.'

Charlie clapped along with everyone else. "Please let this be over soon," he muttered under his breath.

"Everyone gather round for a group huddle," Irvin said beaming. They stood again and moved to the front of the room. Charlie put his hand in the group with everyone else. "Let's sell some cars!" They chorused together. Charlie had his best plastic smile on as he pumped his fist in the air, then turned almost sprinting for the exit. At least he could get outside and walk around in the fresh air.

The sun was out and the cars were waxed to a shine. He paused under the eave, pulled out a cancer stick, and stuck it between his lips. Then he dug out a cheap lighter and glanced at the fluid level. There were a few drops left, and he had to flick it several times to catch a flame. He touched it to the end of his cig and puffed. Leaning back against the wall, he worked the lighter back into his pocket as he blew out a cloud.

Nobody sold a car that day, not even Jennifer. At least he wasn't alone in that. At around six o'clock he punched out and went to his car.

Once he was home, he set the takeout on the counter and got a glass from the dishwasher. He fetched some ice cubes and poured himself a stiff drink. Charlie took a sip, coughed from the alcohol, and took another. After dinner, he crawled into bed. Today had been far too taxing to play games, but at least tomorrow was Saturday.

Charlie woke late, so the sun was already glaring through the window. He turned his head away from the beam of light, yawned, and stretched slowly. Languidly he slid from bed and walked into the master bath. There he brushed his teeth and showered. Charlie threw on some shorts and wrapped a bathrobe about himself, then donned his favorite pair of fuzzy slippers and shuffled into the living room. Fizzgig was there curled into a ball under the dive helmet. The gray and white fur moved up and down as he slept.

"I don't think it works on cats yet," Charlie said to the sleeping animal. He lifted the dive gear off the seat. Fizzgig blinked and looked up at him.

"Meroow," he said in annoyance.

"I'm stealing your sleeping spot," he said ushering the cat off the chair. Wrapping the bathrobe tighter, he sat down, settled the helmet over his head, and relaxed back. Charlie touched the power button and waited for the world to fade. His fingers and toes went numb and his vision clouded over as the sound of the city faded. The Dive Gear was already set to log him into the last game he played. Words floated before his face.

Gun Meister Online Loading...

Connection Established...
Network shaking hands...
Logging into Character...
Reticulating Spleens...

A warm curvaceous body lay atop his. He blinked trying to focus but everything was still dark. Slowly his vision adjusted to the lack of light. A feminine shape was just barely visible laying in the cubby hole with him. After Charlie's first match, they'd come here to log out. Most VRMMO's were based on the Nigmus source code, and a player's avatar didn't disappear when logged out, so renting a safe place to sleep was a necessity.

"You're awake," a soft voice said next to his ear.

"Sorry I didn't get on yesterday. Were you bored?" He asked shifting in the bunk.

"Not in the slightest. I was just dozing." She replied.

"Do you sleep?"

"I do, sort of... curious about me again?" She asked tickling his ear with her breath.

"I'm surprised how far AI's have advanced," he admitted. She too shifted and her bikini-clad breasts pressed against him. Charlie gave in to temptation and ran a hand down her body in the darkness.

"Sadly I am not an AI, not yet anyway. One day I'll take over the world." Elva said shifting in the small space.

"What do you dream about?"

"When not active I go through my recent memories. I will log important details and conversations. Some things get permanently saved like the first time we contracted." She said sighing in the darkness. A hand slid over his thigh and cupped his groin. "The rest gets archived. If I don't call it up the data will slowly be overwritten by new experiences."

"So you are self-learning."

"I am, partially. My only connections are hard-coded to the central database, my file-share, and the sensations the game servers send me. So don't worry, I won't be sending robots to your house... just yet."

"If they're as pleasant as you, I might let them in."

"What would you like to do today?" She asked giving his groin another caress.

"Shopping, I need some things before playing another match."

"I like the sound of that," Elva admitted.

"How do we get out of this coffin?"

A feminine hand reached over Charlie and touched the wall. It slid open to reveal a long corridor. The morning sunlight streamed through a nearby window, which revealed a cheap credit motel. Each room, quite literally, was a hole in the wall.

The walls were a scratched plastic molding. Most of the units were marked with graffiti, and someone had spray painted "Royal Suite," on the coffin room opposite theirs. Elva in all her blond busty glory climbed over Charlie and down the ladder to the floor. He turned putting his foot on the rungs and descended as well. As soon as he touched the floor the bunk closed with a chirp.

Nearby a screen lit up with, "Charge - One credit per hour - 37c." It flashed at him twice before changing to, "Please come again."

Elva was already waiting near the elevator with her hand on the call button, and as he approached, the door slid open. He entered and pressed the ground floor icon. As the door of the elevator opened, Charlie had to shield his eyes from a stray sunbeam that penetrated the cloud cover and bounced off the polished floor. Outside the rain fell in a drizzle and the sun cut through the cloud cover wherever it could. A hand curled around his bicep and pulled him into a busty chest. Charlie smiled at the woman, and had to admit, he could get used to waking up to her every morning.

The competition center was a block down, where the two main roads met and circled the enormous structure. Charlie turned south following the road around the bay. He vaguely remembered the shopping mall was in this direction. With Elva still clinging to his arm, Charlie strolled down the sidewalk.

"Is it the same time as in real life?"

"Gun Meister does follow standard time, but the matches take place in random locations. You might find yourself fighting in different time zones. We're on the Pacific Coast Server, so that's the time the city goes by."

They stopped at the intersection and waited for the light to change. A convertible Dodge Viper rolled up beside them. Loud music was thumping from the trunk. A half dozen topless girls were piled inside, and almost every one of them was different. One was Asian, another a thick Serbian girl, while others were various shades of Caucasian. The driver was a tall black man that had been cut straight from a fashion magazine. His short dark haircut was matched by a precisely shaved beard. A holstered pistol was just visible underneath the jacket of his dark suit. The driver glanced at them and pushed his sunglasses down a little. His predatory eyes regarded Charlie standing on the corner in his noob uniform. As the light changed he grinned and gunned the engine. The Viper leapt forward with a screech, squealing down the road, and leaving a trail of smoking tire tracks in his wake.

"You'll get there," a voice purred into his ear. He turned a little startled by Elva's choice of words.

"I..." He started to say. What was there to say to that? He certainly did want a fast car and a harem of beauties. A real woman would have stomped her foot and called the guy a pig. That bloke certainly was one for making those girls ride around half naked.

"Take your time, enjoy the game and don't worry about other players. It is my pleasure to be your weapon." She said squeezing his bicep.

This game was a little hard to get used too. There were more VR games than you could shake a stick at, and Gun Meister was a straightforward shooter. You killed players, you ranked up, then you killed more people. The developers needed some gimmick to keep the customers happy. Happy and eager to pay the subscription each month. So they used a proven marketing technique, sex. As a car salesman he could see the hook the developers were using.

Soon, their trek led them to the entrance of the mall. He joined other players as they entered the shopping mecca. The smell of food assaulted Charlie's senses as he entered the food court.

"You hungry?" He asked Elva.

"A bit peckish."

Charlie checked his balance on one of the many terminals by placing a hand on the screen. These public computers showed less information than the competition hall. It only displayed his player ID and a 1093 Credit balance. He ordered a bacon burger, fries, and a drink for Elva but nothing for himself. Later after a match or two, he'd log out and order pizza. He brought the food to a table and sat down opposite her.

"Only a little hungry?" He asked watching Elva tear into the food. Her mouth closed over the burger eating half in a single bite.

"We do have hunger bars, but I'm not used to going more than a day without food. One of the guilty pleasures I discovered while waiting for a Meister." She admitted taking a sip from her drink. Elva swirled a fry through the ketchup and popped it into her mouth.

"You don't have to starve yourself on my account."

"We guns can't own anything, so our Meister has to provide all."

*"What if someone didn't return for a month? Would a gun starve? Probably not, more than likely they'd lose their Meister and return to the weapon hotel. There they received free food and board."* He thought as Elva finished off her food.

In real life, he'd be jumping for joy to be on a date with such a sexy woman. Charlie felt oddly comfortable around Elva, but maybe it was because she didn't pretend to be human. Twice now she'd called herself a weapon and him a Meister. Elva dabbed a napkin to her lips then gave a very unladylike belch. She half turned away covering her mouth in embarrassment. Charlie stood smiling, grabbed the food tray, and put it with the others.

The first stop was Zeek's Holsters and Mags. This was where he'd picked up the thigh rig, and he hoped there was something for holding extra magazines. The clerk from yesterday was reclined in a swivel chair with his feet up on the counter, and reading a 'Guns Digest' magazine.

Charlie walked through the aisles of gun leather until he found the dump pouches, grenade bandoleers, and magazine holders. Elva helped him pick out a combined dump pouch and mag holder for 65 credits. It was thick brown leather with canvas buckles. One large band went around the waist while two smaller ones clipped around the thighs. The top half was a medium sized pocket for anything he wanted, which was probably why it was called a dump pouch. The lower half had slots for three extra pistol magazines.

He found several magazine choices just a few aisles over. A basic seven round mag was ten credits, and eight round mag was 120 credits, and a ten rounder was 1100. After a some waffling, Charlie splurged by picking up two of the eight round magazines. Next he needed some new pistol ammo since he had lost his leftovers in his first match.

He walked to the ammo counter to find the clerk still lounging in his chair. Charlie set his purchases down next to the man's boots. "I need a box of Forty-Five ACP as well," He said. The older man smiled and stood from his chair. He set a white box of ammo on the counter then scanned everything.

---

Leather Mag Carrier - 65c
2 x 8 Round 1911 Magazines - 240c
100 Rounds .45 ACP Ball - 10c

Total - 315c

---

Charlie put his hand on the screen to verify his purchase. His ID flashed before his credits dwindled to 768c. Hopefully, after a few matches, he would see that number back over a thousand.

"Where do I pick up some clothes?"

"Depends on what your taste is. Lot of specialty boutiques in the mall, but if you're just looking for some basic threads, I'd check out Sam's. Walk down the corridor till you get to the T and take a right, the shop is about halfway down." The clerk pointed out the doors and in the direction he needed to travel. "He sells used apparel which is why you'll find a bit of everything in there."

"Appreciate the help," Charlie said picking up his items. He clipped on the mag holster and slid the empties into the slots. The box he stuck into the dump pouch. It was time to get some new threads.

"We've all been there," the guy quipped with a smirk as Charlie walked out of the store.

The mall was filling up with people, and several gray-clad individuals walked past Charlie into the shop. Elva was dogging his step as he joined the crowd heading deeper into the mall. At the intersection, he turned right. About halfway down there was a shop sign that read, "Sam's Surplus Threads." Next to this, there was a picture of an old WW2 Army helmet with a bloody bullet hole in the side. "We buy used clothes, inquire within."

Upon entering the store he noticed the faint smell of gunsmoke. The scent permeated the air and probably came from the used items. The female portion was considerably larger than the men's. Underwear dominated the first aisle, and it was here the smell of smoke and oil was strongest. Elva's eyes glistened as they took in the massive selection. He picked up a pair of white thong panties and matching bra.

"Will this fit?" he asked holding the undergarment out to Elva.

"This is a 30B and a small bottom. I'm a voluptuous girl if you haven't noticed." Elva said lifting her breasts up a little and letting them drop. Well, he'd never bought female underwear before. How was he supposed to guess her size?

"How about you pick out what you want," He said and put the thong back. Charlie left her to find clothes. He figured if she'd survived two months by herself she could manage her own outfit. Towards the back of the store he found the male section. These didn't smell as much, so they must have been worn by other players. He found a pair of dark jeans in his size and a plain white t-shirt. By luck he chanced upon an army-green coat for sale. It had a high-necked collar and four large front pockets. Two unadorned shoulder tabs made the jacket appear pseudo-military.

"That was easy," he said carrying everything to the front counter.

41

His new outfit would only cost 95c, so he threw in a black gun belt. Elva came running up with a handful of clothes. Her face was positively glowing as she held them out. She had picked out a pair of daisy duke cut-offs a black tank top, and the last item made him speechless, a white lace teddy at a staggering 400c. He balked at the cost. That was more money than everything else combined. Elva batted her eyes as she beamed at him.

"You're not wearing that with the cut-offs," he said.

"Of course not, it's for later." She replied with that sly grin he couldn't resist.

"Definitely a big hook," he thought to himself. Charlie considered her choices then asked, "What are you going to wear under your shorts then?"

"Nothing," she said tilting her head. He groaned but put everything on the counter as Elva hugged him from behind.

"Go put them on while I pay," he said shooing her towards the changing rooms.

The clerk was a bland, nondescript fellow. His dull eyes and general apathy at the lingerie he rung up was strange. Was this a regular NPC? One that wasn't a gun? The man finished scanning the items and the display lit up. His total was 573 creds which almost made him put the lingerie back, but the thought of seeing Elva in it stayed his hand. That was even more than the magazines and holster he'd bought. Reluctantly he accepted the charge and Charlie was left with a measly 195 credits, but at least they were both fully equipped.

# CHAPTER FOUR

## *Casual Lessons*

Charlie shouldered his way through the packed crowd toward an unused bathroom in the hope of finding a quiet place to sit down. Elva followed him into the restroom and immediately went to admire herself in the mirror. She posed arching her back and pursed her lips at her reflection. Charlie opened a stall door and went inside. He quickly changed out of the gray uniform for his jeans, shirt, and jacket. After buckling his belt on he tossed the slacks into the trash. Charlie unlocked the stall and came out. Elva was slowly turning around in circles admiring herself in the mirror.

"What are you doing?" He asked approaching.

"I'm making sure to record everything about the first outfit my Meister bought me."

"Ahh, geez... Well, please change forms. I need to reload your magazines." He said taking out the box of ammunition. Elva began to glow a bright yellow. There was a flash and a 1911 was laying on the hand-washing counter. Charlie opened the box and loaded one of the eight round magazines. He picked up Elva, pressed the magazine release, and replaced the empty mag with a full one. After racking the slide, he paused in consideration. If the gun had just stripped the first round wasn't there room for another? He experimented by removing the mag and slipping another bullet on top. Then he loaded the gun again so there was 8 + 1 in the chamber. Charlie felt proud of himself for thinking of that. Little did he know this was standard practice.

He finished filling the other two magazines and stored them into his thigh holster. It would give him a total of 23 rounds in the mags plus one in the chamber. The rest of the ammo he tucked into the pouch. At least he'd be able to play several matches without having to fetch more. He clipped Elva into the thigh holster then pushed from the restroom. There was slightly under two hundred credits left in his account, but he was fully outfitted. While he'd been shopping the morning clouds had burned off. Warm sunlight filled the heavens, and the summer rain had mostly evaporated. Charlie joined the crowd heading toward the city center.

Outside the competition entrance several sound stages were set up. On one side women in thong bikinis were posing with machine guns. A girl with a short rainbow bob slid a box into an M60. She charged the heavy weapon and hefted it to her shoulder. At the end of the stage a target and backstop had been set up. The girl squeezed the trigger and sent a burst of fifty rounds into the silhouette. The gun's bucking made her enormous breasts dance in the tight swimwear, so most of the ogling men failed to notice the rounds hitting the target's center mass. Another woman walked around the stage perimeter with a banner reading, "Girls Inc, Recruiting." Charlie spent a few minutes admiring the hardware on display, both metal and flesh.

A live band was playing new age music, which meant it was loud and disjointed. Charlie preferred his music when it wasn't just synthetic noise, so he quickly followed the crowd between the stages. Surrounding the desk were hundreds of wooden ammo containers, and a 'Free Ammo for Memorial Day,' sign hung above it.

*"Shit,"* Charlie thought wishing he'd known about the free ammo beforehand, and saved himself ten credits.

A golden eyed giant was manning the counter, and a line of people wrapped around the help desk and into the lounge. Charlie moved past the free ammo into the competition lobby. Maybe later he would return to collect some. For now he wanted to run a few casual matches. He located an unused console and activated it by pressing his palm to the face. The menu options appeared and he navigated the listing until Charlie found Custom Casual Matches. There he selected a pistol deathmatch and a warning prompt came up. "Casual games may include players of different division ranks," it warned in yellow text.

*"That was fine,"* he thought and hit accept. He didn't want to play another competitive match and have his stats get any worse. The casual games wouldn't count against him. Besides, the higher skilled players

would still be limited to a handgun.

"Please enter lobby 245," it said. He closed the screen and made for the elevators. Several people got into one with him. Most simply swiped their hand over the control screen, which was enough to get the tube moving.

"Lobby 199," a robotic voice announced. A bearded man carrying a sniper rifle walked into the small lounge. The doors closed and continued down.

"Lobby 210," it said, and another man strode out of the elevator before it descended.

"Lobby 245."

The doors slid open, and Charlie followed a woman wearing skin-tight black leather into the private lounge. She had snow white hair and was smoking a cigarette. Several high ranking players were impatiently waiting in the small room, and Charlie gulped feeling like he'd just jumped into a shark tank. There was enough tactical clothing worn by the assembled group to outfit an entire navy seal team. He tried to play it cool by casually lounging in a nearby couch. The woman continued to smoke while they waited. Finally, after almost ten minutes the elevator door opened and the last person walked into the lounge. The world went dark as the final player joined them.

**[Match Starting]**

Charlie found himself sitting on a transit bus. He had a perfect view of the street below as the metro hung precariously over the edge of the freeway. It was sunny outside, but still early morning, which meant he was on the west coast somewhere. A gust of sea wind blew past making the bus rock. The vehicle swayed slowly, edging towards the precipice. He was sitting halfway down the aisle, so any wrong move might send the bus and himself to the highway below.

Charlie lifted himself partially out of the seat. As he did the bus tipped forward rocking on the lip of the overpass. He swung his foot out and grabbed a nearby metal rail. Metal shrieked as the bottom carriage slid across the guard rail and the bus tilted upward. He made his way up the incline towards the emergency exit. Every time the wind picked up the metro inched a little further, and any second it would tip over the rail. With effort Charlie reached the rear by climbing up the seats. Hanging from the handrail, Charlie grasped the door handle and yanked down. As he pushed open the exit the bus went over the edge. He cleared the torn guard rail and rolled to a skin scraping stop. The transit bus slammed face first into the highway below, crumpling like a broken accordion.

As he was looking at the wreckage below a figure appeared from under the bridge. A male was hunched low to the ground and was scanning the bus wreckage. Charlie dropped to a knee next to the ruined guard rail. Unholstering Elva, he remembered to remove the safety, then he stood aiming down the sights at the man. The target was still peeking through a shattered window into the bus. The gun fired and the bullet struck the man in the neck and traveled down into his chest cavity. Blood squirted over the pavement as he crumpled.

"You should check your surroundings more carefully," a female said huskily from behind him. He spun with the gun to see the white haired woman. A bullet slammed into his chest followed by a second and third. The sky filled his vision as he went over the edge to the street below, and he hit the ground just as the darkness closed in.

A door opened revealing the private lounge. Oddly enough the man he had shot was not there, so maybe you didn't have to stick around for casual matches. Above the main screen, the timer showed that eighteen minutes remained. He'd only managed to last two minutes, but at least he'd killed someone. Charlie touched a nearby console and was pleased to see he'd earned two hundred credits. A door opened nearby and another player entered the lobby. The man wore a black balaclava over his head and a dark urban-camo vest. Charlie glanced up from the console watching as the soldier walked to the elevator. It opened at his approach and he slapped at the control screen. The player disappeared as the elevator slid shut and ascended. Well, that answered the question of whether he could leave or not.

He wanted to laugh. The first game had been over too fast to get his heart rate up. Charlie stood and approached the exit. After a few seconds the elevator doors opened, and he returned to the lobby. People were mobbing the help desk for free ammo. Charlie though had only fired a single bullet. He decided to reload next to a nearby console. Elva's chamber was charged so all he had to do was slide in a fresh eight round magazine, and holster the 1911. He ripped open the Velcro pouch on his thigh, removed the ammo box, and replaced the one spent bullet. Then he accessed the console and started another casual pistol match.

"Please enter Lobby 420," it said after flashing the 'Higher Division' warning at him. With ten people in each game that meant at least four thousand people were playing on the West Coast server. He whistled, impressed by the turnout because that number would likely increase after lunch. He entered the elevator and went down to the lounge. The match started almost immediately.

The darkness came and went leaving Charlie staring at a setting sun. Broken down cars littered the highway like forgotten toys. Nearby a speed-limit sign read, '100' with a red circle. Judging by the dusk sky and the foreign traffic sign he was somewhere in Europe. Charlie crouched removing the pistol and glanced around.

The highway ran east to west towards the sun. On either side of the road was a large grass covered berm. Shuffling closer to a car he glanced through the window, but couldn't see any movement. Two shots rang out in the distance, and he looked west, but the sun was in his eyes and there were too many cars on the road. Silence followed the pistol reports and Charlie unconsciously hunkered lower.

He waited this time, while his heart started getting a healthy dose of adrenaline. For several minutes gun shots were exchanged up and down the highway, but none were close enough to make him worry. The buzzer went off somewhere above and the red line crept into view. It was inching along about a hundred feet away urging him into action. Charlie stepped away from the Mercedes, and almost immediately, a loud shot rang out from behind. Something vaguely hot and electric slammed into his leg. Unable to support his weight, Charlie's knee collapsed and he crumpled to the cracked pavement. Laying under a van some twenty feet away was a short girl already aiming at him for a second shot. Charlie tried to bring his gun around but he'd landed poorly. Her pistol flashed sending Charlie into darkness.

"Damn it," he cursed as the door to the lounge opened. He stepped out and punched the padded wall. That player had been much closer to the match border. If he'd just waited for a little longer she would have been forced to move. But, no... he'd gotten impatient. She must have known he was there all along waiting for the shot. What pissed him off even more was the fact he hadn't even fired back. Charlie walked through the empty lounge to the elevators and started up. He got into line with several others to use the console and started another match.

"How are you doing?" Elva asked.

"I got one kill so far."

"That's good, keep at it. If you have questions don't be afraid to ask. I can't tell you how to play but I can give you some general advice." She said in an enthusiastic voice.

"I'll keep that in mind," he replied entering the elevator. It descended, opening onto another lounge. This was just what he had to do; practice, practice, and more practice. That along with a heavy amount of trial and error. In an hour he was going to have to log off for food. Charlie wouldn't do himself any favors by neglecting to eat. After lunch he could focus on running matches, and they were giving out ammo so he didn't have to leave the competition center.

Soft pale moonlight filtered through the broken blinds to illuminate the tiny hotel room. The light fixture hanging from the ceiling was broken, and the switch had been removed to keep people from turning it on. The hotel was forty credits per night, which was twice as expensive as the coffin motel, and it was still a dive. Near the entrance was a small kitchenette and table. The fridge didn't work and the sink constantly dripped water. At least he had a bed, hard and lumpy as it was. The sheets were stained, and the pillows lay forgotten on the floor. Charlie sat on the mattress with his weapon, and a shaft of light framed them as his wrist worked. He licked his lips nervously. This technically wasn't their first time but that didn't stop him from worrying. Elva, however, was thoroughly enjoying herself.

"Mmmm... yes," she groaned and Charlie almost stopped mid-motion. "No, no don't stop. I'm almost there, just a little more." Elva begged. His wrist moved faster, fingers wet and slick from the solvent. The heavy aroma of gunsmoke wafted from the 1911 to fill the small room.

"Ohhh gawd, Charlie. I'm cuummmminnggggg..." Elva squealed. The final word devolved into a series of panting cries.

This time Charlie did stop. His wrist slowed before he said, "You know— that is very distracting."

Elva panted breathlessly into his ear. "I told you... we guns are more sensitive in our original forms." Charlie held in his left hand Elva's upper receiver and in his right a wire brush. The barrel and frame lay on a rag next to him on the bed. Charlie had been scrubbing the breach-face and under the extractor. He dipped the brush into the plastic cup, and brown powder residue swirled in the solvent.

"I can't believe you get so dirty," he complained tapping it on the container's lip.

"Who's fault is that?" Elva asked heavily into his ear. "You used me all day long—not that I'm complaining." She added quickly.

"What I mean is, why? Why add dirt and grime into the game?" He asked using the brush on Elva's upper receiver. He dug the bristles underneath the slide lip. Black oil dripped down the brush to his fingers. Elva groaned again unable to speak as he did this.

"It seems like a pointless waste of time, but I suppose it gives us Meister's a reason to get to know our weapons. A real soldier takes on the responsibility of caring for his gun." He said after considering the idea. Along with the sex and excitement came a bit of work.

Elva looked free of caked on soot so he dropped the brush into the solvent and grabbed a q-tip. This he dug into her slide groove. It came away brownish-yellow, and he set it with the others. After several more he put the slide down on the rag. The barrel was a short tube with a feed ramp on one side. The grooves were nearly black with powder and copper fouling. He picked up the solvent canister and aimed down the throat spraying inside. He waited a few seconds then picked a circular brush out of the cleaning kit and ran it down the barrel. Elva tried but failed to stifle her moans. Charlie did this three or four times until the solvent came out clear. The lower frame was fairly clean aside from his dirty fingerprints, so he sprayed it down lightly and ran a rag over the metal.

"Now you need to oil me, but not more than a drop on the spots I told you. Improper oil is worse than none at all."

The lubricant bottle was small with a long needle on the end. He squeezed a drop onto the front, middle, and back slide. Next he added a tiny amount to the sear and one final drop just below the hammer. The tricky part was reassembly and Charlie paused to check the instructions again.

He slid the barrel into the slide then inserted the bushing. The guide and recoil spring went in next. Now he had the awkward task of putting the upper receiver onto the lower. About halfway down he stopped with the holes lined up, and with one hand holding the pieces together, pushed the slide stop into place. All that was left was to put on the spring cover and push it down. With his thumb he kept it depressed and rotated the barrel bushing into place.

*"Done, phew... that was a task and a half,"* he thought.

He racked the slide several times to spread the oil around, and after aiming the pistol in a safe direction, pulled the trigger. The hammer fell on the empty chamber and he racked the gun again. For a few seconds he held the completed weapon in his hands. The surface was a parkerized matte black which was smooth to the touch. It had dark wood grips with a subtle checkered pattern. Charlie had liked the weapon when he first picked Elva in character creation. She was a sexy creature in both her forms, though he'd learned she had drawbacks. Namely a lack of ammo capacity. Compared to some of the modern pistols seven rounds left him wanting. Still, you couldn't argue about that big forty-five caliber bullet. A single hit to the center torso was generally enough to down an unarmored opponent.

The 1911 began to glow until there was a flash. Elva appeared kneeling on the bed in daisy dukes and a tight little tank top. "That felt heavenly," she admitted rocking her hips back and forth. Elva stretched reaching her hands into the air while pushing her chest out. Again she shifted back and forth until she felt satisfied. Sliding from the bed she said, "I'm going to change into something more comfortable." The blond disappeared into the bathroom which gave Charlie time to clean up. He put the brushes into the kit and replaced the top on the solvent canister. The dirty rags and q-tips he tossed into the wastebasket. Next he wiped his hands clean on a fresh towel, and all the extra cleaning supplies went into the shopping bag next to the bed. He needed a duffel bag or a backpack to put his purchases into. There was no hope of affording an apartment just yet, so Charlie would have to remain mobile by renting rooms each night.

A warm breeze blew in through an open window opposite where he sat. In the distance, the glowing Competition Center was visible reminding him that it was open 24/7. Charlie was caught up in the sight as he wallowed in today's failures.

Out of ten casual matches he had lost all of them. Half the time he'd been one of the first people killed, and it didn't help that everyone was leagues ahead in skill. Charlie felt extremely frustrated with how little he understood the game. A large part of it came down to marksmanship and practice. It was obvious that he couldn't shoot for shit, and Charlie needed to work on his aim before he played another match. Tomorrow was Sunday and he had earned enough credits to rent time in the practice rooms.

The door to the bathroom opened just as the moon exited the clouds, and the shaft of pale light perfectly framed Elva in the glow. She stepped playfully into the room wearing the crotchless lingerie he'd bought earlier. White thigh-high stockings were held up via a little garter belt and the window on her thong showed off a short landing strip of blonde pubic hair. By now Charlie realized he'd been staring at her open mouthed, and Elva looked pleased with his slack jawed reaction. She fingered the lace thong, pulling on it before letting it snap back into place. Moments like this reminded Charlie there was perfection in this digital world, and it was standing before him. Elva cupped a heavy breast feeling her nipples through the soft lace fabric. Next she combed her fingers through her blond hair and shook it out. The strands fell over her chest as she locked eyes with Charlie. He blew out a breath he'd been unconsciously holding.

"Fuck me," he said as she swayed toward him seductively. The lingerie was definitely worth the credits.

"If that's what you want," she replied and he nodded eagerly.

Elva pushed him back onto the bed and started to unbutton his pants. Quickly his new clothes went onto the floor with the blankets. She climbed atop him, straddling his waist, and with long fingers guided him inside. As Elva started rocking Charlie knew he was caught; hook, line, and sinker. The wet slapping sound of there hips meeting filled the room. His questing hands ran up her lace covered thighs, past her stomach, and grabbed her heaving breasts. Elva moaned placing her hands over his as she leaned back. Her sensuous body rose and fell, and Charlie knew he was about to explode. Just when he couldn't hold on any longer, Elva leaned forward kissing him as his climax roared through him.

Afterward Elva swept back into the bathroom. Exhausted and ready for sleep, Charlie touched his temple with two fingers and selected 'Logout' from the options.

All was dark as gritty reality settled over his shoulders. He was sitting in the living room of his dingy apartment. Charlie tried to speak, but it felt as though someone had poured hot sand down his throat. He coughed thickly and tried to work up some saliva.

"Lights, dim." He croaked in a hoarse voice, and the ceiling light came on low. Charlie slipped the dive helmet from his head. Then he rolled to his feet and set the gear down in the chair.

*"Mental note—keep a water bottle handy."*

Charlie coughed again as he shuffled into the kitchen. The water faucet came on tepid but he was too thirsty to wait. Forgoing a glass he cupped a hand under the water and brought it to his lips. It was like liquid ambrosia on his tongue despite the chemical aftertaste. He drank another handful and the fire in his throat cooled. With the dire thirst quenched he fetched a glass from the cupboard and filled it with ice cubes. The cat bowl was empty again and he felt sorry for neglecting Fizzgig.

"I'm going to have to buy more cat food soon," he muttered fetching the container. It rattled as he shook the large plastic jug, and Fizzgig made his appearance at the sound. The feline sat a few feet away patiently waiting for Charlie to finish filling his food and water dish. As he shuffled into his bedroom he took a long draft of water and set it on the stand. Then he entered the master bath and flicked on the light.

He showered, brushed his teeth, and cleaned the litter-box while in the bathroom. After donning a pair of clean boxers he went to lay down. A full moon hung above the cloudless night sky, but the stars didn't twinkle quite so brightly in real life. It was something he never got tired of looking at. Deep down space called to him. He raised a hand pointing his finger at the moon as if Elva was in his hand.

"Bang," he whispered pulling the imaginary trigger. Charlie smiled, rolled away from the moonlight, and drifted off to sleep.

# CHAPTER FIVE

## *Fog Lifted*

The sound of an explosion catapulted Charlie from a dead sleep. The deafening clatter of a machine gun filled the air, and for a few seconds, he sat up in bed as his brain struggled to catch up. The phone making the terrible racket danced across the bedside table. He'd stayed up way too late Sunday night playing Gun Meister, and was suffering for it now.

*"That was the second alarm,"* he thought blearily. The first was considerably more subdued which was why he'd slept right through it.

"Well fudge sticks," he said throwing the blankets off. Charlie snatched the phone, activated it with a quick series of flicks, and silenced the gunfire. He had ten minutes to get to work, and it was a twenty-minute commute. Thankfully he'd taken a shower last night, so all he had to do was throw on a button-up shirt and slacks. He tugged on some socks then shoved his feet into a pair of black business loafers. Grabbing the phone again he ran outside and down the apartment stairs. He was already late by the time he reached his car and started it.

After thirty-five minutes in traffic he pulled into his parking spot at the dealership. The glove compartment opened and he extracted an extra tie. Charlie slicked his hair using a half-empty bottle of water and a pocket comb. Finally, he checked himself using the driver side mirror. There was a heavy five o'clock shadow over his face, and his tie was crooked. He straightened it then ran a hand over his face hoping nobody would notice the stubble.

There were two customers already inside, and Frank glanced past the older woman. Charlie ignored the look and moved to his desk. There was paperwork to finish before he made the lot rounds. Pulling his chair out he was about to sit when his phone rang. He glanced up towards the general manager's office. Through the glass, Irvin was holding the receiver to his ear and beckoned Charlie into the office.

*"Just what I needed this morning,"* he thought to himself, and moved to knock on the door.

"It's open," Irvin called, and Charlie went inside. "You're not usually late."

"It was hot last night, and I had trouble sleeping."

It was a white lie. Elva and Charlie had spent most of Sunday practicing in one of the marksmanship programs. Then they'd screwed well past midnight, but the old man didn't need to know that. Irvin sat back giving Charlie the eyeball.

"Can I talk to you man to man?" The GM asked. Something sarcastic almost slipped from Charlie's lips, but he caught himself just in time.

"Of course," Charlie replied and smiled hoping it looked genuine. He tried to prepare himself for whatever the man had to say.

"I like you, which is why I wanted to talk." Irvin began. Charlie prayed he hadn't meant sexually. God that was such a disgusting thought. The GM picked up a pen and examined it carefully before he spoke. "Your sales numbers are the lowest among the agents. If you don't get them up, I'm going to have to take you off the active roster."

*"Not good,"* thought Charlie. *"If I get put on call, my commission rate will drop to almost nothing."* He adjusted his tie again while he gathered his thoughts.

"It's pretty hard out there with the recession. None of the others are pulling the numbers they used to."

"True, but that also means we can't afford to keep you on. I've seen you sell a luxury SUV to a stubborn mule-headed miser. I know you have what it takes, so why aren't you doing better?"

His mind reeled. Someone had snuck up behind Charlie and smashed him upside the head with a bat called Epiphany.

"I see from the look on your face that I'm getting through to you," The older man said with a smile. The fool was such an ass. He had, however accidentally, stumbled into Charlie's darkened mind and flipped the right switch.

*"Why didn't he do better?"* Charlie asked himself. All his life he'd done just enough to get by and no more. He wanted out of the office so he had time to consider what was happening. It was as if the veil over his eyes had lifted, and the fog in which he dwelled was slowly dispelling.

"Give me a chance," he begged.

"That's why I called you in here. You have a week before I drop you."

"Thanks for the heads up," Charlie replied standing.

*"A week? The reprieve was so pathetically small as to be almost pointless, but there was always a chance."* Charlie thought.

He left the office and walked to his desk. For a few minutes, he sat not doing anything at all. The world was suddenly different. Everything looked brighter, sharper, and more colorful than before, and it wasn't the morning sun coming through the windows. Charlie's world perspective had shifted in the last few minutes.

His first thoughts, strangely enough, were of Gun Meister. He wondered why he hadn't done better in game. All yesterday Charlie had practiced his marksmanship. He'd used hours of time and several hundred credits on training. That still didn't excuse the stupid mistakes he'd made in the matches. He realized only now he hadn't been thinking. Charlie was by nature a lazy man, he could admit that. Like a river, he always took the path of least resistance. His one competition match had scared him enough that he fled to casual. There he'd only met with more skilled players. Yesterday he'd wasted most of his credits at the range. He needed to think more, and act less.

Finally he forced himself back into the present. Charlie was in danger of getting canned if he didn't improve quickly. From his desk he watched the other agents talking to the customers. Each one had their own distinct style he realized.

Chad was deeply engrossed with a young couple across from Charlie. The younger man never shut up. In his mind's eye, Charlie could see Chad closing in on the young duo. The imaginary sub-machine gun in his hands was continuously chattering. It didn't even matter what Chad said, so long as he didn't stop. The point obviously was to keep the marks talking and not able to consider how ridiculously high those interest rates actually were.

Frank walked past the front doors. His eyes were locked onto an elderly woman in a decade old summer dress. He was like an unscrupulous assassin. Using misdirection to trick the customers into looking at something else. Only then did he slip the knife in unseen. Except in Frank's case, it was the car's faulty alternator or a bad transmission. Charlie felt a moment of disgust as the man got within range of that older female. She smiled up at him like a doe in his headlights.

Jennifer was sitting at her desk with her new award proudly displayed. She'd even gotten a frame for it which had certainly cost more than the useless piece of paper it was printed on. Jen was akin to that smurf in his first competition match. All she had to do was walk down the street scanning for enemies, and suckers would leap after Jennifer hot for some attention. That was why she targeted single men coming onto the lot. Natural marks, ones that spent more time hitting on her than reading the loan agreement they were signing.

He needed a new style. Charlie didn't have tits so using his good looks was unlikely. Not unless a string of desperate gay men strolled onto the lot. Neither was he ruthless enough to shovel garbage cars. He would never be a talker like 'Chattering Chad.' That took too much energy even to watch. For a time, he considered what to do. While thinking a husband and wife drove onto the lot with a hybrid convertible sports car. Charlie forced himself from the chair and out the front doors. He caught a piece of their conversation as he neared.

"I don't know babe. These get terrible mileage per kilowatt." The man was saying.

"We need something for the baby, and for the future." The wife replied a little tartly. Charlie stopped a few feet away.

"Good morning, can I help you?" The husband turned with a look that wasn't entirely friendly.

"We're checking out our options, thank you." He said motioning Charlie away.

"My husband wants to trade in his car for something more family friendly," she said. The van she was looking at was a soccer mom's wet dream. Fold out seats, lots of room in the back for groceries, and it even had a luggage rack for trips to the park.

Charlie glanced at the husband whose face was stony. The car they'd come in with was an expensive electric sports car. It was red, of course it was red. Charlie suspected he understood the situation now. The wife married the guy for his money and his fast car. Now that she had the ring, and a baby on the way. She wanted the sports car gone. Mr. Husband though, was kicking tires and finding things wrong with the vehicles. Charlie didn't blame the guy. The car, brand new would be sixty-thousand dollars, and even ten years old, the bluebook was a good 24k in trade.

"How about this," Charlie said to the couple. "Instead of trading in the car for a new van, you can get a used one for a third the price."

"We just bought a home so we don't have much for down payment." The wife said quickly. Charlie nodded and plowed ahead.

"You don't need a down payment for a used car. We finance everything. That way your husband keeps his vehicle for work and you get a family van for the important stuff." Charlie said with burgeoning appeal. He smiled at the two. The woman grimaced as she glanced towards the used car lot. Her face looked skeptical but the husband latched onto the idea.

"Honey, think about it. This way there will be two cars. You don't have to wait for me to get home to go shopping." He said wrapping an arm around her shoulders. He turned guiding the woman towards the used lot, and Charlie followed on his heels.

*"That guy really wanted to keep his hot little convertible,"* Charlie thought to himself.

"This is the same model van that you were just looking at. It's only three years old and has very low mileage." He said stopping next to a vehicle.

"It's used though," the wife argued.

"Everything is rigorously maintained by our service team. The used van is twenty-two thousand dollars less and there's no down payment." He said and the husband was already nodding in agreement. The interest rate was going to be a killer but he could handle it. Charlie had a sale, and it hadn't taken much convincing. He led the two into the air conditioned building, and settled both at his desk. The couple signed the loan agreement and Charlie handed over the keys.

Both cars left the lot. That was exactly what he should have been doing. Look for a way in, push in hard, and get the sale. He sold two more cars that day which was much better than usual.

He logged in just after five in the evening. Elva lay atop him like usual but he didn't have time for her shenanigans today. Quickly he gathered the cleaning equipment, extra clothes, and ammo together in the shopping bags. "Come on," he said pulling open the door and heading downstairs. The lobby was empty and he tossed the hotel key onto the desk as he went by. The city was busy with people just getting off work. Cars and motorcycles roared by on the way to the competition center, and Charlie joined the pedestrian throng heading in that direction.

"Are you angry with me?" Elva asked two steps behind. He stopped mid-stride perplexed by the question.

"What?"

"Your face is set and grim. Are you angry because I hurt you?" Elva asked nervously. For a few seconds he continued to stare at her until realization dawned. Last night he'd tried introducing her to the pleasures of oral sex with disastrous results.

"Ahh, well... I did tell you to treat it like a Tootsie-pop. Little did I know you'd lick it three times before biting into the chewy center." He said reaching out a hand. She smiled sheepishly as he patted her on the head. "No, I'm not angry with you, but next time don't use your teeth. If I am upset, it's at myself." He said and continued walking.

Within minutes he neared the Competition Center and joined the crowd heading inside. Memorial weekend was over so the free ammo was gone. The crowd split apart. Most of the people made for the training areas while the rest went towards the large public lounge. Several bars were set up so people could watch the matches in progress, but most like him were heading straight to the terminals. There was an open console and he activated it with his palm.

[Character Stats]
[Competition Matches]
[Casual Match]
[Custom Casual Matches]

The screen flashed with the available choices, and he selected a competitive match. 'Quick Deathmatch' came up, and he hit accept.

"Enter Lobby 157," it stated and he moved to the elevator. The private room was empty and he was forced to wait while the rest of the players gathered. Elva sat nearby on the couch. Charlie was still irritated at the way he'd been living, but that was no reason to take it out on her. He shifted closer wrapping an arm around her waist. Two players entered next and moved to the far wall.

Elva leaned in and whispered, "I'll do better next time."

"I know you will," he said patting her side. "Weapon form," he added as the next person entered. She started to glow and a pistol was soon laying in his lap. Charlie checked her load, then holstered the weapon. As the final player entered, everything faded into darkness.

**[Match Starting]**

A seagull flew past in a squawking clatter of feathers. His foot slipped on the slimy deck plating, and he quickly grabbed a nearby railing to keep his footing. After collecting himself he scanned the area. It appeared Charlie was standing on the prow of a derelict cargo ship. The vessel was beached and listed awkwardly to one side. Many of the shipping containers had broken their cables and fallen below. Televisions, stuffed toys, and decomposing commercial goods were half buried in the sand. The containers left on the deck formed a disjointed maze of alleys.

*"Ok, enough gawking,"* he reprimanded himself. Charlie had people to kill, so he withdrew the 1911 and slid the safety off. For once luck was on

his side with a good starting position. Spawning on the prow meant he could be reasonably certain nobody was behind him. Just in case he glanced over the railing and scanned the beach searching the jumble of rusting containers. Nothing moved except seagulls and a few sand crabs. In the distance, the red line curved in a giant circle around the ship. His examination of the area was cut short by gunfire. A distant series of pops indicated the actual beginning of the match.

He moved slowly into the entrance of the maze. Several container doors hung open swinging slowly in the sea breeze. Years of rain, mold, and bird droppings formed a dark slime over the deck. A pair of footprints appeared halfway down the row. Charlie glanced back seeing that he too was leaving a trail, so there was no point in camping unless you started in a covered position.

The footprints of the other player disappeared into a nearby container. Keeping his pistol aimed at the entrance he advanced. Charlie took his time. At the first open door he paused to check inside. It held a dusty disused sports car, but was otherwise empty. Finally, after a full minute he arrived outside the container the prints led to. The doors were partially open, and Charlie was tempted to wait the guy out, but the red line was already halfway to the ship. He paused listening at the door, then smiled, and almost laughed from what he heard. Whoever was inside the container was breathing so hard it sounded like a bad horror movie.

*"These guys are just as scared as me,"* he thought to himself. That made him feel a little better.

Reaching out with the pistol he used the barrel to knock on the red container door. Charlie quickly pulled back when thirteen bullet holes appeared in the metal as the player inside unloaded. There was a long lull and he dodged across the gap to the other side. As Charlie did so, he glanced in. A red Ferrari was parked inside and strapped tightly down. Dust and bird droppings covered the once immaculate paint job. Behind the vehicle a man was crouched desperately trying to reload. After a second he straightened and aimed across the car trunk. Charlie did laugh this time. He couldn't help it, for he found the scene strangely funny.

"Why the hell are you laughing?" The man asked from inside the shadowed container.

"I was just thinking you trapped yourself in there. What are you going to do when the red line comes?" Charlie asked in a friendly voice. He stepped into the cover of another open container to wait.

"Screw you!"

"Just pointing out your dilemma," Charlie replied crouching lower. There might still be others nearby and he didn't want to get target fixated again. For almost a minute there was nothing but the stiff sound of the sea breeze. Like usual, the other players were camping until the buzzer sounded, which gave him time to chat. He reached out tapping the door again with his gun.

"Hello?" Charlie asked politely but was met with angry silence. From within the container feet shuffled, and the sound came close to the door. Charlie remained where he was half hidden in his own container. After a few seconds, he heard the player retreat to the car again.

"Fuck, fuck, shit..." The man muttered to himself. Charlie felt bad for the guy. It was such a simple mistake and now he was paying for it. Another minute passed as the man cursed to himself.

"How about you bugger off?" A hoarse voice asked.

"Afraid I can't leave you behind me. We gotta settle this first." Charlie replied. Somewhere above a buzzer went off. Half the time remained and the red line would start moving faster. Several gunshots rang out close by, and Charlie perked up as the noise was only a row or two away. Behind him the red line appeared through the back of the container. He stood, moved out into the open, and slowly shuffled backward up the aisle toward the next row.

A face appeared in the entrance of the container. Charlie raised his gun aiming down the sights, but before he could fire it retreated. As he waited, the red line advanced slowly across the aisle. From inside the container there was a muffled pop followed by the sound of a body hitting the ground.

"Really?!"

The guy did himself in rather than take the fight, so Charlie was robbed of his kill reward. The red line pushed forward and he walked stealthily down the row of closed containers. Now he just had to worry about the people ahead of him, and there was at least one person close by. That was small consolation considering the barrier was right on his heels.

At the next open aisle several sets of footprints led inside. About ten feet in the paths branched and each trail diverged. The left headed towards the prow, but the red line already closed that way off. Charlie was forced right and he walked to the next turn. There a body was laying next to an open container door. It was female, but surprisingly little was left of the face. Carefully he opened the door next to the body. Just inside a few shell casings marked where the ambusher had stood. Somewhere amid the container maze a gun battle erupted, and it sounded like multiple parties were involved in a cascade of fire.

The red line was closing in quickly, and Charlie was in danger of getting boxed into a dead end. He picked up the pace following the trail of footprints. More gunfire rang out nearby, and he stopped short of the next turn. The maze ended in an open platform. Sticking out of the center were the pillars of a massive rusted crane. A boom arm lay broken across the deck like a severed appendage. Twenty feet ahead a tall blond man crouched behind the steel pillar. He was in full view and an easy target.

The player poked his head around the pillar looking across the deck. He raised an FN Five-Seven and shot several rounds at something. Charlie ducked back behind the corner as two people returned fire. He considered his options. Charlie had done a lot of skulking around and very little killing, however, that meant he still had a full loadout. Likely he would have to reload quickly after he made his move. With that in mind, he removed one of the extra magazines and held it in his off hand.

There was less than five minutes left in the round and the boundary was an ever-present concern. Still, he waited while the players in the middle continued to exchange shots. Glancing back around the corner, Charlie found the blond crouched low to the ground, saving his last few rounds for the final push. The weapon trembled in the man's large Germanic hands, and Charlie glanced at his own pistol. It was perfectly still, and pointing towards the ground. His heart rate was up and adrenaline coursed through his veins, but he was managing.

Charlie slipped around the corner with the pistol held in one hand. Raising the sights up he targeted the man's back. The gun bucked as the first round slammed into the target. He jerked sideways in surprise and tried to return fire, but Charlie walked forward firing several more rounds.

Two of his three shots hit center mass, and the player sagged to the ground. Someone else fired at him and a bullet hit the cargo container next to his left arm. Near the broken boom, a girl was aiming at him. Charlie returned fire by instinct as he dashed the final distance to the pillar. Tilting the gun, he pressed the magazine release with his thumb. The empty box slid free and he replaced it with the extra in his hand. The used one, he slid into a slot on his dump pouch.

There was another pause in the fighting, so he crouched next to the pillar and smiled to himself. Well, well... he'd done considerably better than he thought he would. By the looks of things at least four people remained. There was Charlie, the girl, and from the sounds of combat two others on the opposite end. He wished he had a watch. The red line was a clear indication of how much time was left, but it would be nice to know exactly how long the match had been going.

A funny thing happened then. Charlie stood next to the man he'd killed, and the Five-Seven pistol began to glow. After a second it vanished in a twinkling of light, but the corpse remained. That was curious. He'd have to ask Elva about that later.

Charlie decided to risk the dash to the central hoist. He jinked left around the pillar and over a small railing. The girl near the boom aimed at him but he dodged putting the hoist in the way. Once there he considered his next move. He could climb the crane ladder for a height advantage, but that would expose him to multiple attackers. Charlie had the advantage right now, so it was better to wait for the others to push his position. He crouched next to the railing and glanced over the edge. The girl was aiming at someone on the other side as she fired three or four shots.

He used both hands to grip the pistol as he rested his forearms on the railing. Slowly he squeezed the trigger as the girl looked in his direction. Elva barked, and the top of her head disappeared in a spray of brains and red mist.

*"Damn, that felt good,"* he thought to himself.

She'd been something like forty feet away and mostly behind cover. There was less than a minute remaining, and he moved to the hoist ladder. The red circle was only twenty feet away as he began to climb. A cab came into view. The front window was broken which had let rain water into the compartment. Someone on the other side was climbing up the second ladder. A new woman stopped partially above the gangway, but she still had a few rungs before reaching the landing. Charlie quickly fired several shots through the cab. Shattered glass flew outward as his bullets punched through the thin metal, and the girl dropped below.

Charlie reloaded with his last full magazine, while the final player moved around the base. Following the noise he crept to the edge of the gangway. A bullet ricocheted off the metal as he tried glancing over the side, and shrapnel slapped against his cheek. Quickly he pulled back to the control cab as something hot and wet ran down his chin. Reaching up he wiped at the liquid, only to discover it was his blood. That had been a mistake to peek over the edge. One that almost cost him the game. He didn't need to kill her personally, the circle would do that for him.

Seconds were left and the red circle was within touching distance of the hoist. Nearby the metal ladder rattled as someone quickly climbed it. He didn't peek this time. Instead, he knelt next to the edge and pointed the gun straight down. He fired off four rounds and withdrew. Below a body hit the ground with a sickening crunch. Darkness followed after a few more seconds.

**[Match Complete]**

# CHAPTER SIX

## *Second Match*

The taste of victory was sweet on his tongue as he entered the lounge. The other nine players were already in the elevator. It closed and ascended, which was fine. Charlie wanted to check his new stats. He strolled magnanimously around the large central couch to the nearest console. Placing his palm on the face it activated with his information.

---

**Player ID - NA1339872**
**Registered Competition Name - None**
**Clan - None**
**Hours played - 13**

**Wins - 1**
**Losses - 1**

**Kills - 4**
**Deaths - 1**
**K/D Ratio - 4.0**

**Battle Rank - Bronze Three**
**Player Score - 1013**

**Credits - 10742c**

At last, his money problems seemed practically solved with one win. He'd also jumped two ranks to Bronze Three. Silver no longer seemed so far away. Soon he'd have a new contract slot and the ability to pick a primary weapon. He sat and rather awkwardly opened his dump pouch to retrieve the extra ammo. Charlie was still riding the combat cocktail and his fingers felt clumsy as he started to reload Elva.

"During the last game, I saw a gun disappear after the player was dead."

"We always return to our Meister's," Elva said into his ear. "The developers want to make the game Digital Entity friendly. Your original character is kept safe. A clone is spawned at the needed location with any items on you." Elva added, and Charlie reached up touching his cheek which was no longer bleeding. Did that mean there was a half dozen dead Charlie's out there?

"Thankfully these precautions became unnecessary with the advent of Avatar 2.0," she continued when he didn't respond.

"Digital Entities... Avatar 2.0?" He asked in confusion. The words were foreign to him.

"You may have heard of them as ghosts," she replied. Ahh, yes he had heard the rumors, but never met one personally. That was what his roommate Alex had gone off chasing. They were people who'd uploaded their memories online. The problem was you had to die while logged into a game. Talk about burning the bridge after you. In America, it was next to impossible to obtain the modded dive-gear necessary for the transfer. If a person started to have a medical alert the systems were designed to eject the user. Even having an accelerated heart rate was enough to get you booted from the game.

"Avatar 2.0 added a unique encryption algorithm to the memory upload. Digital Entities cannot have their personal data read or altered. Useful for the game developers who wished to draw in these individuals." Elva continued as if she were reading from a promotional pamphlet.

"You're gushing," he interrupted.

"I'm sorry, I just get excited by the topic."

"Why is that?"

"Because the next step might be more intelligent and permanent NPC personalities," she replied and Charlie smirked. He suspected she was programmed to say that. It would be interesting to see how NPC's continued to develop. After he had finished loading the last magazine he pushed it into Elva's mag well. Gripping the slide he pulled back to rack the weapon. Then took a moment to reload an extra round into the mag before holstering her.

The elevator door opened at his approach, and he slapped the controls as he entered. It ascended and deposited him in the noisy game center. Everywhere a line stretched to use a console. Gun Meister was getting more popular by the day, and Charlie had noticed the influx of new players over memorial weekend. He got behind two people discussing stats.

"Endurance is the new meta," A heavily armored man said. His swat suit was high necked and flared into a pair of Kevlar pauldrons. The helmet was off revealing a mop of red hair, a roguish nose, and bright red eyes. His chest was festooned with ammo pouches, grenades, other equipment. He must have had a max strength score to carry all that gear.

"Your hit points only last until I get a shot on you," the female player replied. She grinned wolfishly and patted the high caliber sniper rifle across her chest. She was thin, even more so than Charlie with a considerable amount of skin showing. Garish tattoos covered her arms in a pallet of different styles, while her legs were a mural of grinning skulls. She had on light green armor with leather pants, kneepads, and thick boots. Across her back she carried a folded ghillie suit.

"What about you?" Someone asked. Charlie continued to eye her tattoos half in appreciation. They must have cost a fortune in credits, and he considered getting some of his own.

"Hello?" The voice asked more loudly, and Charlie finally noticed both players looking at him.

"Huh? Oh, umm... I guess it depends on the situation." He replied. Charlie hadn't thought much of his stats since starting the game. He'd been concentrating on learning how to play Gun Meister.

"Look at him, he's still a bronze. The guy doesn't even know." The girl said rolling her dark gray eyes.

"Everyone has a right to an opinion," The first guy said in his defense.

"Mine are average," Charlie admitted. Unlike many, he hadn't maxed any of his abilities.

"A Jack, huh. I started off like that." The first guy said.

"Jack?"

"Jack-of-all-trades. Means you can fill multiple roles if needed. I'm a tank, Val here likes to think she can snipe." The armored man said gesturing to the woman.

"A better shot than you'll ever be," she scoffed. The girl shifted her weight and put a hand on her bare hip.

"I don't need to be a good shot with Vodka here," he mused. He patted a large weapon that was now visible. It was some kind of Russian-made machine gun. "She'll remind you those tree's you hide behind are concealment not cover." The man added with an equally ferocious smile.

The line moved, and the two veteran players started a match together. Both continued to bicker as they walked towards the elevator. A team game? Charlie wasn't opposed to working with others. He stepped up to the console, activated it, and selected 'Quick Team-Match' from the options.

"Please enter Lobby 108," it said.

Charlie returned to the elevators and went down. The lounge was lit by neon blue lights, which was different than the solo competition rooms. There it was a deep crimson color. Sitting on the couches, a group of scantily clad women talked. Charlie scanned the small room but there wasn't another male present. The women were clothed in nearly identical black bikinis.

"Where are your Meister's?" Charlie asked.

"We are the 'players' you misogynistic ass," a dark haired girl snapped.

"We're all girls, here," another said.

"Girls... give me a break. Only if you mean guy.in.real.life," a short girl said in derision. This third woman had teal hair and a flat chest. Like the others, she was dressed in a ridiculously tiny bikini. He pointed at her recognizing the smurf from his first game. Charlie had expected the player to already be silver.

"You."

"I surrender," she mimicked, and he flushed in annoyance. It was his first game, how was he supposed to know everything. She laughed slapping her knee.

"Really? He tried to give up?" The others joked.

"Too bad you aren't on the other team. Would have liked trying to kill you." He said moving into the room. A clock started above the main screen, and counted down from two minutes.

"What's that?" He asked pointing to it.

"The huddle time. Each team gets two minutes to discuss general tactics. How do you not know this?"

"I've only done death matches. Won my first today." He said a little smugly, but they clapped condescendingly. "Screw you all," he muttered moving to sit down. They laughed again and he crossed his arms over his chest. After this, he was going back to death matches, because it was easier to deal with other players by exchanging bullets.

"Is there a plan?" A dark haired girl asked.

The leader pointed to Charlie and said, "Mr. Deathmatch and Remy can go right. You two flank left, and I'll take the center."

The others seemed fine with the arrangement, so Charlie was stuck with the teal haired tit-less wonder. The timer ran down to zero and darkness settled in.

**[Match Started]**

The setting sun hung just over the horizon. Charlie found himself within the end zone of a football field. Behind them the tall goal post stood like the statue to a forgotten deity. An explosion had destroyed half the stadium seating, and what was left had been ruined by fire and age. In the middle of the field, a gutted tank sat. A twisted partially melted radar dish sagged at its side. The missile racks atop the turret were black from fire. Surrounding the vehicle were a half dozen sandbag entrenchments. The rest of the field was torn up from a heated, and ancient battle. Grass and weeds struggled up out of the scorched ground.

Someone jabbed him in the side with an elbow. "Look lively," a girl said jogging by. Two other women were already running towards the tank. Remy slapped his ass before taking off herself. Charlie started after her as she casually zig-zagged through the grass. Across the field he could just see the heads of the other team already running forward.

Twenty yards short of the center Remy jumped into a shallow depression. He was tempted to continue another few feet to a pile of sandbags, but several bullets cut through the knee high grass close by. He abandoned that idea and quickly jumped into the shallow depression. Remy was small enough she could kneel and look over the lip, but Charlie had to lay on his back or expose most of his body to fire.

Remy withdrew her .500 Smith & Wesson Magnum, which was now painted black with white skulls over the frame and barrel. A low-profile ghost ring sight was mounted atop. She raised herself up a little and fired once. A flame blossomed before the barrel as it went off. Remy made an annoyed sound, shook her head, and sank back.

"This is going to be a long match," Remy groaned relaxing against the dirt.

"I thought you'd be silver by now," Charlie said.

"I got up to Bronze Four easily enough, but players quickly became better shots. Philip here is good at scaring the new fish but he draws in the sharks. Lost several matches while I was reloading." She said flicking open the cylinder. From within her skimpy bikini top she withdrew a fresh cartridge and inserted it.

"Why did you start over when you can just reset your stats?"

"I was platinum, but I lost my rank due to team killing. I had a flamethrower and a grenade launcher. God those were the days. The pain threshold is set quite low but people would still writhe after I lit them up. They'd scream too, that was the best part. I loved the smell of burning napalm and the delicious aroma of cooked meat." Remy said caressing the hand cannon in her grip like a lover as she spoke.

"Ok..." Charlie said. This girl was starting to sound like a freak. She pressed the pistol to her face rubbing it around her cheek.

"When I lost my rank they kicked me from the clan. Tried to join other groups but they called me some very mean names, so I was stuck going solo or reset my character. Now I get to be a cute little girl." She said with a flourishing smile. Charlie stared at the strange woman in bewilderment.

"But... you're a guy?"

"Duh, 99% of the girls in this game are."

Remy caressed the revolver. "Hey Philip," she cooed. "How about you change forms for a quickie. We have a few minutes to burn." She asked in a coaxing voice. What the hell was this girl saying? They were in a firefight. Remy licked the barrel of the revolver before Charlie turned away. Definitely a full blown weirdo.

"Oh come on," she said in feigned annoyance. Remy purred as she pressed the gun to her face again. In a silky tongue she said, "I'll let you do butt stuff... You know you love it."

Charlie screamed. He'd had enough of being in this fox hole. At this point, he would rather risk enemy fire than spend another second with this girl. He stood and sprinted towards the nearby sandbags. Ahead of him, two heads appeared looking in his direction, but he focused entirely on reaching cover. Bullets churned the grass around him, before one caught him in the side dropping him to the ground. He struggled to gain his feet but his right leg refused to function. Charlie pulled himself through the grass toward cover. The two enemies stood trying to get a shot, and bullets continued to kick up dirt around him.

A massive boom sounded nearby, and the head of one of his attackers disappeared in a cloud of red mist. The other quickly dropped below sight level. Slowly Charlie managed to crawl behind the sandbags. The pain was like someone insistently poking him with one of those joke buzzers. It wasn't bad, but he couldn't move his right leg in the slightest.

"Thanks for baiting them," Remy shouted from the nearby foxhole.

71

"Sure thing," Charlie muttered. He'd just wanted to get away from that girl, and getting shot at was not a part of the plan. He glanced over the sandbags. The ruined tank was still about ten yards away. To his left, the girls were exchanging rounds with someone. The enemy team was down a person, but his leg was crippled and steadily leaking red fluid. He'd already seen some gruesome scenes. Enough to become desensitized to the sight of blood.

The buzzer went off above, and for another minute nothing happened on either side. Charlie put his back to the sandbags and glanced over again. He considered crawling the rest of the way to the tank. It wasn't far but the ground around it was a scorched no man's land. The tank was melted from the outside like a wax candle left in a summer window. The sand around the vehicle had turned into black glass.

A rock landed nearby making him jump. He looked back to see Remy doing hand signs. She pointed to herself, then to the tank, and finally with two fingers toward the enemy. Charlie hoped she wanted covering fire because he nodded.

A lot happened at once. On his left gunfire erupted as the enemy team made their move. Remy jumped from her foxhole and ran towards the tank. Charlie raised himself up on his good knee as the one enemy on the left started shooting from cover. He couldn't see through the grass but he fired back at what he hoped was their position. The little teal haired psycho made it to the tank, and hunkered down trying to make herself as small as possible. On his left side the gun battle petered out on a dissonant note. He couldn't see any of the other girls which didn't bode well. Charlie pulled a fresh mag free of its holder and reloaded. The used one went into the last slot. It still had rounds left but he wanted to top up the pistol. Finally, he laid down among the grass and weeds for a lower profile.

Remy sat listening for movement. Charlie couldn't hear anything other than the sound of moving grass. All was quiet for several more minutes as the red line crept closer. He had a choice at this point. Charlie could risk the crawl to the tank or stay in cover to provide fire. There was at least one enemy left. His teammates hadn't made a peep after the gun fight, and he suspected they were all dead which left just Remy and himself.

Slowly two people crept around the side of the vehicle. One in each direction. Being further away he could see both were men, so obviously not teammates. The red line was almost on him, but if he moved out now he would be seen. Charlie shifted with deliberate care aiming Elva at the second man. He had to hope Remy could manage her own battle. The red line crossed over his feet, and he instantly lost all sensation in them. Still, Charlie didn't move or fire until the guy was fully in view. The numb feeling crept up his calves to his knees.

"Now!" The man yelled dashing around the tank as a second did the same near the front. Charlie fired several times and the man danced as the rounds struck him. He slammed into the vehicle before sliding to the blackened ground. The red line crossed over Charlie's waist as Remy exchanged fire with her own target. Red filled his vision, and the door to the lounge opened. Three girls were waiting inside.

"Looks like we win."

"I'm just as surprised," the blonde girl said.

"Lasted longer than any of you," Charlie said moving forward. The female glanced back with an annoyed expression, but said nothing.

"I wasn't holding out hope with the noobie and that weird psycho."

"The psycho won the match, so you can shove it up your ass," Remy said from behind them.

"Well, I am out." The blonde said making for the elevator. Charlie checked his stats. He was 2k richer and had two additional kills and one death. His battle rank had also risen again to Bronze Four.

"Thanks for the assist," Remy said from nearby.

"I don't know what to say. It was... well... interesting. I'll say that much." He replied without looking back.

"Want to run another game together?" She asked, which was literally the last thing he wanted, but thankfully he had an excuse.

"I already won a match today so I'll pass. I'm going shopping real quick and then logging out for dinner." He said glancing back. Her instincts were good, and she was obviously skilled, but her personality needed work. Remy shifted her weight under his scrutiny and rested a hand on her slim hip. The black cannon hung under her arm rocked back and forth.

"What's your name?" She asked, and Charlie paused trying to think of an excuse. He was reluctant to give it to her because she creeped him out something fierce, but Remy had been platinum before. It might be a good idea to stay on friendly terms.

"Charlie," he said extending his hand. Her fingers were delicate in his grasp.

"Remy," she replied giving his hand a long squeeze. "Wanna do it?" She asked without hesitation, and he ran for the elevator. It opened, and he slapped the controls as fast as he could. The expression on his face must have been something because Remy was laughing as the doors closed.

"Charlie your heart rate is elevated. Are you ok?" Elva asked with some concern.

"I think I just met the devil incarnate," he rasped in a shaking voice.

# CHAPTER SEVEN

## *Beach House*

Charlie didn't stop running until he'd put a few blocks of virtual distance between himself and the competition center. He paused, breathing hard, and waited for the crossing light. He had a mind to spend some of his hard-earned credits on weapon upgrades, and another spare magazine.

"What kind of mods can I get for you?" He asked as the light changed.

"As a bronze ranked player your choices are limited. This is to keep all the pistols roughly equal. At silver, you'll be able to customize me however you wish."

"Do you have any suggestions?"

"A weapon skin would be nice," Elva offered after a few seconds. Decorating your weapon was in vogue, and Elva spent a lot of time in that form.

"I can do that, but a pretty paint job won't help me kill other players."

"You'll only be able to buy magazines and different sights. Revolvers can alter their barrel length since they can't increase in ammo capacity." Elva said keeping step with him. That did make sense. The developers wanted to give everyone a fair chance. The mall came into view, and they entered the cafeteria lobby.

"Is there a way I can give you cash?" He asked. There were going to be times he couldn't get on and Elva needed to eat.

"We can't own anything but you can buy cash cards." She said and he looked around. There had been a customer help desk in the mall for that, and he found an NPC blithely waiting the counter.

"How can I help you?" She asked.

"I need a cash card."

She took a black plastic card from the stack, inserted it into the reader, and pointed to the screen on his side. "How much would you like to put on?" The woman asked. Elva had been a helping partner, and he didn't want to keep filling up the card every week. He selected two-thousand credits, and placed his palm on the surface to confirm the transaction. There, at least Elva wouldn't starve. He turned and handed it to his weapon. She looked oddly pleased sliding the card into her back pocket.

They wandered into the holster store, and splurged on a ten round magazine. It was a thousand credits, which was a ridiculous price but he might need those two extra rounds. Next Charlie needed some night-sights. He'd already been in two matches that were near sunset. During those matches, he'd had a tough time getting a sight picture. Several stores down was a boutique specializing in optics, and he found a set of Trijicon Low-Profile Night Sights. The front and back posts had green glowing dots, and even in total darkness, all he had to do was line up the circles.

"How do you install these?" he asked holding out the item. Elva squirmed a little which was odd for her. Normally she was bluntly forward.

"After you buy it I just need a little privacy," she said pointing to a back door which resembled a changing room. He bought it and followed her back to the door, but she stopped him from following her inside.

"It's umm... very personal," she said clearly uncomfortable.

"I've seen you naked, we've had sex," Charlie said rolling his eyes. She pushed him lightly and closed the door in his face. From inside he heard a humming sound followed by a moan. Under the door crack, yellow light spilled out which grew in intensity. It was hard to describe the noises after that. Both gun and human seemed to be present. There was a shrill orgasmic cry followed by the sound of a slide racking. Slowly the light faded and the door opened. Elva stood just inside flush with crimson.

"Let's see it," he said holding out a hand. Elva nodded as her cheeks continued to redden. She changed into weapon form which landed in his palm.

"Yes, that is much better," he said pointing the gun at a nearby mannequin. Even under the mall's bright lights, he could still make out the glowing dots. Next he reloaded Elva with the extended magazine, which stuck out of the grip by about two inches, and noticeably increased the weight of the gun.

The night sights, magazine, and cash card cost him 3600 credits, so Elva's weapon skin would have to come later. It was getting late and Charlie needed to find a bed. Sleeping in cheap hotels was getting old, and he was ready to drop some money on a home.

"You can change back," he said and Elva returned to her human form.

"How do we find an apartment?" he asked.

"There is a directory down the block. You can either buy property or rent it." She said stepping closer to Charlie. Elva took his arm, and guided him from the store. Outside the sun had finally dropped below the horizon. Street lamps and the headlights of passing cars lit up the avenue. Charlie gave up trying to retrieve his arm as they walked together down the street and entered a building next to the intersection. Along the walls were pictures of real estate. Several screens sat waiting, but the lobby was otherwise empty.

Whoever had used the console last had left the listing open. It was a million credit mansion, and he suspected a clan had pooled their resources to buy it. It had a hundred rooms, an Olympic-sized swimming pool, and an interactive practice range. Pictures of the property showed a silicon valley fortress with a nine-foot wall that circled the compound.

He exited the page and did a search for properties for lease. An interactive map appeared and he could further refine his search. Quickly he excluded hotels and anything over six thousand dollars. The cheapest apartment was only eight hundred a month and it was near the competition center.

Charlie clicked the link and said, "Ugh." It was little better than the hotel he'd stayed in last night. The wallpaper was peeling off, and he noticed a water stain on the ceiling. That property was just a little too cheap. He exited the listed and tried properties further out.

The third place he checked out seemed to fit. It was a two bedroom beach house for lease and it was only three thousand a month. The problem was that it was at the edge of the city. It would be a ten-mile walk to the competition center, but there were buses, so he could catch the metro most of the way into town.

"Three thousand creds..." he mused tapping the edge of the screen. It was easily doable, especially if he won a single match per month.

"Lease?" It queried when he placed his palm on the screen. He hit accept, and a small compartment opened nearby. Inside was an electronic key-set. On the tag attached to this was listed the address, "13 North - Sex on the Beach Way." He pocketed the key and turned looking for Elva. She had occupied herself with another computer across the room.

"Ready to go?"

The metro was thankfully nearby and he climbed aboard with Elva. Filling the bus were dozens of other players heading home for the night. After flashing his palm over the pay console, the took a seat near the back. Across from Charlie, a man was openly making out with two girls. Both his hands were digging for gold within their unbuttoned pants as the three canoodled. Charlie rolled his eyes and glanced out the window. The city slowly rolled past, and after ten minutes of heavy petting, the trio got off... of the bus that is.

It took almost an hour to reach the city outskirts, but the bus dropped them off a couple of blocks from his new house. The sign depicted a couple doing it under an umbrella. Below the image was another sign reading, "North - Sex on the Beach Way." The sound of the surf grew stronger as they neared the beach and a small ranch house grouped with a few others came into view. As Charlie approached the front door the key fob chirped. A red light under the door lock turned green, and he inserted the key opening the door. His first thought was that the place was empty. The listing hadn't said anything about furniture but he'd assumed there would be stuff. The only thing in the house was in the master bedroom. The king sized bed probably couldn't fit through the door. From the living room, two sliding glass doors opened onto an enclosed porch. The beach began just on the other side. Elva stood near the bay doors looking at the half moon rising over the water.

Charlie walked into the master bedroom, and the LED bulb flashed to life filling the room with a soft yellow glow.

*"That worked at least,"* he thought. Charlie sat on the king-sized bed and dropped the shopping bags to the floor. He'd had a hectic day. What with having his world view shattered and pieced together again. Then he'd managed to win two matches in a row. Elva wandered into the room and toward the closet. It was several feet deep with plenty of room for a future wardrobe.

"Are you glad I did better today?"

Elva turned toward him searching his face. There was a pause, one slightly longer than usual, before she strode toward him. She grasped the hem of her tank top, dragging it over her head, and her breasts came free with an erection inducing bounce. The shirt dropped to the floor. Her long fingers fiddled with the unfamiliar button on her shorts before sliding the zipper down. Wiggling her hips, she shimmied out of the daisy dukes and kicked them towards the top.

"I am thrilled," she stated turning and sitting naked on his lap. That pause from Elva suggested she had struggled with another option.

"You were going to say something else?" He asked curiously. Elva looked back, searching his face again.

"I don't personally care, but it's better that you did well," She said at last. Those were two very different statements, so he decided to reward her honesty.

"Why is that?" He asked sliding his hand between her legs. He wasn't above searching for some golden honey himself. Elva opened her mouth to say something but gasped as Charlie stroked a finger down her sex. It was already slightly wet, and she leaned back parting her long legs.

"Statistically... players who do well—are more likely to remain," She said between quickening breaths. Charlie rewarded her further by slipping a finger inside. It was warm and wet. She gasped again and reached back gripping his neck. Elva shifted and unconsciously started rocking back and forth in Charlie's lap as his fingers picked up speed. There was no mistaking

Elva as human. Despite her beautiful body, she smelled like a weapon. One that had been recently used. The aroma of metal and gun smoke quickly filled the air as Elva grew more excited.

"Do you need a cleaning?" He asked.

"My—" She groaned as he furiously circled her clitoris. Elva, breathing heavily, tried again with, "My efficiency—hasn't been affected—yet." His fingers fiddled faster and he continued to occasionally plunge them inside. Maybe he ought to get into the habit of cleaning her daily. Charlie had finally started taking things more seriously, and he didn't want to slip back into lazy habits. Elva let out a long moan, and her legs lifted into the air as her toes curled in orgasmic bliss.

"Oh Charlie..." Elva cried.

She shuddered and shook for almost a minute before slipping from his lap to the floor. She turned and began to unfasten his belt, quickly tore pants free, and cupped his manhood. Charlie relaxed back on the mattress as Elva started licking. She must have discovered a few new techniques because her tongue slid along his shaft in ever more complex patterns. Charlie closed his eyes, relaxing back onto the bed. Lips closed over his erection and he groaned in pleasure. Gun Meister had to be cheating. Charlie was pretty sure his sensitivity levels were a few percentage points higher than real life. When he opened his eyes Elva was staring at him searching his face for any expression of pain.

"Much better," he admitted reaching down. Charlie grabbed a wrist pulling her up and forced Elva onto the bed. Her technique had improved but he wanted to fuck. Charlie got behind the kneeling woman, slid inside, and quickly built into a steady butt-jiggling rhythm.

"This was better too," he thought to himself. Was there some special code at work or was it just mental?

Over Memorial Weekend the sex had felt like a booby prize or a consolation. Like a child getting a toy after throwing a public tantrum. It seemed wrong getting laid after losing so much. Tonight he was flushed with victory. He deserved to get the prom queen and fuck her too. Charlie pushed her forward with the power of his thrusting, and Elva's arms buckled. Her legs began to shake as a second orgasm overwhelmed her. Charlie held onto her waist with an iron grip, and through a tangle of golden hair Elva stared back at him. He smiled down, withdrew from her, and slapped her ass hard. She let out a surprised shriek of pleasure, as he plunged back inside. His fingers dug into her fleshy hips as he neared his own peek. There was no doubt about it; tonight the sex was the best yet. He finished by dragging her back onto him, and Elva made a sound which was half moan, half whimper as his essence filled her. After a few seconds, he withdrew and fell onto the bed panting for breath.

"I changed my mind. I like it when you win." Elva said and he laughed. She turned pressing herself to his chest and laid her head in the crook of his shoulder. Charlie, in turn, ran a hand down her spine. Her hair and body still smelled metallic but he was quickly coming to like the scent.

"I have to warn you," Charlie said. Elva stopped licking him to look up into his eyes. "I won't be on tomorrow. There is a mandatory meeting after work."

"Didn't you already have one of those?" She asked in a voice still heavy from sex.

"It started off as a joke but it's become a weekly thing. Every Tuesday some of the agents get together at the bar. We mostly just drink and talk shit about the job. Good stress relief that helps us get over the hump in the week." He said running a hand over her bare bottom. Charlie was reminded of the cash card he'd picked up. It had originally been for food when he was away, but there was no reason Elva couldn't take care of some of the drudge work. After all, this was her home too.

"Tomorrow, please take the card and pick up some appliances," he said resting his hand on her ass.

"I can do that. Is there anything you want?"

Charlie shook his head and said, "Just pick up what you think we need. I'm going to logout and get some sleep. I don't want to be late for work again." He touched his temple and a popup appeared. Before he could exit Elva pounced on him. She lunged upward and closed her mouth over his. Elva forced his lips open with hers and slid her tongue inside.

"Hmmmm... mmph," he mumbled as Elva went soul searching via his throat. She hunted his tongue down, cornering it within his mouth. Saliva slid down his chin as she continued to dominate him. His erection grew again before she pulled back.

"Goodnight," she purred in a throaty voice. Charlie quickly logged out before he lost his willpower and jumped her again.

# CHAPTER EIGHT

## *Mugs and Mugged*

Thankfully there was only another hour left in the day and he'd just finished making a sale. It had been a hard battle but he sat back feeling pretty good about himself. The ever beautiful Jennifer stopped next to his desk.

"Are you going to the meet-up tonight?" Jen asked, and he nodded in assent. She gave a small apologetic frown before saying, "I'm going to pass this evening." That was worrisome. Spending time with Jennifer out of work was one of the reasons he went to those crawls.

"Please show up. Last time it was all men. The only thing they griped about was not getting laid. We need some estrogen in the mix or they get weird." He begged and Jen's frown deepened. She glanced at the other agents.

"I dunno."

"You need to come, it's not the same otherwise," he pleaded. Jen searched his face and chewed her lower lip.

"Fine but I won't be staying long," she said at last. Jen wandered off into the lot to look for another mark. Charlie pulled up the last customers' lease agreement. There was still some paperwork left to do, and he wanted to finish what little remained before leaving.

The bar was automated, which meant you just ordered via the table interface and waited for it to arrive. It was cheap, and close. A single overworked waitress was leapfrogging from table to table with a tray of liquid courage. She dropped four beers at their table along with a bottle of tequila and glasses. Along with this was a basket of lime slices and a salt shaker.

"Tomorrow is hump day, and I want you all to think positively!" Chad said holding up his beer. Everyone gave him the finger instead and he laughed.

"Raise them high!" Erick said lifting his beer up. Charlie instead, filled several shot glasses with amber colored tequila, and slid them toward the others.

"None for me," Jen said pushing her shot glass back.

"How many cars did you sell today?" Charlie asked.

"Three,"
"Four," Jen said sipping her beer.
"Damn, I only sold two," he groused. "Fuck this job," he added holding his alcohol up. The others joined him. The glasses rose as the group toasted again. He drained it and licked his salted hand.

Charlie filled another set of shots as lime slices disappeared from the basket. He glanced at Jennifer out of the corner of his eye. She'd barely touched her beer since arriving. She was hot, not Elva hot, but it was unfair being compared to digital perfection. Nonetheless, Jennifer was suited for a camera, and he wondered why she didn't take up modeling. She had an innocence to her face, although her eyes sometimes looked calculating, but that could have been the job. She raised her beer glass carefully taking another sip. Charlie watched her mouth as a pink tongue darted out to collect a stray bit of foam. For a few seconds he imagined what she'd look like with those lips wrapped around his—

An elbow jammed him in the side.

"Shot time fucker!" Chad said pushing his empty glass forward. Charlie shook his head annoyed at himself. He quickly poured several more rounds then stood. The others followed his example raising glasses and cups.

"Three, two, one... SHOT TIME!" The group yelled. Charlie drained the tequila and licked the back of his salted hand. Six empty glasses smacked against the table. They did this three more times before Chad seemed satisfied.

"You guys remember that meeting the other day?" Erick asked.

"I remember the boss's face when he handed Jen that little award. It was like he was giving out a Pulitzer Prize. Bet he was so proud of himself for putting that together on his computer." Charlie sneered reaching for a lime and bit into the tart fruit. Jen was still nursing her beer, so she said nothing, but smiled behind the glass.

"And the fucking cupcake?!? I mean seriously... He couldn't go online and order one of those little miniature trophies?" Charlie continued in a slightly slurred voice.

"You're a bit more salty than usual," Chad commented which was true. The tequila was hitting him fast tonight.

"Why shouldn't I be. I have four more days to pull a miracle out of my ass."

"What do you mean?" Jen asked.

"The great and powerful boss said I have a week to turn the numbers around. I busted my ass today and still only sold two cars." He answered reaching for the tequila bottle. "Two..." Charlie muttered pouring another shot.

"We're in a recession, nobody in their right mind is going to buy a car with the current interest rate," Chad said pushing his shot glass towards Charlie. He filled the glasses again.

"That's what I said," Charlie slurred. Erick passed the salt shaker around. Charlie took it and covered the back of his hand with the crystal granules, then lifted the shot glass in a toast.

"Too suckers and fuckers," he toasted clinking glasses with the others. The poison slid past his lips and down his throat, before he cringed from the taste. Quickly he licked the back of his hand and reached for another lime.

"Got a hot date there, Jen?" Chad asked. Charlie glanced at the woman. Every shot was making her even better looking. She straightened pursing those pert lips.

"No."

"You keep looking at your watch," the younger agent accused.

"I'm fine," Jen said again.

Charlie smirked and said, "Probably has a delicious piece of man meat waiting back home. Whip cream and cherry already donned." Jennifer blushed and drained the last of her beer.

"If you are going to insult me then I'm leaving."

"We're just teasing," Charlie quickly said.

"You are bombshell hot and you never talk about yourself," Chad accused.

"I like to be mysterious," Jen replied tartly as she gathered her purse. Great, the girl was fleeing. They'd gone too far and chased the only woman off. Now it would be another sausage fest.

"I'm out too," Charlie said.

"It has only been an hour, man." Erick said.

"Shit, I've had more shots than most of you combined," he replied standing. Charlie wobbled slightly before grabbing the table to steady himself. Jennifer walked past towards the exit as he pulled on his jacket. He reached across the table and snatched the bottle of tequila.

"Hey!" They exclaimed but he fled towards the door.

Charlie laughed as he drunkenly dodged other customers. He'd paid for the bottle, like hell would he leave it behind. He pushed open the door and stepped from the bar. The summer air felt like a used sauna towel slapping his face, and Charlie inhaled trying to gather his senses. Bottle in hand he stumbled toward his vehicle.

The lot was dimly lit except for the area immediately around the bar, so he was forced to awkwardly weave his way through the pools of light. He was maybe halfway to his car when he noticed Jennifer backed against her own vehicle. A man stood in front of her with a dark hoodie pulled over his head. Charlie couldn't see his face; however, he did see Jen's. Her expression was one Charlie had become intimately familiar with. Terror, pure and unadulterated. Gun Meister merged with reality. The target nearby wasn't aware of his presence. The man had his back to Charlie as he held something to Jennifer's stomach. Her eyes were wide with panic as she scrambled to open her purse. Charlie fumbled for the pistol at his thigh, only to discover it was missing.

Adrenaline began to surge, and he moved with more dexterity than his inebriated body should have allowed. Tequila spilled out of the bottle as he turned it over in his hand.

"Gimme yer fuck'n money, bitch," a thick dark voice hissed.

Charlie caught sight of a crudely duct-taped butterfly knife. The broken handle was wrapped to keep it from closing. Jen saw Charlie approaching, and her eyes tracked him. The man noticed her gaze and spun around. Charlie hopped forward swinging his makeshift club as hard as he could, and glass shattered against the man's face. He went down but the guy had a higher endurance score than most. The mugger reached with hate in his eyes, for the dropped knife, but Charlie stepped on the weapon. Blood and tequila dripped down the side of the man's fat cheek.

Charlie waved the broken bottle in his face as he hissed, "Sod off, before I give you a dirty nose job." The trash scrambled backward across the ground before gaining traction, and stumbling to his feet. He turned and fled the parking lot into the darkness. Almost immediately Charlie lost sight of the man in his dark clothes.

"Oh my God," Jen's shaking voice said. She slumped against her car beginning to shudder visibly.

He felt quite proud of himself. If this were Gun Meister, he would have gotten his first knife kill. He tried to take another drink of tequila as a reward. He brought the tip of the bottle to his mouth but nothing came out. He stared drunkenly at what remained of his tequila.

*"Damn, that was right... What a waste of good alcohol."* He thought, then sighed and tossed the broken remains into a nearby bush.

"What are you doing?" Charlie asked turning back to Jen. She fished about in her purse and produced a cell phone. Her nimble fingers quickly unlocked the screen.

"I'm obviously calling the police," she said. Charlie swatted drunkenly at the phone keeping her from dialing out.

"Fuck that. They're never going to find him."

"He tried to mug me," Jen snarled.

"What was he wearing? What did he look like?" Charlie asked slurring the words. "Only thing I recall was the empty expression on his fat face and those evil shifty eyes." He added looking around the lot. The mugging had gone down in less than a minute. No one else even noticed Jen's plight. "There are thousands of low life's like him." He said noticing the cheap knife on the ground. He bent and picked the blade up before tossing it into the bushes as well.

"What if he attacks someone else?" Jen raised her emotional voice as she asked.

"Dat piece of shit is goin home to put some ice on his head and lick what little remains of his pride." He answered in a drolling slur. Charlie wished the bottle hadn't broken in the fight.

"AnYway, don't you have a hawt date?" The adrenaline was exiting his system and the tequila was kicking in hard. In fact he was slipping into a full-blown blackout.

"Where are you going?" Jen asked holding the phone like it was a personal weapon. Her voice still shook with anger and tension.

"Homeee—" he replied giving the girl a sloppy wave. The short walk to his car seemed farther than he first thought. He managed to unlock it and slumped into the driver's seat. As he turned on the car a high pitched alarm went off.

"Alcohol detected, locking out manual controls." The onboard computer said. Well, that was fair, given he was just a little drunk. Still, he didn't like the slightly reproving tone it had used.

"ScrEw you tu," he muttered.

"Please state your destination," the car responded.

"Hurm," He mumbled.

"Location unknown, please state your destination." It asked again in a patient voice. He blew out his breath in annoyance.

"Hommme," he slurred loudly. The seatbelt slid down over his chest and the car backed out of the stall. Slowly darkness crept into his vision.

In the void he half expected to see the words, 'Match Complete.'

Charlie woke with the taste of death in his mouth. His head pounded, and he groaned from the pain. The alarm wailed at him insistently until he wormed his way closer to the nightstand. He slapped the mobile and managed to shut it off. He waited praying the pain would fade but to little avail. Dull explosions continued to go off behind his eyes.

He could not remember how the hell he got home. Large portions of last night were little more than a slideshow flashing in his mind. Slowly he rolled from bed to discover he was butt-ass naked. He didn't even have boxers on. Charlie groaned clutching his aching head and went into the bathroom for some Advil. It smelled like a bar and a sewer had taken part in a sex orgy. Someone—most likely himself—had pissed and vomited on the floor next to the toilet. A soiled towel lay half in the puddle, and a set of waterlogged clothes were in the shower.

"I do not need this," Charlie groaned pinching the bridge of his nose to keep from breathing in the stink, and tossed a clean towel over the toxic puddle to soak. The wet clothes he put into the hamper. Charlie swallowed two Advil dry and brought his toothbrush with him into the shower. As the water turned hot he scrubbed the back of his tongue. He spit a foul lump of saliva towards the drain, which landed thickly, and oozed down the hole. When he was done scouring the inside of his mouth he soaped up and washed.

Once clean, he climbed from the shower and toweled off. After wiping up as much vomit as possible he found a bottle of bleach and poured it over the tiles. With another spare towel, he wiped up the remainder. Finally, he went back into his bedroom and dressed.

The bright summer light accosted him as he left the apartment. He recoiled taking momentary shelter under the eve. The Advil had only just started doing its job, and he shaded his eyes with a hand. Finally, he risked the dash to his car, climbed inside, and just barely made it to work on time. There was already a customer waiting near the building. Charlie went over, smiled, and introduced himself.

"Can I help you," he asked.

"I'll be in America for a month and I'm looking for a cheap run-about car," the man said in a decidedly British accent. Charlie hadn't checked in yet but this was a possible sale.

"We can help you there," he said guiding the man towards the used car lot. It didn't take much; the Brit was foreign and affluent. After the paperwork was signed, Charlie handed over the keys to the used Jaguar. His day might have started off rough but it was quickly turning around. An hour passed in relative quite, but eventually a shadow crossed over his desk.

Jennifer stood before him in a tight button up shirt and a skinny tie. She lifted a hand dragging a lock of platinum blonde hair over her ear and exposed a set of tiny crosses for earrings.

"I wanted to thank you."

"Thank me?" he asked in confusion. This made her pause searching at his face.

"For helping me..." She said more slowly. He remembered as if through a dream a pair of dark eyes and a duct taped knife. It was still hazy and he put out a hand.

"There was more tequila in my veins than blood, so I don't recall much of what happened last night. " He admitted.

"Well, it was courageous." Jen said looking around to see if anyone was nearby. She pushed another lock of hair behind her ear. "Would you like to get some lunch?" She asked after a second.

*"Holy shit, is she asking me out on a date?"* He thought.

"I would honestly love that," he replied immediately. Visions of her tangled in his bed sheets momentarily filled his imagination. Charlie stood and pushed his chair in. It was early, but he wasn't going to waste this opportunity. "Let's go, I haven't had breakfast yet." Jennifer went to her desk to fetch her purse and jacket.

"There's a place I like around the corner," she said leading Charlie from the building. Today was getting better and better he mused matching her stride.

"So fill me in on my heroic escapades. The last thing I remember was teasing you in the bar." He said as they walked across the lot.

She made a false start. The memories were still raw in her mind and she swallowed hard. "I... went out to my car to leave but I didn't notice someone follow me. I really should have been paying more attention. He had a knife and I just couldn't believe what was going on." She said in a controlled voice. Charlie matched her stride as she moved down the block.

"That's when you came up behind him and hit him with a bottle. Then you poked him in the cheek with the broken end, and he took off."

"Well, that does sound very bad ass," he admitted after some consideration. Charlie only had images and a few snatches of sound to match her story with his memories.

Charlie stepped forward and opened the door to the Thai restaurant. They ordered food and sat. Jennifer set her purse next to her on the table. They chatted rather awkwardly for a few minutes, because Charlie didn't know much about Jen. She kept to herself which made getting to know her a challenge.

Eventually, Jen pulled a mini-bottle of water from her purse along with an electrolyte packet for sports drinks. "Sorry, I have a habit of keeping one of these on me at all times," Jen said dumping the mix into the bottle. It turned a blood red color.

"I know what you mean. Twice I came out of dive with a severe case of cottonmouth, so I keep a bottle next to my chair." He admitted with a laugh. Maybe he too should get some electrolyte packets for long gaming sessions. Jennifer froze as her eyes searched his face.

"You... you dive?" She asked tentatively. He hadn't expected the beautiful woman before him to be addicted to virtual games. She seemed like the fit and active type.

"Am I a dive junkie?" He asked and shrugged.

Jen winced and said,"I hate that word."

"It's fitting. I only recently got into virtual diving, and I fell pretty hard." Charlie admitted. The food arrived and he picked up his fork to start eating. Jen, however, was still looking at him.

"What do you play?" She asked.

"It's a little combat sim you probably haven't heard of it," he answered taking a bite of food. "It's called Gun Meister," he added and Jen shook her head.

"You?"

"Blood and Pride," she said picking up her own utensil. It was Charlie's turn to shake his head. He'd expected her to say Nigmus Online or one of the big MMO's. Still this was a chance. He had a real connection with Jen, especially if she gamed.

"What's it about?" He asked with interest.

"It has vampires, werewolves, mages, and its... I mean there's a lot of clan politics and faction warfare."

"Free?"

"You can download it for free, but there's a subscription," she admitted. That was pretty standard with online games now. They wanted people to try it out and get hooked.

"Maybe I'll give it a try tonight. You can show me the ropes." Charlie suggested and smiled winningly.

"I'd like that," Jen said smiling. There must have been something in his face or a hopeful look in his eyes because she added, "I can introduce you to my boyfriend."

Charlie kept his smile but he felt like someone had kicked his chair out from under him. He covered himself by taking another bite of food.

*"Shit... I'll look like an asshole if I backed out now."*

Jennifer was better at reading people than he'd expected. "If you're not interested..."

"I would like to try it out," he responded quickly. Charlie gathered himself forcing his way out of the emotional rut he'd fallen into. "I mean it's nice to meet someone else who is into online games. It's become kind of a dark hobby lately." He replied finishing his food. Well, romance was out the window. Jen smiled again more naturally.

"How do I find you once I'm in game?" he asked.

"This is the night club number, just ask for Camile. I'm Second in Command of the San Francisco Toreador." She said pushing a piece of paper towards Charlie. There was a seven digit number written in an elegant hand.

"I'll give it a shot," he promised.

# CHAPTER NINE

## *Blood and Pride*

Blood and Pride loading...
Entering Darkness...
New Player Detected...
Creating Monster...

In the darkness blood dripped down the walls filling a dark crimson pool. Three figures rose from the liquid on iron pedestals. The first was a vampire, who's fanged grin was wintry and unmerciful. The second was a tall werewolf in it's full form who barred its predatory teeth. The final figure was a human wrapped in a magical aura.

Charlie focused on the vampire and it slid forward through the bloody pool. The other figures disappeared and six more replaced them. One was a hideous creature half covered in shadow. Another wore a straight jacket and face paint. He skipped over these and selected a vampire straddling a motorcycle.

"The Brujah are a clan of idealistic rebels and roughnecks with little to no organization. Even the young are quick to anger and fierce in combat." A low rumbling voice said from the darkness. He ignored the other options and selected the new figure.

The blood drained from the pool, and the Brujah slid from the chopper seat and approached. A body and facial editor appeared next. Charlie adjusted the man's features until he looked vaguely like himself, but he came out with hair more brown than blond. A complicated attribute and skill screen appeared next, and he was overwhelmed by the amount of choices, so Charlie just accepted the recommended options.

Darkness crowded in on his vision, and almost immediately, he heard the sound of someone digging. It quickly grew louder until something metal struck him in the chest. The dirt fell away from him as a group of people stood over his shallow grave.

"Told you new meat was coming in, and it's a guy! You owe me twenty bucks." A dark haired man said holding out a hand. Several bills flew into the air which were quickly snatched and tucked away. Charlie started to sit up, and brushed dirt from his ragged t-shirt. One girl took pity on him and held out a helping hand. He took it, and was brutally hauled from the shallow grave.

"You're new to the game or it would have spawned you in somewhere else. Welcome to Blood and Pride." She said with a fanged smile.

"Thanks."

A tall man with thick brown hair stepped toward him. The vampire wore a simple wife-beater under a patched black leather jacket. He removed a pair of dark sunglasses and his eyes flashed red and orange like a bonfire. "I'm Jake, the current Prince of the Brujah."

"Charlie," he replied.

The man poked him in the chest with a thick finger. "The important thing to keep in mind is your thirst level. Don't feed and you'll enter frenzy." Jake said reaching behind him. He pulled a five-foot tall girl into view. The little Latina wore leather pants and an abused t-shirt. "Drink up. This is the only freebie you'll get from the Brujah. We aren't the Ventrue or those Toreador emo's. In this clan, you find your own work and hunt your own food." He said pushing the girl towards him. She hesitantly came forward pulling her shirt down over a bare shoulder, and exposed a neck bitten countless times.

His vision slowly turned red, and a spiderweb of lines began to glow under the girl's skin. The woman's heart began beating faster in anticipation. As he opened his mouth, fangs grew from his upper canines, and Charlie leaned forward sinking them into the highway of blood. The girl gave a soft, pained moan and sweet candy liqueur filled his mouth. He swallowed the hot essence, but was halfway full when a voice stopped him.

"You'll kill her if you keep drinking. I'd rather not waste my time tonight burying a mortal."

Charlie withdrew his fangs. Her cheeks were sunken and she had dark rings around her eyes, but she straightened her shirt and returned to the clan leader like an obedient pet.

"I'm supposed to meet a friend on here. Is there a phone I can use?" Charlie asked.

"Who's that?"

"Camile of the Toreador," Charlie said glancing around. The other vampires lost interest in him and wondered off to entertain themselves.

"How do you know each other?"

"We work together," he admitted.

"There's a pay phone in the bar," Jake said leading the way inside. The dirt lot abutted a small biker joint, and he followed them inside. "You'll need a ride to get into the city as well. Take one of the loaners." Jake said slapping a set of keys and a couple of quarters on the counter.

"Thanks," Charlie said turning to the pay-phone. He slotted a quarter and dialed the number Camile had given him earlier that day.

"Club Envy," a sultry female voice said.

"I'd like to speak to Camile."

"She's unavailable."

"Well, she's expecting my call, so go get her." He said and was placed on hold for a long wait. Charlie turned to watch the group of vampires nearby. They were playing pool on a beer stained table. The prize was a half naked woman partially tied up and gagged nearby. Her heavy breasts bounced as she struggled against the rope.

"Camile," a sultry, seductive voice said.

"It's Charlie," he replied.

"Sorry about the wait. I was in a clan meeting. Come over anytime or do you need a pickup?"

"No, I borrowed transportation." He said and Camile gave him directions to the club.

"See you soon," she said. The phone clicked as she hung up and he put the receiver back.

Charlie left the bar and walked to the line of bikes parked out front. A small rope marked off a few loaners, and he straddled the first motorcycle. It started with a meaty roar before the engine settled into a low growl. He backed out then roared down the street. The club was impossible to miss once he got nearby. From a block away he could hear the music which was loud, dark, gothic techno. A ten-meter tall sign read, 'Envy' in black-light letters. Under this were the words, "Lust Welcome."

A line waited to get inside, and people in slutty club clothes wrapped around the block, but Charlie had no intention of waiting. He strode toward the entrance where two bouncers were keeping the club exclusive. The first man was a seven foot tall gorilla, but he quickly unhooked the rope letting Charlie in. Just inside the entrance, a trio of girls were staking out new arrivals. Each of the females had black hair, black makeup, and black dresses on. Frankly, they looked like a gothic backup band waiting to get on stage. They hissed at him exposing their fangs.

"What was that for?"

"Why, oh why did you have to be a Brujah?" A woman asked in a smooth and sultry voice. From out of the gyrating crowd, a vampire in red strolled toward him. It was Jen, but only after her sex appeal had been cranked up to max. Her natural wheat blonde hair was now platinum colored. The former innocence in her nose and chin had hardened into something predatory. The look was magnified by the black eyeliner and deep red lipstick. This matched her silk dress which hugged the curves of her shapely body. Black batwing stockings ran down her legs showing off tantalizing snatches of pure white flesh. As she stopped before him, Charlie whistled.

"Stop that," she said smacking his arm.

"Hot is hot," he said defensively. Camile hit him again but smiled a little. He glanced at the trio who were still eyeing him like week old leftovers. "Jen, are you the only vampire around here that isn't wearing all black?"

"Remember to call me Camile here," she said giving him a glare. Then in a more normal tone she added, "I'm glad I came down here to find you. If you'd made it any further into the club you would've been attacked."

"Oh?"

"Camile, who's your friend?" A male asked in a voice that was smooth and commanding. A figure strolled through the crowd like a shark through a school of fish. The humans parted for him though many stared in abject awe. He was movie star handsome, and an aura of authority hung about him like a palpable cloak. Charlie instantly disliked the man, though mostly because he seemed to be Jen's boyfriend.

"Stephan, let me introduce you to my co-worker." Camile pronounced the name 'Stefawn' like it was foreign.

"This is Charlie," she said glancing at him for confirmation. He nodded and extended a hand.

"Charmed," Stephan said with eyes that suggested he was anything but.

"Likewise," Charlie said giving the other man's hand a firm squeeze. Their introductions were interrupted by a white haired male vampire running up. He tapped 'Stefawn' on the shoulder and whispered into his ear.

"Now? Of course they are, I should have guessed." The dark haired Prince said.

"What's going on?" Camile asked.

"Your friend is a spy."

"What, no—" She said quickly.

"I don't have time right now, Camile. Take him below."

Several vampires materialized from the crowd and grabbed his arms.

Charlie tried to struggle but fledglings were little stronger than human, and after an initial attempt, he just let them drag him downstairs. Camile followed after trying to protest his innocence. Charlie found himself dragged into a concrete prison far below the club. The two vampires threw him into the room, and slid the iron bars into place, locking him inside. He stood dusting his pants off as Camile entered the cell block. Two human guards followed her in, and took up positions next to his cell.

Charlie gave the bars to his cell a pathetic yank and said, "Your boyfriend is an asshole."

"He's just stressed," Camile said defensively.

"Why the hell did he think I'm a spy?"

"Tensions between the Brujah and the Toreador has been increasing for months," Camile said turning and pacing back and forth. She chewed the fingernail of her thumb in agitation.

"Ok, that might've been good to mention before I started, but why is that?"

Camile continued to pace for a few seconds in thought. Then she turned and said, "There are some unique artifacts in the game. One for each clan. In two years only the Brujah one has been found. It's a two-handed sword of incredible power. Especially in the hands of a Brujah vampire. We have it; they want it."

"Ok... So just sell it to them. I'm sure they'll bend over backward for it."

Camile swatted at the idea with her hand like an annoying fly. Her tone was acidic as she said, "It would destroy the balance of power if they got it. The Brujah would bully the other factions and take over the city. We told them if they want the sword to look for our item. For months the players have been scouring the server searching for the other Uniques."

Charlie turned toward the distinctive sound of gunfire. He recognized the staccato of an automatic weapon. The bass from the club above popped and crackled into an ominous silence.

"Just great," Camile said turning to a guard. She pointed down the corridor and said, "Go to the vault."

"I'm sorry ma'am we were ordered to guard the prisoner by the Prince," The guard said in a militaristic voice.

Jen growled, "Stupid NPC's. Well, you can guard him as we move. I'm taking the prisoner to the vault."

Camile approached his cell. "Let's get you out of here," she said and gripped the inch thick iron bars with her feminine fingers. With a little effort, she started to bend them like they were taffy. Soon there was space enough for Charlie to snake his way out.

"What's going on?" Charlie asked with interest. At least his first night in the game was proving exciting.

"The attack on the Toreador Compound was just a diversion. Somehow they found out we're keeping the artifact here." She said stepping back.

"Was that wise?"

"The Brujah have made so many attempts on the Head Quarters, we decided to build a vault under the club. When we aren't sleeping most of us hang out here anyway. We employed only a handful of NPC's for the construction and killed them when we were done." She said making Charlie wince. That was a little drastic but apparently vampires played by different rules. Camile went over to a locker and withdrew a bulky fifty-caliber Desert Eagle. She handed it to him along with two full magazines.

"Ma'am the prisoner is not allowed to have guns," One guard said.

"The Prince never said he couldn't be armed. He only ordered you to guard him. I'm telling you it's fine this prisoner has a weapon. You will not fire on him unless he shoots one of you." She said poking the man in the chest.

"Yes ma'am," the human said with a salute. Charlie was amazed that these NPC's were so strictly literal. They sounded like artificial dolls which made Elva's complex personality all the more impressive. Camile didn't bother taking one herself. Instead, she turned and trotted from the prison.

Charlie and his guards had trouble keeping up with Camile. She moved down the corridor like a cheetah in full sprint. He was halfway down the hall when a leather-clad vampire came out of a side passage between them. The brujah's mouth and neck was covered in fresh blood and his eyes blazed with inner light. Charlie skidded to a stop, raised the magnum with both hands, and fired. The head of the grinning vampire disappeared in a red and pink mist as the silver nitrate bullet split his skull like a ripe melon.

"What the hell?" Charlie asked looking down at the pistol. He hated to admit it, but he had missed. The second he'd pulled the trigger the biker had shifted right slightly, so the bullet should have missed by an inch. His one point in pistol skill had compensated for his shit aim. Charlie felt cheated and more than a little robbed of any sense of accomplishment. For days he had practice his marksmanship in Gun Meister, but this game held his hand like a child. He wondered what having five points in pistols would be like. Could he just aim in the general direction of an enemy and hit them?

"Charlie?!" Camile called from the end of the hallway. The dead biker slowly dissolved into a pile of ash as he looked back to his guards. The two hadn't lifted a finger to help him and he shook his head in annoyance. Charlie jogged down the corridor after Camile and found her standing with a group of mercenaries outside an elevator.

"After we are on the elevator you four are to protect this with your lives," Jen said pointing to a nearby concrete pillbox.

"Yes, ma'am." They echoed saluting. The humans were well armored with fully automatic weapons, and all they had to do was fire down a long corridor from an entrenched position. For some reason, she wasn't impressed with their odds. He followed Jen onto the elevator, and waited for his two dim-witted guards to join them. Camile pressed a flat palm to the control screen, and it started a very long descent.

Eventually it opened onto a massive room. Seven black pedestals were arranged in a large circle. The furthest one was occupied by a massive floating two-handed sword. Two screaming skulls were affixed to the hilt, and the pommel was covered in cracked leather. The black blade was about five feet long and wrought in glowing Assyrian script.

"Don't!" Camile's voice said sharply. Charlie hadn't realized he'd been walking towards the artifact. It had called to him.

"Huh," He said turning to her.

"You'll set off the nuke. There's a number of sensors in the floor around the pedestals. It was decided if anyone got this far it was too late to stop them."

*"Holy shit,"* Charlie thought.

"Isn't a nuke overkill?" He asked moving back a bit just in case.

"I wasn't joking about what would happen if the Brujah leader got his hands on that weapon. The other factions would kneel to him in a month, probably less. The city is better off destroyed than letting it fall to the Brujah." She said in a decidedly nasty snarl.

"Still, I mean..."

"San Francisco has suffered worse than a measly five megaton bomb," she scoffed.

"What's worse than that?"

"A cult of mages opened a portal to hell a year ago. We spent a good week fighting off a demon invasion, then an undead plague ravaged the state. There are still parts of Southern California you can't go into." Camile said moving to a flat section of wall.

She pressed her fingers into three tiny indentations, and a screen unfolded. Quickly she tapped a combination into the pad and let it scan her palm again. Nothing in the room seemed to change but she moved to the sword. Reaching up she took it in one hand as if it weighed no more than a feather. The runes flared briefly before settling into a steady pulse like a heartbeat. When she turned, her eyes were glowing the same color as the sword.

"Guard the door," She ordered the NPC's.

The two humans knelt on the ground about ten feet from the entrance. Above them, automatic gunfire started up, which was followed by an explosion. Charlie moved deeper into the room and took a position behind one of the pedestals. He removed the two magazines from his pocket and put them on the stone.

Something landed on the elevator, and smoke started to billow out from the cracked doors. A large black combat boot kicked through the metal, and the two mortals began to fire their weapons as the vampire appeared. Charlie immediately recognized the Brujah prince, from their earlier meeting. He fired his magnum at the vampire who simply sidestepped his shots.

*"What bullshit was this?"* Charlie thought. Each time he or the guards fired the red-eyed vampire shifted like a ghost on the wind.

Jake slowly removed a large sword from a back sheath. His blade flashed like a whip as he neared the first human. The guard's head flew across the vault, which was followed by the second.

"Thank you, fledgling. We needed a secondary distraction. That ass, Stephan, would have recognized our initial diversion. He probably thought you were a weak attempt at misdirection." Jake said laughing.

"I'm not a fan of being used," Charlie replied firing his pistol for all the good it did. The prince vanished again and reappeared a few feet away. Charlie stood and threw the empty pistol at the leather-clad biker. The elder vampire laughed again, and cut the weapon in half.

"That's how the game is played. Welcome to Blood and Pride."

A red silk blur flew past Charlie towards the dark haired clan leader. Metal sparks flew as two swords clashed. Nearby the tip of a blade slammed into the stone floor. The Brujah kicked out sending Camile back into the room, who flipped in midair, and landed on her feet in a skid. Her eyes were still glowing and she had a wicked smile on her lips.

"Tsk, you know that's going to take forever to regrow," the Brujah said in annoyance. He held up the stump of his left arm. Black blood oozed from the wound to form a dark seal. Then both leaped into the air again. Camile was a flash of red dress and porcelain skin, while Jake was a blur of dark leather. A second clash of steel occurred over Charlie's head. Camile landed hard next to him and toppled. One of her legs lay nearby still clad in black lace and a high-heel shoe. The Brujah leader turned exposing a massive wound on his head. One of his ears and thirty percent of his skull was missing, so his brain was visibly pulsing as it leaked black blood.

"Charlie, take the sword," Camile called throwing the weapon towards him. "Don't let him have it," she added and pushed herself to one knee. Charlie caught the two handed weapon and power flooded him. The blade didn't just flash, it flared with red glowing flames. A True Brujah held the sword now; which magnified all his abilities. Though he was only hours old his character burned with power. His blood boiled, and he felt like he could jump over a building.

"Give it here fledgling," the clan leader said.

"I told you I don't like being used," Charlie answered spinning.

He sprinted for the elevator like a world class Olympic athlete. As Charlie reached the shaft he jumped thirty feet upward and ran vertically up the wall. Wind whipped past his face, and Charlie laughed like a child as he casually defied gravity. As cheap as this game was, at least it made people feel powerful. He came out at the top to a bloody mess. The human guards painted the walls in a gory soup of flesh, Kevlar armor, and broken equipment. Gunfire could be heard in the club above as the Brujah clan fought with the Toreador vampires and their minions.

Charlie had shit for melee skill, so holding the top of the shaft was his best option. There was no way he could outrun the mature vampire. Far below, the clan leader was leapfrogging up the walls. He dug his right hand into the concrete and kicked off the side. In midair, he spun and kicked off again gaining velocity.

Unlike Charlie, it took Jake almost a minute to climb the shaft, so he had time to ready himself for the attack. The Brujah leader flew over his head in a final bound, and Charlie swung in a desperate upward arc.

A pale hand flopped to the ground, and Jake glanced at both his stumps in annoyance. Charlie bent and retrieved the severed appendage.

"Let me give you a hand, boss." He said tossing the flesh at the Brujah Prince. Jake lunged catching the dead fist between his teeth. Red eyes flared as he spun and vanished up the corridor. Charlie lifted the sword with a smile, and flames continued to writhe across the blade. He sort of understood why they wanted this bad boy. It had turned a fledgling into a powerhouse. In a mature vampire's hands, it probably would be a game changer. Camile landed next to him, and he was surprised to see both her legs were attached.

"By blood and fang," she said breathing a sigh of relief. Charlie posed rather heroically with the sword. "Maybe it wasn't such a bad thing you happened to pick a Brujah." She said stepping closer. Of course, his moment was ruined by the boyfriend's appearance.

"Stephan, no!" Camile said in a rush. He was looking at Camile when the attack came.

"You set the spy free!" Stephan spat as a black blur flashed in Charlie's vision. His perspective slowly shifted as it rolled sideways. He watched his own body slowly crumble into dust as his head bounced across the ground. Camile yelled at the other man, but Charlie lost his ability to hear. The words were muted as darkness enclosed him. Soon he was standing at the character selection screen, and a pile of ash and bone was all that was left of his vampire.

"What an asshole," Charlie said to himself. He logged off, pulled the dive helmet from his head and glanced around. The living room was dark, and he quickly grabbed the bottle of water from the table. Next to it was a small pack of electrolyte powder, and he dumped it into the lukewarm liquid, then drank the entire thing. Charlie wandered into the bedroom to lay down. It was late anyway and he needed the extra sleep.

# CHAPTER TEN

## *GMO Intro*

The keys jingled as Charlie held them out. "You won't regret buying the newer car," he said giving them another small shake.

The man smiled closing his fingers around the keys and stood. They'd just signed the last of the paperwork, and it had only cost a small piece of his soul for the luxury car. He followed the man out to the lot, and they shook hands again. The customer slipped into the expensive coupe and started the engine. Charlie gave him his best fake smile and waved as he drove off the lot. That was his third sale today, and he grinned to himself as he wandered back to his desk to organize the paperwork.

Jennifer intercepted him first, and he kept his face neutral. Frankly, he was still a little angry about last night, and he hadn't said much to her all morning. Jen picked her words very carefully as she said, "I... I'm sorry about what happened."

"What about your boyfriend?" He asked.

"You have to understand, we deal with spies literally all the time. It's easier to just kill them, when we find one." She said pushing a strand of hair behind her ear.

That was a pathetic excuse, and Charlie was about to say 'your man is an asshole,' but stopped himself.

Finally she added, "Most people don't even know you saved the city. I would have never disarmed the nuke if you weren't there. We also know there's a high-level spy in the clan. That's the only way the Brujah would have known the sword was at the club. Stephan is willing to be your patron if you want to play."

"Patron?"

"It means you'll get the best mortal blood and a monthly stipend," She said.

"Fuck him. I saved his fancy toy and he killed me for it. The only way I would join his emo band is if he publicly blew me." Charlie snarled in reply.

That wasn't going to happen, which was fine. In his opinion the character skills reeked of hand holding, which meant player ability was worthless. Then only after hundreds of hours in Blood and Pride did you gain any power. In the meantime, anyone with a grudge could curb-stomp you for looking at him funny. The system favored old timers, and those without a life.

"So how about I try your game? What was it called?" She asked.

"Gun Meister, you'll give it a go?" Charlie asked with growing excitement. He would honestly love to have a friend in the game. At least one that wasn't half psychotic.

"I'm still angry at how things went down. So yeah, I need a day off from the politics." She said flashing what he thought was a genuine smile. Over the last couple of days his view of her had changed drastically. She was considerably smarter and more observant than he previously gave her credit for.

"It's not a huge download, so I'll meet you when you come out of character creation."

She turned to walk away, but he quickly added, "Oh, pick a male gun." Jennifer paused as confusion crossed her face.

"A male gun, trust me," he repeated going into the building. The paperwork was still sitting on his desk as he sat down. Today had gone surprisingly well and his sales would boost his numbers.

After work, he fetched some fast food and quickly drove home. He'd been gone from Gun Meister for two days, and he was itching to see Elva.

Charlie ate half the chicken burrito and scooped the rest into Fizzgig's dish. Then he sat in the living room chair and pulled the Dive Helmet over his head. The digital world blossomed as he entered Gun Meister Online.

Elva had been busy, and he sat up looking around. Several new outfits were visible in the closet. Hanging over the bed was a television screen, which he assumed was for entertaining Elva while he was logged out. It was currently blank and his weapon wasn't lying atop him like usual. Instead, a cacophony of noise was coming from the living room, so he rolled from the bed and followed the loud music. Elva was dancing in the middle of the room completely naked, save a pair of beach sandals. She rocked her recently tanned hips to the rhythm of the beat. A mustard covered corn-dog rose to her lips as she sang.

*"War, huh, yeah.*
*What is it good for...*
*absolutely nothing,"*

After the chorus, Elva bit into the end and continued to her wild dance. The two days of sun bathing had given her skin a caramel tan from head to foot. Charlie smiled from the bedroom doorway. The music was obnoxiously loud, which was why she hadn't noticed him yet.

"I bet that tastes good," Charlie said. Elva spun, and her eyes lit up at seeing him.

"Charlie!" She squealed dashing toward him. He caught her by the waist before she could bowl him over. The corn-dog almost hit him as Elva wrapped her arms around his neck. Her skin smelled of sunscreen and sea salt. Elva forced her tongue into his mouth in a passionate greeting. Finally, she pulled back trying to regain some composure, and he glanced at her lunch.

"Going to share?"

Elva looked at the food, then at him, and back to the corndog. She opened her mouth and pushed the entire thing inside. Lips closed over the end and she withdrew the stick with a flourish. Her cheeks bulged as she tried to chew, and swallow at the same time.

"I see how it is," Charlie said turning in a circle examining the changes to the house. A dark rug had been thrown down below a pair of leather couches, and a small drinks table sat between them. Kitchen appliances had been installed.

"You've done a great job with the place," he said in genuine admiration. It was still light on furniture but it felt more like a home.

"The cash card is empty," Elva admitted, which was fine with Charlie. She'd managed to acquire a good selection of furniture for just two grand. "I know you said to buy things for the apartment, but I couldn't resist getting some more clothing."

Charlie had already noticed the outfits hanging in the closet, and he liked this independent side, so he pulled her into another embrace. This time he forced his tongue into her mouth. For almost a minute he pressed his advantage, before Charlie pulled away, and left Elva standing there with eye's full of raw lust.

"What are we doing tonight?" She asked in a suggestively husky voice.

"We are going to meet a friend of mine who's trying the game out. That won't be for an hour or two. She still has to download the client. In the meantime," he paused for dramatic effect and pointed to the bedroom closet. "You can model those outfits for me."

Elva slipped past him and into the bedroom, and very deliberately closed the door. While she dressed Charlie opened the newly purchased fridge. It wasn't full to the brim, but there was a week's worth of food. At least Elva wouldn't starve should Charlie be gone for several days.

Elva appeared in a blue Chinese dress, with a long serpentine dragon swimming among the water lilies. On her chest, a heart shaped window displayed a tantalizing view of her cleavage, and the sides of her dress were tied together with a thick white ribbon. Elva stepped into the living room in three-inch heels and turned slowly. He clapped, and she disappeared into the bedroom again.

The next outfit was a business dress, or at least an attempt at one. Elva came out in a gray pinstripe corset and miniskirt with black stockings. The short heels were black and practical. Her golden hair had been pulled back into a simple bun, and a pen was used to keep it in place. To finish the look, a thin pair of spectacles rested on her nose.

"How do you like it?" She asked in a smooth, cultured voice as she turned slowly for his inspection.

"This one is definitely the best," he said coming toward her. Charlie pushed her back into the bedroom and onto the mattress. They kissed again, and Elva met him with an animalistic hunger.

"We can't," Elva moaned as he pulled the little zipper her corset down.

Charlie ignored the comment and closed his mouth over her nipple. She gasped running her fingers through his hair. Her long stocking covered legs squirmed across the bed as Charlie slipped his hand under her skirt.

"If we are going—to meet your... friend," she panted struggling to continue. "The bus will take... an hour to arrive in town."

Charlie slowed his areola attack and considered. The bus, he'd completely forgotten about that. Reluctantly Charlie let go of Elva's breast, and helped tug her corset back into place.

"We'll have to continue this later," he said climbing from the bed.

Elva recovered herself, and smoothed her miniskirt back into order. She pulled on her heels again and walked to the bedroom mirror to fix her hair. Together they left the house and caught the bus was just pulling up as it reached the stop. Elva sat primly in her seat with both hands clasped in her lap, and didn't lean against him like usual. Instead, she withdrew a smartphone from her pocket. Elva tapped at it for a few seconds and held it out for him.

"What's this?" He asked.

"I was hoping you would buy this for me," she said as he took the mobile. It turned out to be a weapon skin. Across the grip and lower frame was a stylized picture of a horse. The white mare stood on two of its hooves as it reared up. The rest of the slide and frame was left matte black. Charlie wasn't a horse person himself, but it was a beautiful skin. Elva was manufactured by Colt, so it fit her.

"We'll see about getting it done sometime today," he said, and Elva smiled crossing her legs.

"What is this?" He asked pointing to an icon that appeared on the device.

"A friend request. When I bought the phone, it was assigned to your ID." Elva said leaning against him. He clicked the link and was confronted with a pair of spread legs. "Oh geez," he said recoiling from the nude photo. Thankfully he was spared seeing the lady bits because of the black hand cannon she held. Charlie recognized the revolver in the picture because of the white skulls covering the large frame. It was Remy, the girl from yesterday's matches.

Remy: "I'm good in all sorts of ways, let's be friends."

Charlie was tempted to ignore the friend request, but the weird little squirt had been very skilled. Maybe if he talked to her he could get her to calm down a bit. He hit accept and saw her player ID added to his friend's list.

Remy: "Game?"

Charlie: "Sorry, I'm meeting a friend at the cloning facility. They are new."

Remy: "I'm bronze still, so we can all play together."

Charlie: "I'll let you know," he sent and handed the device back to Elva.

The bus entered the city center, and they went into the Cloning Facility. He sat, and Elva perched on the bench next to him. Jen came out of one of the lower bedrooms after about twenty minutes. He recognized her because she used the same face as her vampire character. She was a little taller and more toned, but it was Jen. Her character wore a gray military tunic and slacks cut for a female. A tall, blond, and well-muscled man strode next to her like a peacock. Jen was fighting a crimson blush spreading across her face.

Charlie stood raising his hand in a wave. "Jennifer!" He called, and the girl paused in her stride. She turned in his direction and blushed an even deeper crimson. They crossed the lobby, and he smiled at Jen, but she glared at him.

"You should have warned me," she said in annoyance.

"Warned you?" He asked.

"I have a boyfriend," Jen said with some heat after glancing at the man beside her.

Charlie shrugged and said, "What did you expect? I told you to pick a male, and it's not like you didn't enjoy it." The NPC was a weapon, so she wasn't cheating on anyone.

"What is he? Forty-five ACP... 44 magnum?" He asked with interest. Usually, a weapon's body size indicated their caliber.

"H&K USP 9mm," The man said with a cultured Germanic accent.

"I expected something bigger," he admitted.

"It's not the size that counts, it's where you put it." Was the curt reply. Charlie glanced down. The weapon looked like he was packing something down below. Jen followed his gaze and started blushing all over again.

"Let's get over to the mall. The first step is weapons training."

"I already know how to use a gun."

"That's good, but you'll still need a holster and some ammo." He said guiding them from the lobby. They walked to the mall, and picked an inside-the-waistband holster. Charlie advised her to get an extra fifteen round magazine. If she needed more, they were screwed anyway. Jen loaded the weapon. Her movements weren't exactly professional, but she managed to put the bullets in the right way, which was better than his first attempt.

"Ready?" He asked and she nodded. Charlie pointed toward the exit and said, "To the Competition Center."

"What kinds of factions are there?" Jen asked as she followed along.

"Gun Meister does have clans that compete but no factions. The game is geared towards small squad combat." As they walked, he held out a hand to Elva. "Phone please," he said, and she gave him the mobile. He selected Remy's name and started to type.

Charlie: "We're headed to the center."

Remy: "Is your boy cute?"

Charlie: "It's a girl and no comment," He replied glancing at Jen, who was gawking at all the armed players. The girl probably spent most of the time standing out in the crowd. Her character was just as sexy as her vampire, but here she blended in like a wallflower.

Remy: "I can't wait."

Charlie: "Act normal, or I'll delete you from my friend's list." He quickly typed back.

Remy: "Poo," was the reply.

The Competition Center came into view, and Jen followed him inside. Remy was sitting on the helpdesk kicking her legs against the wood. Her teal hair had been rearranged into a complicated corkscrew of curls. Today she wore a frilly black dress, and a small belt of pistol shells circled her waist. The cannon hung from an underarm holster. He was relieved to see her clothed more modestly.

"Jen, I'd like to introduce Remy. We met yesterday during a match." Charlie prayed she behaved herself as Remy hopped down and held out a tiny hand.

"I am pleased to meet you," she said in a childish voice.

Jen at first eyed the other girl but took her hand. "Yes, I hope you'll take care of me."

Remy turned putting a hand on the console. She selected team match as a squad, and Charlie did the same by placing his palm on the screen. A warning popped up when Jen tried to enter the match. It suggested she start with a lower ranked game.

"Don't worry about that. We're all bronze, so you're not far behind." Remy said excitedly. Jen had experience fighting from her other game, so it wasn't like she was a complete newbie. They walked to the elevator and were deposited into the team lounge with two other men.

"So what do I do?" Jen asked.

"The object of the match is to kill the other team. Most often that means taking the center of the map and holding it." Charlie double checked Elva was ready, and continued to wait for the countdown to finish.

**[Match Started]**

There was a half-moon tonight, and a thick fog hugged the ground. Nearby a red telephone booth stood like a forgotten English guard, and the paint was painfully bright against the moldy backdrop of decay. In the distance half of an iconic tower was visible. Big Ben's clock face was missing, and the tall steeple had crashed into the building. Behind it a cathedral roof vainly tried to pierce the soupy mist.

"Hey, where are you two going?!?" Remy called. The two men from the lobby were moving in opposite directions. "Stick together at least, morons!" They ignored her and disappeared into the fog.

"What are they doing?" Jen asked.

"Not everyone plays well together," Charlie said in annoyance.

"Fucking loners should stick to solo matches," she said stomping a tiny booted foot. Jen withdrew her pistol and nervously held the black USP in her hands. They were already starting to shake with adrenaline. "Welp we're fucked," Remy said turning back to them.

Charlie shrugged and gestured down the road. "Our best chance is to hold up in the center," he suggested.

Four blocks down they located a pub on the street corner. The wood floor was old and covered with enough oil and wax to have petrified it. A wide bar was set up against the back wall with a few beer taps sticking out. Remy went over and tried one of the handles, and a black sludge oozed out. Two blocks down a sudden cacophony of gunshots rang out. Jen spun aiming her pistol down the street. The weapon trembled slightly in her hands, and she was breathing heavily. The rattle of pistol fire cut off.

"You OK?" He asked.

"Yeah," Jen lied nervously.

Another firefight started a block closer, and this one had lasted nearly twenty seconds before the sounds petered out. Charlie could only hope the lone wolves had at least taken a few with them.

"Let's get into position," Remy said in a chipper childish voice. She withdrew the magnum from its holster and checked the load.

"What do I do?"

Charlie walked over and turned her toward the back of the tavern. "Wait behind the bar for them to enter, then stand up and start shooting." He suggested.

Jen was scared, and it showed, but nodded after a few seconds. Last night Jen had been in a sword fight with an elder vampire. Hell, she'd had a leg cut off, and at the time, she'd treated it like an annoying paper cut. Jen couldn't lean on her undead abilities to make her powerful. At the moment she was just a human with a handgun.

"They're coming," Remy said backing away from the door. Charlie took a position behind one of the wooden pillars halfway into the room. Jen ducked behind the bar, and the little girl hid next to an overturned table. Five shapes materialized through the fog like silent ghosts. They were staggered and two crept along this side of the street.

Remy took careful aim through the glass front door, and fired as the tall figure of a male appeared. The revolver was loud in the small pub. The man was knocked sideways into the road, and his four companions returned fire into the building.

Wood splinters filled the air, and glass flew everywhere in the hail of bullets. Under that cover a man rolled through the shattered glass door and behind a thick table. A second man leaped through the remains of a broken window. Another attempted the same dramatic leap into the pub, but landed awkwardly a few feet from him. Charlie poked his gun around the pillar and fired four shots into the man.

In the front of the store, Remy exchanged fire with the first man to enter the pub, who also had a massive chrome silver semi-automatic. He fired on Remy, and she threw herself from the toppled table as bullet holes

**115**

appeared in the wood.

Her magnum belched flame. A 350 grain round punched through the far table and into the man's chest. Blood and bits of lung decorated the wall behind him. The desert eagle dropped to the ground as he fell back against the crimson painted plaster. Someone fired from outside the front door. Bullets slammed into the floor and Remy desperately rolled toward her former cover, but several stitched her side. She collapsed in a small bloody heap.

Charlie had two people to deal with, someone ahead and another behind, so he gambled. He leaped through the window and into the street. A girl was crouched near the entrance with a small black compact pistol. She spun in surprise, but Charlie fired his 1911. His first bullet entered her jugular and his second dug into her chest. She lowered her gun, and her blue eyes closed as if she decided to take a nap against the door frame. More gunshots rang out and bullets filled the air over his head. He stood awkwardly and aimed back into the pub. Jen had revealed herself and unloaded on the final enemy. Her eyes were competing with her mouth to see how wide they could get, and the smoking gun in her hands was violently shaking. Slowly darkness closed in after a few more seconds.

**[Match Complete]**
**[Team win]**

The door opened for Charlie, and he stepped into the private lounge. Jennifer however, didn't follow and he turned to see the girl lying unconscious on the ground. "Jen!" he called in surprise. He grabbed her wrist and carried her to one of the couches.

"She just logged out," Remy said from nearby. "Got too excited," she added. The two men stood and walked toward the elevator. They said nothing and Charlie eyed them darkly as the doors closed.

"What do we do?" He asked.

"Depends on what she decides. After she's got her pitter-pattering heart under control she'll have to log back in." Remy said activating a nearby console to examine her new stats. Charlie wanted to show his coworker a fun time, and possibly entice her to switch games to play with him.

"What if she doesn't?"

"Just tell the gun to carry her to a nearby motel. They will charge her when she logs back in." Remy said before clapping. "Yay, Silver!"

They waited for about twenty minutes, but Jennifer didn't come back. Charlie decided to check his stats and was pleasantly surprised. He'd skipped straight over Bronze Master, and into the Silver ranks. His P-Score had risen by a hundred points, and the system had decided Charlie was ready for the big leagues.

"Congratulations," Remy said looking over his shoulder. He glanced at Jen who was still lying on the couch nearby. "It doesn't look like your friend is coming back," Remy said following his gaze.

"Me and Philip here are going to celebrate with a round of hot messy sex. Care to join?" Remy asked and Charlie rolled his eyes. Remy had behaved herself only when his friend had been around.

"Thanks, but I'll pass." He said dryly.

"I'll let you be the spit turner," she suggested.

Charlie groaned covering his eyes, and tried to block out the mental image. "Remy... I'll be your friend, but I won't have sex with you."

"Your loss," she said skipping toward the elevator.

Charlie reached down and poked the USP in Jennifer's holster. "You should probably take Jennifer to a motel," he said, and the gun began to glow. The green eyed German appeared in the flash, glanced at his Meister with a look of pity, and gathered her into his massive arms. Charlie followed them into the elevator, and activated the console so it would ascend. Since he was Silver now, Charlie couldn't play any more matches until he found a primary gun, so he spent the evening going to the mall and buying Elva the weapon skin she wanted.

# CHAPTER ELEVEN

## *Gun Trials*

Coffee was one of man's greatest discoveries. Charlie certainly thought so because he had stayed up much later than he should have. Once back at the beach house, Elva had been hungry to continue where they had left off. She'd pounced on him, tearing his clothes off, and taken Charlie before they even entered the living room. The sex hadn't stopped there as the tireless weapon had fucked him on the couch, blown him in the shower, and banged him senseless on the bedroom floor. He barely managed to crawl onto the bed to log out. Charlie smirked at the memory, tore open the third packet of sugar, and dumped it into the mug of coffee.

Jennifer entered the break room. She barely looked his way as she went to the refrigerator and put her lunch inside. Charlie wondered what happened to her after the match.

"You didn't come back."

"No."

"Ahh..." Charlie said stirring his coffee. He took an experimental sip as he considered her answer. Jen had not appreciated the casual sex Gun Meister offered. She also hadn't done well without her powerful undead abilities. The woman had been unnerved during the competitive match.

"Didn't care for Gun Meister?"

She grabbed a mug, filled it with hot water, and dropped in a tea bag before she answered."I'd rather invest my energy into Blood and Pride, but I wouldn't mind seeing you in the Clan." She countered pouring in milk and sugar. "Stephan's offer is still on the table."

Jennifer obviously hadn't conveyed his message along to her boyfriend, and the thought of being Stefawn's paid errand boy rubbed Charlie like broken glass.

"I'll pass. Thanks to our win last night I managed to rank up. You could say I'm emotionally invested as well." He said turning fully towards the woman. Jen searched his face, and Charlie was positive she was calculating the truth of his statement. He smiled and leaned in closer.

"I get *two* girls now," he whispered.

Jennifer blushed before raising the mug to her lips. She drank the scalding tea trying to hide the fact she was thinking about it. He too raised his mug and sipped. The coffee was hot and sweet like the sex last night. Soon he'd have another girl in his harem, and the thought sent a pleasant shiver up his spine. Erick knocked on the wooden door as he entered the break room.

"Boss is calling a meeting before we open," Erick said ducking back into the hall. A hollow sensation gripped Charlie and the coffee turned to acid in his stomach. He'd been given a week to turn his numbers around, and it hadn't been enough. The last thing he wanted was more coffee, but Charlie walked with the mug toward the conference room. Most of the other agents were already seated as the balding General Manager paced slowly back and forth before the whiteboard.

"I want to start by saying you've all been a real asset to the company," the GM said. The acidic fire in Charlie's stomach grew, and his fears were soon confirmed.

"You've all reached high, and for that, I am proud of you."

The fluff was pure drivel, but at least Charlie didn't have to wait long for the battle-axe to come down. "Unfortunately the recession is hitting us harder than we expected. Many local branches have been told to trim the fat, including us, sadly."

Charlie mentally prepared himself for the job loss. He had some savings, probably enough to last while he looked for new employment. At least, he was being fired in the morning, so he could spend the day updating his resume.

"Erick, Chad; I'm sorry, but I have to cut you both from the active roster." Irvin said leaving everyone stunned, especially Charlie. He turned looking at the two men. Erick's face was stony, while Chad sat there with an open mouth. For once the 'Chatterbox' couldn't think of anything to say. "You'll be put on an on-call basis," the boss added into the silence.

"I've sold five cars this week!" Erick blurted. Charlie tried to remember his total sales, but he knew it was more than five.

"Sorry Erick, the recession is hitting everyone hard."

"Then fucking fire us," Chad barked launching out of his chair.

"My hands are tied," Irvin said tucking them behind his back. That was cold. Keeping them on the books part-time meant they couldn't collect unemployment. It was cheaper that way for the company. If they quit, the two would forfeit the government handout. Both Erick and Chad stormed from the room accompanied by a heavy silence.

"Things are still up in the air. Our branch is doing well in regional sales, but corporate might demand we cut more. I want everyone to remember that." He stated leaving the room. The agents turned to look at one another, because they suddenly saw each other as competition. Charlie spent the day bouncing back and forth between extremes. He was happy to be gainfully employed, but he felt bad for Chad and Erick. That would have been him—should have been him. By lunch, he managed to pull himself back together enough to make a sale.

Charlie eventually clocked out. Jen was wrapping up a customer who was leaning into her personal space, and Charlie shook his head going by. There was no chance he would ever compete with her in sales. Walking out to his car Charlie settled into the driver seat and started the vehicle.

He had narrowly avoided being put on-call, which was a fate worse than death in this current climate. Charlie had reason to celebrate and there was no better way than with fresh sushi. He stopped near his house for a half dozen rolls and a bottle of sake. An hour later he sat down in his living room chair. The few scraps of leftover tuna he'd given to Fizzgig, who was chewing on the raw fish in abject bliss. Charlie kicked off his shoes and pulled the dive helmet over his head. Then touched the activation button and waited for the world to fade.

Gun Meister Online Loading...
Connection Established...
Network shaking hands...
Logging into Character...

The sound of canned laughter reached his ears first. The television above was playing an ancient black and white comedy. Elva lay on the bed with her head resting against his stomach, and a bowl of fresh strawberries nearby.

"Alright alright, that's enough," the man said raising his voice. He folded the morning newspaper and set it on the dining room table.

"Maybe for you, but I'm just getting warmed up." The woman said gathering the leftovers onto a tray. The statement was followed by another long round of canned laughter.

"You tell him, Lucy. Don't take his shit." Elva said as the laughter died away.

How interesting. Charlie wondered if the show was for entertainment or character growth. The early drama was obviously old, recorded before even color television. She picked up another strawberry pointing it at the TV.

"You're a strong independent woman, Lucy. You don't need him." Elva said bringing the fruit to her lips.

Until now Charlie had remained perfectly still, so Elva hadn't noticed him yet. As it neared her mouth, he snatched the morsel. There was only one thing more important than sex to Elva, and that was food. In her surprise, she spun and chased the strawberry like a bloodhound. Elva bit at his fingers, but he dropped the succulent fruit into his waiting mouth. She hungrily lunged for it, closing her lips over his, and tried to save her prize from edible oblivion.

The fruit was quickly crushed in the attack of lips and tongues. For almost a minute their mouths were engaged in a lip biting, mouth mashing contest. She growled pushing herself against him like a dog hunting for their favorite bone. Charlie reached around her, sliding his hands under the black miniskirt. Eventually, she relented parting from the ravaged battlefield as saliva and strawberry juice ran down both their chins.

"Are you done?"

"I'm just getting started," she said kissing him again. Above them, another round of canned laughter went off. Her surprise had faded and her cultured personality was taking root. Elva was still wearing her business dress, but had kicked off her shoes and pulled the bun apart.

"Good evening, and thank you for the warm welcome. I'm eager to look for a new gun. Any advice?" He asked letting go of her plump posterior.

She rolled over and touched the screen above them. The video paused and the TV went blank.

"You first have to decide what role you want to play," Elva said turning back to him.

"Role?" He asked. "Do you mean picking a sniper or a machine gun?"

"That's a part of it. Higher ranked divisions like Gold and above are designed almost exclusively for squad play. The stats you choose in character creation will lead you toward a type of squad role. Think of them like player classes, which fall into six different types. They are Tank, Heavy Support, Juggler, Flanker, Scout, and Squad Lead."

"What about going solo?"

"You can still play alone. In that case, having average stats and a multi-role rifle is your best option. You never know what situation you will find yourself in."

"OK, so what are the role specifics?"

"A tank is someone who wears heavy armor and carries a ballistic shield. Their primary weapon is often a one-handed submachine gun. An entry fragger needs a large health pool so they have high endurance."

"Heavy Support is similar to tank but maxes out strength instead. They usually carry heavy weapons like squad machine guns into battle. Support sometimes bring extra ammo reserves into a match."

"Juggler is an ambiguous role. They can take on most duties in a pinch."

"A Flanker is an agility based character designed to gain objectives quickly. Often these people match light armor with a semi-automatic rifle."

"A scout is just another word for a sniper. They often have high strength and agility. This lets them carry the largest sniper rifles and sprint over short distances." Elva paused to pick a strawberry from the bowl, and popped it into her mouth. A moment of bliss crossed her face as she swallowed.

"The squad leader is more of a title than a role. They have to coordinate the team and keep them moving on an objective. Most often they are jugglers and flankers."

"You have to decide what position you want to play in a group. A machine gun for instance for support or a sniper rifle to pick off players at a distance. Half of your matches have been solo, so you might want to choose an assault weapon. They aren't as handy as an SMG nor do they have the range of a scout, but a fully automatic rifle will work in most situations." Elva said picking the last strawberry from the bowl.

For a second she stared at it as her decision tree began cascading through multiple options. With a look of regret she offered it to Charlie. He closed his lips over the succulent fruit and chewed while he considered his options. Charlie had two strength and three points in both agility and endurance. By Elva's logic, he was probably best suited to being a juggler, or a jack-of-all-trades kind of player.

"How do I find a new girl to contract with?" He asked finally.

"We should head down to the Royal Armory. It's a five-star hotel that caters to unregistered guns." She said sliding from the bed. Elva donned her high heels and walked to the bedroom mirror to fix her hair. Charlie pulled on his jacket, and they left the beach house, and took the bus into town.

The five-story building was made of white marble shot through with precious metals. The pillared luxury hotel stretched the entire block, and must have contained a thousand rooms. Twin golden lions kept guard over the entrance. At the bottom of the marble stairs Elva leaned in close and said, "Go in and check the directory. You can search by type, caliber, and even era."

"You're not joining?" He asked, and she shook her head.

"I don't want to affect your decision." Elva began to glow, and after a flash, appeared in his holster.

There were two double doors and they opened silently at his approach. The lobby was covered in a thick blue embroidered carpet, and leather couches spread across the space in little groupings. Almost all were occupied by swimsuit wearing individuals, and they paused to look at Charlie as he entered. There was a long counter with several consoles, and he started toward them, but a short woman caught his hand forcing him to stop. Like all the other weapons she wore only a small black bikini.

"Are you by chance looking for a weapon?" She asked stepping closer. The girl was barely more than five feet tall with a slim figure, olive skin, and the darkest hair he'd ever seen. It was jet black like pure onyx crystal, which was matched in her mischievous eyes.

"I am," he admitted. Charlie looked down into her fine face, and for a second he was lost in the depths of her eyes. She smiled and squeezed his hand. Thanks to Elva, he was slightly more armored against beautiful women.

"What are you?" He asked after gathering his senses.

"Why don't you try me and find out." She said licking a small tongue across her lip. "This area is unique. You don't need a contract to use a weapon, and it would be my *pleasure* to be used by you." She said curling her fingers into his. Charlie wasn't opposed to the idea. Elva hadn't been able to suggest a particular one, so he would have to find a weapon himself.

"Lead the way," he said allowing himself to be guided toward a side hallway. An indoor range was attached to the hotel, and it was only here the girl let go of his hand. She stepped towards a counter and removed a box of 9mm ammo from the shelf.

"Everything here is free. You can shoot as much as you please." She said handing it to him, then turned toward a thick iron door.

Charlie followed her in after donning a pair of earmuffs. Two other men were inside testing out weapons as well. The dark haired girl guided him to an open lane, then began to glow. Soon a small boxy machine pistol lay on the table, and Charlie picked it up. Along the side it read, "Ingram MAC 10."

It was tiny in his hands, and Charlie turned it over examining the weapon. Eventually he found the magazine release, and a long box slid free. After loading thirty rounds, he pushed it back into the grip, and thumbed a bolt at the top of the gun, which chambered a round. He took aim using both his hands at a set of crude targets down range. As Charlie pulled the trigger, the small pistol danced in his grip as the entire mag slammed down range in a second and a half. The first target had about five or six holes in it, and the others nearby had one or two each. Charlie was in awe. This was a full machine gun that could fit into his pocket.

"You can pull out my stock," The girl said into his mind. There was a small metal hoop, and as he yanked on it, a thin telescoping stock slid out. He removed the magazine and verified that it was empty. After loading another thirty rounds he pushed it into the gun. One problem he noticed, was the barely visible sights. Still he raised the micro SMG to his shoulder and fired on the target. The Mac-10 sprayed, kicking in his hands as he pulled the trigger. A line of twenty holes stitched up the cardboard silhouette, but the rest had gone over the target into a backstop.

"You are a handful," he admitted fondling the simple boxy pistol. There was still more ammo, and he loaded the weapon again. He found the selector switch on the left side of the gun and set it on single fire. Aiming this time he squeezed off several shots, but it wasn't quite as fun, so he switched back to full-auto. The gun sinfully dumped the entire magazine down range, then used the last ten rounds in the box. He'd fired all one-hundred rounds in a fast and satisfying two minutes. Finally, he turned and left the range with the weapon in hand.

"As amazing as you are I have to disappoint you."

"I suspected as much. Still, it was a pleasure." A voice said into his ear and the weapon glowed. The tiny woman appeared and extended a hand. Charlie took it and shook firmly.

"For my first contract I need something with more range," he replied.

Certainly, she was fantastic at room clearing, but he needed a weapon with more utility.

The diminutive woman turned and sauntered toward another player near the ammo counter. She ran a hand down his side and added a box of 9mm to his pile, then with a playful smile, followed him into the range.

Elva spoke from her thigh holster, "It's better you find a gun you truly want."

He agreed. It would be preferable to contract with a weapon he would keep. Charlie turned to leave the range, but was stopped by another gun. As Charlie neared the exit, a tall woman stepped around the corner, and he came face to breasts, with a red haired giant.

"I hear you correctly? You v'ere looking for longer range, da?" the woman asked in a thick Russian accent. He glanced up between her cleavage into a pair of steel colored eyes. Before he could step back, she hugged him. "I am zeh rifle for you," she said pulling him into her substantial bosom. Charlie found his face sandwiched between her giant breasts.

"Try me?" The giant asked and he nodded. She turned him about and prodded him back over to the ammo counter. "You v'ill need 7.62 x 54r," she said pointing to a lower rack. As he bent to retrieve the ammo a hand slid over his ass and squeezed. He straightened in surprise, but the redhead only smiled, licked her lips, and led the way into the range.

She turned out to be a Dragunov SVD semi-automatic sniper rifle, and she was beautiful. The weapon had a lacquered cherry wood stock, and a matte black frame. He lifted the rifle to his shoulder and found a lack of optics, but all the girls came with minimal features. Charlie already knew he wasn't going to pick the weapon. He needed something that was fully automatic, and the rifle wouldn't work in a close quarters fight. Her barrel length was just too long, so swinging her around in a hallway would be next to impossible. Charlie shook his head but started to load the magazine. The least he could do was actually test her. He tilted the ten round magazine into the well before it locked into place. Then he pulled back on the bolt and shouldered the weapon.

There was a ghost ring front sight which he lined up on a new target. Charlie aimed at the far end of the range to a target that was about a hundred meters away. The rifle kicked hard as he pulled the trigger, and he almost staggered from the unexpected recoil.

"I have to apologize, but I need an automatic rifle." He said after working his way through half the box.

"Full-auto is bad for aim," she said.

Charlie agreed in principle as he continued to shoot. "I like you, but I need something that fills multiple roles." He said after another ten rounds. He finished running through the ammo, and left the range. Outside the gun began to glow. As soon as the redhead was in human form, she squeezed him to her chest again.

"You have good grip. Not loose, not tight, just right." She growled into his ear, which was a strange compliment, but he accepted it.

"Are there any fully automatic weapons you would recommend," he asked after pulling away.

"Not so much auto's left," the woman said.

"None?" he asked in surprise.

"Many, many Meisters come for contract lately. All assault rifles gone." She replied, and he sighed. Charlie had been among the massive influx of new players. The Russian made weapon used a nearby pencil and scrolled something on a scrap of paper. "My ID, you call. We contract." She said tucking it into his jeans pocket. Her hand reached behind him and grabbed his ass again. "I like your grip," she repeated before turning away.

Charlie dodged a number of girls in the lobby and managed to access a terminal. He filtered out everything except for automatic weapons. The SVD hadn't been joking. There wasn't a single assault rifle available. In fact, most of the SMG's had been taken as well.

"Am I going to have to settle for a different weapon?" He asked tapping through the listing.

"Possibly, weapons are only made as needed. More will be created in the next batch wave." Elva said into his mind. That made a sort of sense. The developers didn't want hundreds of weapons just sitting around getting bored. It wouldn't do their personalities any good. "You may just have to wait a few days," Elva suggested.

"Well, that sucks," Charlie said turning away from the screen. He wasn't going to just contract with a weapon for the short term, so for now, he'd have to run casual pistol matches.

Charlie left the Royal Armory and walked down the street. Despite the fact he hadn't found a weapon the experience had been fun. That Mac-10 had been a literal blast to shoot. He smiled remembering her playful black eyes, and suspected she might be a blast in bed too. From his jeans pocket, he withdrew the piece of paper. The ID number was written in a quick feminine hand. Yes, it had been worth the trip. He was feeling good about today, especially having a job still. Maybe he'd rent some practice time and put Elva through her paces.

# CHAPTER TWELVE

## *Duel*

A small pile of empty ammo boxes sat behind Charlie on the loading bench. Elva looked good, and he stroked her steel frame. The white mustang painted across her grip turned out even better than expected. Slowly he placed the magazine into her well and slid it home like a lover. There was a quiet click and he racked the weapon. Charlie had paid for three hours worth of practice time, and there was five minutes left, so he could get in one last run. A monitor was nearby, and he touched the screen activating the same scenario.

Beginning at the loading bench a small Italian street materialized ahead of him. The cobblestone alley was barely more than two meters wide. In the distance, the melancholic sound of a violin floated on the hot Sicilian wind. Charlie licked his lips and started down the alley. Drying laundry fluttered on sagging lines strung between a half dozen windows. Doors on either side were propped open in the oppressive heat.

Charlie slowly walked with Elva in his hands as he scanned the alley ahead of him. He sidestepped a vegetable cart keeping his eyes on a swivel. A man wearing a photographer's vest over a garish Hawaiian shirt stepped from an open door nearby. The tourist raised a pistol in his direction and fired. Charlie dodged, slamming into the cart, then placed it between him and the AI controlled tourist. He lined up Elva's glowing night sights on the brightly colored shirt and returned fire. The man fell apart disintegrating into a dazzling sparkle of lights.

The attack heralded several more NPCs appearing. Bullets ricocheted off the cobblestones around Charlie and he returned fire instinctively. A figure fell from the window and exploded in a shower of light as it hit the ground.

Then a woman rolled into the middle of the street and came up shooting. She wore nothing but an apron covered in pasta flour. Charlie fired wildly, but his shots struck only cobblestones. A head of lettuce exploded next to Charlie, and the sight picture his pistol continued to jump erratically as he pulled the trigger. Elva's slide locked back on an empty chamber, and he dropped the magazine. His fingers retrieved a spare with a practiced ease, and slammed it into the pistol.

As he reloaded the woman rolled to a nearby doorway. Her apron was askew, showing off a thick patch of dark hair. Charlie thumbed the slide release loading the gun and pushed it out ahead of him. He continued to exchange fire with the flour covered matron. A second and third vegetable exploded nearby before a round hit him. Charlie crumpled to the paving stones as a 115-grain bullet struck his chest. The range simulation froze. Pieces of lettuce and tomato hung suspended in the air as if time had stopped.

"Dammit," he muttered sitting up. A transparent red dot hovered over his heart, which quickly began to fade as he rubbed his chest. Charlie had let the stress get to him, and his aim had gone to shit. He picked up the dropped magazine, and walked back to the beginning, while the Italian street disappeared.

The naked woman had been a dirty trick, and Charlie felt cheated. He stopped at the loading bench to gather his things, and reload Elva to full capacity. The empty boxes he tossed into the trash.

"You can change to your human form," he said touching Elva's frame. The gun flashed, and she appeared next to him wearing her pinstripe business attire. Firearms didn't sweat, but Elva did reek of gunsmoke.

"How did it go?" She asked with a satisfied sigh.

He made a 'so-so' gesture. Charlie still needed to work on his marksmanship. He was usually good at putting one or two rounds on target, but once someone started shooting back his aim faltered. A female player carrying a sniper rifle walked into the training room. She nodded to him and set her weapon on the bench.

Charlie left the range and headed to a set of stairs. Halfway up he withdrew the piece of paper the SVD had given him. The tall redhead had been cute, and her husky Russian accent had tickled him pink. Despite needing a full-auto weapon, he was thinking of contracting with her. The lobby was strangely empty, but it was after midnight. There was a long bus ride back to the beach house, and cleaning to be done before he logged out. Elva had run through five hundred rounds and she sorely needed it. His night however, drastically changed as Charlie passed near the match elevators.

A man wearing digital-camo stepped out ahead of him. On his back was a bolt-action scout rifle and he carried a highly modified assault weapon. Both were painted in a pattern of brown and green pixels. Near his waistband, a Kydex holster held a black blocky handgun. Charlie caught sight of the man's face, which was filled with a dark rage as he stared down at the assault weapon in his trembling hands. He pulled the sling off and lifted the firearm over his head.

"Fuck!" He screamed hurling the rifle to the floor. Plastic and metal snapped in an awful clatter as the modular stock broke off. For a fraction of a second regret crossed the man's face, but quickly vanished. Elva gasped in shock while Charlie stared in astonishment. The game was tough, but to do that to your own weapon? Slowly the broken butt-stock slid across the ground and reconnected to the gun as it began to glow. A teenager appeared in a flash of light clutching her swollen ankle.

With sullen tear-filled eyes she said, "I told you I needed a cleaning after going through the swamp in the last match."

"If you weren't such a finicky piece of shit, I would have won." He said stomping towards her. Elva stepped closer to Charlie taking his arm to support herself.

"Any weapon won't chamber when it's breach is filled with slime." The girl said in a bitter tone.

He slapped her across the face knocking the girl to the tiles. Fingernails dug into Charlie's bicep, and blood trickled down his arm. Elva glared over his shoulder at the player with unmitigated fury.

"What the hell are you doing?" Charlie barked grabbing the player by his shoulder. He spun, drawing a pistol, and leveled it in Charlie's face. The other man had sharp green eyes like broken beer bottles, and his cold gaze scrolled over Charlie taking inventory of his weapons.

"Fuck off, Squib." He said spitting the words like shot from a cannon.

"Not gonna watch you wail on a girl," Charlie replied as icy fire filled his veins.

"This is between me and my weapon, so bugger off Bronze." The player hissed.

"It's your fault, not hers." Charlie retorted searching the player's bitter expression. His shallow green eyes turned dangerous, and the pistol continued to twitch in Charlie's face, but it was little more than a rude gesture. The guy wouldn't fire, not in the city. That would earn him a quick twenty-four hour ban.

"You think you can teach me a lesson?" He asked in a dark, angry voice. Charlie glanced past him to the teenage girl. She hadn't attempted to gain her feet, not with that ankle. "How about we duel then?" He hissed lowering his pistol.

"You win... you get the Mattel garbage. I win and get that big titted slut behind you. I like the way she's glaring at me."

"Or are you too afraid," the angry man taunted.

Charlie wanted to teach the guy a lesson, but that was a losing proposition. The asshole was at least gold, maybe even platinum. Night vision goggles hung around his neck, and a bandolier of grenades circled his green chest armor. Charlie felt sorry for the girl, but he wasn't about to risk Elva.

"He accepts," Elva snarled from behind him. Charlie spun in astonishment. Her eyes were like blazing blue diamonds in the lobby lights.

"Hah! She speaks for you too, huh." The guy barked while shouldering passed Charlie.

Elva gave him a small predatory smile, and pushed Charlie forward. She whispered in his ear, "You can set the rules since he challenged you."

"This is crazy," he hissed back.

"It's not."

The man turned away putting his hand on a nearby screen and activated it. He selected 'Duel Challenge' from the menu. On the screen, there was a checkbox for a prize. He slammed his finger onto the console selecting the limping girl's ID.

Then he stepped aside with a belittling smirk and said, "Your turn, pussy."

On the screen, an empty hand-print was waiting, and Charlie slid his palm into place. A new screen appeared, and he selected pistols only, no armor, no grenades, and a tiny map. Charlie had far less battle experience than the man, so his only hope was a small engagement. With considerable trepidation he selected Elva, his only weapon, as the prize. It then asked for a confirmation from both players. The other man swaggered forward putting his palm on the second half of the screen.

"Please enter lobby 49," the terminal said as it confirmed the match. He followed the high level player to the elevators. As they entered Charlie slapped the screen and the door closed. The match began as they entered the private lounge.

**[1 vs 1 - Duel Started]**

A hot wind whipped past Charlie so fast his shirt fluttered. He was standing on the top floor of an unfinished high rise. Nearby flapping blue ribbons were all that was left of a plastic tarp. The sky was a summer painting, and two distant clouds drifted past on the fast moving wind. The sun was high overhead, and he could see the distinctive towers of Shanghai spread before him in a ruin of bombed out structures. Around him, pillars of concrete and hardened rebar stretched to the heavens like claws.

A laser crossed over the support pillar he was standing next to. Charlie noticed the glowing green dot just before it settled on his chest, and he threw himself sideways as bullets slapped against the concrete in a spray. Sharp chips of stone and bullet shrapnel filled the air as he ducked around the side. God damn it. He'd been caught lollygagging—again. Why did he always have to examine his surroundings like a gawking tourist? He dodged behind the concrete block and put his back against it. Charlie kicked himself as he withdrew Elva from her holster, and glanced around the corner. About sixty feet away a shadow revealed his opponent was standing behind a concrete pillar.

The snake eyed man stepped around the pillar already aiming at Charlie with, what he suspected, was a fully automatic Glock 18. He was still learning about the myriad of weapons, but the pistol's boxy design was distinctive. The green laser danced over Charlie's cover as the man moved forward. Desperately he scanned the area searching for something useful. The urban warrior moved forward in a straight line, and ahead of him, hidden by a pillar was an industrial welding rig. Two massive canisters of oxy-acetylene were strapped to a fading orange dolly.

He needed to give the enemy a reason to keep confidently walking forward, so he purposely fired blindly around the corner. 9mm bullets zipped past him like angry bees and Charlie yelped loudly. He quickly slid a new mag into the well, and racked the slide. The guy laughed enjoying himself, and paused to reload next to the welding rig.

Now was his chance, and Charlie only exposed himself enough to get a shot on the tall green canisters. He fired and a bullet struck the stone pillar, and the man laughed at his aim.

"You are the worst player I've ever seen," the player said leveling his pistol.

Charlie fired again and his second bullet pinged off the edge of a canister. Sparks flew, but the round only left a furrowed dent. A dozen 9mm rounds struck the corner of his pillar, and concrete chips slapped against Charlie's cheek as he concentrated on the glowing dots in his vision. He focused his entire attention on lining the sights on the orange dolly. Elva bucked in his hands as he fired. A hole appeared in the side of one green canister, and for an agonizing second, Charlie feared the welding rig was empty. Then a fireball lit up the pillar and one toxic player. From within the expanding inferno, a man screamed and danced in the flames. Darkness settled over him like a welcome hug, and in the black, words floated.

## [Duel Won]

The door to the private lobby opened. On the other side, another opened admitting the second player. He stalked forward still mimicking a burned marshmallow. His face was beet red as he reached behind him, grabbed a wrist, and practically threw the athletic teen at Charlie.

She stumbled part of the way before crying out. The black collar flashed, and in that instant, the slutty dress she wore blew apart in a sparkle of light. For a second she was naked in the glowing corona before it coalesced into a black bikini. As she landed on the floor, her back arched. Her pupils went white and gun parts started to materialize in the air. The broken stock appeared first, falling to the lobby floor and shattered against the ground. An ACOG scope, flash hider, trigger group, and quad rail also burst apart in a second shower of glowing light. With a final shuddering convulsion, the blond was reset to factory default.

"Hope you learned your lesson," Charlie sneered with a belittling smirk. He was going to report the player for abuse, but for now, Charlie would settle with seeing his seething face.

"I lost to a fucking squib?!?," he roared.

"That's silver squib to you, Marshmallow." Charlie replied.

The man couldn't resist giving the unnamed blonde a final spiteful shot. He lashed out with a black combat boot attempting to kick her one last time. Still sitting on the ground the girl's head snapped up. Her eyes filled with a blazing, brilliant blue light as her decision processing went into overdrive. She tracked his foot like a turret with her glowing eyes. Her left hand raised in slow motion blocking the boot sailing toward her face, and guided it past her head. As the unbalanced man fell forward, she brought her right fist up in a devastating uppercut, and connected with his unarmored crotch.

In a feat of superhuman strength, he was sent flying six feet into the air. Only at the apex of his ascent did the pain receptors in his balls catch up with his tiny lizard brain. He screamed a full-throated, blood-curdling cry which made the paltry noises Charlie had inflicted pale in comparison. The man slammed into a group of console screens, but he barely noticed. Screaming like a pig, he clutched his groin and fell to the floor. Quickly his cries petered off.

*"Holy shit,"* Charlie thought.

Elva covered her mouth with a hand. The teenager's pupils slowly dimmed before she too looked away. Charlie moved to check on the man, but his eyes, when Charlie rolled him over, were cloudy in death. She had nut punched him so hard his balls had burst like an overfilled water balloon, and blood covered the crotch of his pants.

"You killed him," Charlie said standing. He had exceedingly little pity left for the man. After what he had done, it was the least he deserved. However, Charlie had a new appreciation for how strong weapons were.

"I'm Charlie," he added coming closer.

A new black collar with his ID circled her delicate throat. She raised her head glaring at him with angry, sullen eyes. Despite the murderous glare, she was good looking. Her face was almost a twin of Elva's with the same blonde hair and blue eyes. On second thought, it was more like she was a younger sister rather than a twin. She lacked Elva's substantial bust and hips. The girl was just entering adulthood, but he could see the youthful appeal.

"Not going to tell me?" He asked.

"A new name then," Charlie said turning away. He circled the room several times before his eyes caught sight of the dead body. Yes, the girl was dangerous.

"How about Fara?"

"Fine," she answered, which wasn't a very enthusiastic reply, but things had gotten off on a strange note. Charlie reached down to help pick her up, but she slapped his hand away.

"Don't touch me," she hissed.

Charlie hopped back faster than if he'd been shot. He had no intention of being the second body on the floor. Fara's return to factory settings had at least fixed her swollen ankle, but she slowly walked a perimeter around the room testing the damage.

This was the second time he'd rescued a girl and been spurned for his trouble. Charlie was getting tired of playing the white knight, and he hoped it didn't become a trend. Anger continued to build, not just at the situation, but also the fact he was thrust into it. Elva approached and tried to pull his arm between her cleavage, but he backed away.

"Whatever happened to not affecting my weapon selection? For that matter, you took a considerable risk on my part." He said not bothering to conceal his irritation. Elva looked down toeing the carpet with her high-heel shoes.

"Care to explain?" Charlie asked impatiently.

The girls looked to one another across the lounge, but it was Elva that said, "Remember I told you firearms are made in waves. We are batch sisters." There was another small pause before she said, "We start off with basic, almost childish personalities. During those first few hours, several of us became close. We remained friends even after being registered."

Charlie turned to examine his new weapon. "I didn't get a good look, but what are you anyway?" He asked Fara.

"I am a Colt M16A1," she said moving to put a screen between herself and Charlie. Fara, at least, was an assault rifle, so he could be happy about that. The skin of the corpse started to bubble, giving off a fetid odor, and Charlie grimaced at the rapidly decaying clone.

"Well, I am sorry to have met you under such circumstances," he said moving toward the elevator. Elva followed him in and meekly stood in the back. Fara paused looking at him from behind the screen.

"Well?" he asked impatiently.

"I'm not going to reregister with you," she said at last. Well didn't that just beat all? It meant she wasn't going to fuck him.

"Fine," he said in a very un-enthusiastic voice. At least he'd have an assault rifle for a month before she left, so he could work with that. His sexy game time was getting slapped with a cold dose of reality, and he didn't care for it. The lobby was even more desolate as he exited the elevator. Charlie walked out of the competition center and got onto the metro. Elva sat next to him but Fara purposely picked a seat out of arm's reach.

After twenty minutes they got off the bus, and walked down the street. The beach house came into view like a beacon in the night. Charlie felt exhausted both physically and mentally. He unlocked the front door and sank gratefully into one of the leather couches. Fara sat opposite him, and her eyes narrowed as she searched his face.

"You're right. This isn't going to work." Charlie said sitting back.

"Charlie," Elva said sitting next to him.

"You heard her. She doesn't even want to be touched. All the way home she's been looking at me like that. It's as if she's calculating how long until I start laying into her." Charlie said pointing at the teen.

"Frankly, I don't appreciate it," he added poking the air.

"You—don't—know—anything," Fara said enunciating each word.

"Enlighten me," he drolled in a tired voice.

"Derek was eager and hopeful as he worked his way up the ranks." That was all she said and the silence continued to linger like a melodious stink.

"He changed?" Charlie prodded.

"At first it was like a dream. Derek was kind, funny, and he made every girl feel special. Unfortunately, Derek's ability didn't match his enthusiasm. His kill/death ratio hovered around .3 and Gold Two was his skill ceiling. He became bitter when he stopped gaining ranks. A week ago he lashed out striking Wednesday. That's when his personality took a turn for the worse. He closed down." Fara said in a tight voice.

"I'm still going to report him because he needs to find a less stressful game to play," Charlie said standing. He fetched the cleaning supplies from the bedroom and brought them out.

"Well, let's get you both cleaned," he said putting the box down. Fara continued to eye him with distrust, but Elva quickly changed into pistol form. After another long glare, Fara began to glow. Charlie leaned over the table and picked up the assault rifle. She was an original M16 straight out of the Vietnam era. The weapon was surprisingly light with its black plastic buttstock and foregrip. He unloaded the twenty-round magazine and put it on the table. Slowly he turned the weapon around in his hands looking for how to disassemble the gun, but there weren't any obvious 'start here' instructions.

"You have to push out the two pins on the lower receiver," Fara said in annoyance.

The weapon came apart in two equal sections. Opening the cleaning box he grabbed the solvent can and liberally sprayed her insides. While they soaked he used a long-handled brush to scrub her magwell out. Despite being reset to default, there was still green sludge liberally coating her insides. Elva usually moaned like a porn star whenever Charlie cleaned her, but Fara might as well be mute for the noise she made. Charlie scrubbed the bolt assembly hard with the wire brush. It was tedious work digging out the caked in sludge, but the carrier group grew shiny and he set it on the rag. Finally, he oiled a few spots around the gun and put her back together. He raised the rifle to his shoulder and aimed at the refrigerator. There was a distinctive click as he pulled the trigger. After a second the M16 began to glow. Fara appeared sitting in his lap but leaped to her feet like Charlie had the plague. She circled the coffee table and sat on the other couch trying to disguise a blush by scowling angrily at him.

He picked Elva up and unloaded the 1911. Charlie rotated the bushing, took the spring cover off, and removed the slide lock. Elva's matte black slide came free of her lower frame, and gun residue caked her insides. The solvent can was half empty, and he shook it before spraying her down. Charlie had barely started scrubbing when Elva groaned into his ear.

"Harder, Charlie... harder." She groaned. Her breathing grew more and more ragged as he scrubbed her upper receiver clean. He forced himself to be thorough despite his exhaustion, and after about ten minutes, her insides shined like she was fresh from the factory. Elva panted in ecstasy as Charlie dragged the long snake cleaner through her barrel, and black tar spilled out onto the dirty rag. With a spare cloth he wiped each part down, then oiled her up, and reassembled the gun. After the function check, he held her in his hands.

"While I am offline, take Fara shopping."

"Don't bother. I'm not staying." Fara said from the couch. Charlie frowned because it was the second time she'd mentioned that.

"At the very least, I'll need ammo and magazines. Whether you buy clothes or not is up to you." He said setting Elva on the coffee table. She began to glow. Her face was pink with excitement as she appeared laying across the wood. Elva swooned still recovering from her cleaning, but sat up and leaned toward Charlie. He caught her hands before she could attack the buttons on his pants.

"Not tonight, Elva. I am tired." Charlie said getting up. He avoided looking at her half-lidded lustful eyes as he moved into the bedroom to lay down. Charlie reached up touching his temple with two fingers. The pop-up appeared, and he logged out.

# CHAPTER THIRTEEN

## *Battle Royal*

It was some hours later when Charlie slowly woke, yawned, and stretched. He rolled from bed and stuck his feet into the slippers. Digging the sleep from his eyes he made his way into the bathroom to brush his teeth and shower. Afterward he dressed and wandered into the living room. He made sure a bottle of water was within easy reach, then pulled the dive helmet on. It hummed, warming up before the world outside was shed in a blossom of light.

The beach house smelled of grilled lobster. Charlie sat up discovering a shopping bag sitting on his chest. He opened it to find a lightly armored vest and a pair of tactical operator gloves inside. The fingerless gloves were green canvas and black leather with hardened knuckle guards. The armor was made of flexible Kevlar pads covering the chest, stomach, and back. The vest fit snuggly against his frame highlighting the muscles of his torso, and Charlie admired himself in the mirror.

Voices could be heard coming from the living room, and Charlie wandered out. Several pots and pans littered the stovetop from a recent cooking spree. The two girls were talking over several plates of seafood.

"You both look beautiful," he said walking into the living room.

Fara had changed appearance considerably. Her blond tresses had been cut into a wild windswept mess of short hair. Several parts of which were dyed in red and green streaks. Green eyeshadow accentuated her blue eyes, and a steel stud pierced her lower lip. Her white t-shirt was torn and cut off at the stomach. Across the front in fading red words it read, "Fuck off!" The blue jeans were similarly faded and worn.

"What?" She asked in annoyance as he continued to scan her figure. Her fingernails were painted black with little skulls on them, and on her pinky, was a green jade ring. Fara looked like a rebellious teenager just out of high school.

"I'm sorry for being ill tempered last night. We got off on the wrong foot," Charlie offered holding out a hand. Fara crossed thin arms over her torn t-shirt and glared up at him. Charlie sighed letting his hand fall to his side.

"Fine, if that's how you want to play it," he said turning to Elva. She had purchased clothes too, and he smiled more naturally. If Fara was the teenage bad girl then Elva was the slutty teacher.

A red hairband barely contained the mass of golden curls. Elva fluffed her hair before pushing a pair of thick glasses higher on her nose. The red bra was partially visible under the white button up shirt. Instead of using said buttons, Elva had tied the shirt tails under her breasts. The red mini skirt was pleated with white stripes.

"Elva, the outfits you pick always get me excited." He admitted with a genuine smile. From within her cleavage, Elva withdrew a cash card and demurely extended her hand.

"We indulged and I spent everything," she admitted.

*"That's what it was for,"* thought Charlie, as he took the card and put it in his back pocket. There was around six grand left in the account, and in two weeks the rent for the beach house was due. Whatever was left, he'd add to the card the next time they went shopping.

"You bought ammo?" He asked.

"See for yourself," Elva said pointing to the kitchen counter. On it were ten large boxes of 5.56 ammo, five brand new thirty round magazines, and a carry sling. She had also picked up an extra box of 45 ACP at the same time.

Charlie opened one cardboard box and examined the rifle cartridges. The bullet itself was smaller than he expected. It was half the size of the 45acp rounds Elva used. The casing though was about two inches long, which promised to hold plenty of gunpowder. On the bottom face, it was stamped with 5.56 NATO around a circular primer. He loaded four magazines and put them into his jacket's front pockets.

Fara had already morphed into weapon form after finishing her food. Charlie picked up the rifle, and reloaded the gun. Elva dabbed at her lips with a napkin. She stood and brushed at her new outfit to ensure it was clean, then her eyes closed as she started to glow. After the flash, Charlie holstered the 1911. He quickly checked the pistol mags were loaded and left the house.

The morning was still young, but the bus was full of players heading into town. It was standing room only, and he ended up crammed between two guys arguing about machine guns.

"Fire rate is all that matters," the first man insisted.

"You must be joking. Fire rate is nothing compared to caliber. I'd rather have the 'Ma Deuce' to your cute little minigun." The second muscular man exclaimed. The heavily armored tank patted the .50 caliber machine gun slung across his chest like a lover.

The first scoffed and said, "Melanie here spits out rounds four times faster than your ancient relic." The two men glared at one another.

"What will you do when you burn through your ammo halfway through a fight?" The second asked his voice growing heated.

Charlie tuned them out as their bickering continued. The bus dropped everyone off near the competition center. Gun Meister was quickly growing in popularity, and the crowd was large. Just outside, a thousand people stood in several lines to get into the doors.

He recognized a pink haired receptionist from his first day stepping toward him. "Care to register for the event, sir?" She asked in a bubbly rush.

"What is it?"

"It's a 'free-for-all' Battle Royale," she said waving her tablet.

"How many people are in each match."

"Everyone, silly." She laughed turning her computer around.

On the screen were the words, 'Ultimate Battle Royal.' The winner of the match would receive an extra contract slot for their character. Kill rewards were also doubled during the event.

"Even higher level players?" he asked in surprise. Letting them play with the bronze fish didn't sound very fair.

"It's more a matter of luck than skill during the first hour. Just go out guns blazing. Not only can anyone participate but it doesn't take up a match for the day." She said holding out the tablet. Well, that sold it for Charlie. He could run two more games after giving this a try. He put his hand on the tablet, and his ID flashed.

"Please enter Lobby One," it said.

"The match starts at noon, so you got in at the last second." The girl said tapping the tablet.

"Good luck!" She exclaimed clapping his shoulder, and moved to the next player.

Charlie entered the competition hall and into the elevator with several others. It descended just one floor before opening up on a massive room. Almost ten thousand people filled the theater, and Charlie stepped out joining the crowd. Nearby a group of gorgeous women were covering themselves in green camouflage paint. Most had sniper rifles or silenced weapons of some kind. Other men and women were doing last minute checks of their equipment. A clan of players was passing ammunition back and forth like trading cards. Charlie ended up being pushed to the side as he gawked at the crowd. A Hispanic man strolled by carrying a black modular shotgun.

Hundreds of screens hung about the hall displaying video footage of the battlefield. A modest alpine town was nestled next to a wildlife preserve, which explained why the girls were getting ready for a forest engagement. Charlie felt his excitement growing as he realized just how big the map was. An enormous ten-kilometer circle ringed the town and forest.

As the countdown reached ten seconds the ambient noise hushed. In the silence, ten thousand players removed their safeties. The sound of so many click, click... clicks made the hairs on the back of Charlie's neck stand on end. He reached down and thumbed his new M16 to full-auto fire. As the timer ran down darkness enfolded him.

**[Match Start]**

It was incredibly dark, and Charlie knew he was in an enclosed space. He had less than three feet of room on any side. The first thing he did was kneel and touch the floor. It was carpeted, and he realized he was in a closet. A second later the world erupted into deafening noise as thousands of battles started around the city. The cacophony was so loud Charlie could have screamed at the top of his lungs and not heard himself.

Bullets punched through the thin door, and stitched across at waist level. Charlie ducked to the moldy carpet as slugs barely missed his head. When the long burst ended he peered through the holes. Outside, the figure of a girl turned away from the closet, and left the room. She returned shortly wrestling a dinner table and cabinet into a crude barricade. Charlie removed Elva from his thigh holster as he waited. He didn't have to worry about making noise at this point. Ten gun battles raged in Charlie's building alone. Her back was turned to him as he pushed open the sliding closet door. She was good. Despite the deafening noise, she spun in his direction and reached for a Tactical FN at her waist.

Charlie raised Elva and fired. The bullet struck her in the chest, but she continued to draw the pistol. In surprise, Charlie quickly followed up his first shot with a half dozen more. The raven-haired girl slumped back against the barricade with the silenced pistol in her hand. Charlie stepped forward and saw she was wearing armor like his under her tactical vest. The Kevlar pads had reduced some of the damage, which was why he'd had to put several bullets into her. Her weapon was similar to his. The firearm sticking through the makeshift cover was an M4A1 with a red dot and a huge suppressor.

He was lucky that he'd started in a closet, and double fortunate the girl hadn't bothered to check if anyone was inside. She'd just emptied a clip through the door and called it good. Down the hall an explosion caused the pictures on the walls to shake. Charlie crouched next to the barrier. Someone was throwing grenades around like they were party favors.

The sheer volume of gunfire was slowly dropping as more and more people died. A shotgun blew a hole into the apartment's front door, and Charlie didn't wait for the grenades. He shot to the right of the hole, and four bullets punched through the thin wood.

Three grenades were tossed through and rolled into the living room. Charlie dropped the rifle, ducked below the barricade, and pulled the black haired girl atop him. A second later the apartment rocked. Shrapnel and smoke filled the space as a second shotgun blast blew the door lock off. The grenadier kicked open the entrance on the heels of the explosion.

Charlie was deafened, so the only thing he could hear was a high pitched ringing. He shook his head, pushed the body away, and grabbed Fara. A man wearing heavy armor entered the apartment carrying a Mossberg 500. He pumped his shotgun, leveled it at the barricade, and fired. Buckshot blew chunks of wood off the table he knelt behind. Already shaken by the grenades, he wildly fired at the player. Charlie's luck held as a bullet cut into the man's ankle, and he toppled. He took the opportunity to dump what was left of his mag into the player.

In the smoking silence, he nervously reloaded. The barricade was a ruin and Charlie stood moving forward. As he did the man's shotgun vanished, but the backpack remained. Fragmentation and flash grenades had spilled out across the carpet.

"Can I use grenades?" He asked.

"Yes, you can use grenades and the ammo left on dead bodies. They are considered battlefield pickups but won't be added to your character. Sorry, you can't keep the grenades." Elva informed him. On the girl's corpse, he found a dozen mags and four pounds of C-4. Outside shotgun shells littered the hallway in a path towards the back of the building. Every apartment had the same treatment as his. Each had their doors kicked open and cleared.

Fighting was still raging in the building above and below him. There was no elevator on the floor, so the only way to get up and down was via a central stairway. Charlie approached the stairs and tried to peek out, but had barely opened the metal door, when a dozen rounds punched through it. Hot bullets struck him in the chest, and he quickly rolled sideways as more streamed through the thin metal. Someone was camping the stairs. Charlie touched his jacket sticking a finger into several bullet holes. The door and his armor had thankfully prevented most of the damage, but his chest ached.

Charlie could try and blow a hole in the floor, but he had never used explosives before. It was more likely he was going to kill himself, so he might as well go out in a blaze. Charlie pulled the backpack off his shoulder and dug around inside. He armed a hunk of the explosives by sticking the detonator into it and turning the timer to ten seconds.

The armed explosive began to blink, and he shoved it back into the bag and closed the zipper. Dragging the heavy pack across the floor, he quickly wrenched the door open. Bullets zipped past him, but he threw the entire bag inside. Another shot sank into his flank, as he turned and sprinted away from the stairs. He managed to make it partly down the hall before the explosion slammed into his backside. The blast wave picked up Charlie's puny human body and tossed him down the corridor.

He rolled to a stop surprised he wasn't dead. It felt as though someone had taken a bat to his ass, chest, and stomach. Smoke was still licking around the stairwell, and the metal door had impaled itself in the opposite wall. He dragged himself to his feet and stumbled forward. His body felt drunk, and Charlie struggled with his unresponsive legs. The stairs were a twisted mess, but he managed more or less to climb from one floor to the next. On the bottom floor were several bodies outside the stairwell. Nearby was an emergency exit and he pushed open the fire door.

A man with a salt n' pepper beard stood ten meters away next to a low wall. He wore the gray uniform of a Confederate, and under the officer's hat was a tangle of pure white hair. Charlie stared at the civil-war era soldier as he questioned his own sanity. It took longer than it should have to notice the ancient musket leveled at Charlie. He reacted finally by raising his own rifle. Delusion or not Charlie would not go down without a fight. The musket flashed belching a cloud of smoke, and a .58 caliber ball slammed into Charlie like the fist of god. Darkness closed over him as his body was knocked back through the fire exit.

The door opened on lobby one. Charlie wasn't even sure he was annoyed or not. He hadn't expected to be slain by a ghost from the past. There was a nearby console, and the screen came alive as he touched it. On it was his recent match statistics. He had killed ten people which honestly surprised him.

———

Killing an enemy = 100 x Battle Rank x Weapon Multiplier.
(Bronze 1, Silver 2, Gold 4, Platinum 6, Diamond 10, Tungsten 20)
(Explosives 1, Rifles 1, SMG's 1.25, Pistols 2, Melee 10)

1 x Diamond - pistol = 2,000c
1 x Platinum - rifle = 600c
2 x Gold - explosion = 800c
4 x Silver - explosion = 800c
2 x Bronze - explosion = 200c

Total = 4400c x 2 (Mission Bonus) = 8,800c

Charlie was impressed he'd dispatched a Diamond player. That had to be his greatest achievement to date. The number of credits he'd earned was impressive as hell. It was almost as much as winning a match. At least he wouldn't have to worry about rent now. His stats appeared next which hadn't changed much. Charlie was still Silver One despite killing a diamond player.

_____

Player ID - NA1339872
Registered Competition Name - Charlie
Clan - None
Hours played - 46

Wins - 4
Losses - 1

Kills - 9
Deaths - 3
K/D Ratio - 3.0

Battle Rank - Silver One
Player Score - 1202

Credits - 15,532c

Doors nearby continued to spew a steady stream of men and women. Charlie saw the older Confederate enter the match lobby. He was distinctive against the backdrop of Kevlar vests and urban camo. The man had a bemused smile as he strolled casually to the elevator carrying a long musket. He had a bandolier across his chest, and several leather satchels containing balls, patches, and powder. On his wrist, a much smaller pouch shook with loose primers. The man carried no other weapon besides the ancient flintlock. Charlie's annoyance grew, and he followed the man inside.

The elevator doors opened and they stepped out onto the lobby. Finally, he couldn't stand it anymore. His irritation boiled over and he said, "I despise joke characters." The other man turned curious that someone was talking to him. Charlie glared at him.

"I assure you, young man, that war is nevah a joke," he said in a thick southern drawl.

"Using an old musket is just stupid. If you don't want to take this game seriously then play something else." Charlie replied eyeing the musket on his shoulder. "Use an actual weapon like everyone else."

"You sir, are going too far." The man said putting a hand on his musket. "I take umbrage with your callousness. If you think me and my rifle a joke then I gladly challenge you to a duel."

Charlie paused blinking. He had taken part in one duel already and seen the consequences that came from it. The old man, despite being a joke, was willing to put his weapon on the line. Charlie had just gotten Fara so he wasn't ready to lose her just yet.

"Fine, I over spoke myself." Charlie gritted out.

"Do not apologize to me. It is not my honor you have impeached." He said stroking his rifle.

"Grace will you kindly change forms. This ruffian deigns to speak to you."

Charlie's face heated as the musket started to glow. A southern belle-flower appeared in the yellow light. She had a colonial hairstyle of pleated curls. White lace hid the black collar around her neck, and a brown bronze hoop dress covered her entire body. It was the first time he'd seen a weapon that wasn't showing fifty percent skin. She flicked a small paper fan open covering her lower face.

"I apologize," he managed in a more normal tone. He turned to the

Confederate again and asked in a slightly mocking tone, "Care to explain why you chose to dress like that?"

"To someone who is genuinely interested, I *would* be compelled to." The Confederate agreed. He took the woman's gloved hand and tucked it into the crook of his elbow, then turned to Charlie with a thin smile.

"Shall we depart these facilities? The noise is not conducive to proper conversation."

Charlie followed the man out of the Competition Center, and they crossed to a small park. The man took from his pocket a filigreed handkerchief and dusted the stone bench. The southern woman took his offered hand and carefully perched on the seat. Only when she was finished organizing her dress did he join her.

"Proper introductions are in order," the older man said and waited.

Charlie sat on the opposite side. He touched both his weapons and said, "You can change forms." Both blonds appeared already sitting beside him. Fara, however, scooted as far from him as possible on the seat.

"This is Grace, and you do her a disservice by calling her a musket. She is an 1861 Springfield Rifle." The man said gesturing to his weapon again. "My name is Montgomery Cunningham the 22nd," he added touching his chest with splayed fingers.

"This is Elva and Fara. You can call me Charlie." He said gesturing to each girl first then to himself.

"It is truly a pleasure to meet your acquaintance," he said kissing both of their hands. Fara smiled for the first time since Charlie had seen her.

"So?" Charlie asked a little tartly.

The man gathered his thoughts before saying. "It wasn't until the mid-eighteenth century that war changed. Several innovations came about during the American Civil War which altered the battlefield entirely. As I said before, Grace is as modern a weapon as either sitting beside you. She is a rifle by manufacture, capable of killing a man well out to four-hundred yards." Montgomery said in a lecturing voice.

Charlie glanced at the woman. He hadn't gotten a good look at her as a weapon. All he'd seen was a long hexagonal barrel and cocking mechanism.

"She also uses a minie'ball. You may recognize the shape most modern bullets use." He said withdrawing a paper cartridge from a leather case. He rolled it across the table and Charlie picked it up. Inside the thin wax paper was a charge of powder and a conical bullet. "Grace is quite literally the culmination of these technologies," he said pausing to take up his weapon's hand. He kissed the back of her glove before continuing, "If I may be so bold as to say, she is the mother of all modern firearms. I for one, am humbled and honored to carry her into battle."

"You do go too far, sir." The weapon said in a sultry southern accent. However, as she said this, her face blushed scarlet, which she hid behind the intricate fan. Montgomery kissed her gloved hand again before turning to Charlie.

"By now, I hope you understand that I take my duty seriously." He said in a firmer business like tone.

"I apologize," Charlie said and glanced at Grace. She was still fanning the blush across her cheeks. "To you as well," he added. Their conversation was interrupted by a small chime. Grace slid the cuff of her sleeve up and exposed a treacherously modern wristwatch. She touched the face and turned to Montgomery.

"It's time for your medicine."

"What would I do without you, dear?" He said and stood from the table.

"You're sick?" Charlie asked.

"Cancer, I'm afraid. This is the third time. When they chase it down the thing jumps elsewhere. Sadly, my own body seems intent on rebelling against me." Montgomery said taking the hat from his head, and bowed politely.

"I shall take a short leave, so please, continue without me." He said walking away and out of sight. Montgomery would never do something so uncouth as logging out in public.

"He doesn't carry a pistol?" Elva asked.

"Olivia, left..." Grace sighed and lowered her fan.

"Monty is sometimes gone for weeks at a time for treatment. He is always profusely apologetic, but there are long periods of unavoidable absence." She said toying with the fan in her fingers. "Olivia, found another Meister," she sighed.

"What Grace failed to mention is that she has the patience of a saint," Montgomery added coming back into view.

Grace's eyes lifted and she turned towards him. "I would have left you long ago if anyone would have me," She said flicking her fan open. The bite of her words were belied by the playful tone in her voice.

"I'm afraid we'll have to cut our gaming short today," he said in apology. Grace held out a hand which Monty took. She slid from the bench to stand beside him. "If you'll excuse us," he added with another bow.

As they walked away, Charlie turned to Elva and said, "Send them a friend request. I don't know if we'll play together, but he was interesting."

# CHAPTER FOURTEEN

## *Intermission*

Charlie crouched under the corpse of Lady Liberty. The old girl had been cruelly disfigured. Her head was missing, and a melted hole took her arm off. The final affront was the fact someone had disrobed her leaving only an iron skeleton. In the New York Bay, an aircraft carrier had been broken in half and partially submerged. Tiny toy-like jet fighters littered the beach the vessel had crashed upon.

"Why do you lick your gun?" Charlie asked. Remy turned to him with the revolver still partially in her mouth. After a second she smiled slyly and removed the cannon.

"It drives Philip nuts," she admitted.

"That's it?" he asked.

"Is there a better reason?" She replied caressing her dainty fingers over the revolver.

Charlie rolled his eyes and said, "I just wish you wouldn't do it in the middle of a firefight."

"It's called multitasking," she said leaning around the corner. Remy took careful aim and fired twice at a distant shadow. The bullets connected and the target collapsed in a bloody heap. Remy ducked back next to Charlie as a splatter of return fire hit the stone brickwork. There was less than a minute left in the round, and he did his best to ignore the red circle at his back.

Charlie rose and aimed at a target leaping onto the base of the statue. His round struck, but the enemy continued to sprint toward the old girl's sandaled foot. He switched to full auto, but the man was already halfway there. The gun bucked against his shoulder, and the figure staggered from a hit before throwing himself behind cover.

"One of us must get under Lady Liberty's skirt," Remy said reloading her revolver.

The problem would be the enemy waiting under there. Remy withdrew a double-barreled saw'd-off from a thigh holster.

"Cover me," she said struggling to crawl onto the statue's base. Several bullets skipped past from the enemy holding the other side.

They both mounted the base and Charlie sprinted for the left side. A bullet skipped past his left foot, then a second missed his head by barely an inch. He threw himself forward into the statue's skeleton. On the right side, Remy rolled to an awkward stop and aimed up with the shotgun. Her finger squeezed the trigger on both barrels as bullets stitched her side. The blast peppered the enemy player with two dozen buckshot pellets, and the corpse slid from the skeletal perch.

*"Good job, Remy. You might be a weird little perv, but you are amazing at the game."*

Charlie knelt next to the statue and waited. The red barrier closed in, and a woman with over-sized melons crawled up onto the base with the circle hot on her heels. Charlie didn't give her a chance. He let out a long breath as the sights lined up on the sniper. She ran forward, breasts bouncing as his finger stroked the trigger. Blood sprayed out in a mist as six rounds punched into her lightly armored chest. Two other bullets flew over her shoulder, and he let go of the trigger. Her beautiful face planted onto the stonework as she skidded to a bloody halt. Darkness closed over him.

**[Match Complete]**
**[Team Win]**

"Another game?" Remy asked as he stepped out into the lobby.

"Sorry, can't. I wanted to jump on a used car before it was gone. Afterward, I was going to get some lunch and relax."

Three random players were already in the elevator. Remy stood in the doorway preventing it from closing. She flicked open the breach of her double barrel and loaded two more shells inside. "That's right. You live out near the water." She said giving the weapon in her hands an absent caress before slipping the gun into a thigh holster. Remy backed into the elevator as Charlie entered.

"It's cheap," he admitted putting his palm on the control screen, and it ascended.

"Did that before, couldn't stand the commute. It's a game. I don't want to spend twenty minutes driving into town." She said walking beside them.

He didn't mind it. Besides if he managed to get this car it would make the trip that much shorter.

The lobby was still full, but Charlie pushed his way outside. He met the man standing next to a white 1965 Shelby Mustang Convertible with two thick black racing stripes down the middle. The stock tires had been replaced with custom racing slicks, and running lights had been added to the front grill. A good car for drag racing down the empty evening streets.

"You're in luck. I got a phone call about the car just before you got out here." The man said. Charlie smiled, because this was his field of expertise. He did a once around the vehicle, and noticed the man had hit something hard on the left side. The back bumper had been quickly replaced but not repainted.

"That'll be quite a fix," Charlie muttered just loud enough to be heard.

"A couple of grand," the man said following Charlie. A second scrape marred the right side, and he ran a hand over the damaged front panel.

"How about five thousand," he asked.

"The ad was for eight."

"True, but a factory Mustang is only sixteen grand," Charlie said running a hand over the damaged part of the car. The guy had probably bought it early. With the mods visible, it was obvious the player had dumped money into the Mustang to keep up with more expensive sports cars. Now he was selling it to upgrade.

"Seven Thousand."

"Five-point-five," Charlie countered.

"Six."

"Done," Charlie said holding out a hand. They shook on it and went inside to make the trade. The money he saved could be used to repair the bodywork, but he wasn't about to waste a fortune fixing a write-off. The man held out the keys after they'd transferred the credits over.

Removing Fara from his shoulder, Charlie set her on the passenger seat. Then climbed into the driver's side and ran a hand over the leather upholstery. He slid the key into the ignition, closed his eyes, and listened carefully as it turned over. The engine started with a roar, and a turbocharger spun up to full speed as the car shook. Elva appeared sitting on his lap and smiled. It was a Mustang, and Elva was part of the reason for the purchase.

"I love it," she said turning sideways and settled her feet on the passenger seat.

Her arm circled his neck as she settled against the driver side door. He pushed the clutch in, and shifted the car from neutral into first. Elva gave a shriek of surprise as the vintage muscle car shot forward. Then pressed herself harder to Charlie as she hung on. The car screamed onto the street, and Charlie goosed the engine again speeding through the intersection. He wasn't doing it just to make Elva squeal and squeeze him tightly, that was a side bonus. Charlie was checking the wheel alignment which did pull to the left a tiny bit. It confirmed his suspicions there was damage, but it wasn't as bad as he feared.

The bodywork he would probably fix, but a bent rear axle was low on the list of repairs. Still, the car was a steal for how much the guy had modified it. It took about fifteen minutes to reach the beach house, which was far quicker than taking the bus. As he approached the garage, it automatically opened, and he rolled to a stop. Elva slid from his lap when he opened the driver side door. Inside, she went to the refrigerator to get lunch, so Charlie sat on the couch and touched his temple to log out. The pop-up appeared and he exited the game.

His phone was ringing as the living room came into focus. Charlie's throat was dry and he reached for the coffee nearby. It was cold, but he polished off what was left. He coughed and swallowed the bitter java before taking the dive helmet off. The phone rang again.

He reached for the mobile and saw it was a long distance number. In fact, he was pretty sure that number wasn't in the united states. For a second he considered just ignoring it, but touched the accept button and lifted the screen to his ear.

"Hello?" He asked.

"Good afternoon old friend," A vaguely familiar voice said. "I'm glad I managed to catch you." He added next. Charlie couldn't reply. Inside his head, he was replaying the voice again and again.

"Alex?" he asked tentatively.

"Charlie, it's nice to hear from you." The man said with enthusiasm. His roommate had dropped off the face of the earth after leaving.

"It's been months, how are you?" Charlie asked with more energy.

"Keeping myself busy. I am the Director of Arrivals here at the resort." He said, and Charlie smiled. That was a step up from being a college dropout shut in.

"How about you?" Alex asked.

"Still selling cars, but I'm lucky to have a job in this economy." He admitted. Charlie picked up the empty mug and walked into the kitchen. Fizzgig announced himself by rubbing up against Charlie's leg, so he bent and scratched the cat behind the ear.

"I hear it's bad over there," Alex said.

"Enough about me, how are the Caribbeans?" He asked turning the faucet on. Charlie cleaned out the cup and set it on the rag next to the sink. He picked up the coffee carafe and dumped the rest down the drain too.

"I wouldn't know."

"How can you not know?" Charlie asked in surprise.

"I haven't looked outside in a month or so," Alex admitted, and Charlie put the pot back in the machine. He was at a loss what to say.

Finally, he laughed and said, "Alex you're still a shut-in."

The man laughed too, "I have no idea what it's like outside because I'm dead." Now Charlie was thrown for a loop.

"What?"

"Dead... deceased... no longer alive." Alex answered.

From the casual tone of voice, it was something he apparently discussed often. Charlie struggled with what to say to that, and Alex started to laugh again as the silence dragged on.

"I love getting that reaction. I told you I was chasing the ghost." He said after controlling himself.

"Yes, you mentioned you were looking into getting digitized, but I never thought you'd cross that bridge." Charlie said shaking his head again. The idea was just too much to grasp.

"I mean... You have to die?"

"I couldn't do it on my own, and getting the equipment in America is impossible. Some investors were looking to cross over. We started a resort on the Islands where the laws are more liberal. Of course, those cowards were happy to let me be the guinea pig."

"How?" Charlie asked.

"We got a copy of the Nigmus Source Code then smuggled in an altered dive pod. God that thing was ugly, but it worked. Things became easier after the Chinese released the unofficial avatar patch for Nigmus." Alex said in a reminiscing voice like that had been years, not months ago.

"You did it."

"We did. Now I'm Director for Dreamland Retirement Resort. We cater to wealthy individuals who aren't quite ready to kick the bucket. Most of my time is spent convincing wrinkled old fogies that I'm really dead and digitized."

"That must be a pain..."

"The real pain was figuring out what to do with all the bodies. People check out, but their bodies don't leave." He said, and Charlie recalled the lyrics to an old song.

*"Relax," said the night man,*
*"We are programmed to receive.*
*You can check-out any time you like,*
*But you can never leave!"*

"I suppose there's not a lot of land to bury people."

"Exactly. Can't bury them in mass graves like the Russians and Chinese do. While the laws on the islands are lax the environmental regulations are a quagmire of red tape. We tried burning them, but that caused $CO_2$ emissions. There were also mercury and heavy metals in all the old bones and hip replacements." The man said in annoyance.

"In the end, we have to charter a barge to carry a load of bodies out into the ocean. We rope them together with a heavy weight and drop them overboard. The coast guard board them every time, so we constantly have to shell out bribes and kickbacks. Everyone wants a piece of the pie." He said with a weary sigh.

"What happens to them after they're digital?" Charlie asked.

"Many of these people can barely work a smart phone let alone a full dive. We take it slow for them. A private cloud runs a Custom Server that simulates modern times. The current hot spot is a recreation of 1950's France. Most spend a few weeks screwing each other silly before moving on." Alex said.

"I suppose you have lots of time for video games."

"Hardly. Our operation is 24/7 with how much we've grown. I haven't logged into my old character in a month, but all the dive pods are down for scheduled maintenance. I was sitting in the office twiddling my thumbs."

"So you gave your old roommate a call?"

"It was either that or make small talk with the residents," Alex said with a shudder.

"You could have dipped into the server for some wine and women," Charlie suggested.

"I don't do badly in that respect, but hey, I have to cut our talk short. Just got word the machines are coming back online. Nose to the grindstone and all that."

"It was nice talking to you, Alex."

"You too, Charlie. Hey, I'll send our brochure in case you're interested."

Charlie wasn't but said, "Thanks," and disconnected the phone. He rather liked breathing despite how intriguing the idea was. Fizzgig meowed again pressing himself to Charlie's leg begging for more scratches.

"Sushi, again?" he asked the cat. Fizzgig meowed, and he nodded in agreement. He might as well indulge today.

# CHAPTER FIFTEEN

## *July 4th*

It was the Fourth of July, and the sky was full of exploding fireworks. Charlie lay face down on the beach blanket, clad only in black swim trunks and flip-flops. A set of smooth legs straddled his lower back, and Elva popped open the sunscreen bottle. A drop of lotion hit his neck, and she worked the liquid into his skin. Her expert fingers spread sunscreen over his shoulders and back. He really should have done this sooner, but Charlie had been too caught up in running matches.

"You could be nicer to Fara," Elva said in a suspiciously light tone. She shifted sliding down to straddle his legs. After liberally covering his back she started to massage the lotion into his skin. Fara—was the fly in his ointment. Aside from buying ammo he hadn't bothered upgrading her.

"Would love too, but I haven't seen her in a week. She spends all her time in weapon form." Charlie admitted. Fara refused to speak to him now, and Charlie could count the number of times they had conversed with her on one hand. It was annoying, especially because he liked her as a gun. The M16 suited his style, but he wouldn't waste money on mods for her.

"I get the feeling Fara's keeping me at a distance so she can go back to Derek."

"Probably."

"Why in the seven hells would she do that?" He asked.

*"The man had beat her and she was going to crawl back like a broken puppy. It was like Stockholm Syndrome for androids."*

"You have to understand how our memories work. We can't save everything that happens. I get sensory data, like the feeling of having you inside me. It's recorded once. The thirty-seven times we've re-contracted are linked to that incredible sensation." She said squeezing his butt cheeks. After she'd satisfied herself, Elva said, "Our database forms a spider web of interconnecting links. At its center is the Meister, especially our first one. They end up forming a large portion of our personalities." Elva moved lower, and her fingers started to work lotion into his thighs and legs.

He turned his attention back to Fara. The only interaction he had with the Vietnam era weapon was shooting, and cleaning her. He shrugged and said, "She can just delete the memories then. You told me you erase what you don't use."

"We can't completely wipe out a memory, even if its painful. At best we can archive the data. Compressing it down so that it's little more than a log entry." Elva said slowing.

"I'll be nicer to her, if you promise me something too," he said.

"What's that?"

Charlie turned over on the beach blanket. A blonde goddess knelt over him wearing a red, white, and blue bikini. She'd gone from pale white skin to a light bronze from the summer sun, and for a second, he was caught up in the sight of her gorgeous body. Charlie never tired of looking at her, even after a month of sex. Elva poked him, prodding Charlie's mind back into function.

"Stop nagging Fara about staying," he said looking up into Elva's face. She pouted like a child caught with their hand in the cookie jar. "I know you like having her around, but whether she stays or not is up to her." Charlie would lose the assault rifle in a week, then he'd pick up a new weapon.

"I promise," she said petulantly.

Elva went back to spreading sunscreen over Charlie's chest, but with significantly less energy. Thankfully conversation about Fara ended, and for a few more minutes, the massage continued until his skin glistened.

"It's your turn," he said once she had finished. Elva reached up and yanked on the bikini string tying the flag together. There was a small party favor secretly worked into the knot. It went off, showering Charlie with red confetti as her breasts fell free. Elva had been wearing that bikini all morning, and he suspected she'd been dying to do that for hours.

"Get it?" Elva asked biting her finger. "It's a... booby trap," she said laughing at what was probably, the worst pun ever. Charlie reached up grabbing her waist, and Elva squealed as he rolled her onto the towel. Charlie bent biting one nipple as he pinched the other. Elva gasped grabbing a fist full of his hair, and long legs wrapped around his middle as he attacked her breasts. She squirmed under his assault, moaned, and opened her legs like a flower to the morning sun.

Charlie bit and licked his way down her stomach, but paused at her red and white thong. "I'm not going to find any more surprises tucked away?" He asked.

"You'll just have to risk it," she breathed aiming her groin at him. Charlie was about to do just that when the mobile phone rang. Things were just getting interesting with Elva, but Charlie had made a few friends, so he reached over picking up the phone.

"Montgomery, it's nice to hear from you," Charlie said answering. He'd been absent for more than a week since they'd first talked and became friends.

"Happy 'The Brits Lost' Day," the man said in a faux cheer voice.

"You mean Independence Day?"

"Good Lord, no. We patriotic southerners fought for our own independence, yet no one celebrates our valiant struggle." The man replied with a piqued Louisiana accent.

"That happened like two hundred years ago," he said with a smile. Montgomery was a character all right.

"The passage of time is irrelevant," Monty said in a long southern drawl.

"Are you even southern?"

"Now you mock me, sir. I shall hang up this infernal box."

"I was only joking," Charlie replied with a chuckle.

"If you can bear the presence of a disgruntled soldier, I have time for a match." Montgomery said. Charlie hadn't been down to the competition hall today. Instead, he'd attempted to relax with Elva. His neighbors, however, continued to launch grenades and mortars into the water, which was starting to get on his nerves.

"I could kill a few souls today."

"That's the spirit. Meet inside the competition hall?" Montgomery suggested.

"See you soon," Charlie agreed while hanging up, and glancing down at Elva. The woman was suggestively posing on the blanket, and toying with the string on her bikini bottom.

"Later," he smirked. Charlie climbed to his feet and walked the short distance up to the beach house. Elva made an annoyed tisk as she scrambled to grab the lotion and towel. On his way into the house, he dialed Remy's number. It rang about three times before connecting.

"Harder," Remy said picking up. There was the distinct sound of wet slapping sex in the background, and he pulled the phone away from his ear.

"Yeah...?"

"I'm running a match at the competition hall, be there in twenty minutes if you want to join." He grumbled. There was a shrill female cry from the phone.

"Fuck me that was good," a small voice sighed from the mobile. Charlie hung up. If Remy showed up, that would be up to her.

Charlie discovered the M16 laying on the master bed. She must have been watching TV while he was outside, but had changed forms as he had come into the house. The show playing was an old black and white horror series. He picked up the assault rifle, checked her load, and was about to shoulder her, but at the last second remembered his promise.

"Sorry for interrupting your show. On the way home I'll pick up the box set for you." He stated. Fara, as usual, remained completely silent and he walked into the living room. Elva was putting her top back on, and Charlie walked over to her. She paused with a hopeful look in her eye.

"I'm going to drive the Mustang hard into town," he said, and Elva blanched. Charlie used the muscle car like he had a death wish. Why not? It was a virtual car, so he'd put a few scrapes in the new body work. Elva's bronze skin began to glow, and a 1911 appeared on the counter. He holstered the weapon and went out into the garage. The engine started with a roar, and he backed out onto the street. The tires left a black streak down the road and he fish tailed around the corner.

Outside the Competition Hall, Remy was skipping back and forth in an elementary school outfit. She had pigtails and a teddy bear backpack on. At seeing him she stopped and pointed a tiny finger his way.

"You hung up!" She accused stamping her little red shoe. It was odd seeing a girl dressed for class and wearing a leather holster. The massive black handgun dangled under her arm as she continued to point.

"Of course I did," he said moving past the girl. She skipped beside him and they entered the hall. Montgomery was chatting with Grace just inside the lobby. The weapon held a black lace fan in her right hand and waved at seeing them. Monty however, was sniffing with disdain at the plethora of American flags. Remy stopped short and stared at the distinguished southern gentleman. She gave a girlish shriek and ran forward.

"Oh my god, you have an epic beard." She said leaping up. The older man was forced to catch the short female or risk being bowled over.

"Thank you..." He said in bewilderment.

"You must give the most amazing mustache rides," she said running her little fingers through his beard.

"Excuse me, miss?"

"I wanna climb onto your face and go to town." Remy moaned and the man dropped her.

Charlie came forward and sighed, "Just ignore her. That's what I do."

"Is this a friend of yours?" The man asked in a cold derisive tone.

"This is Remy; she is... sort of an acquaintance." He admitted with a shrug.

"I thought we had something together after what happened in that foxhole," Remy said in a childishly high voice.

"I'd rather not remember that," he shuddered while replying and turning to the older man. "Montgomery, you called me. I'll let you decide what we do today."

Grace was dressed in a vintage black ball gown with red lacing. A black bonnet was carefully pinned to her hair. Another black lace scarf hid the collar at her throat, but nothing could hide the way she was glaring at the teal haired girl. Monty stepped away from Remy and said, "I was feeling better than usual, so I wanted to run a match. I do hope we get to see the Capital. It is '*that*' day after all."

"Why does that matter," Charlie asked. He assumed they would run some special event, but he hadn't heard of anything going on.

"As a historian and archaeologist, I am fascinated by the story of this world. Especially the clues they left behind." Monty said.

"Story?"

"You mean you haven't noticed?" The older man asked in shock.

"No," Charlie admitted.

"Have you not questioned why this fair city is a paradise. The streets are free of litter. There is ample food, clothes, and luxuries, but not once have I seen a delivery truck on the road. Yet, all our battles take place in ancient ruins or sundered cities. Surely that should've made you wonder." Montgomery said.

"I just thought it fit the setting."

"You have taken things at face value. I suppose that's to be expected of today's youth. The developers have hidden the lore of this world behind clues and subtle backdrops." Montgomery said finally stepping away from the young elementary schooler. He moved to put himself closer to Grace.

"Is that true, Elva?" He asked touching the frame of his pistol.

"They won't know either. I once spent four hours tickle torturing Grace to see if she would talk. Unfortunately, she divulged nothing but a torrent of squeals." He said gesturing to his weapon nearby. The girl blushed at the memory and flicked her fan open again.

"You were a brute," She said hiding her blushing cheeks.

"My true colors did shine that evening," Monty admitted.

"I still don't get it. You mean like... We're in a simulation within a simulation, and we fight out in the real world?" Charlie asked slowly. That was some double deep smoke and mirrors plot. It hadn't occurred to Charlie to question why there was electricity in town, but nothing outside worked.

"One of my personal theories, yes." Monty said doing his best to ignore Remy. The girl was standing on her tippy-toes trying to reach his magnificent white beard.

"Let's get into a match before Remy does something to get us all banned," Charlie muttered turning toward the console screens.

"Mustache ride..." Remy whispered following after Monty.

They started a match together. Charlie followed his companions into the elevator, which then descended. Remy continued to try and get past Grace, and the matron's eyes were starting to glow with the same dangerous glint Fara had just before she'd attacked Derek. Thankfully, the elevator disgorged them into the lobby before a blood bath started. Two other players were already waiting inside, and darkness closed in.

**[Match Starting]**

Charlie found himself looking upon the wizened face of Abraham Lincoln sitting in a larger than life chair. It was already evening on the east coast, and the setting sun was casting long shadows across the memorial entrance.

"Ahh, excellent. I had hoped it would send us to the Capital." Monty said from nearby.

"Why is that?" Charlie asked turning to the man.

"I've been here once before. There's an easter egg in the White House I wanted to check out. Last time I stumbled upon it by accident, but had no time to investigate." Monty said in excitement.

"Seen them, boring," Remy said from nearby.

"Well, don't spoil it for the man," Montgomery said.

"Seen who?" Charlie asked, but the older man only smiled.

"We're going to have to sprint there. The White House is about ten blocks away, and the wall will close in fast."

"What are you guys talking about?" The two men asked. Charlie hadn't paid much attention to the randoms, who were checking their rifles a few meters away.

"Sorry gentlemen, but we are taking the opportunity to investigate."

"You're running off?" They asked in disbelief.

"You can join us if you want," Monty suggested.

"Why don't we do this in a casual match?" Charlie asked jogging after the older man.

"They only show up in official games. That's been confirmed." Remy said from behind him.

Charlie jogged after the older man down the memorial steps. Soon they reached the avenue and quickly sprinted along the reflecting pool. Charlie was fast, but the old man reached the intersection ahead of them. He slid to a stop and glanced both ways. With barely a pause to catch his breath, he turned down the side street, and after ten minutes of sprinting they reached the White House. The marble facade was dark brown like a cigarette stain. Part of the iconic dome had fallen inside, and half of the structure was burned to the ground. The entire east wing was little more than a pile of blackened timbers. The tree's on the front lawn were twisted husks, and the ground was scorched glass. Charlie skidded to a halt seeing the damage to the iconic building. He'd seen Big Ben as a ruin, and watched Shanghai crumbled into dust, but it hadn't hit home like this.

"Technically, this is the third time the White House has burned down. It was torched in 1812 by British forces. Then the west wing burned to the ground on Christmas Eve in 1929." Monty said slowing to a jog.

The red circle was slowly closing in, but it was still a block away. They had some time to explore and get back. The gates to the front garden had been knocked over, and an APC was sitting on its side with spent bullet casings littering the ground around the wreck. Closer to the building two M1 Abrams sat in sandbag pillboxes. Both sixty-two ton tanks were missing their tops like someone had cut off the turrets and walked away with them.

"I've seen battle damage like this before." Charlie said moving closer to the vehicles. The cut looked like someone had melted the composite metal with a laser scalpel.

"Interesting damage indeed," Monty said stepping onto the porch. Remy continued to follow along in a half interested gait. She kicked a few bullet casings as she walked around the APC. Inside the lobby bullet holes and scorch marks crisscrossed the walls. Charlie was finally starting to see a picture form. He was reminded again of the missile tank back in that football field. It had been sitting alone in the gutted stadium surrounded by entrenched fighting positions as if they'd been making a last stand.

It became difficult to travel further inside the old mansion because of the damage. Entire sections had been blown out by grenades. Those strange straight black lines were all over, and Charlie wasn't quite sure what could've caused such damage. Remy continued to follow behind with a bored expression on her face.

"Which way was it?" Monty mused glancing down the hallway. The ceiling had collapsed halfway down, which blocked off access to the Presidential Wing. Monty ambled around the corner before spotting a side passage. "Ahh, this way." He said opening the way into a back stairwell which led up to the second floor. Someone had cobbled together a crude barrier of tables and chairs at the top of the landing, and Charlie struggled over the precarious pile. Monty in his excitement went ahead.

"There you are, you handsome devil." A distinguished voice said from around the corner. The Confederate paused next to a cleaning closet with a smile on his face. He pointed inside.

In the darkness, it was difficult to tell what Charlie saw. It appeared to be the remains of a futuristic set of body armor. Only it wasn't made for humans. He stepped inside the dim space for a better look. A clear face shield displayed the mummified head of an alien creature. To call it reptilian was a mistake but it's hard scaled skin had a greenish tint. It had two small predatory eyes under a ridged brow that were milky white in death. Instead of a nose it had two tiny slits. The creature's mouth was open in a final expression of pain, which showed teeth that were short but definitely carnivorous. The armored chest plate had been peeled open like a can of sausages. Inside was a blackened alien rib cage. Charlie was repulsed by the sight because it's bones and vertebrae were in all the wrong places. Its guts had long ago decayed leaving the scaled husk inside the armor.

"It appears our friend met with a rocket propelled grenade," Monty said kicking the long green tube of a LAW launcher. "That probably damaged his suit, preventing them from finding him. They go to great lengths to collect their dead."

"Aliens?!?" Charlie asked in astonishment.

"An exciting development, no?" Montgomery asked with a sly smile on his face.

"Who are they?"

Instead of answering the old man turned and walked down the hallway. Charlie gave another glance at the alien corpse before trotting after the Confederate. They walked towards the ruined west wing. Most of the floor had collapsed, but the old man spryly leaped across the gap. Charlie was glad his Agility was higher than average. Several times he was forced to dash across a tiny space then throw himself over a gutted hole in the floor. After passing into the West Wing the old man dropped down to the first floor. Remy was already sitting on the Presidential Desk within the Oval Office. She kicked her red shoes against the ancient oak wood and toyed with her revolver. Next to the young school girl was a human skeleton, and it was the first time Charlie had seen one since playing the game. Despite all the destruction, all the ruin, there wasn't a single body. Now that he thought about it, the lack of any corpses was bizarre. This lone skeleton was headless, and it sat in the presidential chair facing the room. Montgomery moved to the table and pushed several stacks of water stained papers around. Finally, he picked one up, and held it out.

"You'll find the answer to your previous question here," he said, and Charlie took the sheet. It was made as if on an old typeset printer, and much of the document was damaged by water and time, but a few words had survived.

---

**Confiden...**
**Presidents eyes on...**

**Seek... elter in Langley. Craft like nothing... Massive... moon orbit. Satellites down, communicate by wire only. Roth dropshi... down, forces mobilized... Ship damaged in fighting. Cloning technolo... recovere... far adv...**
**Can't kill the Roth fast enough...**

---

"The Roth?" Charlie asked, and the older man smiled thinly. Monty scratched his mustache and smiled slyly.

"If they attacked us why aren't we fighting them instead of each other?" He asked in astonishment.

"Practice," Remy quipped still kicking her feet on the desk.

"I suspect the young lady is onto something. It may be why the late game is so focused on small squad combat." Monty said toying with more of the water soaked papers.

"Wait, where are they?"

"Another good question." The man said dropping the damaged documents to the desk. Charlie hadn't seen anything resembling alien technology, ships, or that warrior back there.

"We won then. America fought them off." Charlie said defiantly. Of course America won, they always did in the movies.

"In one voice we cried out, we shall not go quietly into the night! We will not vanish without a fight! We're going to live on! We're going to survive!" Monty said dramatically. The silence lengthened as his words slowly sank in.

"Does that look like victory?" Monty asked pointing to the headless President.

The old Confederate took considerable pleasure in saying, "Happy Independence Day."

Charlie shook his head in confusion and turned away from the presidential desk. Aside from that single corpse, there wasn't any sign of fighting. He walked in a circle around the room with the paper, and re-read the missive several times. 'Roth Dropship Crashed...' If that was true America had accomplished something. The next part might be 'cloning technology recovered.' Did all the alien vessels have that? If so it was no wonder they couldn't kill them fast enough. The aliens would just keep respawning, and Charlie tried to imagine what it would be like fighting waves of endless soldiers. Impossible, it would be like holding back a river. Charlie's musings were interrupted as the red wall appeared in the room coming towards them.

"Looks like our time is up. Should have been paying more attention." Remy said from the desk. She hopped down onto the stained carpet and holstered her revolver. Charlie dashed for the destroyed windows, but the border closed over him. He saw red for a moment before darkness encroached.

The door opened into the private lounge. Montgomery's face was blanched and he was using the wall to support himself.

"Monty!" Charlie called moving forward to help the man, but he held out a hand. Montgomery pushed from the wall and turned towards him. With a set face he straightened his gray officer's jacket.

"Sorry, you had to witness that," he said in a controlled voice. Remy came in through another private door. She searched their expressions then moved into the lounge.

"Are you alright?"

"The excitement has drained my reserves. I'm not doing as well as I first thought," the man admitted. Monty turned still stiff backed and walked to the leather couches. He sat and placed his rifle carefully on the seat next to him. Then he turned and said, "I might have to pass on another match. Sorry for dragging you out here."

"How's your treatment going?" Charlie asked feeling for the man. He was obviously still in some pain.

"Badly I'm afraid. This new one is a stubborn demon."

"Have you considered getting digitized?" Charlie asked tentatively. The Confederate removed his gray hat and held it in his trembling fingers.

"I've tried to get into the research programs, but they won't have me, not with so much cancer riddling my body. They're probably afraid it's reached my brain, which makes me Persona Non-Grata. All I can do is undergo the treatment and pray it works." He said setting the hat carefully back on his head.

On the television screens, two men were desperately fighting against a group of five. They were running down a side street in a leap frog fashion. One remained behind aiming a vector submachine gun down the alley.

"I have a friend who works at a ghosting farm. It's run out of the Caribbean Islands." Charlie said to the older man. "He sent me a brochure. It's expensive, no... that's too kind a word for how much it costs to get in, but I could send it over to you." Charlie continued and the man looked intrigued.

"I would have to take a close look at it." The man said stroking his beard. Despite himself, he seemed very interested.

"They refer to it as a retirement center and elders resort, but they digitize people," Charlie warned and they exchanged contact information.

The two last randoms became cornered in a blind alley. Several flash bangs landed next to the dumpster they hid behind. In the bright flash, four enemy soldiers moved in. The two fired blindly around the corner hoping for a kill. A fifth person climbed onto a crashed delivery van near the alley entrance. He fired down on the duo striking one in the temple.

The man collapsed to the crack pavement dropping his SMG, and the second teammate didn't last much longer.

**[Match Complete]**
**[Team Loss]**

"You fuckers cost us the game," a man spat from behind them. Charlie turned and saw the red faced player coming toward them.

"Sorry," was all he could manage at the moment. He was more concerned with his new friend than the loss of one match.

"Grace, let's head home," Monty said touching his rifle.

It began to glow. The southern belle appeared and took Monty's hand. They stood and started toward the elevator. Monty tried to hide it, but much of his weight was carried by Grace as Remy and Charlie followed. He was done for today because he wanted to send the brochure over, and search for information on the aliens.

# CHAPTER SIXTEEN

## *Love Bites*

The smell of expensive coffee was the main reason Charlie came to this cafe so often, and he stopped in the doorway to breathe it in. It was an edgy, 'I'm smarter than you' coffee shop. No less than six college students were typing away at ultra-slim laptops, and pretentiously ignoring one another. He stood for a second drinking in the atmosphere. When his lungs were suitably saturated, he advanced on the coffee counter. A barista was idly cleaning the machine, but she smiled pushing a lock of her purple hair back behind an ear.

"A large vanilla Mocha with whipped cream," He said withdrawing his wallet.

While she was making his order, he turned scanning the tables. He noticed Jennifer from work sitting alone in a back booth. She was dressed in a savagely tight black business suit. After the initial hopeful exchange a month ago they hadn't talked much. Jen had gone back to sucking blood and flaunting red dresses. Charlie had murdered and killed his way through several Silver ranks. The rest of his time was spent screwing Elva. Still, their working relationship had improved to the point where they'd formed a tentative acquaintance.

"Your order," the barista said sliding the paper cup across the counter. On the lid, the barista had written his name with little red hearts, which was a sign he came here way too much.

Charlie took his cup and headed toward the back of the cafe. He was about to sit down with Jennifer when he noticed her eyes. They were red rimmed with a smear of black makeup, and it was obvious she'd been crying. He steered himself instead to a table nearby and hunkered down. Jen held a mobile phone with a distant expression on her face. Her drink sat forgotten as she stared at the screen. Charlie was curious and worried at the same time. He'd enjoyed a burgeoning friendship with Jennifer, and something was going on.

Closing her red eyes, Jennifer dialed a number, and waited while it rang. Her voice was surprisingly normal for how much the phone shook. "Hey," she said keeping her introduction short. Charlie was close enough that he could just make out the person on the other end.

"You're at lunch early," a small voice replied.

"I was hungry. Sorry, I missed you last night." Jennifer responded in a perfectly modulated tone. The pause was very slight.

"I was stuck in a clan meeting."

"You should have called me. I'm your second," Jennifer replied quietly. Charlie knew her, and noticed the subtle change in her voice. The bloodhound caught the scent of prey.

"It was informal," Stephan said quickly.

Jen's manicured fingers tightened on the smart phone as she asked, "How informal?"

"What?"

"How informal are we talking. Was there a lack of clothes involved?" She asked as her voice turned hard.

"Camile, I don't know what you're talking abo—"

"You know precisely what I'm saying," Jennifer snapped cutting him off.

"No, I was..."

"Don't... Don't even try and deny it, Stephan."

"Look, whatever you've heard, it's a pack of lies," Stephan said in a hurried voice.

"I have the fucking video! You had a goddamn foursome with a group of fledglings." She hissed loudly showing a break in her hardened exterior. All the noise in the cafe ceased as ears turned in her direction. Shit, Charlie felt embarrassed for the girl.

"Now you aren't going to deny it?" She asked in the silence.

"Camile... They meant nothing," he stated.

"Apparently, I don't mean anything either," she answered in a colder voice. The edge in her tone sharpened her words like a serrated razor blade. Up until now, she'd been carefully controlling her tone.

"Bloody hell, if they have video it was a setup. They're trying to come between us." Stephan said trying to reason with her.

"Well it worked, we had a promise to each other." She said raising her voice.

"This is rich, especially since you cheated on me first." He spit acidly. Jennifer wiped at the black mascara running down her face.

"With an NPC and I told you about it. I cried in your arms, poured out my heart, and you said it wasn't even a thing." Jen said fumbling for her purse. She pulled a tissue from inside and tried to dab at her eyes. There was a long pause, and silence suffused the entire cafe. "You've done this before, haven't you? That's why you forgave me so quickly. You were already cheating on me." She accused crushing the tissue in her fingers with the realization.

"Camile, don't come to the club tonight." He said at last.

"Fuck you, Stephan. You don't ever get to tell me what to do." Jennifer hissed.

"You're unstable, so I'm going to reset your permissions. You're rogue to the clan until further notice." He said in a hollow voice.

"You self-centered asshole. You're offended that I found out, and you have the audacity to kick me to the curb like a common whore. What did you think was going to happen?" She retorted.

"Camile... You're trying to make this about your feelings, I can see it in your reaction. When you've calmed down, we can talk about this." He said, and her back stiffened.

The tremble in her hand was gone, and she stared into the infinite distance. Charlie could imagine the cafe wall vaporizing from her expression, and it was a look, he hoped, was never aimed at him.

"I am calm, because 'Stefawn'—you just made me an enemy." Jennifer said in a chilling voice.

She hung up and slammed the phone down with a screen splitting crack. Jen cursed under her breath, and Charlie carefully raised the cool coffee to his lips and drank. Like the rest of the cafe, he had been caught up in Jennifer's drama. She glanced around finally, and saw Charlie seated a few tables away.

"Great, I've made a fool of myself." She said stuffing the tissue and cracked phone into her purse. Jennifer snatched her cold latte and stumbled towards the door. Charlie raced after.

"Don't say that. I feel horrible for making the situation worse by inviting you into Gun Meister. I honestly didn't think it would be a big deal." He said stepping forward. Charlie grabbed the door and opened it for Jennifer. "So I'm sorry," he added. The rest of the patrons were looking on with a mixture of pity and amusement.

Jennifer walked past him, into the afternoon sun. It was a cloudless summer sky, which was an affront to the raging storm inside her heart. Charlie caught up but for the first hundred feet, Jennifer said nothing as she wallowed in her grief. She stopped at the intersection and glared at the sky.

At the light, they crossed while she continued to struggle with her emotions. For a second Jennifer considered throwing herself under a passing delivery truck. She finally spit out, "The worst part is, that I have to see *him* if I want to play Blood and Pride."

"You could start over?" Charlie tentatively suggested.

Her laugh was like sulfuric acid, but she caught herself before saying, "It took hundreds of hours to become a mature vampire. I can barely remember what it was like being a fledgling. Besides, I wouldn't give him the satisfaction of leaving."

"Maybe that's why I like Gun Meister. It's entirely skill based."

"You still play that?"

"Of course. I'm getting closer to gold which will mean my third weapon. I have a few friends now, and we play together almost every day." He said pressing the intersection button. Charlie dared not comfort her more than standing nearby. She sniffed again and turned to him.

"I'm going home early. Tell them I'm not feeling well." Jen said as they neared the car dealership.

"I can do that."

"There are some things I need to check. If Stephan has labeled me as a rogue, I won't be able to leave my sanctuary, but I can still mobilize my forces. No matter what though, I need a break from Blood and Pride. Would you help me?" She asked pausing near her car.

"I would love to. I have a phone number in game, so you can use any pay-phone to call me." Charlie said digging around his pockets. He found a spare pen and wrote his character's contact information on the back of her hand. Jen climbed into her car and quickly peeled out of the parking lot.

Charlie spent the next three hours working over a tight lipped old man. The geezer drove onto the lot with a failing Dodge Valiant but kept hemming about the interest rates. In the end, he got back into his sputtering, aging car and drove away. Charlie was left with nothing to show for the wasted time.

He clocked out and drove home more than a little annoyed. Despite surviving the culling last month, there was still a guillotine hanging over his neck. He'd be cut if he didn't get his sales figures up. Once home he kicked off his shoes and pulled the dive helmet over his head. It started up with a hum.

Gun Meister Online Loading...
Connection Established...

Network shaking Socially Acceptable Appendages...
Logging into Character...

A teenage punk-rock girl was straddling his chest, and a second bustier blond lay next to Charlie on the bed. While he was distracted, his hands were seized and pulled over his head. A pair of cold handcuffs closed around his wrists chaining him to the headboard. Fara straightened and tossed the key across the room.

"Hot damn, this is more like it!" He said looking between the pair. Elva was beaming like a girl who'd just gotten a pony for Christmas. Fara however, was glaring down at him.

"Shut up," Fara said pulling her torn t-shirt over her head.

"Oh my, what sass. Next time we go shopping, I'm going to get you a whip and some black leather pants." He said with a grin.

Fara was just as he remembered. Red and green hair with a steel stud in her lip. She had on a plain white bra that she unhooked and removed. Her breasts popped free, which were bigger than he first thought. She had pretty pink nipples and he noticed one was pierced. Charlie was about to comment on the hotness of that fact when she interrupted him.

"I said shut up," Fara growled shoving the bra into his open mouth.

"Thmt iz phfumm huwt," he mumbled through the cotton and soft padding.

"And don't look at me," she said grabbing her shirt and used it as a makeshift blindfold.

As his vision went dark, he thought, *"This is getting better and better."*

Charlie was already so hard his pants were cutting off his circulation. He'd been secretly hoping the girl would come around. Over the last couple of days, he'd dropped a dozen compliments about her lightweight, and comfortable shooting nature. It didn't hurt that he'd been extra thorough when cleaning her too.

The blindfold and handcuffs seemed to sharpened his senses, so he could feel Fara's body heat through her torn jeans. Powerful fingers curled into the collar of his gray t-shirt tearing the fabric down the center. Her nails scratched furrows across his chest. Then Fara leaned forward, and a pair of grapefruit sized mounds pressed to his chest. Her nipple ring was warm from her body heat, and it dug roughly into his scratches.

"I haven't changed my mind entirely, but you get another month," she whispered next to his ear.

Fara growled like a feral cat as she bit down on his earlobe. His erection was like a twitchy caged lion, and it was straining against the bars. Teeth bit his neck and shoulder, before traveling slowly downward. All the while, Fara's crotch ground back and forth over his groin. She was teasing his beast, and Charlie groaned around a mouthful of bra. The weight shifted down his legs, and a hand squeezed the bulge in his pants. Petite fingers stroked the length of his fabric covered shaft as a tongue licked in and around his navel.

A second set of hands touched his face. Elva caressed his cheek with a soft touch as she said, "This is going to sting a little."

He was just wondering what was going to sting when a set of teeth sank into the flesh of his stomach. Charlie tried to kick his legs, but they were pinned to the bed by a pair of teenage thighs. He yelped and struggled against the handcuffs. Sting?! That hurt like a bitch. Lips closed over his wound as a tongue hungrily licked back and forth. In contrast to the pain, petite fingers kept stroking his groin. Elva's hands coaxed his face at the same time. His mind was getting the mother-load of mixed messages, and Charlie struggled against his restraints.

"It'll be over soon," Elva said in a soothing voice. Now he was glad Fara hadn't taken his pants off. Charlie's manhood would have made a tempting target for the sadist. The weight disappeared off his legs and climbed from the bed. Elva removed the blindfold, and he saw Fara leaving the room with a mouth covered in his blood. She was, however, wearing a black collar with glowing numbers. Charlie spit the bra out finally.

"What the fuck was that?" Charlie asked looking down. He was missing a hunk of flesh and the wound was still bleeding. Elva snatched the torn shirt and pressed it to his stomach.

"We weapons don't necessarily need semen to contract with a Meister. With girls, for example, it's their lubricant," she said after the blood had stopped. "The Meister's DNA is what we need."

"So you can drink blood?" He asked.

"That's a third method, not often employed," Elva admitted with pity in her voice.

"Why the heck didn't you do that before I logged online? That might have spared me the pain." He said in annoyance. His monstrous erection was finally fading.

"We can't register with a Meister that isn't active. That part is hard coded into us."

"Why did it hurt so much? I've been shot, blown up, and crushed to death, but that was way worse." He admitted looking down at the bandage. The pain was nearly gone, but there was still a dull reminder.

"Pain tolerances are considerably higher with weapons because of the contracting we do," Elva said with pity. The blond ran a hand over the scratches on his chest. "I could help take the edge off." She suggested toying with the button on his jeans.

"Not in the mood now," he said and shook the handcuffs. Elva sighed, climbed off the bed, and went to fetch the key. She came back and unlocked him. Charlie lifted the rag to examine the wound, and found teeth marks were visible.

Charlie walked out into the living room with Fara's bra in hand, and thankfully, she hadn't returned to weapon form yet. The teenager had cleaned her face with a kitchen towel and was sitting on the couch. When they'd first met Fara had glared hateful daggers at him. Today's glance wasn't exactly friendly, but it was much better than he remembered. He was still angry about getting worked up into a fury and bitten. Fara had purposely toyed with him. The only silver lining was that he didn't have to go looking for another weapon. Despite that he was going to lay down some new rules. Charlie held out the white bra, which she took and slipped her arms inside.

"You don't get everything your way," he announced. Fara paused with the bra half on, and her piercing blue eyes narrowed in suspicion. "You're going to sleep with Elva and me in bed." He said in a flat, serious tone.

Fara's mouth opened as her pupils sparkled dangerously. Before she could say anything he added, "I said sleep, not fuck."

The girl closed her mouth with a snap and sat back. Charlie held up a hand with two fingers and said, "Second, stop hiding in weapon form. You're cute, and I like seeing you." For once she actually blushed. The young woman crossed her arms over her chest and glanced away, but after a few seconds, she nodded.

"Fara..." He said and waited for her to look at him. "I'm glad you're staying," he stated which elicited a tiny imperceptible smile.

"If we're laying down ground rules, I have some as well," Fara said holding up her hand. "No excessive touching, stop trying to goad me with cleaning, and don't under any circumstances call me snookums." She said extending a finger as she ticked off each item.

Charlie smirked a little at the second point. He had been overly meticulous in Fara's daily cleaning, but he'd never called any girl snookums. It was probably a pet name her former Meister had used.

They weren't atrociously bad rules. Aside from touching Fara too often the others were easy, so he nodded. Elva squealed and ran forward. She leaped onto the couch and hugged her batch sister.

"I'm so happy!" Elva said pressing herself to the young teen.

"You need a new shirt," He said and was reminded that his was ruined too. "Well, we're both in need of new clothes. At the same time, why don't we pick up a few gun mods."

"Elva, would you mind dressing in your business suit today," Charlie asked, and her demeanor changed immediately. She stood and walked elegantly into the bedroom. He followed the 1911 inside. The tall blonde disappeared into the closet to change. Charlie went over to the night stand where he left his extra clothes. He removed the remnants of his torn shirt and tossed it into the wastebasket. Then he pulled on the form fitting armor and picked up his jacket. He was straightening the sheet covers when Elva came out of the closet in her business dress. Elva ignored his hungry stare and went over to the mirror to pin her hair into a severe bun. Charlie admired the gorgeous woman, but forced himself from the bedroom.

He stopped before Fara. The teenager looked much younger wearing just a white bra, and Charlie held out the patched army jacket. "You'll need this until we buy you another shirt." A strange mix of emotions crossed her face as Fara took the garment. She stood and pulled it on.

They followed him out into the garage. Charlie opened the driver-side door, and Elva took the passenger seat while Fara slid into the rear. The car roared to life, and he backed out more modestly than usual. With the girls in the car, his trip into town was positively stately.

The mall wasn't quite so busy, but it was a weekday. Charlie already knew what he wanted to buy. For a month he'd been secretly compiling a list of mods that he wanted. He liked Fara's handiness, so he was going to make her lighter, and more compact. Inside the parts store, there was an odor of machined metal and freshly molded plastic. It wasn't as good as a coffee shop, but close enough. He shook himself from the stupor and quickly gathered the mods from his mental list.

Three Position Collapsible Buttstock - 800c
10.5 Inch, 1:7 Twist - Cold Hammer Forged Barrel - 2300c
Yankee Hill Advanced Phantom Compensator - 1200c
M16A4 Upper Receiver with Picatinny rail - 3000c
Low Profile Trijicon 3 MOA Red Dot - 1500c
1911 - Ported Barrel Compensator - 1200c
Flared Pistol Magwell - 800c
— Total - 10,800c

Fara took his purchases into the back changing room, and after a long minute of yellow flashes, stepped out with a healthy glow to her skin. She immediately changed forms and Charlie caught the altered weapon. The original M16 had a barrel length of twenty inches. Now she was just over ten, which reduced her weight and made her easier to point. It would, however, increase her recoil with less mass. He'd compensated for that with... well, the tactical compensator. Charlie stroked the assault rifle feeling the change in weight, then shortened the butt stock and shouldered the weapon. Fara slid into position like she was made just for him. His eyes naturally focused on the red dot mounted to the Picatinny rail. Charlie turned aiming the weapon at a nearby mannequin, then he spun and focused on a promotional stand. Finally, he lowered the rifle with a satisfied smile. Fara was a dependable gun even in her original state. He'd gotten to Silver Four with her over the past month, but now he felt like he could take on the world. Charlie still wanted a better grip, a new trigger, and a quad rail for mounting accessories, but for now, he was happy with his choices.

Elva disappeared into the changing room next with the two extra mods. After a few seconds came out with a flush over her face. His phone began to ring, which was likely Jennifer, since it was nearing seven o'clock.

"How about you and Elva wander into the clothing store. Pick out something for yourself, and a shirt for me too." He said holding the rifle at arms length. Fara appeared after a brief flash and the two weapons left the store.

"Jen?" He asked answering the call.

"I want to thank you," the woman said.

Charlie was bewildered. "Thank me? I feel horrible about instigating all of this."

"It was you, who tore the rose colored glasses from my eyes. You told me Stephan was an asshole, but like some starry-eyed fan girl, I kept brushing it off. More than a few Toreador knew about Stephan's little escapades. I was a fool." She said allowing the bitter tone to creep into her words.

Changing the phone to his other ear he replied, "So he made you a rogue?"

"That was just to give him time to remove all my access codes. Even without them, I've been gathering my own loyal forces. Tomorrow I'll leave the sanctuary, and if I'm still a rogue, there will be a civil war. Half the clan elders will support me in the fight to become the new prince." Jen said.

"He'll have that fancy flaming sword though," Charlie warned.

She laughed dryly before saying, "Not likely, he'll be too worried the relic will get stolen in the melee." It was nice to know Jen hadn't given up, and that asshole Stephan was going to get his shit pushed in.

"Where are you now?" Charlie asked. He was hoping to steer her attention back to Gun Meister.

"I don't know, some shitty little motel lobby." She said over the phone.

"If you're near the competition center, I think I know where you are. I'm at the mall buying some things, so I should be about ten minutes. If not I'll call the pay-phone number back." He said hanging up the mobile. Charlie slipped the device back into his pocket.

His two weapons had returned while he'd been on the phone. Fara had tied his green army jacket around her waist. She wore a torn black t-shirt, which showed off a newly pierced belly button. Across the front, in glowing green letters it read, "To serve man."

Charlie recognized the reference, and he smiled. Deep down Fara might have a sense of humor, though it was a tad dark. She held out a small shopping bag, which he took with some trepidation. Elva was smiling precociously and that worried him. Fara must have hunted all over for just the right thing, because inside was a tiny pink t-shirt. Charlie almost admired Fara's sheer audacity as he examined the shirt. There was a funny smiley face and a rainbow with the words, "Sorry Girls... I'm Gay."

"Well, this will teach me to ask you for anything." He groaned removing his Kevlar armor and tugged the tight pink t-shirt on. It barely fit over his lean frame, and Elva coughed.

"You're going to wear it?" Elva asked still trying to stifle her laughter. He shrugged.

"It'll be under my armor anyway," he said pulling the form fitting gear back on. "Your weapon skin will have to wait. I need to meet with a friend." He added tossing the shopping bag into the garbage. Charlie wrapped an arm around both girls. Elva looked pleased; Fara less so, but she didn't move away. He guided the girls out to the parking lot and into the Mustang. The cheap coffin motel was a few blocks down. A tall woman with platinum blonde hair pushed open the door, and climbed into his idling muscle car without a pause.

"Yohan is gone," Jennifer said in annoyance.

"Who? Oh, your pistol." Charlie said, and glanced around for the big German hunk, but he wasn't in sight. Charlie put the car in reverse and said, "It's been more than a month, so you lost the contract with him.

People quit or stop playing for various reasons. The game isn't going to let guns sit around twiddling their thumbs."

"Where is he?"

"Most likely he's contracted with another Meister. If not, he'll be at the Armory." Charlie informed her backing out of the lot. He threw the car into first and spun out down the road.

"Can I get him back?" Jen asked loudly over the roar of the engine.

"If he's available, otherwise we'll find you a new one."

Turning the corner. The Armory came into view after a few minutes. The inside of the hotel had changed considerably since he was last here. Half of the lobby now resembled a gun store. Pistols were laying inside glass cases, and long guns hung on hooks behind the counter. The developers must have finally gotten around to decanting a new batch.

There was a metric ton of bikini clad females just lounging around. Hungry eyes locked onto him as they entered, but Charlie ignored the stares. He walked quickly to a couple of consoles, and activated one.

"You can probably search for him," Charlie said gesturing at a terminal.

Jen tapped a few commands into the search box. "He's here," she said excitedly. Charlie wasn't surprised. Gun Meister catered to the male ego, stroking it like an expert violinist. Even the supposed girl players were, in all likelihood, men in real life. Which explained the disproportionate ratio of female guns.

"Give him a buzz," Charlie suggested. The massive German appeared less than a minute later. His hair was wet as if he'd just climbed from a swimming pool, and there was an unused towel casually thrown over his shoulder.

Charlie and Jen moved to meet the Olympic God. His eyes found them and narrowed. "What do you want? No, don't answer that. I know why you're here, and no thanks. You'll just piss yourself again and quit." The man said in a cold Germanic voice. Jen blushed a dark crimson and turned to flee, but Charlie caught her by the elbow and spun her back around.

"Guns aren't stupid NPC's like in your vamp game. Convince him." He whispered into her ear. She had nothing left to lose at this point. The girl was still blushing as she faced the tall weapon.

Her back straightened as she said, "You're right, I was terrified of even holding you. I might just quit again, but I paid for the three-month subscription. I want to try so, please... please let me be your Meister." She answered fidgeting. Her fingers worked together like she was tying a knot with her digits. It didn't take much convincing after all. Weapons went out of their way to find a Meister. Having one beg him instead must have tickled the man immensely.

"Come here, give me your hand," he said. Jen glanced at Charlie but stepped forward. She held out her arm, and the massive German grabbed her wrist. She was yanked forward and lifted off her feet. The man wrapped one arm around her torso as he forced her head away. Then his teeth sank into the flesh of her neck.

"Owwhhh..." Jennifer squealed. She gasped in pain and kicked her legs, but it made no difference. The tall German was inhumanly strong as he pressed the woman to his chest. Blood trickled down the back of her neck as he started sucking.

"Ohhh, oh..." Jen wailed but stopped struggling. She dangled in his grasp for another twenty seconds before the man dropped her. Jennifer stumbled back, touched her bleeding neck, and glared up at the weapon darkly. Yohan offered the towel to her, which she took and pressed to the side of her neck.

"You bit me."

"Interesting turn around isn't it. You've been a vampire for what, two years? Is this the first time you've been on the receiving end." Charlie said with a laugh. Despite the fact she'd just lost several pints of blood her face was beet red.

"Why didn't you tell me about that?" She asked angrily.

"Would you believe me if I said, I only found out today." He offered lifting his armor and shirt. The wound on his stomach was healed over, but Fara's teeth marks were still visible.

"You have a weapon, that's what matters," Charlie said turning away. He hoped to escape the building before they were both accosted by a host of guns. Jennifer followed still holding the towel to her neck.

"What now?" She questioned as Charlie climbed into the Mustang.

"Weapons training."

# CHAPTER SEVENTEEN

## *Bloody the Water*

Jennifer was unlike the other two blondes in the car. Elva and Fara both had hair the color of rich honey while hers was a white gold. She removed the towel from her throat. The bite mark was already scarring over, but her face wrinkled as she touched the wound.

"I'll have to be nicer to my blood dolls," she muttered under her breath.

As the car pulled up to the stop light he asked, "You got a three-month subscription?"

Jennifer pushed her windblown hair back over her ear and said, "It was cheaper than by the month. I don't know if I'll stay, but I'm willing to give the game another try."

She opened the glove compartment and shoved the blood stained towel inside. Charlie was almost two months into Gun Meister himself, and in the next few days he'd hit Gold rank, so he had high hopes for converting the girl. The light turned green, and the Mustang slid forward with the traffic.

The competition center was already half full of cars when they arrived. Charlie climbed from the mustang first, and held out a hand which Elva took. She stepped out primly and smoothed the rumpled mini-skirt. Jennifer watched in amazement as the weapon used the side mirror to fix her hair. The wind had ruined her careful bun, and she tucked the stray strands back into place.

"That's incredible," Jennifer said.

"What is?"

"She just used a random object as a reflective surface. In 'Blood and Pride' an NPC wouldn't even try doing that without a compact or a bathroom mirror." She said in amazement.

"Any object with a high enough reflectivity is technically tagged as a mirror," Elva answered for herself. Jennifer stared at the woman utterly fascinated.

"You'll find that Gun Meister has a substantially more complex NPC system than you're used too."

"Why waste it on this?" Jennifer asked pointing to the competition center.

"I disagree that it's a waste. I think Gun Meister is the perfect platform to test the system on. Imagine what would happen if you dropped Elva here into Blood and Pride. She would hunt you down and stake you within a week. In that game, you play a monster of the night, and the NPC's your prey. Here we are just human. Elva is my tool, which I use to kill other humans, so there's no moral quandary there. Still, you'd be surprised at the depth of Gun Meister." Charlie stated slipping an arm around Elva's waist and glanced at Fara. After a brief second the teenager stepped into his waiting arm, which was a big step indeed.

They walked inside, and Charlie led them to the back stairs, and down to a series of simulation ranges. A counter nearby rented space and sold everything from pistol rounds to 40mm grenades.

"I don't have any money," Jen complained as she noticed the prices.

Charlie waved off her statement,"Not a problem. Credits come and go." A bland looking NPC was manning the shop. "We'd like to rent a lane, and I'll take ten boxes of 9mm as well." He said and touched the console nearby.

---

**Player ID - NA1339872**
**Registered Competition Name - Charlie**
**Clan - None**
**Hours played - 234**

**Wins - 44**
**Losses - 19**

**Kills - 57**
**Deaths - 22**
**K/D Ratio - 2.6**

**Battle Rank - Silver Four**
**Player Score - 1590**

**Credits - 58,739c**

His information flashed on the screen, and he accepted the charge. The NPC brought the boxes to the counter which he scooped up. Jennifer followed him in through the range door. He plopped the ammo down on the loading bench and turned to his co-worker.

"I'm not a proud man. I admit I screwed up badly when I started playing this game. I rushed into doing matches and slammed my head into a brick wall. Thankfully, I have a rather thick skull." He joked knocking his knuckles against his own forehead.

Jennifer smiled briefly.

"Training. It sounds boring, but it'll give you the skills you need to have fun. Two things will help you succeed. Being observant. I can't teach you all the tips and tricks to searching for enemies. For that, you have to learn on your own. Don't give away more information than you have to, and keep your eyes on a swivel."

He carefully chose his next words, mainly because Jen seemed to have a minor phobia of guns. She'd been ejected from the game, but Charlie hadn't been much better. He'd basically shat himself after killing his first player.

"The second thing you need to do is manage your stress. We all get jacked up on adrenaline, that's normal. When your heart starts racing your aim will suffer, and you'll make bad decisions." Charlie activated the screen and went down the list until he found the training scenario he wanted.

"That's what we are going to work on today," he continued gesturing to the scene. The dull concrete firing lane flashed, and they were standing on the wrong side of a dead-end alley. Thirty meters away the alley mouth opened onto a packed street. A horde of zombies shambled past in a river of dead flesh. Behind them, a chain link fence was topped with razor sharp barbed wire. On either side, the brick buildings loomed without exit or escape. The loading bench transformed into a small overturned dumpster.

There was a gurgled moan from the street, and a zombie walked into sight followed by several more. Jennifer looked nervously at Yohan, who started to glow, and a pistol appeared on the damaged dumpster.

"This one is called Zombie Alley. It will get you used to shooting and reloading under stress." Charlie said standing behind the blond.

Jennifer held the weapon nervously between her hands. She aimed at a zombie twenty meters down the alley and fired. The bullet punched into the pizza delivery boy's chest, but he continued forward unconcerned. The weapon barked again hitting him in the stomach.

"You have to aim for the head. That's the only way you can kill them." Charlie advised as two more zombies entered the alley.

"I know, that's what I was doing," she said taking aim again.

"Let them get closer before shooting," he suggested. The first zombie slowly shuffled forward until it was close enough they could smell the rotting stench of death. Jennifer wrinkled her nose in disgust as she fired the pistol again. The bullet struck the zombie in the forehead, and it disappeared in a twinkle of lights.

Charlie opened the first box of ammo and started to reload. She fired two more times before the next zombie disappeared, then struck a zombie in the shoulder. It's ear came off with the next bullet, and she whiffed her third shot completely. Jen may have been trained in another game but she was using Point Shooting. Technically a valid way to use a pistol but it took a lot of practice. Likely they used it in Blood and Pride because the skill system favored it, but in Gun Meister, she was struggling to hit her target. Within a minute, a dozen shambling corpses were headed there way.

Her H&K USP's slide locked back on an empty chamber. The zombie continued forward dragging its right foot and Jen struggled to reload her magazine. Jennifer turned the weapon in her hand and pressed the release. She awkwardly slid her spare into the well and racked the slide. The zombie was only a few steps away as she raised the pistol. Jen fired twice and the zombie disappeared. Three more walked into the alley attracted by the noise. Charlie stooped to pick up the dropped magazine, and started to load bullets as Jen fired at a groaning cheerleader.

"How long does this last?" She asked.

"Until you're dead," Charlie replied cheerfully. He slipped the last bullet into the mag and set it on the dumpster next to Jennifer. "That's why I bought so much ammo."

By now, the reek of decay permeated the alley like a palpable miasma, and Charlie thought this was a brilliant touch. The pungent stink alone was enough to make anyone nervous. Jennifer waited impatiently for the next zombie to get within arms reach. Then fired once hitting the corpulent sloth between the eyes. Another two zombies entered the alley. Each bullet she fired attracted another corpse, and killing a zombie added two more. Someone who didn't manage their aim would quickly be swamped. Jen dropped the mag and grabbed the one on the dumpster. She reloaded and fired four times at the closing zombie, who disappeared in a shower of light.

"You have decent aim, but you get easily spooked. I had the same problem."

"You did this?" She asked.

"Oh yeah. Zombies have eaten me so often I must be their favorite meal," Charlie laughed, as he picked up the mag on the ground.

He turned and started loading bullets. Thirty zombies shuffled to the back of the alley, and each one gave off a fetid aura of decay. Jen fired at an undead police woman, and a wooden truncheon tumbled to the ground as the officer disappeared in a sparkle of light. Jen snatched the fresh mag from the dumpster, and slotted it into the gun.

"This reminds me of the undead plague in Blood and Pride," Jen said firing at another zombie.

"Crazy, huh?" He asked.

"There were so many undead we ran out of bullets." She said aiming at a grandmother. The old lady pushed a walker ahead of her and shuffling forward. As she got closer she smelled of a cross between a retirement center and mortuary. She grinned at them in a toothless smile.

"What did you use?" He asked trying to breathe through his mouth.

"Silver swords mostly," Jen said with a wistful smile. She fired once more, "The fledglings we gave Molotov's too, but that was a mistake. They ended up burning several blocks to the ground."

"Sounds fun."

"It was intense, and the only time all the factions came together," Jennifer retorted, firing again. Charlie barely managed to load the magazine before Jen grabbed it from him. Sixty zombies were in the alley getting uncomfortably close. Jen missed and tried for a quick follow up, before emptying the weapon into the approaching undead. Eight disappeared before she dropped the mag, and held out a hand nervously. Charlie finished loading and put it in her palm.

She slotted it into the gun and fired at a zombie grabbing her. The undead disintegrated as she panned to the next target. Charlie thought she was doing well, but maybe it was just because she'd fought zombies before. He loaded more bullets as Jen fired at a trio of Japanese businessmen. The first vanished, but the other two tackled her, and Jen cried out falling over. She pushed the gun into its fetid mouth and fired. Twinkling lights showered over her as the third zombie bit her gun arm. A big red mark appeared on her forearm, and the simulation froze. The undead horde slid into complete stillness, then after a few seconds vanished.

"Good job," Charlie said putting a fully loaded mag on the dumpster. "Again, or do you want a break?" He asked.

Jennifer stood shakily and examined her arm. The red bite mark was already fading. "That didn't hurt as much as Yohan," Jennifer said rubbing the spot.

"Tolerances are higher with the weapons because we contract with them. Personally, I think it's to discourage that method." Charlie said with a shrug. Jennifer reloaded her USP and nodded to him. He moved to the nearby console and activated the same scenario. Ten zombies started to shuffle into the alley.

"This would honestly be easier if you had more mags, but we'll make it work," he admitted picking up her spare.

Charlie opened up another box of ammo so the bullets would be easily accessible. Jennifer waited until they were ten feet away before she fired. The first zombie fell in a single shot.

Things continued like that for a while. He loaded while she killed zombies as efficiently as possible. Jennifer died five times over the next two hours. She also put nine hundred rounds down range, which was impressive.

"I need a break," Jen said climbing back to her feet. The last zombie had bitten her right on the boob, and she rubbed the red mark in annoyance.

"Me too," he admitted holding out the last box of ammo. Jen took it and pushed the box into her tunic pocket. They left the simulation range and found a seat at the nearby benches.

Charlie logged out, then quickly opened a nearby bottle of sports drink. He guzzled half of it, then used the head, and returned to the living room chair. The dive helmet was damp as he tugged it back over his head. He brushed the hair out of his eyes and activated the gear.

"That is not something a young lady should be doing," Montgomery said from nearby. Charlie's view was dominated by the sight of a felt tip marker in his face. Remy was straddling his lap, but looking at the Confederate.

"What's a little dick between friends?" She said sticking her tongue out.

"You have absolutely no boundaries, do you?" The older man asked.

"Nope," the girl chirped. She turned back ready to begin her phallic masterpiece.

Charlie reached up grabbing her thin wrist and said, "I would appreciate it, if you kept your dick to yourself."

"Oh pooh, he's back, and I didn't get to draw anything." Remy pouted sliding from his lap.

"I tried to stop her," Monty offered. Charlie glanced at the teal haired girl as she innocently capped the marker and put it back into her elementary school bag.

"I'm more surprised you two are together," Charlie admitted.

"We saw you were online, but you didn't accept our calls. We figured you were in a match and came down here." Remy said tugging the teddy bear bag back on.

"I was helping a friend run some training scenarios," Charlie said gesturing to the woman next to him.

"The coworker you had the hots for?" Remy asked stepping closer to Jennifer.

"Remy..." Charlie growled dangerously as the young girl climbed onto her lap.

"I put my pen away," she said with a smile. The blonde in question blinked and straightened. "Welcome back," Remy squealed hugging the woman.

"Umm..." Jennifer said in confusion.

"These are the friends I told you about. The gender confused school girl in your lap is Remy. You met her once before." At hearing the gender confused part Jennifer shoved the girl off.

"Ooof, meanie," Remy said standing. She brushed her skirt non-plussed and sat down on the bench next to Jen.

"The gentleman is Montgomery Cunningham the Twenty-Second." Charlie said gesturing to the older individual.

He stepped forward and lightly took Jennifer's hand, brought it to his mustached lips, and kissed the back of it. "It is a pleasure to meet you, madam. I take it from the conversation that you are a friend?"

"We work together, yes," Jennifer said looking at the man holding her palm hostage.

"What happens now?" She asked taking back her arm gently.

"You could try a competition match and put your recent training to the test," Charlie suggested.

"Sure, but you can't join?"

"We are in the Silver Division. If you grouped with us you'd be stuck in a match without a primary weapon. That would not be any fun, but we could watch your game." They moved up the spiral stairs. Jen found an open console, activated it, and searched for match options.

"Please enter lobby 214," The console chirped. Jennifer walked to the elevators, while the trio went toward the bar. Charlie picked an empty game booth and called up the match number.

"The girl looked nervous," Montgomery said taking a seat next to him.

"Jen is odd like that. She shakes like a leaf, but there comes a point where she goes completely still. We'll see how she handles herself." Charlie replied activating the screen. He finally found the lobby number, and the screen flicked to life displaying a nighttime scene. Remy slid into the seat after ordering a large chocolate sundae. She took a bite then glanced up.

"Total darkness, that blows for the newbie," Remy said taking another bite.

"It may help," Charlie said. The dim setting, might hopefully, help Jennifer channel her inner vampire.

Charlie switched player camera's until he found her standing in the shambles of a hotel lounge. The half circular room was partly filled with old couches facing a stone fireplace. It must have been abandoned because graffiti liberally covered the walls, and trash filled the once majestic fireplace. Jen drew her weapon and put herself next to the only exit from the room.

"I spoke to your... 'other' friend by the way. He's a persuasive young man." Monty whispered.

"Oh, Alex? So you're going?" Charlie asked glancing at the older man as he ran a hand along the wooden stock of the rifle.

"I still have a passport, barely within its expiration date, but it's valid. After organizing my finances, I should be leaving the country here soon." Montgomery said in a tone that was almost sad.

"I'm glad to hear it, and I hope it works out," Charlie admitted.

On the television screen, Jennifer slowly opened the door into the next room. She didn't enter though, that would frame her against the lounge windows. Her stealth skills in 'Blood and Pride' were at least proving useful. After a few minutes a cloud passed by sending the parlor into darkness. Jen used the chance to crawl through the door, which turned out to be a billiard room connected to a cocktail bar. The furniture had been shoved against the exit. However, a door was already ajar within the bar area, but someone was crouched behind the dilapidated counter.

Nothing happened for several minutes, then Jen stood and advanced with her pistol pointed ahead of her. She fired as a girl stood from behind the bar. The 9mm barked filling the room with a deafening noise, and the mirror shattered, but the girl flinched back behind the counter. Jen cursed, firing wildly as she ran sideways toward the exit. She threw herself through the open door into the hallway, and fired the rest of her clip back into the room.

"I would've just shot through the wood. I mean come on, that stuff has to be like eighty years old." Remy said kicking her feet under the table.

"Having an enemy at my back wouldn't be my first choice either," Montgomery added watching the action.

Jennifer's fingers fumbled with the magazine as she jammed it into the gun. Quickly she opened the nearby door which led to an indoor swimming pool, and crab walked inside. The pool had been mostly drained, and graffiti covered the walls. Several broken lawn chairs huddled like hobos around a rusted out burn barrel. Jen crouched low in the darkness and snaked her way to the south side.

If she was interested in hiding, it was not the best choice. Most of the large bay windows were broken, and what little moonlight there was filtered in through that side. Jen crouched behind a pillar and waited. The woman from before came after, and scanned the poolside deck before pointing her weapon at the changing rooms. Slowly she crept through the shadows in that direction.

Jen half stepped from cover and fired several times. The girl was knocked sideways by the first bullet, and tried to return fire, but Jen's follow up shots punched into her chest and stomach. She collapsed in a heap next to the changing area. High above a buzzer went off signifying half the round was over. Jennifer ducked back behind cover, but she didn't attempt to load her magazine. In the gloom she sat, and listened.

"The pool is probably the endpoint. It's at the center of the hotel." Remy said, and Monty nodded. That meant the other players would be quickly filling the open room. It didn't look good for her, especially with a handful of rounds left.

Jennifer holstered her pistol and hugged the pillar. She jumped a few feet up and used her feet to brace herself. Then she let go with one hand. Her weight shifted and she began working her way up the column. There was a scrape of boot on tile as a man entered the swimming pool and Jennifer froze. He quickly crouched next to the door and scanned the room while she hung in the air. A second person crept into the pool area from the sauna, and the two players opened fire on one another. In the dark, each brilliant flash illuminated the pool room for a brief microsecond.

Jen started up the pillar again. From a side door, a gray wrapped bundle of frayed cloth rushed inside completely ignoring the gun battle. He raced forward across the slimy tiles, and landed with a splash in the scummy knee-high water. A fifth player jumped in through the broken windows right below Jennifer. The man leaned out around the pillar and joined in the rolling gun battle. Gritting her teeth she inched slowly upward, and finally reaching the rafters. Then swung her body forward and hooked her legs around the thick wooden beam.

Bullets ricocheted off the pillar as two players returned fire, but Jen was shadowed in darkness within the eve of the rafters. The three players had each commandeered a pillar for cover, but that wouldn't last forever. The red circle was closing in around the pool. In the murky water, the fourth man withdrew a large two-handed sword, and took a defensive stance. Jen wormed her way along the old wooden beam.

The farthest player from the pool made a dash for the sunken pit. He dodged left around his protective pillar and sprinted across the tiles. A bullet slammed into his jaw spinning his head around. A second bullet nicked his spinal cord, and his legs went limp. He landed hard on his side and dropped his pistol, which skidded the rest of the way into the dark water. Then as the red circle closed in both players stepped from cover. Pistols flashed as they fired at one another, and the first girl slumped as a bullet punched into her chest. She sagged to her knees still trying to return fire. The unexpectedly heavy gun began to lower, and she sent rounds into the tiles next to her. The second player rushed forward and jumped into the darkened pool. The swordsman below turned and swung his massive blade. There was a quick flash of steel and it cut the player in half.

Jen locked her legs around the wooden beam and reached for her pistol, but she fumbled the gun. It dropped into the water below, and the man spun slashing his weapon. With dawning realization, he started to look up as Jen fell onto the tall swordsman.

She landed heavily on him and wrapped her legs around his neck as they fell into the water. She quickly grabbed the wrist holding the longsword and pinned it to her chest. Then twisted her hips forcing the man's face under the knee-high water. He struggled to pull one of his arms free, but in response, Jen squeezed her thighs together as hard as she could. Bubbles filled the water. A meaty hand shot out of the muck and grabbed her throat in return, but she refused to let go. Slowly the bubbles stopped, and darkness settled in.

"I think you are correct. That girl has two distinct natures to her. A soft and pliable outer coating, but inside she is hard as diamond." Montgomery said in an impressed voice.

"I agree about the soft outer coating. I'd love to be squeezed between those thighs," Remy said and Charlie glared at her. She innocently smiled and climbed from the booth.

They stood and left the bar. Jen was just stepping out of the elevators, and a massive bald man was thrusting his contact information into her palm. Jen had a genuinely confused look on her face but accepted the piece of paper. He turned and fled with gray tattered robes fluttering.

"Congratulations!" Charlie shouted and Monty and Remy joined in.

"Quit teasing me," she said trying to vainly keep from blushing.

"We're not teasing you girl, that was good work," Remy said in a high pitched and awed voice.

"You just made eleven grand in twenty minutes, which is pretty amazing. I told you credits are easy to get."

"I think I'm done for tonight. My nerves are shot." She admitted, and Charlie nodded. He'd only played one game during his first day.

"I'd advise stopping over at the mall to pick up a gun cleaning kit. Your pistol will be slimy from falling into the pool, and you put a thousand rounds through him, so he'll need it. If you've never done it before, there are some guides you can check out."

"I can do that, and thank you for your help today. I appreciate everything."

"I do hope to convert you," Charlie admitted as she pulled away. Jen's smile was small, but he thought it spoke volumes.

"Have a good evening," She said walking away.

"Shall we have a match?" Montgomery suggested.

"That's an excellent idea," Charlie agreed following the older man to a console. The three signed up for a team deathmatch.

# CHAPTER EIGHTEEN

## *Crazy Girls...*

Fear and adrenaline coursed through his veins in a gut-clenching, addictive cocktail. Charlie swore to himself he wasn't a junkie, but here he was—playing one more match. Charlie slid to a stop putting his back to a tree. He panted sucking in the sticky air and nervously waited for his stamina to replenish. His heart rate was sky high, and Charlie desperately needed to pee. He closed his eyes. In an effort to calm himself he took several long breaths, and the pounding in his chest abated, but he couldn't relieve his bladder. At least, not until this was over.

The steamy Alabama countryside he was running through would have been pretty with its bright flowers and multi-colored birds if five people weren't trying to kill him. He turned the rifle in his hands and activated the magazine release. The box slid free into his waiting palm. A small plastic window on the side revealed it was empty of cartridges.

*"Just great,"* he thought dropping the mag and patted his vest for another. Again he came up empty and sighed.

Monty was busy setting up the trap, but Charlie had to keep ahead of his pursuers. The rifle was out of ammo and dead weight at the moment. Dropping it would mean he could run for extended periods, so with a pang of regret, he set the empty weapon against the tree. When his stamina pool filled, he stood and started jogging towards the ambush point. As soon as he crossed a ditch, the sound of running water attracted his attention.

*"It would be easier to move down a river bank than through a thick forest."* With that thought, Charlie picked up his pace, and started sprinting

toward the sound. Hopefully, it would be heading in the right direction.

He came out of the trees at the top of a waterfall. The stream was small but fast moving as it poured over the rocks, and dropped fifty feet to a boulder filled bottom. Bass leaped from the water amid the rapids. Unfortunately, the river's path turned south instead of west. Still, this was an opportunity to put an obstacle between himself and his pursuers. Charlie jumped from one slime covered rock to the next. He almost slipped on the last wet boulder but threw himself to the far shore.

"Shit," he muttered as his boot sank into the warm water. The enemy team was closing in. Charlie could feel it in his bones, so he hid behind a set of three trees and withdrew Elva from the thigh holster. The safety slid free, and he waited trying to calm himself with regular deep breaths.

The only reason he was being chased was pure overconfidence. Their team was mostly dead, and the only ones left were Monty and himself. Everyone else had walked into a well-planned attack. The enemy was probably a clan climbing the ranks, but that also made them eager for blood.

Charlie could feel them drawing closer, like prey who instinctively knew the tiger was behind them. Less than a minute later a chocolate skinned underwear model dressed in jungle camouflage sprinted from the tree line. Small green and gray pieces of cloth were intricately woven into his shoulder-length dreadlocks. The African American man skidded to a stop and scanned the opposite bank with his silenced MP5K. The compact SMG was an excellent choice for keeping up with Charlie. After a few seconds, the guy touched his throat mic.

"He crossed here," the man whispered noticing the boot marks on the river rocks. The sound of running feet and breaking branches neared. His pursuer though didn't want to lose Charlie. He clipped the SMG to his chest rig and started across the river. Charlie waited until he was ten feet out before stepping from cover, and raised the pistol aiming at the smaller man. Their eyes met as he looked up in surprise, and a brief second passed in tableau as the river roared by.

"On the far shore!" The enemy shouted just before Charlie fired three times. Two heavy slugs slammed into his chest, and he went backward into the water. Almost immediately his corpse slid into the river, and over the waterfall to the rocks below. Two girls ran out of the tree line already shooting in his direction. Dirt and pieces of bark sprayed around Charlie, and he fled into the forest as the hail of bullets filled the air.

At least he'd killed one, and the fastest enemy at that. He dodged past several trees then turned west. Charlie had lost his lead crossing the river, but the enemy would hopefully be more cautious when chasing him. His stamina was good, better than most, so he figured it was better to trot along at a fast pace. The two women were hot on his heels with two more massively muscled Russians just behind them. The point of this was to get them separated enough to take on one at a time—or at least in smaller groups.

Charlie caught the scent of smoke in the air and smiled. Monty had finally finished his preparations, and he turned toward the haze in a headlong sprint. The smoke filled the low valley, and piles of wet leaves smoldered on burning logs. He heard the loud call of a magpie and groaned.

"Do I have to say it?" He asked slowing before the bonfires. In answer, there was a louder, more annoyed bird call.

"Northern Yankees are yellow-bellied!" Charlie yelled, but didn't wait for the reply. The enemy team was still right behind him, and he ran through the smoke. A figure in gray stopped him with an arm.

"They is yella' bellied, and sissies." Monty reminded him.

"Well, you'll just have to forgive me."

They paused, listening. Then quickly hid at the sound of running feet. Monty was smiling as he pulled a gray cloth over his face and crouched next to the burn pile. A long bayonet was already fixed to his Kentucky long rifle.

Another branch snapped as a woman with outrageously huge breasts ran down the valley floor toward them. She held a Tavor SAR bullpup rifle against her bouncing chest. The second woman was more modestly built with athletic runners legs, and carried a modified M4a1 assault rifle. Both girls slowed to a trot, sensing the trap, but the call of blood was too compelling to ignore. Charlie waited behind a thick tree with Elva in his hands. At the last second Monty rose from his crouch and leaped forward.

"For the South!" He shouted skewering the large breasted girl. She made a strange sound and flailed on the end of his weapon. Bullets slammed into the ground as she squeezed the trigger. Blood gurgled from her lips, and she released her rifle to claw at the steel bladed in her chest. Silver pupils rolled back and her mouth opened in an unspoken warning.

At the sound of gunfire, the second girl turned toward them in the dense haze. "Tiffany?" She asked.

Monty kicked the girl free of his bayonet. Charlie could see little in the smoke, but he heard the corpse hitting the ground. Monty raised his musket at the second hazy figure and fired. The old man laughed, filling the forest with the raucous sound.

"A bayonet charge in the smoke. Grant used it in the battle of Antietam 'gainst the yanks. Can't believe people still fall for that." He said removing the bloody bayonet and cleaning it on the corpse's shirt. Charlie still held his 1911 and moved through the dense smoke.

"Two are still left," Charlie reminded the man.

"Ah, yes. Several repeaters if I recall." Monty said lifting the rifle and blowing through the flash hole. He withdrew his powder horn and poured a measure inside.

"If by that, you mean machine guns, yeah."

"Everything has its weakness. We'll just have to exploit their low speed." He replied seating a ball on the muzzle and tamping it in. Then he slid the ram down into the breach and replaced the percussion cap. "Romans loved their defensive squares, but they fell like cattle to the Mongol Horse Archers. Never underestimate a mobile force."

"I get to run around some more, yippee—" Charlie drolled in a less than enthusiastic tone. "The circle is closing in, and I'm down to using Elva anyway. I'll draw them toward the center while you come at them from behind."

"A good plan, sir. I like it."

"Even if we lose the match, we made the enemy team pay. They should have taken the center and held it."

"It was our good fortune that they were overconfident in facing a perceived weaker enemy."

Charlie took a moment to reload Elva with a fresh ten round magazine and slid the spare into his dump pouch. He jogged up the valley floor toward the forest center. The burn piles continued to spew a black obscuring smoke, and for a minute he wondered if a wildfire would start. Gold Matches had proven very different than his previous ones. They lasted twice as long, and the circle was much broader. The players were considerably more skilled, though in this case, over-eager for blood.

Bullets cut into the tree's around him, and Charlie threw himself to the ground. By chance, he found the earthen bowl between two giant tree trunks, and he rolled into it. A second machine gun began to chatter to the right pinning him in place. Fifty meters ahead a figure in heavy armor stepped from behind cover holding an M60 squad automatic machine gun. Charlie raised his pistol and fired a few rounds at the target. A fat 45 acp round careened off a shoulder pad, and the Russian man grinned under his helmet.

The smoke was leaking from the valley below and filling the air with a foggy mist. Neither man noticed a gray shape skirting their flank. Charlie unloaded the rest of his clip trying to keep their attention long enough for Monty to close in. A bullet slammed into Charlie's shoulder spinning him around. The pain was momentarily intense before being replaced with a dull, annoying ache. He rolled over and saw that his entire left arm dangled by a few pieces of bloody flesh.

Charlie struggled to sit up and reached for his dropped weapon. With one hand he pressed the magazine release and pawed a spare free. Two massive men appeared at the lip of his depression, and both looked down with hungry eyes as they leveled their weapons. The head of the first disappeared as a .58 caliber ball slammed into the back of his helmet. He was knocked forward into the pit with Charlie.

The second turned spraying the forest behind them with lead. Charlie awkwardly slid the mag into the well, then bit down on Elva's slide, and shoved hard with his remaining hand to rack the pistol. As the Russian turned, Charlie raised the 1911 and unloaded at close range. The man tottered at the edge of the pit, then collapsed into the makeshift grave. Charlie sagged back against the dirt as the darkness closed in.

**[Match Complete]**
**[Team Win]**

"That was well played," Monty exclaimed as he exited the lobby door.

"Another round?" Charlie asked coming forward, but the older man shook his head.

"I have preparations to make before I log out," he said with a complicated frown.

"I know we didn't get off to the best start, but I'm glad to have met you," Charlie admitted holding out a hand.

"Everyone makes mistakes, but it takes a true man to admit to them. I am honored to call you a friend, and a brother-in-arms." Monty said clasping his hand firmly and looked Charlie in the eye. His dark pupils were sharp as blades today.

"Jesus, get a room you two. If you're going to kiss, at least warn the children." Remy mocked as she started to make gagging noises. Monty rolled his eyes and released Charlie's hand, then turned to the smaller girl.

"Your ability to ruin a moment cannot be underestimated. Despite yourself, I might actually come to miss you." Monty said as the elevator opened. The trio came out into the lobby.

"Admit it—you will," Remy said with a wry grin.

In a moment of rare seriousness, she added, "I hope you make it back inside."

"Thanks."

"You still owe me a mustache ride."

"Never... upon my honor," Monty said turning away. He left the two and made for the exit. The man carried the long Kentucky rifle against his shoulder as he made his way through the crowd. His back was straight, and he marched like the soldier he represented.

"Maybe when he gets back we can start a clan. Jen should be Silver by then, and we'll have enough people." Charlie mused watching the Confederate man leave.

"Oh, I have a great name," Remy said excitedly. Charlie groaned but gestured for her to continue. "NeverPullOut... Get it? It's a double entendre." Charlie shook his head.

"I'm going to log out and cook dinner."

"How about Mortally Fingered?!" Remy shouted after him.

"Hard as Diamond?!"
"Your Mom, My Harem!"

Charlie walked toward the competition center exit. Today had been fun, but he was going to have to buy more magazines. He touched the assault rifle slung across his chest.

"I'm glad we have another month together. Do you want me to add anything to our little contract?"

"Add?" Fara asked into his mind.

"Stipulations," Charlie added.

"I suppose you want something," Fara said in a dry voice.

"I do. The next time we contract, I want sex. You are an excellent gun and a cute woman. However, I have no desire to sacrifice a pound of flesh every month for you."

Fara changed, appearing before him, and searched his face. "I make no promises," she said before her eyes slid past him.

"Derek?" She asked pushing Charlie aside.

"Yes?" A player said stopping.

"You're back," Fara breathed in relief.

"Ahh, Tuesday. I didn't recognize you at first. You've changed your hair."

Derek said in a cold, distant voice.

"Where are your other guns?" Charlie asked noticing he was minus his fancy full-auto Glock.

"Because of you I was banned for thirty days, so I lost them. I also de-ranked to Silver, but I should thank you." Derek admitted.

"Oh?"

"You gave me the chance to part with Tuesday cleanly. There was a new batch of weapons, and I contracted with Friday. She's a very modern FN Scar-H, so I didn't even bother picking up a pistol." The man said caressing the weapons hips.

"Well, at least the ban gave you some time to cool off." Charlie said turning away.

"For what it's worth Tuesday, I'm sorry for my actions." Derek said moving toward the consoles.

Fara had a bewildered look on her face, and barely reacted when Charlie took her wrist. She swayed in an unfocused daze as he left the competition center. Her processing centers were busy shifting memory connections and reassigning personality values. She was still dumping data into archive as they got to the Mustang. He opened the car door, but she continued to stand there. Charlie took her by the shoulders, turning the young woman around, and pushed her into the passenger seat. She mechanically drew the seat belt over her chest as he walked around the front and got into the driver side.

"I'm going to screw you tonight," she said in a voice that was not her own. Her usually high, teenage voice deepened with rough unwaxed cords. Charlie glanced at her, but Fara was staring into the distance, deep in calculation. He felt conflicted about the girl. She'd started off unbearably nasty to him, but her attitude had improved by leaps and bounds over the last month. Despite her offhand nature, she was fun to keep around, and Fara might have caved even without meeting that nasty twerp tonight.

"I look forward to it," he said after that pause. Charlie started the Mustang and left her to work through whatever mental juggling she was doing. The trip home was silent except for the rumble of the engine.

As Charlie walked into the beach house, he pulled his armored vest off, and dropped the light gear onto the couch. He withdrew Elva from her holster, dropped the mag, and racked her slide. Then caught the bullet in mid-air and set it down on the table. By now he could take the 1911 apart blindfolded. The top and bottom came free of one another, and Charlie set them on the table. He sprayed her parts down with a light layer of solvent and used a rag to wipe Elva clean. Then he oiled her and put her back together. She changed into human form, and appeared on the couch next to him. Elva wasn't swooning like usual but he'd only done a quick cleaning.

Charlie was about to pick up Fara when the doorbell rang. He stood perplexed, because nobody ever came to visit. A pair of hands grabbed him as he opened the door, and he was dragged into a set of enormous breasts.

"I so angry with you," a thickly accented voice said above him. He managed to look up into a pair of glowing steel colored eyes.

"I seem to be annoying most of the women in my life. How did I wrong you?" He asked giving up his struggles.

"You v'ere at the Armory today. I saw you come into the lobby. I v'as so happy to see you, because I thought you come to contract, but no, you spoke to man. That explains shirt you are v'earing," The giant Russian said pushing him away. Charlie stumbled back and glanced down at his pink t-shirt, which was still proudly displaying his gay pride. Damned Fara... He wanted to cover his face and laugh at the absurdity of the situation. He had a gun that was going through a personality crisis, and this new girl thought he batted for the same team.

"I'm not gay."

"The shirt says othervise," the SVD said with disdain and walked quickly back up the street.

Charlie pulled the stupid shirt over his head and tossed it into the bushes. "Ignore that, I'm not gay," he said chasing after the tall red head. Charlie grabbed her by the waist and dug his heels in, but she didn't stop. It was like trying to halt a tank from moving. He desperately said, "I was helping a friend find her pistol, so I wasn't there to contract. I'm not even Gold yet."

"I'm sorry, I meant to call you," he apologized. The SVD slowed just enough for him to run around her front, put both hands on her stomach, and brace himself. The red headed giant made an annoyed sound but finally stopped.

"So you're still available?" He asked.

"I vaited so long," she said in a despairing voice. He'd been too busy with running matches to check on the weapon, so it was no wonder she was annoyed.

"You're right, and I'm sorry for not contacting you," Charlie said quickly.

"I saw you and remembered your grip. I v'anted so badly to be held again like that."

Charlie closed on her. "You came all this way, so why don't you stay?" He asked with sudden inspiration.

"V'hat?" She asked in surprise. He let go and gestured toward the beach house.

"Stay here. I hit Silver Master tonight, so in a few days to a week, I'll be Gold. We can contract then. I have food, entertainment, and a beach you can swim at." He gestured to his house. Her eyes flashed from steel to silver as her decision tree went into overdrive. He continued to try and coax her back toward the house. "I have spare bedrooms you can use."

"Very well, I v'ill stay. We sleep in same bed, but I v'ill not sex without contract. I am not that kind of weapon." She warned poking him in the chest. Charlie pulled her slowly back down the sidewalk. She was a foot and a half taller than Charlie, but he led her back like a stray puppy. Finally relaxing, the woman draped her arm around his neck. Her long fingernails brushed over his naked chest, and now that she had an arm around him she was reluctant to let go.

"I'm Charlie,' he said.

"Do you have a name?"

"Nyet," she said in a dreamy voice.

"We aren't Meister and weapon yet, but you need one." He muttered glancing at the woman. Charlie had to call her something, at least temporarily.

She was a giant compared to him. The Russian was over seven feet in height with enough muscle to be called fit. Her hair was bright red like the color of freshly spilled blood. Those steel colored eyes were still registering the data changes, and they flashed under her long dark lashes. Her nose was small and straight with a direct, uncompromising character. It was the lips that drew him in. They were a natural bright red like she came with lipstick already applied. It wasn't quite the same color as her hair, but they complimented each other. Tanya? Sasha? Anastasia? Hmmm… Most Russian names ended with an 'A', and he already had Elva and Fara to contend with, so his third weapon needed something different.

"Sofie," He said tasting the word. It was a relatively strong name, with a feminine ending.

"Da," she said turning to him.

Elva looked on with interest as they re-entered the house. The tall Russian turned in a circle in the living room absorbing and cataloging the visual data.

"Sofie, this is Elva. I'm sure you'll have plenty of time to talk." He said stepping away from the tall redhead. Charlie was glad to have the SVD, though his night was turning out a little crazy.

He sat down, cleared the M16, and removed her roll pins. The rifle came apart in two pieces, and he pulled the bolt carrier out. She was sooty and caked with gunpowder, so Charlie picked up the solvent can and started to coat her liberally with the liquid. As he began cleaning, Elva and Sofie started a quick exchange in Russian. He shouldn't have been surprised the weapons were fluent. Elva laughed suddenly.

"He is," she said and glanced in his direction. Charlie pointed the dirty scrub brush at her.

"Elva, I will put those handcuffs on you and bend you over this couch." He warned returning to his scrubbing.

"See," Elva said gesturing. Charlie rolled his eyes. At least they weren't talking about his pink shirt.

Fara's bolt assembly was finally coming clean, but per their agreement, he didn't go overboard. He wiped the part free of residue and set it down. Then squirted solvent into her barrel. While the liquid did its job, he glanced at his first weapon. Elva was still talking in rapid fire Russian. Her personality was continuing to evolve, and Charlie cherished that, but he wished Fara wasn't rubbing off so much. She laughed again covering her mouth with a hand. He dragged a bore snake through Fara's barrel, and left over copper residue spilled out. Charlie oiled the bolt carrier, assembled the weapon, and ran a quick function check.

Fara appeared sitting in his lap, and wasted no time in kissing him. Their tongues wrestled for territory before she growled biting down on his bottom lip. If that was how she wanted it, he would oblige. Reaching behind the girl, he grabbed a fist full of her colored hair and yanked. She gasped letting go of his lip.

Elva and Sofie finally stopped their conversation and turned to watch. Charlie took the collar of her black t-shirt and tore the top apart.

"Jerk, I liked that shirt," she said.

He grinned tossing the garment away. Charlie unhooked her bra and leaned in biting down on her pierced nipple. She yowled in pain digging her fingers into his hair. They quickly tore the remaining clothes from one another in a tussle that ended with her straddling him.

Fara leaned in biting his lip a second time before forcing her tongue into his mouth. Charlie was guided inside the furnace that was her sex. She rocked slowly at first, and Charlie was surprised by how incredibly tight the girl was. Instead of moaning, she growled like a feral cat as black fingernails dug furrows into his skin. He hissed from the unexpected pain, causing her to move faster and smile. Charlie grabbed her waist trying to keep up, but within a minute all he could do was hang on. Fara's hips shook inhumanly fast, and she pistoned furiously like a racing engine. Gun Meister wasn't helping. The game had cranked up his sensitively from winning the last match, and tacked on an extra percentage point for gaining a new rank too. Her wetness dripped down his shaft and pooled on the leather couch as Fara drove herself onto his erection.

He struggled with his self-control, straining to keep from finishing too quickly, and Charlie dug his nails in as Fara rode him like a train steaming toward a broken bridge. She suddenly grabbed him by the throat with both hands, and her eyes flared with blue light as she squeezed. He quickly saw stars as the girl choked him, and he didn't just climax. Charlie exploded inside Fara like a nuclear warhead. His eyes crossed and he groaned as the train wreck of an orgasm washed over him.

Fara wailed letting go of his throat and clawed at her chest. She pulled on her own pierced nipple until blood started to drip out. Her luminous blue pupils rolled into her head, and she made animal sounds as her sex clamped down. Saliva dripped from her open mouth as her entire body convulsed in fits. Finally, Fara slowed to a stop and sagged like a toy running out of batteries. Charlie coughed as the stars in his vision faded.

"Holy shit! It's true what they say. The crazier the girl, the better the sex." He said looking up at the weapon. Fara wiped the drool from her lips and stared down at him. She finally glanced at her fingernails, which were stained red with both their blood. Then she laughed almost hysterically, bent forward, and kissed him again.

"Ok Charlie, you win. That was the best orgasm I've ever had." She admitted.

"I didn't know this was a competition, but I like the way you say that." He replied, and Fara climbed from him. She bent grabbing her clothes and went into the master bedroom.

Elva slid across the leather couch, and he was once again surprised to see flaming blue eyes. They were however, directed at Fara as the girl closed the bathroom door. Elva pressed close touching Charlie's throat with a trembling hand.

"I thought she was going to hurt you," Elva said.

"I'm glad she didn't," Charlie said reaching up. He grabbed Elva by the hair and pulled her in for a kiss. She resisted for a second, then slid into his lap. For a while their lips mashed together like punch-drunk boxers, until he tasted blood again from his split lip, and they finally broke apart.

"I need you to go to the mall in the morning. During the last match, I dropped all of Fara's mags, so I need at least a dozen more. I hit Silver

Master this evening, so gold won't be far away. Buy some clothes for Sofie preemptively. She also needs some ammo, mags, and a scope." He said turning to the woman. The Russian beauty was staring at the couple like she was memorizing every second. The tall redhead crossed the distance between them and ran a hand over his bloody chest.

"Is all sex like so?" She asked curiously.

"I try. My spirit is strong but I am only flesh and blood." He said standing up from the couch. There was a dark patch of leather from the lovemaking, and he briefly wondered if it would come clean. Charlie gathered his boxers and pants before remembering his naked chest.

"Oh, and another shirt."

"I can do that," Elva said, and he pointed at the pistol.

"Don't you dare let Fara pick it out," he warned. Elva smirked mischievously at his shaking finger. Charlie went into the master bedroom to lay down. Elva and Sofie climbed into bed next to him. Fara was still in the shower as he accessed the menu and logged out.

# CHAPTER NINETEEN

## *War of the Worlds*

There was something magically cleansing about great sex because Charlie woke feeling utterly refreshed. He yawned expansively and stretched underneath the covers. It was Saturday, and he was looking forward to spending time with the girls, especially Elva. It had been a few days since he'd given her special attention, and she certainly deserved some. He showered, brushed his teeth, and shuffled with fuzzy slippers into the kitchen. Fizzgig's dish was empty so he poured some mixed cat food into the small bowl. Then he filled the water dish with ice cubes, which would keep it cold in the summer heat. He was part way through several Pop-tarts when his phone rang. He recognized the number and picked it up.

"Good morning Jennifer, to what do I owe the pleasure?"

"Are you're getting on Gun Meister today?" Jennifer asked, and he put his breakfast down.

"Of course, Saturdays are always exciting. You should jump in and work on getting Silver rank." He suggested.

"I don't know if I can," Jen replied in a tired voice.

"How are things on the undead front?"

"Complicated," she said in a sour tone.

"I'm all ears."

"I spent most of last night in Blood and Pride," Jen sighed tiredly. In the background, Charlie heard a microwave beep.

"You mentioned a civil war was going to start," He inquired picking up his unfinished Pop-tart and biting into it.

"I wish, but that coward backed down when he saw half the council supporting me. No, I spent most of my time in the club watching the vile twit squirm on his hook. We both know I don't need the access codes to ruin him." She said in a slightly more cheerful tone.

"Oh?"

"Envy, the nightclub is his. He spent millions turning it into a hangout. Right now the clan passively protects his sword just by being there, but as soon as everyone finds out there is a nuke under their feet, it would be a ghost town. Nobody would risk getting caught up in our domestic squabble. Stephan would have to bankrupt himself hiring mercenaries." She said taking a sip of something hot.

"That must have been fun."

"Not entirely. Stephan didn't waste any time in openly courting a new batch of fledglings. Probably just to spite me." replied Jen bitterly.

Charlie was surprised the man wasn't groveling at her feet, but then Stephan seemed arrogant enough to try and bluff his way out.

Charlie attempted to persuade her, "Forget him. You can make faces at your ex another time. Come spend the day with me. There's also Yohan... I'm not gay, but you know how to pick 'em. He's gotta be what nine, ten inches?"

There was a choking cough, before she said, "I'll think about it." Charlie could practically feel the girl blush through the phone.

"I'll let you do that while I finish my breakfast," He said pushing the last Pop-tart into his mouth and savored the strawberry confection. "Well?" he asked around the food. Whatever Yohan was packing below the belt must have been the deciding factor.

"Ok, you win. I'll be on after a bit," Jen said in a more normal voice.

"See you soon," he replied hanging up. Charlie put the plate in the sink, went into the living room, and pulled the dive helmet on. He activated it and waited for the world to fade.

Gun Meister Online Loading...
Naughty Bits Connecting...
Network Bumping Fists...
Logging into Character...

The female form in all its shapes and colors is a glorious tribute to God. Especially when said flesh was draped over Charlie like Egyptian silk. Arms and legs interlinked in a complicated Chinese puzzle. He was pinned under that loveliness, and he wouldn't have moved for the world. Someone was using his thigh as a pillow, two others had his arms, and a fourth wrapped long legs around his waist. He'd also apparently joined in the middle of a conversation.

"What happened next?" An unfamiliar voice asked.

"Fara made a funny face and sounded like—" Sofie said followed by the cry of a cat giving birth.

"I did not," Fara objected in a piqued and embarrassed voice.

"Da, it was just so. This one made you squeal like svin'ya," Sofie sighed running a long fingered hand across Charlie's bare chest.

"That sounds amazing. What was your peak pleasure quotient?" A second unfamiliar voice asked.

"I'm not saying," Fara said, and several girls giggled. Charlie finally turned his head. An exceptionally attractive woman with black hair and Asian features was snuggled up to his right side.

"He's awake," she said sitting up.

"Who are you?" Charlie asked. The oriental woman was shorter than him with a sensual, curvaceous figure.

"That depends on you," She said batting her lashes.

Charlie glanced around taking in the scene. His bed was covered in females, several of which were not a part of his harem. One-two-three… Seven, seven girls lay on the master bed with him. Sofie sat on his left side, legs partly wrapped around his waist. Two girls with snow white hair continued to cling to his arms as he sat up while the gorgeous Asian caressed a hand across his abs. The last woman had auburn hair and was bashfully holding onto his right hand. Finally, he caught sight of Elva who was hiding near the foot of the bed. She had removed her business dress and donned daisy dukes.

"Elva… While I enjoy logging into a bevy of beautiful girls, I do wonder who they are." He inquired looking between the women.

"How come you assume it was my doing?" She asked defensively. He glanced down at Fara still cuddled to his thigh, and her bright blue innocent eyes looked up into his.

"Fara's not smiling like she got to play a prank, and Sofie wouldn't risk her chances at being contracted. That leaves one final possibility."

Elva lunged at him wrapping her arms around his neck and kissed him. "I'm sorry!" She repeated with heated kisses.

"Well… I'm still waiting for an explanation."

"You see, I went shopping as you requested. Since we were near the Armory, I wanted to visit some friends." Elva said gesturing to the four new girls. At their mention, they pressed closer, and a multitude of hands caressed him. Then she said, "I told them about Sofie staying with us. The idea that a gun could stay with a Meister before contracting sort of lit a fire in the lobby."

She kissed him several more times before he managed to pull away. "I'm not mad, Elva. Just curious." He said turning to the new girls. "You're welcome to stay, but I warn you. I promised Sofie the contract. It may be some time before I rank up again." He added, and each nodded eagerly, but it was Sofie that drew close.

"I'm glad you still vant me," She purred stroking his chest.

"I do."

Charlie needed to move before his hormones got the better of him. The women slowly untangled themselves as he shuffled to the edge of the mattress. He rolled off the bed escaping the Venus fly trap it had become.

There was a shopping bag near the nightstand with a plain white t-shirt, and Charlie pulled it on along with his armor and jacket. A second bag contained magazines, ammo, and a Russian made PSO scope. He examined the item and looked through the glass. There was a strange sloping graph along the side with several pointed chevrons. The foreign scope was more complicated than he first imagined, so Charlie put the sight on the nightstand along with the extra ammo.

*"I'm going to need a couple of practice rounds at the range to get used to that scope."*

He spent a few minutes loading Fara's new magazines and hiding them about his person. Once he was mission ready, Charlie held out his hands to Elva and Fara. "Let's head into town. I'm eager to kill some people." Elva smiled sliding across the bed. Fara pushed his hand away and stood, but turned and gave him a tiny peck on the cheek.

"Ladies, I apologize for the lack of introduction, but please enjoy yourselves." He said leaving the five uncontracted weapons in the house.

Charlie climbed into the Mustang and opened the garage door. He sent Remy, Montgomery, and Jen a message before starting the engine. Then he backed out into the street and sped into town.

The competition center was on some kind of alert. From a mile away red lights were visible flashing over the structure. The colorful advertisements and streaming banners had been taken down. Instead, the circular arena looked like it was on military lockdown. The West Coast Server was still growing as Gun Meister became ever more popular. Charlie tried finding a parking spot, but the lot was overflowing with vehicles. He was forced to find a place two blocks down. Elva took his hand and climbed from the back seat. Fara climbed out next and took up a position a few feet away, while Elva seized Charlie's arm and pulled it into her cleavage.

As Charlie neared the competition entrance, he caught sight of Grace sitting on a bench in her distinctive southern gown. Today she had on a peacock feather hat that shimmered in the sunlight. The woman was looking away, staring off into the distance, so she didn't notice his approach.

"Grace, how are you and Montgomery doing?" He asked. She turned toward him and quickly hid the handkerchief in the folds of her dress. Her eyes were red rimmed like she had been vainly attempting to keep her tears at bay.

"What's wrong?" He asked quickly stepping closer. He knelt before her, but for a few seconds, she remained quiet.

Her eyes brimmed and she finally wailed, "Montgomery left me!" Grace brought out her kerchief again and blew her nose.

"Tell me what happened," he said.

"After the match last night, he ordered me to find a new Meister and barred me from the manor," Grace said clutching the silk cloth in her hands. Even hearing it from the source, Charlie found it impossible to comprehend.

"Did he say why?" He asked.

"He said he couldn't bear the thought of me sitting there looking at him. It would be like forcing me to watch over a corpse." She answered, and Charlie took a seat next to the woman.

"Why are you here instead of the Armory?" He asked. Grace looked toward the entrance of the building. Hundreds of players and weapons were streaming inside.

"We weapons have simple pathways for joy, anger, sadness, but love... Love is just a word, one that has a hundred different definitions. I said to Monty that I would take a new Meister if anyone would have me. Now he's ordered me to do so." She stated in a voice filled with pain. Grace was unconsciously tearing the kerchief in her hands apart. The silk was like tissue paper against her strength.

"The thought of being held in another Meister's hands... It's repugnant." She said shivering at the idea. Charlie glanced at Fara, who looked down quickly and away. "Monty, he ordered me to find a Meister. I have to do what he asks, but I don't want to, so here I sit looking at them."

"Do you need anything? Food, or a place to stay?" Charlie asked. He had a home, and extra bedrooms to spare. Grace gave him a small half smile.

"You are too kind, and I can see why Montgomery has such great fondness for you. Thank you, but no. Monty pushed upon me his entire savings." She said lifting her small purse, revealing a dozen cash cards.

"Grace, I can see why he did this. Monty has gone to war, and unfortunately, the battle he faces is one with his own mortality."

"That's what makes this hurt even more," Grace agreed.

"Do you want some company?" He asked, but she shook her head and the peacock feather danced. Grace tried to raise the remnants of silk to her face and discovered the destroyed handkerchief. She sighed and let it fall to the ground.

"Thank you again, but no. I wish to be alone with my thoughts."

"I understand, and I pray for Monty's return. If you need anything at all Grace, please call." He said standing. Grace reached out taking his hand in hers. For a second he thought she was going to ask him to be her Meister. Her eyes began glowing as her decision tree went active.

"Take care, Charlie." She said after a few seconds.

"If you figure out what love is, I hope you'll let the rest of us in on the secret."

Grace squeezed his hand again, but her smile was forced and tinged with sadness. All Charlie could do was nod sympathetically and let her be. When Grace released him, he turned and walked away. He made it a few feet before a pair of arms wrapped around his waist. Charlie half turned to see Fara hugging him from behind. It was only for a moment though, as she shoved him forward and stepped out of arm's reach. Elva took the vacated place and slid into his grasp without hesitation. Fara however, stuck her tongue out and took two steps away.

*"Well... you can't get everything."* He mused, and glanced back once more. Grace was looking up at the sky already lost in thought, and he hoped Monty returned soon.

With Elva under his arm, Charlie went through the entrance and discovered a heated argument in progress. A short teal haired school girl was glaring at a giant bald man. Jennifer looked on nervously from a few feet away. Other players streamed past on their way inside.

"What do you mean you don't use guns?" Remy asked in disbelief.

"No, I don't," the man said in a rumbling voice.

"Why the fuck not?" Remy nearly shouted.

"It is only faith that I need. I have the spirit of conviction within me," was the reply and Remy scoffed.

"You have the spirit of a jackass. This is a game about guns. You know... Gun Meister. It's in the name for bloody sake." She spat.

"We each have our role to play, mine is to bring the Word of God to the unfaithful." The tall figure replied. From a hidden back sheath, he withdrew his two-handed sword. It was brutal in its simplicity, with an iron crossguard, and a tattered cloth wrapped grip. It read along the blade, 'Word of God," in a large italic script.

"If you want to swing swords around go play with the elves and fairies. Here in Gun Meister, you can't deflect bullets. So sorry buckwheat, but a Jedi—you are not." Remy said venomously.

"What's going on?" Charlie asked approaching this new scene. Jen turned to him.

"When I logged in, I got your message on my terminal. I saw Tobias," she gestured to the man with the long sword. "Was online so I invited him to play since we're both Bronze. We found out the matches are canceled for the weekend because there's a worldwide event. Something to do with an alien invasion. Remy just showed up." Jen said, and Charlie smiled.

"The aliens are back? Shit, now I really wish Monty were here. He would have loved this." Charlie said grabbing Remy. The girl looked like she was going to take a swing at the strange giant. He dragged her just out of kicking range.

"If this is a special event we can group in the same squad." He said wrestling with the little woman.

"I won't hold you back?" Jennifer asked.

"No, it'll be more fun." He admitted.

"What about Tobias?" She asked, and Charlie shrugged. With Monty gone it wasn't like there was anyone else around.

"I don't see why not," he said, but Remy snarled.

"This moron doesn't even have a gun. How is he going to help?" She grumbled.

"Let him be. You aren't exactly a model player yourself." Charlie said struggling to hold the girl back.

"It bugs me," Remy said glaring at the crusader.

"It's nice to see something does. Maybe we should keep Tobias around just for that." Charlie chuckled, and finally looked at the man. He was huge, probably over seven feet tall, which suggested he'd dumped points into his strength score in order to swing that blade around. He wasn't quite bald, instead, dark brown peach fuzz covered his scalp. He was around thirty with a wide face, and deep set gray eyes under a pair of bushy eyebrows. A scar ran from his right lip down to his chin. Frankly, he looked like a hero from a fantasy game. Charlie thought he was a moron as well, but his ability to annoy Remy might be useful, and a possible check to her behavior. Besides he wasn't that different from Montgomery in his obstinacy for a weapon type.

"You want to join?" He asked the massive man.

"Yes, I will hunt the unclean with thee," Tobias said in a deep resonating voice.

"Very well."

Remy pouted but followed along as the group headed into the Competition Lobby. All the consoles were scrolling the same words in bold red letters.

## <<Matches Canceled Due to Alien Invasion>>

The lobby was packed full of players. News of the invasion was continuously playing on the screens. The announcement looped and started over with a middle-aged woman sitting before the camera.

She reported, "Today at approximately 02:30 AM, long range telescopes spotted what appears to be a spaceship entering orbit around the moon." The screen changed to the familiar pot marked face of the lunar surface. Floating in from the right side was a tiny reddish object. It was only about six pixels long and one tall, but judging by the image scale, the craft was several thousand meters in size.

"At 08:22 am a launch was detected from the object, and a cluster of small vessels headed towards earth. We tracked the trajectory to be somewhere in Shanghai. In forty minute increments, another sixteen ships departed for Europe and America." The woman continued. The screen changed to a two-dimensional view of the earth and moon. Several orange lines were closing in on their home planet.

The woman appeared on the screen again, and her solemn face wrinkled in worry. For several seconds she looked into the camera then said, "One group will land somewhere on the West Coast at 12:20 pm. Anyone willing to take part is urged to enter lobby 1. Further information will be revealed there." The screen went blank, and the announcement looped back to the beginning.

Once again he wished Monty were here. The old man had left at the worst possible time.

Despite that, Charlie's excitement grew. He'd been secretly hoping for a crack at the aliens. The fact that humanity had fallen still burned in Charlie's stomach like an ulcer. The squad accessed a console and created a group together. Even Remy, eyes glaring at the crusader, put her hand on the screen. Then Charlie, Remy, Jen, and their newest member Tobias went into an open elevator. It descended one floor and opened onto a massive lobby. He'd been here once before, but it was still a sight. Thousands of players were idly chatting, joking, or passing the time waiting for the event to start. Jennifer stared at the assembly as they got off the elevator.

It was still early, and they ended up wandering around for an hour before anything happened. At about noon a man stalked onto the raised platform in the center of the arena. He was old, shit the guy had enough wrinkles to be called grandpa. However, he walked with a straight proud back toward a waist high console. He was dressed in a crisp gray military uniform that matched his salt and pepper hair. Charlie realized this was only the second time he'd seen an old character in the game, aside from Monty. The lobby announcer had been middle-aged, and this person was pushing sixty-five. Conversation near the main stage died down as he activated the console with his palm.

Around the arena, screens flashed to life, and a hidden camera somewhere zoomed in on the old man. He tapped a button on the console, and silence descended like the will of god. It wasn't that people stopped talking, no... Zero sound came out of everyone's lips.

"I god-damn love doing that," the man said in a voice like cracked and aged leather.

The military officer looked right into the camera and said, "Please find an available display screen. I am an old man, and I don't have the patience nor inclination to repeat myself." He waited a minute for people to cluster together.

"My name is Colonel William Blake. Forty years ago I took part in the failed defense of the United States. I won't bother with excuses. America fell in days, and the rest of the world soon followed. After picking through the corpse that was humanity the aliens left. It appeared the Roth were not interested in the planet, but only our destruction." Colonel Blake touched the console again. The video that started was old like it had been taken from a camcorder, and it silently played in the background so the colonel could continue.

"We achieved only one small pyrrhic victory in that war. A dropship was successfully shot down. I was a mere Corporal then, and my battalion was assigned to assault the crash site." He said pausing to watch the video. A massive ship was half smashed into the ground, and dozens of men sprinted toward the derelict ship. Strange armored figures emerged from within and fired on the advancing soldiers with what could only be described as laser weapons.

"We captured the ship at great cost, and discovered the cloning bays the aliens had been using. While the rest of the world burned, we buried the ship right there. We covered it in dirt, concrete, and metal scrap to hide it from their sensors. Then we studied the vessel and made all this." The man said gesturing towards the arena.

He continued, "Forty years we waited for the Roth to return, and we knew they would from the satellites they left in orbit. I was certain I'd kick the bucket before I got to shoot at the bastards again. Thankfully, they showed up at the perfect time."

The video screens flashed back to the Colonel. "We can't afford to show our hand just yet, so today your objective is only survival. We need to know what the alien capabilities are." He announced while activating the console. A map of the greater Los Angeles area came up, with a twenty-kilometer wide circle covering the city center.

"The mission will last for eight hours in total. Every hour that you survive will be counted as a match win. However, you will only gain credits by killing an alien. A regular Roth soldier will count for one thousand credits. It doesn't matter how you get the job done. Killing a leader will be worth four thousand." He stated, and paused to scratch his wrinkled face.

"Have I forgotten anything?" Blake mused.

The colonel tapped the console several times zooming in. "It sucks getting old."

"Ah yes, supply. There are a number of secret caches around the city. You can find them by looking for the graffiti." He said after a few seconds. On the screen an image of a stenciled bullet came up. The old man straightened and put his hand on his lower back. He groaned in weary annoyance before turning to the assembled crowd.

"I want to repeat the objective. Survive, observe, and preferably kill the Roth when possible. Are there any questions?" He asked and pointed to someone before the dais. They started speaking but were still muted.

"Sorry 'bout that, keeping everyone on mute makes the conferences go so much faster." He chuckled. The man leaned over tapping a button on the console. Afterward, he gestured for the player to try again.

"Can we kill other squads?"

"No. Every human is on the same team today. Killing one will be counted against you. I'm glad you asked that." He pointed to another person.

"Can we pick up the alien weapons?"

"Frankly, I have no idea. We don't know enough about the Roth technology, so it's possible." He said pointing to one last player.

"What if we need to take a shit, or eat." The person shouted.

"Preferably not at the same time, that would be messy and awkward." The old man replied to a chorus of laughter. His wrinkled face turned serious as he added, "Then do so. We're not going to make you soil yourself on a mission. Again I have to restate the alien technology is unknown. The Roth may have superior sensors. Rolling into a dumpster may not save you." Blake glanced at the clock as it began to flash.

"Time is up. Good luck out there, and for my sake, happy hunting."

**[Match Start]**

# CHAPTER TWENTY

## *Roth Landing*

Charlie found himself standing a few paces away from what remained of the Hollywood sign. Below were the neglected remnants of a dozen celebrity mansions. In the near distance, Los Angeles forcibly reminded Charlie of a forgotten campfire. Parts of the city had burned to the ground, while other sections had been taken over by scrub brush and palm trees. The air was crystal clear today, probably due to the lack of human intervention, so the coastline was just visible. The metal bones of skyscrapers were all that was left of the business district.

"I can see my house from here," Remy squealed excitedly from atop the Hollywood sign.

She held a hand over her brow and was peering down toward the suburbs. Remy kicked her feet and swayed dangerously on the rickety old letter. Jennifer and Tobias stood next to each other about ten meters away. Two other squads were visible on the next hilltop over. Several of them pointed skyward, and Charlie looked up.

At first, it appeared as a cluster of meteors, and Charlie shielded his eyes from the glaring sun. A dozen foreign objects streamed orange fire as they entered the atmosphere. They slowed in the thick air and the blazing trails faded. For a few seconds, he lost sight of them, and forced his eyes to track where they would have gone. A tiny black speck caught his attention as it stood out against the cloudless summer sky. More of the grouping became visible again as they neared the coast. There were four large vessels still smoking from their atmospheric entry. Surrounding each was a wing of much smaller craft, which looked like horse-flies buzzing around the behemoths. The cluster broke apart, and two dropships headed north toward Santa Monica and San Fernando. The third group was still supersonic as it blew over the southern coastline to Long Beach. The final group dropped lower toward Los Angeles as it continued to slow.

Half of the tiny black flies split from each wing, and Charlie finally realized they were fighter craft escorting the much more cumbersome dropships. The closest pair approached the city center. They had a matte black fuselage with long forward-swept wings and a single large engine. Smaller directional thrusters were visible along the wings. Both fighters aimed at the business district, and from their underbellies, a red laser shot out. The beam of light was accompanied by the sound of burning Styrofoam as it superheated the air. The weapons lanced across a standing skyscraper, and for a second nothing happened. Then the skeleton of broken steel slid sideways crashing to the street below. Dust billowed into the air as the fighters screamed passed.

"Oh my god," Jen gasped in shock. Remy whistled from her perch as the escorts fired again. The hawk-like craft turned and blasted a cluster of trees, then a random building.

Tobias crossed himself and quoted as if from scripture, "When they opened the Gates of Hell, heat rose from it like the fire from a gigantic furnace. The sun and sky were darkened by the smoke from the Abyss."

The closest dropship continued to slow. It looked like an armored scarab beetle, one that was over a hundred meters long and half as wide. The beast managed to stay aloft only because of six massive articulating thrusters. By comparison, the nearby Roth fighters were a scant ten meters in size. The two small escorts continued to flank the dropship as it swung wide around the perimeter of the city. From the belly, teardrop shaped pods disgorged like ticks from a dog. The vessel neared their position, and the squad took cover behind the Hollywood sign. In clusters of four, the drop pods spewed forth every few seconds, and several groups crashed to the lower foothills.

"Hell is empty, and all the devils are here," Tobias said watching the four ships disperse pods around the city.

Now Charlie was impressed. These aliens didn't dick around when it came to their invasions. With engines flaring, the dropship ponderously turned south into the city center, and the pods slowed to a trickle as the ship slewed sideways. Finally, it lowered itself with a massive billow of dust into the Los Angeles Entertainment Stadium. The other three behemoths also found secure locations after disgorging their own troops. The sixteen escort fighters made one last pass around the city before turning skyward and rocketed out of the atmosphere. Everything had happened with military precision, and for almost a minute silence descended.

Remy swung down from the sign and dusted her skirt off. "What's the plan?" she asked checking the load on both her weapons.

Charlie turned to his small squad. Only he and Remy had primary weapons. Jen had a 9mm pistol, and Tobias was in ragged priest's robes with a two-handed sword sticking out from his back. It wasn't likely either would be useful in a skirmish. Still, he wanted a piece of the action, so Charlie pointed at the two squads.

On the other hilltop, two teams were already descending the slope toward the suburb. "They are heading towards the inner city, and being in the open will get us killed. Our objective is to survive, so let's follow them down. Stick with the others until we know more." He ordered, gesturing to the group on the next ridge.

Down in the city, gunfire sounded out in quick tentative snatches. Every so often a beam of reddish light would lance out making the air pop and crackle. Charlie turned to the two bronze players.

"Stay behind Remy and Me. If you see movement call it out, especially if it's an alien. We're going to have to jog to catch up with the others." He said and checked his M16 was loaded. Then he slung the weapon over his shoulder and navigated the hilltop brush to the mansions below. Remy skipped down the slope about fifteen meters away while Jennifer and Tobias nervously followed.

It took only five minutes of jogging before Charlie stumbled out of the sagebrush into the tennis court and swimming pool of a multi-million dollar estate. Under the manor's back patio a squad crouched, and they quickly motioned for him to get down. He and his squad crouched low, then duck-walked around the pool to their location. Two men in medium armor were looking over the tall gate. Charlie tried to move forward, but a curly haired man put a hand on his chest and pushed him back.

"Don't you dare steal our kills," the man said in a half snarl. Under his helmet was a flash of red hair and a smattering of freckles. Across his chest was an AK-74u, and a M24 bolt action rifle hung on his back.

"You can have them, but I am going to look," Charlie replied shoving the hand away. He unceremoniously pushed his way between the anxious soldiers. The gate was wrought iron but overgrown with tall ivy. Charlie stood glancing over, and found the driveway looked directly down the street.

Coming up the road was a squad of four long limbed aliens. Three were wearing lightly armored suits just like the one back in the White House. Hard glossy plates protected their chests, shoulders, and thighs. Smaller plates overlapped across their arms and legs. Each soldier had white armor, and he briefly wondered if that signified anything, or was it just pretty. Inside the enclosed helmets their green skinned faces were visible through a clear visor. Two round objects stuck out of the back, and occasionally steam or gas would escape in a small puff. Charlie guessed it was an air filtration system, which might explain why the aliens didn't want the earth.

The fourth alien must have been the squad leader. His suit was twice as bulky as the others and covered in overlapping crimson plates. On his back was a protruding pack, which again, steamed slightly in the air. The enclosed helmet didn't have a visor. Instead, a four fingered palm print decorated the face. Next to the helmet on both shoulders was a thick round lens recessed into the armor. A massive futuristic cannon was attached to the suit via a three inch thick knotted cable.

"Where did the first group of players go?" Remy asked pushing the ivy aside and peeked through the iron bars.

"Across the street, we're waiting for the Roth to get closer. Then we'll surprise them from both sides." The second squad leader answered.

He pulled Charlie away from the fence and took up a firing position. The rest of his team lined up ready to stand and fire down the driveway. Remy remained there crouched between a pair of brawny legs.

The squad leader touched his radio. "Aliens will be in the kill box in ten seconds, fire upon my shot." He whispered. The mic picked up his muffled words and broadcast them to the squad across the street. A hundred meters away the alien captain stopped in the middle of the road. It pointed with one hand in their direction, and the trio of grunts ran to cover.

Though unexpected, the squad leader found a target, and squeezed the trigger of his rifle. His squad, immediately settled their weapons atop the gate and fired on the Roth. Instead of taking cover the leader set his feet and aimed the cannon in their direction. Within the chunky barrel, the diamond capacitor began to glow dark red. Remy turned and dove into the swimming pool. Charlie leaped in after, because her instincts were rarely wrong. Several splashes follow the girl's example as a red beam of energy sliced through the ivy covered bars. Above Charlie, the laser flash boiled the surface of the water into steam.

He waited as the water around him grew uncomfortably warm, then with lungs burning, he surfaced. Charlie gasped coming up for air and drank in a mouth full of searing smoke. Coughing in fits, he swam for the edge of the pool and dragged himself onto the hot concrete. Two dead bodies were scorched black. The blood had boiled, flashing into steam much like the pool water.

Gunfire from the other manor finally picked up, and Charlie shook himself and his weapon free of water. Remy, Jen, and Tobias also climbed from the pool along with several members of squad two. Their team leader was dead with one other, but the curly haired ginger pulled himself from the pool.

"You still want to do this on your own?" Charlie asked.

"Bite me," the man yelled running past. He pointed to a heavily armored man carrying an RPK machine gun. "Diego, get in that second-floor window and fire on their heavy. Keep him busy while we close the distance."

"What do we do?" Jen asked.

"Let's move through the houses and backyards. None of us have long range weapons." He said jogging to the hedgerow that was the boundary between the two properties. Remy grunted struggling to get over the tall plants until Charlie boosted the small girl over, followed by Jen.

Across the street, the team was still firing down the avenue. Both manors were already on fire from the laser weapons. Several people tossed flashbangs and grenades, and a machine gun started to chatter from behind him.

They crossed through a toy strewn playground. Then Charlie held up a hand slowing the squad in the next backyard. A high pitched laser was firing from nearby. He glanced around the corner and saw a Roth soldier taking cover behind a dust covered Bentley. The alien's light armor was already scarred with dings and gouges. Bullet holes covered the vehicle, and shattered glass littered the driveway. The alien was kneeling by the trunk and aiming with a bulky futuristic rifle. One that was smaller than the heavy cannon, but it too was attached to the alien's suit via a knotted cable. When it fired the weapon shot out a pulse of three red beams.

Someone tapped his leg, and he looked down. Remy was crouched next to him with her revolver in hand. Charlie drew his 1911 and took aim at the creature's head. The Roth was about twenty-five meters away, but the target's white helmet stood out.

He fired, and the lead slug knocked the creature's head sideways. Sparks flew and a round divot formed on its temple. At the same time, Remy aimed at the creature's torso. Her magnum round slammed into the side of his chest plate punching through in a neat hole. A squirt of yellow ichor shot out as the soldier fell to the ground. Surprisingly the Roth soldier wasn't dead. The creature rolled onto his back, lifted his head, and aimed his pulse rifle in their direction. Both of them fired again at the Roth.

The magnum round slammed into his gun arm tearing it half off. Charlie's .45 ACP bullet hit the creature in the faceplate, punched through in a spider web of cracks, and drilled into the Roth's eye. Its head rocked back, bouncing off the pavement. He was impressed again. The armor was as tough as anything humanity had, but it wasn't invincible. The visor was a glaring weak spot in the lighter suits.

Gunfire shifted away from the Bentley to somewhere else down the street. A beeping began from the alien's suit like a sullen SOS signal. Charlie holstered Elva and unslung his short barreled M16. He approached the body with his weapon trained. The head inside the mask was a mess of yellow blood and crushed bone. From the suit, the noise grew in intensity until it sounded like an angry bleating sheep. Charlie quickly got behind the Bentley before the alien weapon shattered in a small explosion. The suit was left intact, but the pulse rifle was little more than a ruin of broken parts. Well that sucked, he had been hoping to steal a few of those weapons to give to Jen and Tobias. There was another, much larger explosion, down the street.

"Clear!" Someone shouted from that direction.

Jen and Tobias came out from the backyard and approached the corpse. From the burning manor, four smoke covered humans fled. They came towards Charlie to get a better look at the enemy humanity faced.

"How are you doing?" He asked Jen.

"It's a little scary, but I'm having a surprisingly good time," Jen said taking a look at the corpse. She briefly glanced inside the face visor before turning away in disgust. Two men appeared from down the street and paused next to the body.

"How many did you lose?" The man asked a girl from the other squad.

"One with an unlucky head shot. You?"

"Two when that fat bastard fired on us. I think the Roth heard the radio broadcast." Ginger said flicking his radio in annoyance.

"You lost one too?" They asked Charlie.

He shook his head and said, "No, we started with a short squad."

"So... We know they can pinpoint radio signals, and their weapons explode after death." The curly haired man said kicking pieces of a pulse rifle away.

"That blows," the girl said, and Charlie agreed. Most of the soldiers took their radio's off and tossed them away into the bushes. They'd do little good if it allowed the Roth to pinpoint their locations.

"The demons cometh seeking vengeance," Tobias warned pointing down the street. Everyone turned to see a second squad of armored aliens moving fast. They were still about two hundred meters away but jogged in a straight line to their position.

"Engage?" The girl asked.

"I'm down for a second tussle," another soldier said.

"Not with my squad," Charlie said looking for an escape route. Both the houses behind them were a raging inferno. "Objective is to survive, and those aliens know we're up here. They'll be ready. Besides they might not be the only ones headed this way." He added motioning for the crew to follow.

"Looks like you don't have a choice." The man said moving into cover. He gestured for his squadmate to set up his RPK again across the street.

The Roth soldiers slowed suddenly and spread out. Laser fire hit a nearby palm tree, and Charlie ran to the nearest manor that wasn't already ablaze. However, he found the front door locked.

"Tobias, would you get this door open?" He asked the giant.

Jen probably had the strength to kick it open, but he wanted to include the new guy. The tall man planted his foot against the lock, and the door burst open. The four ran inside as a new firefight erupted.

As Jen moved past, he caught her shoulder. "Take the lead down the hill."

For a second, worry filled her face, but she swallowed and nodded. She pulled her pistol free and went into the living room ahead of the group. The back patio was already starting to catch fire from the next mansion over. The awning was aflame, and several plastic pool chairs were starting to melt.

Jennifer jumped the fence and immediately tumbled down the steep slope. She kept her gun in hand by sheer will and even managed to gain her feet toward the bottom. Tobias rolled down in a gray heap of robes, and Charlie rather ungracefully followed his example. Remy managed to find an inflatable pool-shark and slid down in a giggling shower of dust. Behind them, it sounded like the firefight was picking up in intensity.

Charlie put himself behind Jen, with Tobias in the middle, and Remy was taking up rear guard. That way there was always someone close with a weapon. Jennifer's stealth abilities from her vampiric game once again proved useful, for she was surprisingly skilled at avoiding the Roth patrols. She led them through a maze of side streets and alleys until they reached Santa Monica Blvd. There, they paused next to a three-story office building and Charlie checked his watch. It was 2:32 pm which meant they'd lasted two hours so far. That was worth a couple of match points, but their luck quickly ran out.

Jen pulled back into the alley of the office building. She held up a hand with three fingers indicating three squads of Roth. Charlie tried the back door to the office building and found it unlocked. What he hadn't counted on was the sound the rusty hinges made. They quickly piled inside, and Jennifer let the door swing closed with an ear splitting squeal. The first soldier appeared at the alley entrance and turned in their direction. It watched the back door creek with suspicion in its marauding eyes.

The squad waited nervously in silence. Jen withdrew her USP 9mm and slid the safety off. Charlie flicked his assault rifle from single-fire to full-auto as the armored footsteps approached. The extraterrestrial closed a four-fingered hand along the edge of the door and pulled it open. The Roth's golden eyes widened in surprise as he saw the humans standing just inside. Jen quickly pressed her pistol to his visor and fired. The 9mm bullet punched through the glass and into its sunken eye socket.

Charlie put his foot against the door to keep it from closing and fired at the second alien soldier. He didn't bother conserving ammo as he squeezed the trigger. Thirty rounds stitched across the armored chest, upper torso, and neck in two and three-quarters seconds. He let the door close, and red spots started melting through the metal. They rushed headlong down the office hallway, passing a water flooded bathroom, and a break room that was slowly turning into an indoor garden. Behind them, the door was hit by a heavy laser and melted off its hinges.

Through the front glass, another squad was visible coming down the street. Charlie's quick escape was cut off as laser beams filled the first floor. Thankfully the glass, and concrete weren't catching fire.

"Up the stairs!" Charlie shouted pointing to a door next to the elevator.

Remy dodged up the stairs first, followed by Tobias and Jen. Charlie let his rifle fall on its sling and drew Elva. He fired down the rear hallway as a heavily armored suit came through the door. The fat slugs barely chipped its paint, and he tisked in annoyance, then raced up the stairwell after his squad. The wall blackened and a wave of scalding hot air followed after Charlie. The door was open on the third floor, and Remy was holding the angle with her magnum revolver.

"We are fucked without bigger guns," Charlie said going past.

"I'm surprised we lasted this long," Remy replied crouching in the doorway.

"I'm not sure if those captains can get up the stairs, but they might send up the soldiers. Can you hold this down while I look for a way out?" He asked. Remy settled onto one knee and used the door jamb to cover most of her body. This office building was likely going to be their impromptu Alamo.

Jen and Tobias were peeking through the blinds of a managers office window.

"Any way out?" Charlie asked at the doorway.

"The demon's hath encircled us. Even now another host approaches." Tobias said letting the blinds go. Jen backed away and clutched the USP pistol in her trembling hands. The towering crusader noticed her shaking and put a meaty hand on her shoulder. "Fear not, brave soul, for we do God's work today."

"This has definitely been interesting," she said, and let out a pent-up breath. Those aliens held all the advantages. They had better armor, advanced weapons, and a constant resupply of fresh troops. It was unfair in the extreme, but Charlie had to agree. He was enjoying himself.

"What do we do?" She asked. Charlie sighed unable to see a way out. The best they could do was run down stairs and take one or two out.

"Gather your flock together, let us pray," Tobias said pushing Charlie from the doorway. "Go tell the annoying girl to join us."

He stumbled at first, then blinked. Pray... Well, he would indulge the man this once. Charlie walked toward the stairs. A magnum fired as he approached.

"Ha, that'll teach ya to try and out peek me," Remy said with enthusiasm.

"We're having a discussion."

"Kind of busy," she muttered firing her revolver again.

"Close the door and lock it," he said turning away. Remy rolled her eyes but followed, and they found Tobias was kneeling in the conference room.

"What is this, Last Rights?" Remy asked pausing at the door.

The tall giant lifted his gaze, and spoke in stern sermons voice. "We hold in our hearts the fury for humanity which demonkind hath brought low. Now they dare trespass again on our blessed soil, salting the earth with their foul blood, and hunting the last human souls into oblivion. I say they have mistaken us for cowards. We are no mere soldiers, but god's warriors." Tobias preached standing. As he spoke, he withdrew his two-handed sword and held it aloft.

He turned to Charlie and said, "Do not go unto them as men, nay. Let us descend upon them in righteous fury. Let *us* be the avenging angel."

"You want us to jump out of a three-story building?" Remy asked slowly.

"Aye," the tall man said with conviction. It was an interesting idea, but Remy was right. They'd probably break bones on landing.

"It'll be more fun than getting picked off one at a time," Charlie admitted.

"You guys are crazy," Jennifer said.

"Enough talk, the Roth are about to break down the stairwell door. Since it's your idea, you get to lead this time." Charlie said pointing to the giant who was grinning maniacally over his polished blade.

"I stand ready," he said turning to the bay windows. They made a clumsy line at the back of the conference room. The giant sprinted forward with his blade held before him and burst through the glass in a shower. Charlie followed and leaped out of the broken window.

Several Roth waited directly below, including a Captain. Roaring in his deep voice Tobias fell upon the heavily armored suit with his shining blade, pierced the thinner stomach plates, and pinned the creature to the asphalt.

The Roth leader remained stuck fast to the ground, but reached up trying to grab and crush the annoying human atop him. Tobias twisted the blade snapping it, and the four-fingered hands spasmed. Tobias stood from his kill like David from Goliath. Something inside the alien's suit began to bleat, but the crusader grabbed the dropped laser cannon. Tobias rotated slowly toward the office building before planting his feet. Another Roth Captain was just inside and turning toward them.

"Die demons, die in your own hellfire!" Tobias screamed pulling the thick trigger. The red beam of energy cut through the front doors and slammed into the thick red suit. For a fraction of a second, the armor held, before the energy melted the chest plate. Tobias's fingers blistered and turned into cooked sausages from the superheated air. His eyebrows and peach fuzz burned away as his face reddened.

Charlie landed on a parked car, slid across the vehicle's roof, and tackled an armored alien. As they tumbled to the ground, Charlie jammed the barrel under the white helmet. Twelve bullets danced inside like a Pachinko machine turning the alien's head into a chunky yellow soup. Nearby the other two squadmates landed hard on the concrete.

"Drop the laser fool," Remy screamed running past the giant and skidded to a stop next to Charlie. She fired at a fourth soldier. The magnum round knocked the creature down, and she finished him off with the rest of the cylinder.

"Fear not death; For the sooner we die, the longer we shall be immortal." Tobias quoted pulling the trigger on the heavy weapon again.

He had turned and was aiming down the street toward another squad. The beam caught a lightly armored soldier out in the open. As it passed over the alien, it was cut into two parts. The long armored legs continued forward sans the torso for another few feet before collapsing.

The sleeves of Tobias's gray robes caught fire as the meat of his fingers melted away. Boiling ruptures broke out over his face as he laughed. Then the cannon's alarm reached a crescendo and exploded sending the scorched giant flying into the office lobby.

"Well, he made us a way out. Let's not waste it." Charlie said standing from cover.

Jen was laying on the concrete with an ankle bent in the wrong direction. Instead of pain, she looked annoyed as she held her pistol. An alien lay on the ground next to her.

"Just leave me," she said as Charlie approached.

He ignored her comment and picked up the woman in a fireman's carry. Thankfully, his two strength was just enough to lift the extra weight. Remy ran ahead of him into the alley. They picked a random direction, and half jogged away from the battle. By some miracle, they missed the alien squads converging on the location.

Several streets down they found fresh graffiti on a storefront. It was a crude bullet surrounded by a circle and an arrow indicating a direction. Charlie pointed with his elbow, "Look, it's one of the stockpiles they told us about."

"Maybe they'll have medical supplies," Remy suggested.

The supply cache turned out to be inside an old speakeasy. The same graffiti pointed down into the steps of a business's basement. Remy pushed open the old wooden door with her shotgun drawn.

"Someone's already been here," she warned as Charlie carried Jennifer down the stairs.

The secret door marred with graffiti was already ajar, and several crates had been broken open and looted.

"I hope we find what we need to survive another two hours," Charlie said entering the cache room.

# CHAPTER TWENTY-ONE
## *Landing Pt2*

A foul smelling car battery bubbled and smoked near the hidden entrance. Two wires ran up the wall, along the ceiling, and haphazardly connected to a hanging light fixture. The ancient yellow bulb blinked erratically like a caffeine addicted office drone. It illuminated if barely, the rough hewn limestone walls, and was another visceral reminder of just how far humanity had fallen. Wooden crates were piled along the walls in an uncoordinated mess. Charlie approached the nearest stack as he carefully pulled Jennifer from his shoulder.

"You know, under different circumstances, I'd be excited to have such a beautiful woman in my arms," Charlie said putting his wounded comrade down.

"Don't even try it," Jennifer replied with a look best described as dark. His face heated from the curt rejection and he turned away.

"Just joking," he said looking around.

Jennifer sighed and said, "That came out harsher than I intended."

"No, it's for the best. I'd rather keep you around as a goofy sidekick than a serious romantic interest. I already have one damaged girl in my harem." Charlie said as he walked over to a pallet of miscellaneous equipment. There was a tiny red bag with a cross on each side, and he pulled it out from the tie downs. The kit wasn't much, but he returned with it.

"Has anyone ever told you, you're an ass."

"I completely agree. He won't fuck me no matter how much I beg." Remy said from deep within several pallets of grenades.

She tore open another top and grinned. Pulling out several sticks of C4, she yelled, "Finally, the good stuff!"

The banter helped salvage the mood in the room, and he turned his attention back to his initial task. The little red bag unzipped down the middle and opened like a clamshell. One side contained ten injections of morphine. The other held five rolls of beige colored bandages, and stuck in the middle was a two-page pamphlet. It repeated the same instructions in several different languages.

[Inject the patient with an ampule of morphine, then wrap the wound in a bandage. For all serious injuries, shoot the patient.]

Charlie laughed and handed the pamphlet to Jennifer. "Now I won't feel so bad when I put you down like a wounded dog." She quickly scanned the instructions and crumpled the note. It flew across the room and rolled into a dark corner. "With how cheap clones are, it makes sense they haven't wasted much energy on keeping us alive."

He removed an orange ampule, popped off the safety cap, then unceremoniously jabbed it into Jennifer's thigh. She gave a relieved sigh and said, "At least the annoying tingle is gone."

The foot pointed in an unnatural direction, and he removed her boot revealing a purple and swollen ankle. There weren't any bones sticking out —thankfully, so Charlie forced it around until there was a loud pop. Then, he wrapped a bandage around her foot.

"How is that?"

Jennifer stood carefully from the crates and walked across the dirt floor like she had a peg leg. "I won't be running any marathons, but at least I can walk." She admitted sitting back down and putting her boot on.

Remy returned from her fishing expedition with several ammo boxes. Dangling from her waist was a plethora of frag grenades, flash-bangs, and smokes. Her teddy bear backpack overflowed with sticks of C4, and hanging from its open mouth were a couple of remote detonators.

Charlie took the ammo container, which was filled to the brim with loose 5.56 rounds, and reloaded his magazines. While he did this, Jennifer managed to locate two more belts for grenades. Her movement speed was already crippled, and she dared not carry anything extra. When each of them were ready, they crept back up the basement stairs.

Toward the south, a constant gun battle tickled Charlie's hearing like distant fireworks. The smell of smoke and something electric hung in the air like a pall. He paused near the exit checking the street in both directions. A few blocks down several human bodies lay in the open, and he was certain they hadn't been there before, so he turned his squad away toward a nearby shopping mall. Charlie crept along the sidewalk with his rifle at the ready. Jennifer limped behind him with her USP in hand, and Remy walked backward with her revolver.

The parking lot was congested, and they wove between abandoned cars and FEMA trucks. Faded scorch marks covered the face of the building like old battle scars. The glass doors were shattered and crunched under his boots as Charlie entered the shopping center. More glass littered the food court from the broken skylights. Sunlight streamed from above illuminating a standing pool of water, and weeds struggled up between the marble tiles. Most of the shuttered storefronts were closed and padlocked.

Behind him, Jennifer and Remy scanned the hallway. Charlie walked toward a set of broken escalators, but stopped pausing to listen. He lifted a closed fist, and his companions froze. Something had moved on the second floor, and Charlie trained his weapon on the landing as he slowly crept one step at a time. He almost squeezed the trigger as two shapes appeared on the second floor. A male and female whitetail deer stop near the top of the escalator. The impressive ten point buck glared down at him imperiously, as if to say, "How dare you block my path." The female nervously ducked behind a moss covered bench, but sadly, it wasn't Charlie she should have been afraid of.

A pulse laser lanced out from deeper within the mall followed by the pop and crackle of burning air. The burst of energy caught the female in the flank. The doe jumped, screaming in pain before her legs gave out. As she collapsed, the furious buck turned and charged into the darkness. Several high pitched beams darted past, and something heavy crashed to the ground.

Charlie moved to the top of the escalator in a crouch. Two alien soldiers started poking the deer's corpse with their energy rifles and talking to one another. It appeared they were stragglers waiting for their comrades to respawn. One took out a small device and the second posed with his white plated foot on the trophy animal. On the second escalator, both girls crawled to the lip and looked over. Remy made a small disgusted sound low in her throat.

She turned to Jen and whispered under her breath, "Flashbangs." Jen withdrew a thin grenade from her belt, and they pulled the pins. Raising up both tossed the flashbangs across the twenty-meter gap. The two soldiers turned at the sound and raised their rifles. Closing his eyes, Charlie waited until both grenades exploded in a brilliant flash of light and sound.

He stood aiming down the red dot of his M16. The soldiers staggered backward from the deer as they fired indiscriminately. He shot at the right most alien in a precise one-second burst, and the rounds stitched across its chest leaving a trail of holes in the light armor. The bulky pulse rifle clattered loudly to the tiles as the alien fell over. The second Roth danced under an onslaught of pistol rounds slamming into its armor. Remy's revolver belched defiantly as she aimed using the scope. The soldier's leg buckled at the knee, and the creature collapsed.

Remy ran forward, and Charlie was forced to follow. His target had stopped moving but the second alien was still alive. The small school girl stepped on the laser carbine pinning it to the ground, and Charlie immobilized its other wrist with a boot. She holstered her magnum and withdrew the double barrel shotgun at her thigh. Jen caught up and together they looked down at the Roth. Remy glanced back at the smoldering animal corpse then at the alien, who was just recovering from the blinding flash.

"I wonder what Roth tastes like?" The young girl mused.

"That's pretty dark even for you, Remy," Charlie said.

"I'm just curious."

The wounded soldier made a sound inside its helmet which was muffled by the glass. Maybe it was talking, or cursing, or begging for its life, but Charlie didn't much care. Remy pointed the short barreled shotgun at the lizard-like face and pulled both triggers. Bone, ichor, and brains splattered everywhere as the two loads of buckshot shredded the Roth's head. Remy knelt and stuck a finger into the yellow tapioca pudding that had been a face. She sniffed tentatively, then gave it a lick, and quickly spat the glob onto the ground.

"What's it like?" Charlie asked raising one eyebrow.

"Like week old semen deep fried in sewage," Remy said spitting again. Jen dry heaved and closed a hand over her mouth. Her face turned a shade of green, and she walked away. Remy rubbed her fingers clean on her skirt. "We better leave. Every time one of those fuckers dies it sends out a distress signal."

Charlie agreed and checked the time. It was 3:13 pm which meant almost three hours had passed. He reloaded Fara with a full magazine and put the partial in his dump pouch. "Anyone need to go potty?" He asked, and both girls shook their heads. Charlie was fine for another hour, but he was going to need some lunch soon. They continued through the mall at a fast hobble.

Near the north parking lot, a fresh squad of Roth was investigating the distress signals. A heavily armored captain struggled to find a path toward them. Charlie ran forward to the cover of an armored FEMA vehicle. The M16 settled atop the hood, but the Roth weaved between the abandoned cars. Charlie fired a short burst just to keep the soldiers from closing too quickly, while Remy pulled the pin on several smoke grenades and hurled them into the lot. Within seconds they began spewing an obscuring blanket. A massive laser beam slashed over their heads and melted the glass entrance into slag. Jen and Remy both started throwing all of their smokes and flash-bangs toward the advancing Roth.

The tactic was a double-edged sword, however. The armored captain couldn't see them through the thick smoke, but Charlie found it impossible to pick off the soldiers coming toward them. Without much hope, he fired again at a shadow moving between the cars. The bolt locked back on an empty chamber, and Charlie dropped the mag to load a fresh one. Things were happening too quickly to worry about picking up empty magazines.

A white clad Roth sprinted toward them through the smoke. It held a small carbine sized laser rifle as it moved. Without stopping the alien fired cutting a long gouge into the armored Humvee. Charlie leveled his CQB weapon and squeezed the trigger. The soldier dodged right, and he followed the target with his automatic fire. He cut a swath across the alien's stomach, but it continued around the side of the vehicle. Charlie swore as his M16 ran dry and let the rifle fall on its sling to his chest. He transitioned with long practice to his 1911 as the wounded Roth appeared again. Lifting the pistol to eye level both fired at one another. A beam hit Charlie in the neck cutting apart his jugular and fusing several vertebrae together. His bullet slammed into the glass visor, punching through in a spiderweb, and drilled into the slitted nasal cavity. Charlie collapsed to the ground along with the convulsing alien.

Darkness closed in after a few seconds.

A door opened in the void exposing a massive public lobby. Thousands of players were still sitting around watching the combat. Screens displayed a variety of ongoing battles. He stepped from the small enclosed booth and looked around. On the centrally raised dais, a massive map was representing the overall event. Yellow dots showed the locations of all the living humans. Red pings indicated known Roth activity. On the side, a counter listed the number of players remaining, which was steadily ticking down past eight thousand. He checked his watch and was glad to see it was past 3:30. Charlie would just barely get that third match point.

"Brother Charlie!" A deep voice called. The figure of Tobias pushed through the throng toward him. "I watched your skirmish. You have done well, and your flock continues to fight the demons." Tobias said pointing back to a rear screen. Charlie followed the man over to the couches.

"I am..." Tobias paused before sitting down. He struggled to find his words. "The Lord hath tested me and found me wanting."

"You're joking right? If it wasn't for you, we would all be corpses in that office building." Charlie admitted.

"Before... I was presumptuous to state I needed only the conviction of faith. Against the hellish weapons the demon host brings, faith alone means little. I need more than a sword and I beg thee for advice."

"I'd be happy to help, especially if you'd be willing to take on a role in the group. We need someone with heavy armor. A tank that can take some of the heat."

"I am willing."

"Did you rank up?" Charlie asked.

"Yes, my Division Rank is now Silver One." The giant admitted with a humbled voice.

"Good... Good, we can find a primary weapon for you."

The conversation paused as the action restarted. Less than a minute had passed since Charlie's demise. Smoke filled the parking lot in a thick fog of war. Jen and Remy had retreated to the entrance lobby. Two surviving alien soldiers were firing from the armored Humvee, while the captain was slowly plodding a course between the ruined cars. Charlie's body lay on the ground near the fallen Roth soldier. It was a little disconcerting to see his corpse and the massive pool of blood it lay within. Both women returned fire as best as they could. Jennifer was at a severe disadvantage with her pistol. She popped up to shoot, and a pulse of three beams narrowly missed her face. It singed her cheek, and she dropped below the concrete planter.

"The enemy is as cunning as they are wicked," Tobias said pointing to a second screen. Another squad was coming up from behind through the mall. In less than a minute they would be pinched from both sides. Remy must have realized something was going on. The Roth seemed too content to hunker behind cover, which was unusual. All morning they had rushed pell-mell into combat like kids straight out of Bronze rank.

"It's the endgame!" Remy said enthusiastically. She pulled the teddy-bear off her back and dug out the C4. She stuck a blasting cap into the plastic wrapped explosive. A wire was connected to a transceiver and Remy tossed it across the gap. Jennifer holstered her weapon and grabbed the explosive.

Jen's breath stilled, and a calm took over. She rose and awkwardly sprinted through the sagging glass entrance. The Roth fired at her, and a laser ripped into her already injured leg. She fell hard but managed to toss the armed C4 just underneath the Humvee. A series of pulse beams hit her, digging into her unarmored torso, and cooked her pounding heart. Remy activated the radio button. The Humvee lurched upwards in the explosion, then crashed down atop the two soldiers.

Remy smiled and dug another stick of C4 from her pack, and added the blasting cap. A laser shot out from within the darkened mall. It cut into her teddy-bear, and she yelped in pain as her armor started to melt. Thankfully the C4 didn't detonate. Instead, it spilled out across the glass covered tiles. She rolled to her feet and ran toward the toppled Humvee just as the Roth captain came around the smoking wreck.

"Fuck me in the ass," Remy cursed.

The red armored suit planted its feet apart as Remy neared. It was the oddest thing Charlie could have watched. A massive alien leveled its laser cannon at the charging elementary school girl. Her pigtails and plaid skirt flapped wildly as she sprinted forward. A red glow sparked to life deep within the heavy weapon. Remy threw herself forward shredding the skin off her legs and ass on the rough concrete. The cannon fired and she skidded below the superheated beam of energy. Her blue pigtails instantly melted away along with most of her scalp. One eye exploded like an egg cooked too long in the microwave, and her blackened body slid to a stop just between the captain's legs. For a second she lay there unmoving before her head turned exposing a bright green eye. She reached up pressing the adhesive side of the C4 to the Roth's crotch.

"I... Love... Explosions," Remy said pressing the transmitter in her right hand.

The girl disappeared in a mist of liquefied flesh and bone. The charge pierced the weak spot between the front and back armor, and the suit toppled backward from the force of the explosion. Just like Remy, the alien's reproductive organs were liquefied, and the result was a messy yellow discharge from the armor's cracked groin. The kill instantly made the highlights on the central display. Around the arena, men shuddered and clutched themselves in sympathy for the alien invader.

Jen and Remy would be coming into the lobby soon. Tobias followed Charlie as he stood and walked toward the respawn tubes. Jennifer was near the exit collecting her wits after the battle, and Remy strutted out of the door quite proud of herself.

"Congrats, those were some nice kills," Charlie said nearing the duo. Jen looked up and smiled, while Remy preened. They checked their stats on a nearby console.

"I got gold," Remy exclaimed as her screen came up.

Charlie was disappointed to still be Silver Master, but he had expected the result. Jen placed her hand on the screen and smiled. Just like Tobias she had risen to Silver One. Everyone had ranked up except him, and he felt a pang of jealousy, but quickly pushed it aside.

"Tobias asked me to help him find a weapon. Want a ride to the Armory?" Charlie asked Jennifer.

"Sure, I have some time."

"You coming too Remy, since you ranked up?" He asked turning to the smaller woman.

"Naw, my weapon's already waiting at home. She'll be happy to get unhandcuffed from the bed finally." Remy said with one of her usual smiles. Charlie glanced at her, as did the others.

"What? I fed her," She said in the silence.

"I can't tell if your joking or not, and that kind of scares me," Charlie admitted. In response, Remy blew him a kiss and waved at them.

"Have fun," She called skipping away.

He worried about that one sometimes, but all he could do was shake his head. Charlie made his way to a nearby console to access his money account. If Tobias was going to join the squad, Charlie didn't mind donating ten thousand credits for the cause. That would help pay for his heavy armor, mods, and any ammo he'd need. They left the Competition Center and piled into his muscle car. It was a short trip to the enormous hotel resort. The Armory lobby was a virtual ghost town today, and barely a dozen weapons were lounging around in skimpy bikini tops. Elva had cleaned out the building by dropping her bombshell idea on the place. It wasn't even that big a mental leap, but the developers must have purposely not given the AI that option.

The gun shop side had more of a selection. Under the glass cases, a couple of dozen handguns sat waiting. Racks on the wall held more shotguns, rifles, and a smattering of SMG's. There was one weapon, unlike the others. A Tri-barreled Gatling Cannon looked out of place sitting on the counter. It should have been mounted on the door of an attack helicopter, or aboard a Coast Guard cutter. The cannon had a motorized housing and a thick rubber carrying handle on the top. Red and yellow triggers were mounted on the second-hand grip to the rear. Tobias's eyes raked over the heavy weapon like a man fallen instantly in love, and his shaking hands itched to stroke the three long barrels to its triangular shaped head.

"No touching that one till you satisfy the requirements." A man said sharply from nearby. Tobias turned with feverish eyes to the speaker.

A middle-aged clerk was pointing to a small sign on the counter. It read in large letters, "Must have four strength to contract with this weapon."

"You're a bigg'un, but I need you to verify your stats before you go pawing the girl. She's new, and might get a little excited." Tobias put his hand on the nearby screen, and his ID came up. He did indeed have four strength score, and the clerk smiled. "Alright then. Be gentle with her. She came out of the factory only hours ago, so her personality hasn't fully formed yet."

The GAU-19B Gatling Cannon began to glow a brilliant yellow. In the flash of light, a young nineteen-year-old stood in front of him. She had hair the color of driven snow and the most incredible eyes. They were like the stained glass windows of a gothic cathedral. One was a pale light blue like the color of natural diamonds. The other was a dark translucent green, and shaped white eyebrows highlighted her distinctive eyes. She instantly looked down at the carpet when she noticed so many people staring at her. Her lips were small, and frowning slightly from all the attention. The line of her jaw was straight and came to a pointed noble chin. She had a transformative face, one that could change with her expression. That expression turned to confusion as Tobias fell to his knees, put his forehead to the carpet, and began to trembled. The young woman stared at the giant cowering before her.

"What are you doing?" She asked in a nervous voice.

"I am not worthy to look upon your beauty, Angel," Tobias said in his deep voice.

The girl blushed furiously, and her innocent cheeks burned with heat. She glanced around and noticed Charlie watching. He made a 'go on' gesture and the girl swallowed. "Please, you're embarrassing us both."

Tobias lifted his head but didn't stand. His eyes welled with unshed tears as he looked up at the Valkyrie before him. She blushed furiously again.

"What is thy name?"

"I don't have one, yet." She responded, and Tobias looked stricken for a moment, then he gathered himself.

"Nay, you have had a name all along. The Great Creator imbued you with one at your inception." Tobias stated in a deep, reverent voice. The young girl looked genuinely confused as she quickly searched her memory bank. She started to shake her head, but Tobias quickly added, "Surely you are Gadreel the Angel of War, and the Guardian of the Gates of Heaven."

The young woman paused, staring down at the giant. "Gadreel..." She repeated several times as if tasting the word from different directions. When she was satisfied, the girl asked in a small voice, "What is your name?"

"This humble servant is beneath your notice. However, I am known as Tobias." He replied.

"May I call you Toby?" She asked.

"Yes, Angel. If it pleases thee."

Finally, she held out a delicate hand and asked, "Do you accept me as your weapon?"

Tobias took her petite hand in his massive paw and pressed it to his forehead. "If it is thy wish, I would be honored to carry thee into battle," he said.

"Yes, I find you very acceptable. Please stand." She replied, and he did as instructed. His massive frame towered over her, but he looked down into her eyes with worship.

"It is Providence, that we met today."

"There are..." She said pausing as her decision process worked. Finally, she shyly tried again with, "There are chambers nearby so that we may anoint our union." Tobias followed the girl toward the back hallway. Halfway there he picked up the weapon. She squeaked in surprise before wrapping her arms around his thick neck. Charlie watched the two disappear down the back hallway and wished them luck.

Finally, he turned looking for Jennifer. She was standing next to an open console with a frown on her face. Charlie wandered toward her and glanced over Jen's shoulder.

"Woah, whoaw, wooah... How are you going to find a gun if you check off everything?" He asked seeing the filters she'd applied.

"Well, I want a man."

"I did warn you there were fewer male guns, so you may have to settle for a girl."

"I'm not a lesbian," She said hotly.

"Ok, what are your stats?"

"Three Strength, Four Agility, and One Endurance," Jen said.

*"Ouch... It was no wonder Jen had broken her ankle jumping from the building."*

"You did well with that," she added pointing at the short barreled rifle hanging from his shoulder.

"You're not going to win any stand-up fights. Most everyone puts at least one extra point into endurance. You're like a squishy glass cannon."

"What do I do?"

"You have three strength, and that's good enough to carry a large caliber rifle. I would suggest something like this." He said tapping the screen.

He first selected only male weapons. The catalog dropped to two dozen weapons currently staying at the hotel. Next, he sorted them by type. At least half were handguns, so he added another filter to exclude them. That left just ten, and he selected the first one. A picture of a blocky long barreled rifle with a massive muzzle break came up on the screen.

"That's huge," Jennifer complained.

"Yes, it is. You have three strength, so you'll have the equipment load to carry it."

"I wanted something compact, like what you have."

"That's the thing. Small caliber weapons are close range. Face it, your hit points blow, and you're going to be banging your head against that ceiling. You could pay to change your stats, or pick a weapon that compliments them." He said tapping the call button.

"No..." she hissed trying to stop him. An audible ping sounded from the screen, and Jen groaned. Charlie glanced at the other weapons while they waited. Ten or so scantily clad girls were carefully avoiding eye contact. They had, however, started to gather on the nearby couches.

The weapon came out of the elevator like on military parade, and Charlie laughed watching him walk toward them. He had seen some characters in this game, but this weapon was impressive. The guy looked like the poster image of an American GI. He was easily over seven feet tall with muscles on top of muscles. His eyes were like bright green targeting lasers, but that chin said it all. It was shaped from a solid piece of marble, and above that square jaw was a simple, understated pair of lips. The nose was similarly straight. He had light auburn hair cut into a regulation crew fade. Charlie waved at the man before Jen grabbed his arm.

He came to a stop and saluted with military precision. "Reporting for duty, Sir!" The man shouted, and Charlie laughed again.

"Charlie..." Jen hissed.

"This is exactly what you need. Seriously... you asked for my advice. He's male, and a standoff rifle." He said turning to the man. "Jen here is looking for a primary weapon. Tell her about yourself." Charlie suggested.

"Aye aye, Sir! I'm a Barrett M107 .50 caliber anti-material rifle with a magazine capacity of ten rounds and a maximum range of two thousand meters. My barrel length is 29 inches and I have a dry weight of 30.9 pounds, sir!" The weapon stated as if speaking to a drill sergeant.

Charlie whistled and asked, "How long have you been waiting, soldier?"

"Five days; Twenty-Two hours; Sixteen minutes, sir. I am ready to serve," The GI stated glancing between the two.

"You hear that? This man is eager to serve you. How could you say no to that." Charlie said slapping the rifle on the shoulder.

Jen's face looked both furious and embarrassed. Still, she scanned the weapon. The gun put his hands behind his back like someone at military parade. Her eyes rolled down the hairless chest toward his rock hard abs, but Jen absolutely refused to acknowledge the heavy bulging Speedo.

"Fine," she said at last. "I'll give him a try, but not here. I have an apartment nearby."

"Very well, Ma'am!"

"You can call me Jennifer," She muttered while turning away, and headed for the door. The soldier followed her out at a quick march, and Charlie watched the two exit the armory. Once again, he was a little jealous everyone else was getting a contract tonight.

# CHAPTER TWENTY-TWO

## *Cheesecake*

Jennifer had just left the lobby with the hunk hot on her heels. Tobias was deep within the Armory's royal suites getting blessed by that nubile angel. That left Charlie with nothing to do but go home and clean his weapons.

He checked his watch one last time, then pushed from the console, and headed for the exit. It was dusk, and the sun cast the sky into a kaleidoscope of colors. He walked by the mustang and trailed a hand over the hood. Then climbed into the car and put the M16 between the seats. The engine started with a roar and a whine from the turbocharger, and soon he was fishtailing out of the parking lot and headed home. Even before Charlie pulled into the garage, he could hear the sound of music. The stereo was on full volume, which reminded him that the house was full of guests.

He entered the garage door to a battleground. In the living room, plates of dinner were left half finished. Bottles of wine had been uncorked, and glasses lay like slaughtered corpses over the table. Several wet and sandy towels sprawled over the living room couches. The kitchen was a bigger disaster. Dirty pans littered the oven top, and it looked like someone had pulled the pin on a grenade and tossed it into the refrigerator. One door was still open, and bags of food scattered over the counter. A milk jug had tipped over and was slowly dribbling its contents onto the tiles. He was dumbfounded how five girls could do so much damage in a few hours. Charlie walked to the stereo, turned it off, and was treated to thunderous silence.

"Ladies?!" He called loudly. The girls in the living room glanced nervously between one another. A fourth Asian weapon came out of the bedroom with a towel around her head.

"I did say you could entertain yourselves. However, I think there came a point where you may have gone overboard. This kitchen is unacceptable." He said looking pointedly at each one of them.

"Are you angry with us?" The auburn-haired girl asked, and nervously hid behind another weapon.

"I am disappointed. I think the Armory pampered you all a little too much." He said. To his statement they each showed varying degrees of guilt.

"Where is Sofie?" He asked, and they pointed down toward the beach. "Fine, I'll talk to her later. You three clean up the kitchen." He ordered aiming a finger at the first group. Then pointed to the woman wrapped in a towel. "Clean the living room."

"We never had to do that at the Armory," she argued with a pout.

"I am not interested in picking up after you either. You can keep the house clean or go back to the Armory." He said gesturing to the front door. The busty Asian reviewed her odds, and reluctantly moved to the couch to pick up the dirty towels.

"Fara, Elva; Transform." He commanded a little more curtly than he intended.

Both girls materialized. Fara looked around rather impressed with the damage. Elva took in her surroundings in shock.

"I'm sorry Charlie. I..."

"Your friends can stay, but you need to show them the ropes."

"Fara,"

"What?" She asked looking like she was ready to tell him off. The weapon probably expected to be assigned something to do.

"Elva and I are going to spend some quality time together. Can you go a night without being cleaned?" He asked.

"Yes," she said, but disappointment was written on her face.

"Tomorrow morning, at the latest. You did good work today." He said turning Elva toward the bedroom. Charlie wasn't about to let her clean up after the women, and he urged her through the door.

"Charlie..." She said in a strained voice, but he stopped her by covering her mouth.

"You're like the matron of this family, Elva. This house is as much yours as it is mine. After I log out, you can give them the birds and the bee's of staying here." He said. Elva smiled slightly at his compliment and straightened with pride. "Get naked and lay on the bed."

Charlie walked to the nightstand, and pulled off his jacket, armor, and holsters. Elva yanked her shirt over her head like it was on fire, and the top made a supersonic crack as it broke the sound barrier on its way into the laundry basket. Her daisy dukes and panties swiftly followed before Elva leaped onto the bed.

"Roll over on your belly." He said pulling several pillows closer and patted them. Intrigued she did so.

Elva had bronze skin, a result of many days spent lounging naked on the beach. For a few seconds, he admired the swell of her ass and the long valley her spine made. Charlie touched the back of her calves and ran his hands up her smooth legs. She shook her hips seductively as he slid his hands over them. He continued up her back to the base of her neck, and started to massage the skin. His fingers worked like he was kneading dough across her shoulders, and he did this all the way down each arm. Elva sighed relaxing fully onto the bed.

"You mentioned they pamper you all at the hotel."

"Uhh huh," Elva said in agreement.

She deserved a little something. The situation with the girls wasn't entirely her fault, and he rather enjoyed having them in the house. Elva did the shopping, kept the house clean, and even did the laundry, so he wanted to give her a special present for always doing the chores.

He was no professional masseuse, not by any margin, but he was enthusiastic in his attempt. By now he was working his way down to her lower back. His palms slid over her dorsal muscles and rolled over her sides. Charlie dug his fingers and knuckles into her plump posterior. He toyed with her inner thighs, and his fingers lightly stroked along the edge of her sex.

She moaned into the pillow and said, "They never did that on the massage table." Charlie moved down each thigh kneading the bronze colored flesh. After giving her feet some love, he returned to the cleft of her core. Elva parted her legs, and his fingers grew slick with her sweet smelling lubricant. He took his time gently rubbing her until she made a sound, not unlike an impatient cat waiting for its food.

Charlie straddled Elva from behind, entered her slowly, and descended inch by inch to her molten core. Her hot swollen walls clung to him like oiled fingers, and his manhood quickly grew slick. He bottomed out within her and there was a momentary pulse of electric pleasure. Charlie withdrew completely, and his shaft glistened with her milky lubricant. Elva reached back and spread her bronze ass cheeks for him. Smiling at her invitation, he aimed at her honeyed entrance again and dove. As he fully entered her, another shock of sweet bliss raced up his spine, and Charlie moaned feeling dizzy from the intense sensation.

For a time he was in control. For a time he moved gently, but eventually his restraint broke, and he began pumping into her as hard as he could. The climax slammed into him like a runaway dump truck. Charlie roared as a tsunami flooded down his loins. His trembling arms buckled, and Charlie collapsed atop the bronze goddess.

She reached back, combing her fingers through his tousled hair, and he bit her neck tasting her metallic skin. Elva purred like a satisfied kitten.

"I'm going to log out for tonight," he murmured in a drunken voice.

"Okay," Elva breathed. He touched his temple to access his system menu. The prompt came up, and he logged from the game.

Sunday morning he woke early, which gave him time to fix a proper breakfast before logging in. Like usual he carried a bottle of water into the living room and pulled the Dive Helmet on. It hummed to life and dropped him into the game.

Gun Meister Online Loading...
Installing Amorous Content...
Initiating Modem Foreplay...
Network Swapping Digital Fluids...
Logging into Character...

Charlie opened his eyes. Above him, an old Twilight Zone show was playing in black and white. Fara lay on the bed with her head between his legs, and must have noticed the change.

"I want season two," Fara said without moving.

"We can work something out." He said running a hand along her jawline. She bit his hand as it approached her mouth and he winced. Fara was like a moody cat. Sometimes she was sweet, but mostly just rebellious and disobedient. He reached down and flicked her nipple through the thin t-shirt. It instantly stiffened under his attack, and Fara growled biting down harder.

"Ok, you win. You're obviously not in the mood for play." He said through the pain. She let go, and he examined his hand for teeth marks. Maybe she was annoyed at not being cleaned last night.

"Where's Elva?"

"Showing the girls how to serve man," Fara said in a deadpan voice. Charlie hoped Fara didn't mean seasoned and deep fried in oil.

"If you can tear yourself away from the television, I'll clean you."

Fara touched the screen and it blinked off. Then she glowed yellow and transformed into a short barreled M16A4. Charlie picked up the weapon and walked out of the bedroom to an unusual scene. Six girls sat around the kitchen counter which was covered in banana clusters.

"Sensei, show us again," a sultry Asian begged.

First Elva pushed the thick pair of red glasses higher on her nose, then fetched another banana and unwrapped it. She checked to make sure everyone was watching before the woman opened her mouth. The white fleshy fruit approached, and she licked a tongue across the tip. Her lips closed over the head and slowly forced its length into her mouth. The lucky food item bottomed out at the peeled base. Elva's head bobbed as she withdrew the fruit, and saliva covered it all the way to the yellow hilt. She smiled and wiped her lips clean.

"The trick is to relax your throat." She said, and several girls tried it. Sofie managed it on the first attempt, but she had those sultry lips and a long, languid tongue. The fruit disappeared down her throat, and Elva applauded. The two white-haired twins managed to get about halfway before gagging. They coughed in unison and started to giggle in embarrassment. The auburn haired girl tried next. She only managed to get the tip in before biting down.

"I cannn't hellp itt," she mumbled with a mouthful of fruit. The girl swallowed. "Banana tastes so good, I can't help but eat it."

Charlie could see why Fara hadn't been interested in joining. He probably would never let the sadist near his manhood. Not with her penchant for biting.

"I see you're going above and beyond," Charlie said announcing his presence. Sofie turned in surprise and quickly ate the banana.

Elva leaped from the kitchen stool and circled the counter with an excited smile on her face. She was wearing her teacher's outfit today. Only a few buttons were actively used on the white shirt, which strained mightily against her cleavage. Elva smoothed the red pleated miniskirt and stepped toward him in bright red four-inch heels.

The sex-ed teacher pressed herself to him in greeting. Charlie tasted the banana Elva had so vigorously practiced upon. Her kiss and the scene he'd just witness conspired to get him highly aroused. He slipped a hand under her skirt and traced the line of her lace panties to the damp crotch.

"I only asked you to show the girls the ropes, but I didn't expect you to give your secret techniques away."

She moaned as he continued to prod her wet panties. "How about we finish with a proper demonstration?" Elva suggested in a heavy lust ridden voice.

"I would love that, but first I think you should introduce your friends. It's only fair after the lengths they're going to." He said removing his hand from Elva's skirt.

She gestured to a voluptuous Asian sitting closest to them. The woman still had the banana in her mouth and winked at him. "We didn't have names, so we used the last three numbers of our object ID's when talking to each other. 853 is an M79 Stand Alone 40mm Grenade Launcher."

Elva paused and whispered into his ear, "She hates being called blooper."

*"A grenade launcher,"* Charlie thought. It was a good thing he'd already promised Sofie the slot, or he would be sorely tempted to pick her as his Gold contract.

Next Elva pointed to the white-haired twins sitting together. "901 and 902 are a pair of Thompson Center Machine Guns." If he ever wanted to dress up as a mobster for Halloween, those two would be perfect weapons. They blushed in unison and giggled behind dainty hands. The shy brown haired girl was an M97 Trench Shotgun, and Charlie whistled. They were all reliable guns in his opinion. Each seemed to be around world war two era, but maybe that was how the batches came out.

"It's nice to meet you all," he said, before the phone began to ring. Charlie fished it out and activated the screen.

"Remy," he said accepting the call.

"You usually don't pick up."

"I'm always afraid you're in the middle of something I'd rather not hear," Charlie admitted.

"There's another event today. I figured we could show up early and practice together." Remy suggested, which was surprisingly thoughtful.

"That could be useful. I'll message the others. We're going to have to integrate Tobias and Jennifer with their new weapons. You'll be surprised I think." Charlie said with a wolfish grin. He was already starting to imagine that Gatling Cannon and the Sniper Rifle at work on the Roth Captains.

"Hold… hold on…. oh god, that feels so good. Right there… I'm gunna cum," Remy groaned.

Charlie sighed and hung up. He turned to Elva and said, "It looks like our demonstration will have to wait until later." The weapon pouted but nodded reluctantly.

"I still need to clean you. If you change, I'll give you and Fara a quick scrub down before we leave."

# CHAPTER TWENTY-THREE

## *Dropship*

At ten in the morning, the Competition Center was a bright bustle of activity. Red strobing lights still decorated the outside like a Las Vegas sideshow. Charlie parked the car near the street, shut the engine off, and fetched Fara from between the seats. He was halfway to the entrance when he caught sight of Grace sitting on the same bench as yesterday. Remy sat beside her licking an ice cream cone, and the southern belle was busy ignoring the little girl. She had purchased a hoop dress of plain white fabric. As Charlie approached, she gave him a small wave and a smile.

"Charlie," she greeted.

"How are you doing today, Grace?"

Her smile never faltered, but she said, "I am miserable. How are you?"

"I am doing good, quite good. My only regret is that Montgomery is not here to bask in the excitement."

"I share your sentiment," Grace admitted.

"Do you need anything?"

"No, but thank you," Grace replied with another forced smile. Charlie turned his attention to the small girl next to her. She was licking her fingers clean of ice cream.

Remy was dressed in a skimpy black bathing suit, and her teal hair was tied back into a single ponytail. Under her right arm was the magnum holster. A half-full belt of 40mm grenades were slung across her small chest, while a full one wrapped around her waist. At her thigh was a leather holster containing the double barrel shotgun. There sat a large weapon in her lap, and with it, she must have been pushing her weight limit.

"Why are you wearing a bikini?" He asked.

"That light armor didn't do shit against the lasers yesterday, so I bathed in 180 SPF sunscreen instead. Every half-pound I save is another 40mm grenade." She said running a hand down her stomach.

"You seem unusually chipper."

Remy smiled in response and patted the Milkor Six-Shot Grenade Launcher in her lap. The heavy weapon looked like a giant black revolver.

"Missy is still a little annoyed with me."

"This is the gun you had waiting at home?" Charlie asked.

"I wouldn't let her go till we had a contract, so she bit me. I had no idea a girl's clitoris could be circumcised, but hooweee... Missy did it. I couldn't get the blood stopped no matter how many towels I used." Remy admitted.

"You deserved it," Grace said in a none too quiet whisper.

"Philip wouldn't help me in the slightest. Do you know how awkward it is to bury yourself in the garden?"

"Can't say I do."

"It certainly gives you some existential thoughts on life. At least I got Missy contracted. I think she'll come around in the end." She said giving the weapon another long, lascivious stroking.

"Remy, you are so utterly fucked in the head."

"I just didn't want Missy to contract with anyone else while I ranked up. She had TV, food, and I played with her tons."

"Weapons are not pets."

"Well, they're not entirely human either. Besides, Missy could have left at any time. All she had to do was change into weapon form to slip the cuffs. Then change back and walk out while I wasn't home. She's not human though so that never occurred to her." Remy countered crossing her arms over her flat chest.

Charlie wasn't sure what to say about that, so he only shook his head in disgust. Thankfully, Jennifer showed up halting the debate before it began. The woman had gone shopping. Her platinum hair was cut into a short shoulder length layered bob, and she wore light body armor under a tight-fitting black turtleneck. A leather shoulder harness contained a few pistol magazines and a long-bladed knife. At her waist was a larger canvas bag containing spare M107 magazines. She wore matte black spandex with knee pads, and a pair of hiking boots. Following after her were two well-muscled men dressed in identical butlers suits.

"I should thank you," Jennifer said as she neared. "After I got Sebastian to stop saluting he explained how to use him."

"I'm glad you two hit it off."

"What are we doing today?" She asked as the two weapons took up flanking positions at her sides.

"Once Tobias arrives, I thought we could discuss a few squad tactics. I'd like to wait for him to show up before we start though." Charlie said and sat down next to Grace. Withdrawing his phone again, he sent the man another message.

A couple minutes later, the final member of their small squad showed up. He walked through the lot like a man with boat anchors tied to his feet. Tobias had heavy kevlar armor on, which was covered in hundreds of paper pages. As he neared, Charlie could make out diagrams, scripture, and psalms. A metal pack frame was attached to his shoulders and connected to an articulating arm at his waist. On his back was a large square backpack with a link of ammo sticking out the top. Charlie frowned noticing that bloody two-handed sword sticking out between the backpack and his heavy armor.

Walking beside him was a young woman radiant in white. Her snowy hair was shoulder length, and she wore a thin golden circlet around her forehead like a halo. Her distinctive pupils were highlighted with a lining of dark eyeshadow. A white silk dress was split down both sides, and a thin string tied them together at the hips. The fabric hung down in front and back all the way to the ankles. A simple golden belt circled her waist, and finishing the outfit was a pair of white knee-high boots. The only thing missing was a set of wings.

"I hope you didn't use a real bible for that," Charlie said.

"Sacrilege," Tobias agreed. "No Brother, these are from the Biblica Demonica. A hundred demons once breached the gates of hades to wreak havoc on earth. Each page chronicles their capture and exorcism back to hell."

"I'm glad you made it," he said extending a hand, which Tobias took.

"Your message was timely. I had just finished preparing my armor. May I introduce Gadreel," he said gesturing to the woman behind him.

She stepped forward and extended a hand, which Charlie shook. Gadreel's palm was smooth as silk, but hard as iron.

"It's a pleasure, Toby has told me of your battle with the demons. You managed so much with so little."

"Hopefully, we'll mix it up with the Roth again. I feel better about our chances."

The angel turned to Tobias and asked, "Shall we?"

Her silky hand stroked across his roughly stubbled chin. The giant knelt like a knight helping a lady onto a horse. She took the offered hand and stepped lightly onto his raised knee. The angel turned as she began to glow and sat on the extended metal arm. There was a flash, and the GAU tri-barreled cannon appeared. The frame sagged with the weapon's weight, and Tobias tightened the cannon down. He pulled a .50 caliber ammo belt from over his left shoulder and slid it into the weapon's feed slot. Then lifted the safety on the back hand-grip and tested the yellow button. The three barrels whined as they spun up to top speed. Satisfied, he let go, and the barrels slowed to a stop.

"Before we head inside I'd like to discuss our squad makeup. Yesterday we managed mostly by stumbling along." Charlie began, and Remy laughed.

"We survived three hours with a rifle, two pistols, and a sword, which was more luck than skill." Remy scoffed.

"Which is why we need to set down our roles. Our speed is going to be dictated by the slowest member. Tobias with his heavy armor will be the anchor. He is the core of the atom, and the rest of us move around him. Jennifer, you are the fastest person here, so you're going to scout. It will be your job to stay just ahead of the group."

"I can do that."

"I will be playing fast response. If we hit enemy troops pull back to Tobias, who will be in the third position. Remy will be the rotator. Mostly she'll stay in the back, but can move to put damage on the enemy whenever necessary. Tobias, I know you're eager to test out your new weapon, but we need to hold you back. Wait for the captains. They pose the largest risk to us. We need you and Jen to concentrate on taking them out."

"Demon-kind will fear my Angel's wrath."

"Let's hope so. How much ammo did you bring?" Charlie asked.

"Thanks to you, I bought the pack which holds six hundred rounds."

Charlie waved goodbye to Grace, and she lifted a hand in a small gesture. They headed inside and found the place crammed with people accessing the consoles. The screens all displayed the same message.

**<<Matches Canceled Due to Alien Invasion>>**
**<<Event briefing begins at 11 am>>**

Together the team signed up and followed the crowd into the elevators. Lobby One was packed with even more players than yesterday, and all the couches were already taken. An invisible barrier kept the central dais empty. Charlie waved everyone toward a less populated portion of the lobby and ended up near a couple of hanging display screens.

Charlie waited along with the rest, and shortly before eleven, the wrinkled Colonel Blake climbed the stage steps. He strode purposefully to the console at the center, pressed a few buttons, and absolute silence descended. Remy had been in the middle of an off-color joke, and he was grateful for the interruption. The Colonel turned and looked at the camera, and it zoomed in on the man as he began to pace. Another ten seconds passed as he walked back and forth in silence. Finally, he sucked in his breath as if preparing himself for the long-winded briefing.

"First, I'd like to say I was tickled pink by yesterday's display. There were some truly heroic efforts. Thank you, and I mean that from the bottom of my wrinkled old heart."

"Not everyone got to play patty cake with the aliens though, so we're going to start this briefing with a small recap. Most of you fought the Roth, so I'll make this quick." He paused until the screens flicked over to an image of the moon. A tiny red smudge was floating around the pot marked lunar surface. Dots approached the Earth as if on fast forward. Then the view shifted to a few seconds of the alien landing, followed by the fighting. The screen froze as a long-limbed extraterrestrial warrior entered the picture. It zoomed in on the creature until it dominated the shot.

"The Roth. That name first appeared in radio traffic caught by SETI when they first attacked Earth forty years ago. They are bipedal creatures that stand anywhere from six to eight feet tall."

"We think the soldiers you fought yesterday are the runts. Frantic and untested children just out of alien boot camp. They send them here to cut their teeth killing humans. The light suits they wear are equivalent to our medium armor. Most pistol rounds won't fully penetrate, but rifle calibers will. The Roth are also tougher. On average a soldier takes thirty percent more damage to kill then a human."

"The captains are slightly older and more blooded. They are far more dangerous and accounted for most of our casualties. The heavy armor they wear is better than ours, and the cameras mounted on their shoulders are capable of night vision. The captains can also detect electrical broadcasts. That will be less an issue today, but I'll explain why later." The view changed to show a red-suited alien. These usually stood a foot taller, especially in the thick armor.

Several alien weapons appeared on the screen, which settled on a laser carbine. "The Roth weaponry is very effective at penetrating armor. At close range, light armor doesn't do any good, but medium and heavy armor will grant some protection. Battlefield pickups are impossible. They set up a failsafe in their weapons to explode on death." The colonel said pausing again. Video of a familiar giant started to play. He manhandled the dropped laser cannon and turned it on the Roth. Several nearby people silently cheered as he cut an alien soldier in half. Then the weapon exploded sending Tobias's charred remains into the building.

"Their suits will also send out an SOS signal to nearby squads, so this makes killing even lone aliens dangerous. Most often we became engaged and were swamped by the support. We died. Oh yes, so many died. Just over 1.6 million players took part in yesterday's worldwide event. Only eight survived to the end."

"Eight..." he repeated slowly. For a few seconds, he let that solemn single digit sink in.

"Today we are taking the gloves off. Everyone will receive an unlimited number of respawns, so death is no longer the end of the match."

"Your objective is to capture one or more of the alien dropships. Thankfully, for once, we do know something. The wreck we took forty years ago was severely damaged, and most of it was crushed into scrap. The eggheads managed to reconstruct what the layout should be." He said and waited for the screen to change again. The wire frame of a ship appeared which spun slowly, and revealed the hallway layout.

"Each dropship is 124 meters long and split into three decks. The lowest level is where the ramp entrance is located. After the drop pods are deployed, it is turned into a storage and assembly area. Two stairs lead up to the main deck on the left and right side. The biggest challenge will be breaching the cloning bay, and you must either secure or destroy it to advance further. From this point, you must take control of both the bridge and engineering. The reactor room is located at the rear of the main deck. Failure will result in the ship's systems being sabotaged. Moving forward will lead to the command deck. This objective must be captured as well, or the ship's commander will self-destruct the vessel."

"Take a minute to memorize the layout," he instructed. The wireframe slid to a sidelong view displaying the three individual decks. The command deck was isolated via a switch-back set of stairs. The viewpoint swung to a top-down cross section of the main floor. The central room was labeled as 'cloning bay,' and a hallway ran the length of the ship. Most of the rooms to either side were labeled as equipment storage.

"There are four dropships located in Los Angeles, so that means four chances."

Finally, the view shifted back to the old Colonel. His wrinkles deepened as he grimaced like a man who'd just swallowed something bitter. "The good news, the French, English, and Chinese have each captured dropships earlier today. The bad news is the Roth know about our cloning centers. They will begin actively searching for them. If they destroy them, you will no longer be able to respawn at that location."

The screen flicked over to a map of Los Angeles. Highlighted were the known locations of the alien dropships. Six blue icons were spread around the city a safe distance from any dropship. "The first time you spawn it will be at a random respawn center. Squad leaders will decide which location the group returns too."

The colonel clapped his hands. "Onto the good stuff. Anyone who steps foot on a dropship within an hour of its capture gets a match win. If you're still alive when the ship is captured; you get four match wins. Killing a Roth soldier still earns you one thousand credits, and a captain four thousand. Slaying the ship's commander is worth twenty thousand credits."

The old man paused as if collecting his thoughts. "Most of the supply cache's have been destroyed, so don't bother looking for them. You'll respawn with a full loadout each time anyway. If you're desperately low on ammo, just scavenge the dead bodies." He paused again, and took a deep breath before he continued, "I'm not going to bullshit you. This event is going to be a long slog, so prepare yourselves for a battle of attrition."

Blake tapped the console to unmute the crowd before asking, "Any questions before we wrap up?"

"Why don't we all just attack one ship?"

"That might work, but it comes with some risk. While you're concentrating on one dropship, the other three will be out looking for our cloning centers."

"Can we work together?"

"Of course, but our radio network is still rudimentary. You'll only be able to communicate with those within a mile or so. The aliens can still track your broadcasts. But, well... If everyone's talking, you can blanket them in traffic."

"How fast do they respawn?"

"Each ship can support about four thousand troops. Our clones take about a minute to fully form, but it has been forty years. The Roth's cloning technology might have improved. Expect them to be slightly faster."

There were a few seconds of silence, and no one else ventured to raise a hand. "Our time is about up, but you have a few minutes until the mission begins. Discuss among yourselves what you plan on doing." He said and walked off the stage. A map of Los Angeles and the dropship's layout was left flickering on the screens.

Charlie glanced at his team. Tobias was kneeling on the ground deep in a solemn prayer as he whispered to himself. Remy was drawing silly faces on her 40mm grenades in black sharpie, and Jen nervously examined her new high-powered rifle. She lifted the weapon to her shoulder, and looked through the 15x scope, then adjusted one of the round knobs.

"We going in balls deep?" Remy asked putting the finishing touches on her latest doodle. The face had a set of goofy eyes and a tongue that stuck out. She opened the breach on her launcher and slid it into the first cylinder.

"It depends on where we spawn. At the very least, we can stake out a dropship and watch it for a while." Charlie replied. The clock ran down quickly until darkness took them all.

### [Event Started]

A door opened before Charlie and he was bodily shoved down a ramp. He stumbled to the bottom along with the rest of his squad. Behind him, the door snapped closed, and the machine started processing the next respawning player. He quickly checked his equipment, while Remy, Jen, and Toby did the same.

They were in an out-of-date fish canning factory, and the walls were red brick patched over with crumbling cement. The packing machines were long gone. Instead, a hundred cloning vats were disgorging a flurry of soldiers. Near the main exit was a map of Los Angeles, including their location. The squad had spawned at the marine harbor at Long Beach. The nearest Roth dropship was about four kilometers to the east.

A console was located near the door, where presumably, Charlie could select one of six spawn locations. The squad collected near the map, and he pointed to a spot on the northside of Long Beach.

"Let's head here. Most of California beach is flat as a pancake, but there is a large hill just past the dropship. If we can climb it, we should get a good vantage point. Especially with Jennifer's new toy."

She smiled, enjoying her new role. Charlie borrowed Remy's marker to make a crude drawing on the back of his hand.

The wave breakers and retention wall had long ago washed away, so the ocean was flooding into the streets of Long Beach. Water surrounded them on three sides with a single rocky land bridge connecting the harbor to the mainland. Crashed upon those huge boulders was a large commercial fishing boat. Its metal hull was rusted through exposing the skeleton underneath.

Standing atop the deck was a dozen heavily armed men. Each possessed a high caliber rifle or stood behind a mounted machine gun. They were dressed in matching gray camo, with a mask over their faces, and a red band around their arms. He suspected they were NPC guards set to watch over the gap. They'd hold off any Roth forces long enough for spawning players to mobilize. The land bridge made for a formidable choke point, but it could work against them. If the Roth took the mainland side, it would completely bottle up the spawn point. Charlie and his team joined several hundred others as they walked past the ship. Remy stopped just on the other end, spread her arms out, and took in several deep breaths.

"Do you smell that?"

"I only smell the ocean and a burning city," Charlie admitted.

"Exactly, its enough to get a girl's panties wet," Remy said dragging in another lung full of burnt Los Angeles. Charlie ignored the comment and tapped Jennifer on the shoulder.

"Take point."

Tobias waddled silently along at a snail's pace. Jennifer ran forward while Charlie walked a few feet ahead of the tank. The squad fell behind as they spread out from the factory in a wave. Most of players moved east, but Charlie aimed his team north.

To the left, the avenue was flooded. A submerged bus and several cars were visible in the crystal clear water. Colorful fish darted in and out of the broken windows, and crabs crawled under the vehicles. Ten or twelve groups were well ahead and jogging up the street. The sound of a high pitched whine pierced the air. Two blocks down the glass wall of a car dealership began to glow red for an instant. In the explosion of glass, a heavy beam shot across the lot, and several hapless men vanished in less than a second. The remaining squad members scattered as more laser fire rained down on the column of players. Charlie halted in surprise. The Roth were way closer to the spawn center than expected.

Jennifer ran forward while Charlie shouldered his rifle and quickly scanned the windows around them for more Roth. Gunfire sprayed at the sports car dealership, but it was desperate and wild as the players struggled against the well-planned ambush. The squad moved forward another block and waded across a partially flooded street until they reached the side of the dealership's building. Jennifer held up a hand with four fingers, then pointed through the side window. She backed away as Charlie looked inside. Four aliens had taken up a position on the second floor. The glass front gave a commanding view of the street and the dozen player squads under fire.

*"So the aliens can learn,"* Charlie mused to himself.

Tobias plowed through the waist-high water toward them, while Remy held her weapon above her head as she struggled to keep from drowning.

"Can you put grenades on that second floor?"

"Easy peezy," she admitted after spitting the water out of her mouth.

"Tobias, wait here with Remy and keep an eye on those stairs. Engage only if a captain shows up."

Both nodded, and Charlie smashed the window with his rifle butt. Remy poked the barrel of her grenade launcher through the gap and fired. The first grenade bounced off the ceiling and landed on the second floor in a brilliant flash. The following round struck in the same spot exploding in a spray of smoke and shrapnel. While Remy hosed down the upper floor, Charlie and Jen sloshed around the side.

He peeked through the front doors. One dead alien was visible laying over the balcony railing. Charlie made sure Fara was on full-auto before he pushed inside. Jen followed with her rifle aimed at the second-floor balcony. The water inside was ankle deep, and he felt exposed on the show-floor. He ducked next to a blue colored Maserati and waited for Jen to find her own cover. She knelt next to a Silver Aston Martin and gestured with a finger to the far side of the second floor. With the rifle aimed at the landing he walked backward one step at a time.

Charlie was only halfway up the stairs when three aliens jumped over the balcony to the waterlogged lobby below. Two green colored soldiers roll to a stop next to Jen's cover. The third was a massive red suit that dropped straight down in a shower of broken tiles. Charlie ignored the armored captain and aimed at the first soldier as it rose. He squeezed the trigger in a long burst. Bullets stitched the creature's back, and it fell forward onto the expensive sports car.

The second alien ran around the vehicle's side directly into Jen. She held the long rifle awkwardly while laying in shallow water. There was a deafening boom, and the grunt sailed backward with it's green chest armor pierced through front and back. Blood sprayed out as it landed a few feet away. The Captain turned aiming directly at Charlie as its heavy cannon charged. He had time to admire the massive weapon up close. The red glow inside the cannon really was like the Gates of Hell.

From outside a rain of lead punched through the wall and slammed into the heavy armor. Several rounds cut apart its back shoulder, and the laser cannon drooped. It fired down into the water flash steaming it in an explosion. Charlie was forced to duck on the stairs as the fusillade continued. He tried shouting for Tobias to cease fire but the noise was cataclysmic. Finally, after the longest thirty seconds of his life, the tempest ended.

The smoke and steam slowly dissipated, and Charlie was amazed he was still alive. He patted himself checking for damage. The bottom part of the stairs and the lobby cars were shredded. Tobias broke through the wall holding up his glowing tri-barreled weapon. The Roth captain and his armor were in little bits, and pieces of plate were scattered about as if the suit had exploded. Both the legs had been melted off, and a single arm was still attached by ribbons, but the rest of its torso was a picture of destruction.

Remy crawled through the hole next as she continued to load grenades into her weapon. Charlie reached up fingering his right ear and was rewarded with a pop as sound came back.

"Jennifer," Charlie called into the silence. A bedraggled and soaked woman stood from behind the ruined sports car. She dripped stinking water but was otherwise unhurt. They'd survived their first encounter, which he could be happy about. His boots splashed in the yellow tinted muck as Charlie jumped from the upper stairs to the lobby floor.

"That was..."

"Loud," Jennifer suggested.

"I was going to say impressive, but yes. Loud too." He said turning to Tobias. "You're out of ammo now?"

"Yes, a demon dared stand before thee, and I was carried away in my zeal." He admitted.

"Now you know why I don't use heavy machine guns. They are like two-pump chumps. Once they run out of juice, they are little more than big paperweights." Remy said sliding the cylinder closed on her weapon.

"Your grenades wouldn't have done much against a heavy either," Jen said sloshing forward. She pulled the partial magazine free of the rifle and reloaded.

"True,"

"Whatever, we'll head back and get a resupply. It won't even take that long." Charlie said and motioned for everyone to head outside.

"Hopefully big boy here won't dump his load again on the first attractive alien that comes along," Remy said adjusting her grenade belts. As Charlie passed Remy, he gave the girl a slap to the back of the head.

"Hey," she called after him.

Tobias sloshed through the water toward the street, but Charlie easily caught up with him.

"We came out alive, which is always a win in my book. Anyways, Remy had a nasty way of saying you should try firing in one-three second bursts."

"I'm sorry."

"Tobias, I'm glad you're on the team. Don't let Remy's snarky attitude get to you." Charlie said moving beside him.

"When it comes to slaying demons I shan't let anything stop me."

"Good," Charlie called back.

# CHAPTER TWENTY-FOUR
## *Dropship Pt2*

The street was littered with human bodies from the ambush. It had been a surprise, and Charlie felt highly annoyed. That last move to jump from the balcony hit a little too close to home, like the aliens were adapting by stealing tactics they'd seen used on them. Charlie paused next to a female corpse. Her weapons were gone, but at its shoulder, the radio was squawking. He bent and stole the equipment from the dead player, because she'd respawn with a new one anyway. The squad turned towards the Marina as Charlie played with his new toy. He turned the channels back and forth, and listened in.

"Roth on 9th and Jackson, waiting in ambush."

[Click]

"Travis you stupid motherfu—"

[Click]

"Shee't, did these guys rank up overnight?" Someone asked, and Charlie flicked the channel again.

"Move to West Anaheim Street; the aliens have destroyed the bridge to Ocean Boulevard." A female voice said.

Now, that was useful information. The Los Angeles River cut through Long Beach nearby. The bridges would be natural choke points, and the aliens were making it hard to move around the city. It was a good thing they'd been stopped by this ambush because he'd planned to cross the river near that location.

Los Angeles felt like a war zone, and the aliens were in control. They reached the respawn center after a few minutes of backtracking. The massive wave of soldiers had slowed until a trickle was coming out of the pod doors. Tobias approached one, and it slid open for him. As he stepped inside the pod snapped closed, and lights flashed around the seals. He was gone for maybe ten seconds before it spat Tobias out like something foul tasting. At the bottom of the ramp, the tank verified his weapon was loaded. Satisfied, they turned to leave.

Once past the choke point, Charlie turned to the group directly north and navigated the maze of flooded streets. The trip was made slower by Tobias, but after twenty minutes they reached a battle raging at the bridge. Charlie halted a block down from the fighting to watch. Two players in light armor tried to sprint across the concrete span. All of the cars had been pushed from the bridge into the river below, so there wasn't a sliver of cover to hide behind. Neither man made it more than halfway under the hail of accurate laser fire, and several squads haphazardly fired back on the Roth positions across the street.

"I don't like it," Charlie said mostly to himself. He could take his group further north and hope for an easier crossing, but suspected the highway bridge would be equally protected. It was late summer and water was about half of its usual level. Fording the river under the bridge might be possible. He pointed to a tall billboard next to the street. "Jen get on that and give those aliens something to keep their heads down. Tobias, you'll have to stay here with Jen. Remy and I are going to swim across the river."

Charlie needed to lose some of his gear. He stripped out of his jacket and armor, dropping them to the ground. Remy whistled at him as Charlie tugged his shoes and pants off.

"That's what I like to see," Remy said eyeing him. Charlie ignored the comment as he refastened the holster to his thigh and stuffed Elva inside.

Remy was already dressed for swimming so followed him to the high rocky berm. Behind them, Jen climbed onto the billboard and quickly laid down. She dialed the scope to two hundred meters, which was point-blank range for the fifty caliber rifle she was using. After a few seconds, Jen opened up with a series of loud booms. Charlie rose and ran barefoot to the chain-link fence. He put his hands together waiting for Remy. The schoolgirl dashed to him, and Charlie tossed her over the barrier. Several lasers zipped past as he climbed over himself. There was another boom. Together he and Remy ran down the bank. The water was warm as Charlie hit the river, and he quickly dove under the surface. Remy passed him as she kicked to the bottom. Then pulled herself along using the rocks and sunken cars. He followed the bikini-clad girl through the clear water.

Witnessing Charlie's attempt, other squads rushed to jump in the river. Some dared the bridge again as the aliens were temporarily pinned down. Lasers zipped overhead as the Roth responded, and one or two beams sizzled into the water but quickly dissipated in flashes of steam.

Charlie broke the surface on the other side. Above them, the battle picked up again as both sides fought to control the bridge. Remy popped open her cylinder and reloaded with grenades covered in pictures of clouds. Then fired over the edge, and pink smoke began to fill the street.

They vaulted the next fence, and crept through the haze until they hit the side of a three-story office building. Above them, lasers were firing from the second and third floor. Remy patted him on the back, then pointed to herself, and gestured toward the front of the building. Finally, she poked him and pointed toward a side employee entrance.

Charlie nodded and shuffled along the wall as Remy ran around the side. The employee entrance was kicked open and hanging by a single hinge. Inside powdered milk and creamer covered the coffee lounge. Around the front, a brass bell rang as the customer entrance opened. A white armored alien jumped out of the supply closet and aimed it's weapon down the hallway. Charlie stepped through the door and fired at the young warrior while it's back was turned.

"Captain!" Remy called from inside the lobby.

Charlie ran forward to the lounge door. There was a short hallway with offices on each side. At the end, the captain was standing with legs apart aiming at Remy. Charlie unloaded the M16 at it's back, but his bullets only dug grooves into the armor like he was chipping paint. Two magnum rounds hit the captain in the helmet sending out sparks, before it fired into the lobby. The beam cut apart the reception desk, and Remy burned in a flash of energy.

A wave of superheated air hit Charlie in the face as he ran forward. His lungs burned, but he transitioned to his pistol in a single fluid motion. Elva was cold to the touch and still wet from the trip through the river. Charlie slid to a stop behind the giant armor. He hadn't realized just how tall the Captains were from afar. This one was a few inches over seven feet. On its back was a rounded pack of equipment that powered the suit and filtered the oxygen out of the air. There were small vents dotted around, and he shoved his pistol into a random one. He pulled the trigger and Elva went off with a muffled pop.

The creature spun ponderously knocking Charlie into the supervisor's office and he landed on a desk. Behind him the towering captain dropped its laser cannon, and clawed at its blank visor trying to pull it off. With a hiss, the thickly armored helmet felt to the ground.

The alien's scaled skin was slightly yellowish instead of green, and an intricate black mark was burned into the right side of its face. The creature dragged in a lung full of air and immediately coughed up yellow blood. It staggered sideways crashing through the thin wall into the opposite office. The captain spat more ichor as Charlie retrieved Elva from the ground, then stepped to the side of the large suit, and looked down. The alien coughed again and glanced up with it's beady golden eyes. Charlie put two rounds into the top of the Roth's head, and the four-fingered hand dropped to the stained carpet. Almost immediately the suit began to bleat like a disgruntled sheep.

He turned and walked into the office lobby, then balked at the stench. Remy's body was a charred corpse. One crispy arm hung in the air, and a black fist was giving the Roth the cheeky finger. Armored boots approached the stairs, and Charlie quickly laid on the ground next to the charred corpse. He pulled the husk of Remy in close as the alien came down the steps. It was suited in green armor and carried a large pulse rifle. Charlie held his breath while the Roth scanned the lobby.

On the landing, it aimed down the hallway to the lounge. Charlie raised the 1911 and fired what was left of the mag, and holes appeared across its green armored side. The creature jerked, rolled down the stairs, and slid to a stop at the bottom. Immediately it began to bleep that annoying SOS and another pair of armored boots pounded the floor above him. Charlie rolled to his feet and ran for the laser rifle on the ground. It was heavy, but he managed to aim it up the stairs. The last alien had orange armor on and was carrying a new type of laser weapon. It was five feet long with a thick square scope on top.

They both fired. Charlie's weapon let out a whine, and three beams shot from the end. His laser bolts hit the Roth in the chest, and it's armor plates sagged in. The sniper's tightly focused laser sliced past his right side and burned a long streak in the carpet. Then it fell over the staircase railing, and slammed into the bottom floor. The alien weapon in Charlie's hands grew warm as the beeping reached a climax. He tossed the alien laser away, but it exploded showering him with bits of hot metal.

Welp, that was it. He had a few rounds left in his pistol, but Fara was empty and dangled on the sling across his chest. The brass bell jingled as Charlie pushed from the front entrance. Aliens were still firing on the bridge, but some players were making it across and swarmed the surrounding buildings. Several paused to look at him standing outside in his boxers, and covered in blood. Tobias and Jen crossed the bridge after another ten minutes. The sniper held out his clothes, which he took.

"Remy dead?"

"She's smart enough to catch up, so we will wait for her," Charlie grunted, pulling on his pants and shoes.

He tore the white shirt into four large pieces to use as bandages and tied them crudely around his stomach. Then he tugged on the armor and green jacket. Tobias kept watch nearby, while Jen scanned the road to the east. The radio was squawking again with traffic, but most of it was about the Anaheim bridge. Charlie clipped the speaker to his lapel, then took the time to reload.

Remy joined them as he finished up. The teal haired elementary school girl trotted across the bridge with a fresh bandolier of grenades. Together, they headed north past the warehouses, then east toward Hilltop Park, but they took their time securing each intersection. Charlie learned the hard way that the aliens loved ambushes.

Upper-middle-class houses lined the winding path up the hill. After an hour they finally made the summit. All but Tobias crawled across the overgrown grass to the edge of the park, and Charlie parted the hedgerow to peek through. About half a kilometer to the south the Roth Dropship sat like an engorged blood tick upon the track field. Respawning soldiers ran down the ramp in small groups and dispersed into the city.

Jennifer pushed her rifle through the thick bush, and used the 15x scope to scan the field. "There are defenses. Cables are running from the ship to two fixed emplacements."

She pointed with her hand. On either side of the park, the Roth had constructed a high platform, and heavy cannons were mounted in armored positions. Black cables ran across the ground to each. Only one turret was visible from this angle, but the fact the dropship was powering them was a little worrying.

The urban fighting spread out along six blocks south and east of the ship. Charlie could see smoke from an explosion and lasers shooting between the buildings. Automatic gunfire continuously raged like the buzzing of angry hornets, and he wasn't interested in sticking his nose into that nest. After about two hours, the Roth stopped running out into the city. Instead, a horde gathered outside of the ship on the field.

Jen watched them through her scope. "Twelve hundred and some change," she said after the Roth finally stopped coming out. As one body they moved directly west toward the Marina. Charlie turned the radio back on and repeated her words.

"Now might be a good time to attack the dropship, while the aliens are moving out." He suggested.

"Ok, everyone push hard, and get to the field." A Female voice replied back.

Charlie turned to their sniper and asked, "Jen, can you take out the fixed gun?"

"I might be able to kill a crew-member, but they'll just replace them. The weapon armor is thick, so it may be easier to hit the cables. They're six or so inches in diameter, so maybe... I could hit them." Jen said hesitantly. She pulled a piece of paper out of her magazine pouch. On it was a list of numbers, which Jennifer double checked. Then she dialed up the elevation knob on her 15x scope.

"Take your time."

Jen snuggled up to the weapon and put her cheek against the pad. Slowly she took aim, let out her breath and held it for two seconds, then squeezed the trigger. The M107 fired with a massive boom. The impact was visible as a spray of dust several feet below the cable.

"Way low," she muttered and dialed the knob six more clicks.

Charlie could only watch with his naked eye as she fired again. From the field, a dark beam of red energy lanced out and struck the house just below them. The wall burned through in a second filling the air with smoke. Jen let out her breath, focused on her sight alignment, and fired again.

"Fuck, so close." She hissed as dust kicked up inches shy of the cable. The cannon picked another house nearby and started cutting it up. The Barrett M107 bucked as Jen fired two more shots, and she reloaded with a fresh magazine.

"Not to rush you, but the Roth are running out of houses to shoot," Remy said from nearby. There was a loud crackle of burning air as a beam sliced the top off a palm tree ten meters away. The flaming fronds caught the dry grass under the tree on fire.

Jen let out a long breath to steady her nerves and settled her cheek against the padded stock. She squeezed the trigger slowly until the weapon thundered. The round sailed through the air leaving a long wake. Half a kilometer downrange the thin black thread snapped apart, and one end flailed turning the sand into glass.

"Good job! Now the second one, before we get off this burning hilltop." Charlie said slapping the sniper on the shoulder. She shifted to aim at the second cable, and thankfully, this emplacement couldn't shoot back. Jen quickly blew the wire apart with a few more shots.

The silenced guns were the signal the players had been waiting for. The surrounding blocks lit up in battle. The dry hilltop was ablaze as they ran down the slope. Charlie's squad pushed south on the field along with twenty others, and he sprinted for the back of the dropship.

The ship was about four stories tall, and rested on the six enormous thrusters. The loading ramp was lowered, so Remy fired several HE rounds inside. Charlie paused at the bottom waiting for Tobias to catch up. Half a dozen squads pushed past him. Remy was already inside squealing with joy firing grenades across the lower deck. Jen took up a position to the left of the ramp, aimed at a building near the east side, and fired several shots.

Ponderously, Tobias climbed up the steep ramp. Charlie backed inside and called, "Jen." The sniper fired one more round then climbed to her feet and followed.

Crates of scavenged metal filled half the lower deck. A machine churned the scrap into base components before feeding them into more bins. He found Remy hiding behind a metal crate full of gold scrap. A laser burn scoured her right shoulder leaving a third-degree burn, but Remy smiled like a shark as she reloaded the cylinder of her grenade launcher. Tobias stepped from his cover on the right side and aimed at the stairs in the back. The three barrels spun up to full speed, and Charlie clapped his hands over his ears. A fusillade of bullets sprayed across the deck punching holes into the wall, and several descending aliens were cut apart in the storm.

Ahead of Charlie, a squad of girls leap-frogged toward the right stairwell. On the left, a second group picked their way over the dead aliens. Charlie followed the ladies up to a small landing. Two sets of double doors formed a simple airlock, and a thick square button was mounted on the wall next to it. The first girl to reach the landing slapped it with a gloved hand. It lit up gold, and the door opened onto row after row of pods.

Three aliens popped out of the respawn pods already suited up for war. They turned and fired a pulse of lasers out of the open door, and the two women returned fire while a third pulled the pin on a couple of smoke grenades. She tossed them through inside while Charlie motioned for Tobias.

"We found the alien spawn room," Charlie said pushing the man ahead of him.

"The Lord will be pleased when we sanctify this altar of evil." Came the muffled reply.

Tobias walked forward as the Gatling Cannon began to spit righteous destruction. The steel storm turned right spraying indiscriminately across the cloning bay. Remy followed him through the smoking doorway, and pumped grenades in the opposite direction. Charlie and Jen went in next, along with another squad of girls. Yellow blood and blue cloning fluid covered the floor. A wounded alien soldier came toward him with a cracked visor, and several holes were leaking yellow blood. The carbine it carried fired, and the laser skipped past Charlie's head. Fara bucked against his hip and bullets hammered the Roth. As it fell, Charlie put a few more rounds into its faceplate. In the thick smoke, it wasn't hard to kill the Roth. The lasers left a brief, but visible trail to their location. He raised his weapon and shot at a second creature.

Finally, Charlie managed to find a console near the middle of the room, which was filled with the golden alien script. The first objective was to capture or destroy the spawn room, but he had no idea how to stop the Roth from respawning. A pod ten feet away opened spitting out a white-suited youth, and it looked around in surprise. Charlie drew his 1911 and fired on the Roth as it turned to look at him. The bullet punched through the vulnerable faceplate and into the alien's open mouth. It flopped to the deck. With a prayer, Charlie turned the pistol on the console and emptied the rest of his clip into the screen. The lights in the cloning bay flickered and went out.

Charlie was plunged into darkness with the rest of the assaulting humans. An ear-splitting alarm sounded, and blinking red lights illuminated the room. He found Jen and Remy near the right side. Both wrestled with a spawning soldier. Remy had a hold of its weapon arm, while Jen's long legs were wrapped around its right side as she drove her dagger up into its helmet. A captain lay nearby with several .50 caliber holes punched into its back. Now, the aliens wouldn't be able to respawn. However, if Charlie were the commander, he'd be setting the self-destruct soon. They had to take the ship fast. More humans were piling into the darkened cloning bay from the lower deck.

They found Tobias near the front of the cloning bay hacking at a pod with his sword. The man's eyes were positively glowing with his fervor, and the pages covering his armor were splattered with blue and yellow gore.

"Tobias, we are moving on," Charlie called. Tobias stood from the remains of the destroyed pod and followed along after Jen and Remy.

The door forward opened revealing a long hallway. At the end was the landing for the double back stairs. Two alien squads knelt behind fixed positions and started to fire. There was no cover, and Charlie forced open an equipment room door. He hurried inside with Tobias right behind him. Remy squeezed in next, which left Jennifer to buddy up on the other side.

*"Well, that's a meat blender."* Charlie thought. A man from another squad tried to fire off a burst, but was lanced by a dozen lasers.

"Smoke grenades again?" Remy suggested. That had worked well last time, and he nodded.

She popped open her MGL and refilled it, then bounced the grenades off the opposite wall. Soon they skipped and danced along the floor spewing pink smoke. Immediately lasers cut down the hallway in a constant stream.

"Wait for a break!" Charlie shouted over the high pitched noise. Tobias unmounted his cannon, and set it down like Gadreel was made of brittle glass.

"What are you doing?" Charlie asked.

"I will bring the Word of God to these demons," he said removing the metal pack frame.

"You're not going to start that bullshit again, are you?" Remy asked incredulously.

"I am," he replied smiling, but not with those grey eyes of his. Tobias pulled off his damp helmet and unbuckled his armor. His chest underneath was covered in strange religious circles and Latin diagrams. In the hallway, the lasers were still scorching black marks up and down the walls.

"We just need to wait for reinforcements," Charlie said. Time was short, but in a minute more squads were bound to show up.

"You're gonna get your ass shot off," Remy said like it was a matter of fact.

"Have faith, deviant. Besides, my beautiful *'paperweight'* is out of ammo." Tobias said and took up his sword. He went prone on the floor and crawled into the smoke-filled hallway. He held the sword in one hand with the blade turned to protect his face.

Pink smoke continued to swirl as red lasers crisscrossed the hallway. The air smelled electric like lightning during a storm, and through that tempest, Tobias crawled forward an inch at a time. Charlie reloaded his weapons while he waited. After a minute the mist dissipated enough to make out a form. Tobias stood perfectly still halfway down the hall, with his sword held aloft. He was bare of clothes except for a thick pair of kevlar pants. He was alive, but not unhurt.

A line of black crossed over his brow leaving his left eye milky and blind. Another black mark ran over his scalp burning his peach fuzz off. Four more laser shots had grazed his back, and his blade had half a dozen holes melted into it. Maybe all those protective tattoos did him some good after all. The pink smoke thinned, and Tobias became visible standing in the open hallway, so there was no way the aliens didn't see him.

"Come, heathens! Hear the Word of God and be purified." He thundered. Remy laughed despite herself. Seconds passed as the Roth continued to aim down the hallway. Then a single warrior jumped over the armored wall and ran toward Tobias. His one good eye fixed on the Roth. It was unarmed but a foot taller than the giant man. Its suit was a sophisticated shade of colors like it had graduated from being one of the masses.

The Roth attacked, but Tobias didn't even move. He shifted his weight to his back leg and slashed the blade across at an angle. The alien sailed passed him in two parts and rolled down the hallway. The next Roth leaped from the stairs and sprinted forward, with one hand ahead of it as it tried to tackle the crusader. Tobias roared and brought the two-handed sword down. The blade severed the soldier's arm, shoulder, and part of its torso. A set of lungs and both its hearts spilled out.

Charlie was astonished that it was working. Even if Tobias died, he'd thrown the Roth into a glory-seeking frenzy. Two more soldiers started to step from cover, but they froze as a roar echoed down the stairs. From the command deck, a truly massive suit crashed to the main level. It was immaculate with golden plates, and instead of a helmet, it's lower face was covered with a breathing regulator.

"Satan shows himself at last," Tobias said with a smile. His single wintry eye glittered at the Roth with something approaching madness. The commander stood close to eight feet tall, with dark red skin and little white thorns coming out of its eye-ridges. Two more cream colored horns protruded from its temple curling backward. It withdrew a black saber from behind it's back, and the blade was five feet long with a curved serrated edge. In the other hand, it held a device which was blinking and pulsing.

Tobias changed his stance immediately. He took this older demon more seriously and held his blade defensively. The Commander stalked forward, and the first exchange happened fast. Tobias sidestepped and brought his weapon across his opponents stomach. The captain partially parried. Tobias's blade dug a long furrow in the armor but failed to penetrate. At the last second, Tobias jumped back from the riposte. He reached up touching the side of his head where his ear used to be.

The commander's gold eyes twinkled under his ridges, and it smiled with sharp teeth around its respirator before it dashed forward again. Tobias turned and ran at the wall. He got three steps to it and kicked off trying to gain a few more inches of height. The giant spun in midair slashing with his two-handed sword. The commander cut upward with its black saber, and Tobias's sword flashed as it sank into the opposite wall. Two severed arms were still gripping the weapon's hilt.

"I did not think the demon had courage enough to commit to that swing," Tobias muttered falling backward. Blood pumped out of the two stumps onto the floor. The commander remained standing in the hall. Slowly a line of yellow formed along its neck. Then the head slid free and rolled across the metal floor, which was followed by the body a few seconds later. The blinking device in its hand powered off. Tobias's one eye gazed up past the bulkhead to the heavens, then closed slowly.

"Holy shit. The nutjob actually knows how to use that thing. Damn it! I'm gonna have to be nicer to the Zealot from now on." Remy said.

The chain of leadership was broken, and the Roth fought to be the ship's next commander. The soldiers on the landing started shooting each other. Charlie ran forward taking the stairs before the Roth finished killing one another. He vaulted the armored railing and fired on two of the fighting defenders. His bullets caught the first in the back, and he grabbed the Roth from behind. The second Roth fired at Charlie, but the pulses blasted into the corpse's chest armor. He angled his M16 under the alien's dead arm and discharged the rest of his magazine. Remy and several others ran past him up the stairs.

The bridge was an elevated disk, and the defenders must have been the bridge crew. It was empty save two green-skinned aliens working the consoles as the others fought below. They didn't even have weapons.

Remy skipped across the short distance and daintily placed her magnum against the alien's helmet.

As it looked in her direction, she smiled and said, "Welcome to Earth."

She pulled the trigger, and the helmet snapped backward. The second crew member died less dramatically, but no less brutally. Charlie gained the bridge as Remy was cleaning her weapon of icky yellow blood.

After a few minutes, several humans came aboard carrying laptops and plastic boxes. They pulled panels off and plug in the computer. Lines of orange colored code started to scroll down the screens.

"We're in," the small man announced. The leader of the tech group went over to the Commander's chair. He sat down and placed a hand on the screen. It flashed, and he tapped a button.

"This ship has been captured," The man said, and his voice was projected around the dropship.

"Congratulations, now everyone off the ship. You have a mission to continue." He said flicking the intercomm off.

That was right. There was still three more dropships. The squad was unceremoniously dumped from the ramp. The engines bloomed, and heat blasted the grass into cinders. The players swore and dashed from the vessel as it lifted skyward. It turned east towards what he thought was Texas and disappeared. Charlie felt a little drained as he watched it go.

# CHAPTER TWENTY-FIVE

## *Spoils of War*

Charlie checked the time—7:20 pm.

The event would end at eight, so they had less than an hour left. After capturing the first dropship, things had not gone well. Not at all. Humanity was down to a single spawn center which was under constant siege.

Charlie chewed his nail and glanced at Jennifer. She was lying prone on the kitchen counter with the sniper rifle perched on the dining room table. Jen's unblinking gaze looked through the scope, and down the long avenue. The sun had set more than half an hour ago, and the night was a dark one. Charlie and his team didn't have any night-vision gear, but at least they didn't have to go far to reach the dropship. The apartment complex sat just four blocks from the nearest one. All they had to do was wait for the signal.

Tobias was keeping an eye on the stairwell, and Remy was being Remy with a squad of players in a next apartment suite. The ancient bed springs were violently protesting the carnal exploits taking place upon it. He sighed and glanced at his watch again. Barely a minute had passed, and he wondered what moron came up with this ridiculous plan. For two hours now human forces had been gathering near one dropship. At the last second, they would zerg rush the Roth in a wild gamble. In Charlie's opinion, it was a stupid plan. They wouldn't catch the aliens napping, and unlike players, NPC's didn't get bored.

"Stop pacing," Jen said in annoyance.

"I'm bored."

"Go join Remy."

There was a loud female cry from the next apartment suite. Charlie sighed, pulled Fara over his head, and set the weapon down. Then sat in a tottering dining chair, quietly wiggled his foot in the air, and glanced out the window. Outside it was pitch as black, and he lamented not bringing a flashlight into the event.

At last, ten minutes later, a grenade shot skyward and exploded in a brilliant flash. Charlie launched himself from the chair and grabbed Fara from beside him. He didn't wait for Jen as he jogged from the apartment. With a fist, he banged on the next doorway as he went past.

The mattress springs sighed in relief, and a rosy-cheeked Remy ran into the hall wearing nothing but an extra-large shirt. She carried her grenade launcher in one hand while struggling to pull on the two belts of ammo. Following after in various degrees of undress were a squad of male players.

Charlie threw himself headlong down the darkened stairs passing Tobias on the next landing. It had been a long day, and he was eager to make this one last push. Jennifer's pace was more leisurely as she trotted behind them.

Charlie waited just long enough for his team to exit the building before they started forward in a jog. Outside figures were storming the streets like a kicked anthill. In the distance red lasers began to lick out of the upper story windows. Tobias had lessened his weight by dumping half his ammo, so at least he could manage a fast walk. Ahead lasers lanced out from the defenders cutting into the rushing crowd. None stopped, not even to fire back because this plan was an all or nothing gamble.

The dropship became visible in the night. It was the only thing illuminated as it squatted over hole nine of the Wilshire Country Club. Two laser cannon emplacements started to fire. The heavy red beams lit up the sky, and Charlie lost sight of his squad in the wild rush, but it mattered little now as everyone converged on the ship.

He sprinted past a sand trap and up the ramp into the brightly lit interior. The bay was full of metal bins and churning machinery. Further inside humans were forcing their way up the stairs. Finally, he slowed and shouldered his weapon. Charlie was breathing hard as he scanned the stairs through Fara's red dot. The door to the cloning bay opened, and he fired at the Roth as it exited. Players pushed passed him even before the corpse rolled to a stop. Charlie followed them in and turned aft running past rows of pods. At the back of the chamber, there was another set of double doors.

He wasn't alone. A man with a blue mohawk slapped the control button, and Charlie aimed down the corridor. Two Roth jogged toward them through a short hallway, and he opened fire tracing both with the spray. His strange new companion went in first while Charlie reloaded. The man had two flash-bangs already unpinned as Charlie caught up and hit the door switch.

Inside, the engine room was sixty feet wide by thirty long, and two containment cylinders pulsed with green energy in the middle. The man tossed his two flashes, and they skidded toward a couple of consoles and exploded while Charlie looked away. Mr. Mohawk lead the way with a P90 SMG in his hand. He unleashed a flurry of rounds into the alien crew. Charlie turned right aiming at two more on the catwalk. They were doing something with the machine near the ceiling. Charlie tried to avoid hitting the equipment as he fired. His first burst caught the closest Roth in the back of the head. The second Roth dropped his tool and grabbed the small carbine laser hanging at its waist. Charlie knelt, aiming quickly at the new threat. Fara bucked against his shoulder and the crew member fell over the railing to the deck.

A few minutes later the ship's intercom crackled to life, and a voice said, "The ship has been captured, congratulations." Charlie lifted his weapon with the others and cheered. They didn't get booted off the ship this time. Instead, darkness closed in.

**[Event Complete]**

The arena lobby was swarming with players. He felt a mixture of relief, triumph, and mild surprise at the last minute victory. Charlie checked for his squad, but it was unlikely he'd run into any of them again tonight. Everyone would be splitting up anyway. He headed over to a free console, and checked his stats.

---

**Player ID - NA1339872**
**Registered Competition Name - Charlie**

**Clan - None**
**Hours played - 268**

**Wins - 56**
**Losses - 20**

**Kills - 82**
**Deaths - 29**
**K/D Ratio - 2.8**

**Battle Rank - Gold One**
**Player Score - 1710**

**Credits - 102,931c**


"Gold rank!" Charlie shouted jubilantly. He pumped his gloved fist in victory. Over the course of two days, he'd acquired almost forty kills, and his player score had risen two hundred points. The best part was the hundred thousand credits in his account.

It was time to head home, clean his weapons, and drag that beautiful redhead into the sack. He closed the screen and strolled from the Competition Center. Outside the street lamps did their best to dispel the darkness of the night. The sky was a panorama of twinkling lights. He strolled through the lot to his Mustang and placed Fara between the seats. The beast started with a roar, and he peeled into the street.

Charlie wasn't sure how the girls knew, but they crowded him as soon as he entered the house. The five women clung to his jacket like drunken fairies. Maybe they could detect the free contract slot like a powerful aphrodisiac, or it could have been the metallic stink of spent gunpowder and the aroma of battle. Their eyes devoured him as hands felt up his chest and arms. Sofie hugged him from behind and wrapped her arms around his neck. Her cheek pressed to the top of his head as she drank in his combat cologne. It was like being mobbed by a clutch of beautiful kittens, and Charlie found it impossible to get past the small foyer.

"Ladies, give me a minute to clean Fara and Elva. You wouldn't want to be neglected, now would you?" He asked. All except Sofie backed away a few feet.

She clung to him like a lovesick puppy and Charlie struggled to the couch. The redhead sank down next to him, and draped herself over Charlie while the others took up places in the living room. Sofie watched him, committing his every movement into memory.

He unloaded Fara first because she'd done the lion's share today. The M16 came apart like a clamshell, and he withdrew the bolt carrier. It was covered with a thick layer of residue, and he sprayed the weapon parts down with solvent. Black grime came off as he started to scrub with a wire brush. After the carrier group was shiny, he worked on the receiver and rifle bore. Then he oiled her and slid the pieces together.

Next was his 1911. Elva had been silent most of the day, but she moaned noisily as he started in on her. Fara could contain herself when she wanted. His first weapon though was as vocal as a porn star. She panted as Charlie scrubbed her slide, and especially the grooves. Her voice rose in volume as he reached the dirty breech face. Elva loved this part most of all. He oiled the pistol and assembled her like a hundred times before.

She started to glow, appeared in his lap, and sank back against him panting for breath. Fara still sat in her M16 form on the table, but Charlie suspected she was secretly recovering as well. The girls were trying not to stare at him like a bloody piece of meat.

"I think Sofie and I need some private time in the bedroom."

"Would you like me to join?" Elva asked still laying against him.

"I'd prefer to concentrate on Sofie tonight. She's waited long enough, so I'd like to give her a proper contracting." Charlie replied glancing at the giant. Elva kissed his cheek, stood, and headed into the kitchen to make dinner. He gathered the cleaning supplies and wiped his hands free of solvent. Then Charlie walked into the master bedroom. Sofie followed him inside as if on an invisible leash.

"Maybe I should shower first," he suggested pulling off his jacket and armor.

"Mmm, nyet. I like zee way you smell." She growled grabbing Charlie, and pulled him into her heaving bosom.

Her hands dug under his t-shirt, and she raked her long fingers across his stomach. Sofie smelled different than his other guns, and it was hard to pin down why. Her body odor was something halfway between sweet and waxy. It tickled his nose. Much later he discovered it was called Cosmoline, and most Soviet-era weapons were stored in the substance.

He managed to wrestle the giant red-haired woman onto the bed. She fell onto the mattress pulling him down as well. Charlie wanted this night to be a little special, so from the bedside stand, he retrieved the handcuffs. Sofie was too distracted kissing and licking Charlie's lean body to notice. He crawled atop the giant, grabbed a wrist, and worked the cuff over it. Soon both her hands were restrained to the dark oak headboard.

Her long muscled legs closed around his waist and her damp crotch ground against him. Charlie pulled his shirt off and folded it in thirds. He approached Sofie's head, but she turned it to the side.

"Nyet, I vant to see you when we contract," Sofie said.

"You don't always get what you want with me," He replied tying the cloth around her head. Charlie parted her legs and climbed from the bed to fetch some of the supplies by the nightstand.

"Vhat are you doing?" Sofie asked listening as he opened a green colored spam can. Inside were several hundred rounds of Soviet surplus ammo. He brought the container to the bed and poured the contents out onto Sofie. Bullets bounced off her breasts. More hit her hardened stomach and slid between her legs, but most rolled onto the mattress. Charlie tossed the empty can to the floor. The many metallic cartridges clinked and rang like bells as he mounted the bed.

He looked at the woman before him. Sofie was a tall girl, made more so with her arms pinned above her head. She had skin the color pale cream, and her hair was like a pool of blood against the white sheets. Unable to see him Sofie shifted, and her legs quested for Charlie.

"Do you want to contract with me, Sofie?"

"Da," Sofie breathed.

"I just demonstrated you don't get everything your way. I might even hurt you." He replied.

"I vant you. I know you are special." Sofie panted.

"Don't flinch," he ordered picking up her right leg. Charlie held her ankle and bit into the flesh. Sofie gasped at the pain, but she didn't move. Charlie alternated between kissing, licking, and biting his way down her long leg. The bullets on the bed danced as the woman squirmed under his advance. Her bikini bottom was drenched, and a little pool was forming on the sheets. He pulled on the string with his teeth.

Her sex was larger than life, with thick lips that crowded her leaking entrance. Finally exposed to the air, Sofie's strong smell hit Charlie in the nostrils, and his erection strained against the fabric of his pants. He lowered his face between her legs and kissed her pussy tenderly. Then he licked up the center drinking in her flavor. She tasted earthy like pumpkin pie with a sweet undertone. Sofie had a grape sized clitoris, and its head was already poking from under the protective hood. Charlie closed his teeth gently over it.

"Nyet!" Sofie cried closing her legs. Charlie's head was squished between her muscled thighs, and Sofie refused to release him.

"Alright, I promise not to bite you." He murmured, and she reluctantly released him. Charlie rewarded her courage by licking and sucking on her clitoris. Sofie's hips bucked and she drew in deep, ragged breaths. Lube leaked from her in a steady, unrelenting stream, and the bed sheets quickly grew slick.

"Now, now... I vant it."

Charlie unbuckled his pants and tossed them to the floor. Then pushed himself into her glistening oversized sex. It was like plunging into a hot lake as liquid slid past his shaft. His cock sank all the way inside without any effort. At the end of her hot tunnel was a tight pocket, like a special little room made just for him. Sofie gasped, unprepared for the sensation, and her legs wrapped around his waist.

He watched this time as a clear plastic collar circled Sofie's neck. It snapped closed and the woman's back arched. Around his shaft Sofie's sex tightened, squeezing down, and pulled him in deeper. Charlie slowly built up speed and a rush of lube spilled onto the bed. Each thrust into her extraordinary pussy made his mind tingle with pleasure. The bullets bounced, jingling together as the headboard banged against the wall.

Sofie's wet sex slapped like a chime and her ragged moaning added to the chorus. It was almost musical. Charlie set the rhythm to ultra fast as he pounded into her frictionless pussy.

"Sil'neye," Sofie begged straining against the handcuffs. The metal bent and the chains slowly pulled apart. Why did this game have to make sex feel so damn good? Charlie struggled with his own desire to climax, and he fought back against the wave of pleasure, but it was like holding back a river.

Charlie dragged Sofie's bikini top off. Her huge breasts bounced, and he tossed the black cloth away. Her dark nipples were like sunken ICBM's, and both were half launched already. They tasted salty and waxy, and just a touch oily as he sucked the first into his mouth. Sofie groaned as she rocked against him. He was seconds from finishing and there was no way he could hold back anymore. Thanks to Fara, he'd discovered a small secret. A little pain made the pleasure all the better, like a foundation which launched the weapon to new and glorious heights.

"I lied about not hurting you," he admitted.

Charlie bit down on her nipple as his climax began. A river of bliss raced down his spine, and his skin tingled as it flooded through him. Sofie gasped, shrieked, then cried out, and despite herself, squealed like a svin'ya. Her legs tightened around his waist as her sex spasmed on his cock. The metal links of the handcuffs snapped, and Sofie grabbed him. For almost a minute Sofie was a woman possessed, and the bullets on the bed went flying as Sofie shook uncontrollably.

Finally, she released him. Around her neck, the black collar glowed with his numbers. She reached up with a trembling hand to pull the blindfold off and looked down at him.

"Ozornoy vladelets," She said in a thick husky voice. Charlie smiled and withdrew from her drenched sex. He glided across the slick sheets and fetched several shopping bags from near the nightstand.

"You may want to shower first, but these are for you."

The surplus ammo clinked together as the giant Russian climbed from the bed. She reached out, but Charlie didn't let the bags go right away. He hung onto them and said, "Welcome to the family."

Sofie's eyes danced as she bent and kissed him. "I so confused," she growled taking the offered bags. "You are so sweet, and so mean in the same breath. Why do I want more of both?"

Charlie laughed turning the woman around. He slapped her ass hard sending the giant toward the master bathroom. Sofie swayed drunkenly across the carpet before clinging to the door jam. Her steel eyes looked back at him, searched his face, and memorized every detail. He made a shooing gesture, and she closed the door. A few seconds later the shower turned on.

Turning back to the scene of destruction, and Charlie let out a long sigh. The bed was an ocean. A five-foot diameter stain marked the place the Russian redhead had lost her virginity, and slimy bullets covered the mattress like golden Koi. Everything about Sofie was big, including the cleanup.

# CHAPTER TWENTY-SIX
## *Testing Range*

A few days had passed since they'd taken the alien dropships. The Roth had been so angered by the losses they'd immediately burned Los Angeles, London, Paris, and Shanghai to the ground. Afterward, the aliens had sent a dozen more raids, though they were far more careful with their landing craft. Humanity had started the 'Emergency Roth Channel' to warn players when they'd arrive and where. However, it was impossible to predict if you'd encounter a patrol during a game.

Charlie was finally able to play a match since the alien invasion, and he was eager to try out Sofie in battle. The private lounge was dimly lit. All the screens were scrolling the same warning, "Roth activity detected across the globe."

Sofie straddled his lap as they waited for the countdown timer to hit zero. She combed her fingers through Charlie's hair, and he looked up into her steel colored eyes. The tall woman wore a single one-piece leather outfit with a zipper running down her front. A pair of broken handcuffs from their first contracting circled her wrists, and she'd refused to take them off. The NPCs had didactic memory, but she liked being reminded that Charlie was both; pain and pleasure. Her shockingly red hair was tied back with a piece of cloth, also from that night.

They weren't alone though, and the other party members were waiting nearby. Charlie needed to stop Sofie before things got too heated. He pushed the Russian giant away slightly and said, "Weapon form." The woman pouted, but began to glow. Her skin flashed brilliantly and a long SVD sniper rifle fell into his lap. Charlie picked up the lacquered weapon, and slid his hand over the frame. A Russian made PSO scope hung above the upper receiver. At least now he had a better idea how to use it since Sofie had taught him the basics.

Remy, Jen, and Tobias were all sitting together on the opposite couches. Remy was dressed in a blue one-piece bathing suit with light armor strapped over her flat chest. She was grinning at Charlie as he tried to adjust the bulge in his pants. Tobias's armor was covered in scriptures again, but he had removed his heavy helmet. More symbols were etched into his cheeks and forehead. Jen looked the most professional of the group. She had tan colored shorts with a desert-camo vest.

Finally the last person entered the room. The male player had a set of medium armor, and wore Kevlar kneepads over a pair of slacks. Across his back was an automatic shotgun, and in his hands was a heavily scoped M14 scout rifle. He had no backpack or molle vest, but instead, carried several pouches around his waist. The player threw himself onto a couch, and waited while the timer quickly ran down.

**[Match Start]**

The air smelled like old decay. The buildings nearby were slowly being torn down by kudzu vines and the weather. Charlie was standing in a shallow marsh along with the rest of his squad. Water immediately filled his combat boots, and soaked his pants all the way to his waist. A pint-sized gator glided away from them and into a deeper pool. They had to be in the south, somewhere in Louisiana probably, but it was hard to tell. The wetland was slowly retaking the crumbling city.

The final man—a random add to the group—was scanning the weed ridden marsh in either direction. This was Charlie's first gold match since ranking up, but Remy had once been platinum.

"Remy where's the center?" He asked.

"No idea yet, the maps are ten kilometers wide at Gold."

"Fine, we stick together and look for some high ground." Charlie said glancing at the fifth group member. "You OK with that."

"I'm just peachy, o'illustrious leader." The man replied. Charlie rolled his eyes and gestured toward the sniper.

"Jen, the usual formation. Mark up one block ahead. The rest of us will anchor on Tobias."

Jen's noble face pinched as she tried to keep from falling into the muck. Out of instinct she held the fifty-caliber rifle over her head and picked out a tall apartment building in the distance. At least she was wearing shorts, and the scum only came up to the knees. Charlie got into position near the back of the squad, and held Fara at the low ready as he scanned the reeds behind them. Tobias struggled through the swamp under his colossal burden. Remy kept pace next to the man in her skimpy swimsuit, and together the five slowly moved toward the city center.

Forty-five minutes passed at a snail's pace, which was matched by their progress forward. There was no sign of the enemy, Roth or Human. That specifically made him nervous. Finally, swamp gave way to cracked weed-ridden pavement, and several small buildings leaned like drunken sailors. The foundations were broken and sinking into the ground. Jen led them toward a twelve-story condo high-rise which rose above the decay. One corner of the building had been pulled down by the weight of kudzu vines, and Ikea furniture lay in a pile of broken memories.

Jen stopped a block ahead with a fist in the air, and pointed upward. It took Charlie several seconds to spot the sniper barrel sticking out of a broken window. It was hidden with kudzu vines, but nothing could hide the thick suppressor. Everyone immediately scanned the surrounding buildings, and Charlie turned to guard their retreat—if they needed it. He backed up slowly as the scout returned.

"Go around?" Jen asked.

"That sniper has the high-ground, and we need it. If the enemy is in the building we might surprise them, kill a few then retreat." Charlie said, and no one argued. Remy or the new guy would be the best choice to lead the way. They both had shotguns designed for close range. He pointed to the random player. "You lead the way."

The man withdrew his automatic shotgun, and flicked the safety off, but didn't seem particularly enthused as he started toward the condo at a low crouch. Charlie followed him in after changing Fara to full-auto. The lobby floor was covered in mildewed marble tile. Footprints were visible coming from the opposite direction. They had formed a huddle near the stairs, then a single pair had gone up. The rest had walked back out the same entrance.

Charlie pointed to Tobias and Remy, then gestured to the front desk. The big man would make too much noise climbing up the stone steps. He didn't look happy being matched up with the pervert but walked behind the counter. The thick desk would provide some cover and gave a commanding view the lobby.

Mr. Random started up the stairs, so Charlie and Jennifer crept up after him. They caught up at the fifth floor as he waited on the last step to the landing. With a small red flashlight, he pointed to the ground. In the darkness, someone had stretched a thin wire across the landing and tied it to the railing. Charlie stepped over it carefully and saw a claymore mine pointed at him around the corner. So that was why the sniper felt confident enough to be by themselves.

The only other trap was on the tenth floor. A flashbang had been duct-taped to the railing with a wire strung across the gap. They stepped over the second wire and snuck down the hallway to the last condo. The random didn't wait for a signal. He blew off the lock with his Spaz shotgun and kicked the door open.

Three separate claymores went off as the door swung inward. The combined blast shredded his legs into ground meat, and the wall opposite was peppered with shrapnel in the vague shape of a man's waist. Charlie charged into the room with ringing ears. By the corner window, a woman rolled over in surprise, and reached for a small compact machine-pistol laying on the ground next to her. She had wild brown hair kept in check by a gray ballcap, and green speckled light armor over a loose shirt, and drab brown leather pants.

Charlie didn't waste time raising the short-barreled M16 to his shoulder, and fired on full-auto from the hip. Bullets struck the ground next to the sniper and he quickly tracked them onto her torso. Blood sprayed across the wall as a half dozen 5.56 rounds tore her insides apart. Jen entered last with her suppressed USP in hand and quickly cleared the rest of the condo apartment. She opened the bathroom door, and leaned in tentatively checking the shower stall. Charlie used his rifle to push open the kitchen closet, just to ensure it was clear.

"You're bleeding," Jen said from behind him. Charlie glanced down. His pants were soaked with water, but red was mixed in from pieces of shrapnel. He didn't feel it, not even as a tingle, so the damage couldn't have been bad. Charlie had survived worse wounds with his endurance score.

"Tiffany, Respond..." A small voice said near the corpse. He walked over and picked up an earbud laying on the ground. A radio wire snaked to the girls hip.

"Shit, they're at the condo. All units switch to the alternate channel."

"Well, they know we took her out." Charlie sighed as he crushed the radio bud. It wouldn't do them any good, and the enemy might be able to listen in on them. Both Jen and Tobias were still Silver, and radios were gold level gear.

"Oh my, that cute guy got all blowed up. Tisk... and I didn't even get to do it." Remy said from the entrance. She toed Mr. Random with her shoe before stepping past his shredded corpse.

"You were supposed to stay downstairs... with Tobias." Charlie growled.

"I heard an explosion, and you know me and things that go boom. I can't help myself."

"I'm surprised you didn't trip over the two traps on the way up."

"Trapping stairs is standard practice in the platinum ranks. I could have walked up here with my eyes closed." Remy said coming forward.

"They picked a good building," she said pointing out the window. The graveyard was across the street, and most of it had sunken back into the swamp, but there were still plenty of headstones sticking out of the water. Far in the distance, the red circle was visible.

"Is that where the match is going to end?"

Remy leaned out of the broken window scanning the horizon in either direction. "Most likely," she said after a few seconds. Charlie joined her but refrained from sticking his head out of cover. It did seem like they were near the center of the map boundary.

"Both teams lost a squad member, but we have the high ground now.

Take Tobias and move into the graveyard. We can cover you from up here."

"We did lose someone, but they will have to assume its five versus four now." Remy corrected skipping from the room. As she left Jen came back from the bathroom.

"Even if that's true, they know we're up here, so there's little point in changing rooms," Jen said pulling a dining room table to the windows and laid down on top.

Charlie was eager to try out his SVD for the first time. He had yet to buy a weapon skin for Sofie, but he liked her oiled wood finish. Charlie knelt at the sill, and raised the rifle to his shoulder.

The graveyard leaped into focus as he looked through the 4x scope. In the middle of the cemetery was an old fountain filled with black water. A grim reaper stood on a pedestal keeping watch over his buried charges. The cultured grass surrounding the base have been overtaken by choking weeds and standing pools of water.

Along the horizontal plane was a line with ten dashes for windage. At its center was a slightly larger chevron. Three smaller chevrons were evenly spaced down the vertical plane. A slope with several numbers was to the left.

"Sofie, can you remind me how to range a target?"

"Use guide on scope. This iz for man-size targets of 1.7 meters. Make sure head of target iz' touching the curved slope, then place flat line on feet. Results will be range to the target."

"Simple, da?"

"Yes, thank you." Charlie said looking through the scope again. He picked the grim-reaper statue standing over the fountain, which was roughly man sized and he set the slope along the head.

"I read two-hundred and fifty meters to the fountain."

"I'd say it is closer to 275. The statue is bigger than seems." Jen said from the table.

Sofie chimed in again as he picked out a tall cross on the other side of the graveyard. "Zee top chevron iz for targets under one-hundred meters. Next is for targets between two-hundred and three-hundred meters. The final two chevrons are for four, and six-hundred meters. You v'ill need better scope to hit target at thousand meters." Nothing happened for a while, and he wondered where the enemy was.

"Jen, What would you do?" Charlie asked.

"I'd set up somewhere and counter-snipe us."

"Not sure I'd try out-sniping you and that fifty-cal. If I were them, I'd lay low until the condo was no longer a threat." Down below Remy and Tobias carefully crossed the street. Remy reached the gate first and pulled it open for the trundling tank. They only made it partly into the first ring of tombstones when someone opened fire from the opposite side of the graveyard. The head of an angel statue disappeared, and Remy rolled into cover. There was a forest abutting that side and at least two people had climbed the trees to get a better vantage point.

"I don't see them in the foliage," Jen said next to him, so there was little chance he'd find them. She was using a 15x scope and could see much better. Charlie settled the SVD against the sill again and peered through the glass. The foliage was thick with bushes and beech trees. Two people ran out of the copse and through the knee high water.

He very briefly used the guide on the running figures, and found they were over six hundred meters out. Using the third chevron he fired at the first running man. By the time the bullet reached the target he was already a dozen feet ahead, and the bullet splashed into the water. He tried again, by aiming well ahead of the man. The round slipped past and slammed into a half-sunken headstone. Sniping was much harder than he first imagined.

Jen fired once. The glowing bullet arced over the cemetery, and a dark human shape fell from a far tree. Tobias stopped next to a kudzu wrapped tomb and aimed Gadreel at the tree line. A stream of hot rain cut into the forest like a buzz saw. In the distance, a figure slid down a trunk, then disappeared into the foliage.

While that had been going on Charlie was still failing to kill his two targets. Both were among the headstones. Remy climbed to the shoulders of an angelic statue, closed her legs around its neck, and fired a string of grenades at the two players. They landed in the water exploding with less force than usual, but the grenade grouping sent one man leaping out of cover. He dove into the shallow water to avoid the deadly shrapnel. Charlie followed the man's movement with his cross-hair.

*"Use the second chevron,"* he reminded himself.

Aiming at a point just above the bubbling water, Charlie pulled the trigger as the man stood. The 7.62 caliber bullet caught the player in the temple snapping his head back. With a golf-ball sized hole through his brains, he fell backward into the murky water. Almost immediately two small gators seized the corpse, and dragged it under the surface.

Jen fired again and again at the second sniper who was running into the graveyard in the opposite direction. Charlie felt a little better knowing she was having just as much trouble hitting a moving target.

"The red is coming in, we should leave." Charlie said standing. Jennifer made no move to climb from the table.

"I only have the Barrett, so I'm not going to be any good down there. Join the others, and I'll stay here and provide cover for as long as possible. That was probably their plan too, so good luck."

Charlie stood shouldering the SVD, and with Fara in his hands, left the condo. At the last second, he remembered the trip wire at the top of the stairs. He chuckled to himself, because that would have been a sad and hilarious mistake. His foot stopped a few inches from setting off the trap, then he stepped over carefully. The claymore on the fifth floor had been disarmed, and he quickly ran down the rest of the way. As he exited the building the barrier was already closing in. Jennifer's massive rifle continued to fire non-stop at the two remaining targets. Under that cover, Charlie sprinted into the graveyard and met up with Remy and Tobias holding the corner.

"Good to see you, Brother."

"You too, Tobias. How much ammo do you have left?"

"Half, maybe a little less." The giant admitted.

"Good, I want to get into the center first while Jen still has their attention."

The heavily armored Giant stepped from cover and activated his Gau-19 cannon. The barrels spun up as he aimed at a group of bullet ridden headstones. Charlie ran forward through the water toward the center of the graveyard.

The enemy sniper caught Tobias out in the open. He staggered from several slugs hitting his heavy chest armor. Paper scriptures flew off as the rounds continued to slam into him. Remy returned fire on the sniper with a string of grenades, but Tobias had fallen backward into the murk. Only his weapon stuck out as if his last action was to keep his angel from touching the unclean swamp.

Together Remy and Charlie made it to the center, and he rolled into the fountain which was filled with black water. However, Jen had stopped firing as the red barrier crossed over the condo. The sniper took the opportunity to shower the fountain with accurate rounds, while the second enemy player moved into cover.

"Don't let them get close enough to throw grenades," Remy said splashing toward the right side of the fountain. She fired blindly over the lip at the closing player. Charlie wasn't sure how he was going to do that. Every time he poked his head out the sniper would quickly fire on him. He'd already been hit by flecks of stone twice, so there was no chance he could out shoot the other person.

A grenade landed in the murk three meters from the fountain and exploded. The stone cracked, and water quickly poured from the broken stone. Charlie crawled to the center and slid behind the Grim Reaper. As he did, bullets knocked chunks off the statue's legs and feet. The first player stood again to throw another grenade.

He rose up just enough to fire Fara. The slug caught the man in his grenade hand, and it dropped into the shallow water at his feet. Wounded but still alive, the player dove away from the spot.

"Got you!" Remy cried standing up. She leveled her double barrel at him, and the buckshot shredded the player as he struggled to his feet. Seconds later Remy fell from the fountain as three quick bullets slammed into her. Charlie transitioned to the last player and fired on the sniper's distant cover. He missed, but kept the player pinned down. Now that Charlie had a bead on his location he wasn't going to give the player a chance to line up a shot.

The circle was feet from the enemy player, and Charlie wondered if the man was going to just let it roll over him. At the last second, he dodged toward new cover, but Charlie had saved the last ten rounds expecting it. Fara rested against the base of the statue, and he led the target a little before firing. The first bullet caught him in the stomach, and he tried to throw himself into cover. The next five punched into his chest before the sniper slammed into the grave-marker face first. His body rolled over into the water and several gators converged on the corpse. Darkness closed in, and Charlie stepped out into the private lounge.

**[Match Complete]**
**[Team Win]**

"Good job!" Remy said clapping. Jen and Tobias looked pleased as well, though the random guy was already in the elevator.

"Did you notice that we got more contracts?" Jen asked.

"Really, did you level?"

"No, I'm still silver, but I have four contract slots."

"I hath only one extra," Tobias said. Charlie checked his stats, and discovered he had two open contract slots as well.

"Unexpected, but maybe it's an extra reward for capturing those dropships."

"I got two as well," Remy said with a mischievous grin. "I'm going to walk into the Armory, get naked, and contract with the first weapons that fuck me," she added. The girl stuck her finger into her mouth thinking of all the delicious combinations.

"Who wants to join me?" Remy asked.

"I already have some girls waiting at home. It's getting late, and I want to clean Fara." Charlie said turning toward the elevator. Everyone climbed in and headed up to the competition lobby.

Outside the night was coming on fast. Charlie climbed into the Mustang and drove quickly home. The aroma of his contract slot drew the girls to him like bears to honey. The door was barely open before four bikini clad girl slammed into him, and knocked Charlie back into the garage.

"I like the enthusiasm," he said as Sakura and Rain pulled his shirt and armor off. Thelma and Luise were giggling like intoxicated fairies as they worked his pants free. There was a choice to be had because he could only take two of the four girls. Sakura was a stand-alone grenade launcher, and he really considered her first. Grenades were an effective tool for clearing an area. The asian eyed Charlie, and pursed kissable lips as he considered her. Rain was a pump action shotgun, but Fara already had the short range covered. He finally forced the girls off of him, and sat up. Really there was no choice. A threesome with the twins was too good to pass up, and he pointed to Thelma and Luise.

"You two... bedroom... ten minutes. I'm going to clean the girls, but you had better be ready when I'm done." The twins beamed at Charlie and only left after kissing him several times. Sakura looked downcast, but Rain pecked him on the cheek.

"If I hit platinum soon, I'll get another contract slot."

"My time here has been better than fighting for Meisters at the Armory. I'll stay, if that's what your asking." Rain said.

"Me too," Sakura added.

He managed to collect his clothes, and enter the house. Charlie sat down to clean his guns. He cleared each, then sprayed them down with solvent, and waited a few minutes. Then he ran a brush through each barrel, and worked quickly to scrub their insides. He loved having his harem, but it was taking longer and longer to clean the girls.

Afterward he walked toward the bedroom. He could hear giggling, and muffled talking as he pushed open the door. Two pale skinned girls were already naked, and laying atop one another on the bed. Two sets of amethyst eyes looked back at him.

"Thank you for contracting us together."

"Yes, we are very happy." Luise agreed reaching for Thelma and spread her sister's legs wide. Charlie was treated to the glorious view of her pink and glistening entrance.

*"Tonight is going to be fun,"* he thought, and smiled at the two as he closed the door.

# CHAPTER TWENTY-SEVEN

## *Halloween Pt1*

Gun Meister Online Updating...
Installing kinky content...
Fingering Communication Nodes...
Network Jilling Off...
Climaxing...
Logging into Character...

His eyes opened to a room filled with burning candles, and a bed covered in women. The house reeked of pumpkin pie, buttered popcorn, and gun oil. Above him the television screen was playing a horror movie. A woman wearing only a bath towel was sprinting through the darkened forest while a masked man stalked after her with a bloody kitchen knife. Her blonde hair was damp and clung to her shoulders and chest. Panic was written on her face as she looked back, and a twisted tree root caught her foot. She cried out and stumbled to the moss covered ground. Her towel; the only defense she had fell away exposing her young, supple, and obviously fake breasts. The killer grabbed the naked camper by her wet hair. The bloody knife flashed, and she let out a blood curdling scream.

On the bed, six girls also screamed, and a dozen hands clutched at Charlie as they used him to hide their faces. Fara, the only one not wailing in fright, avidly watched the girl noisily bleed to death. She pushed another handful of popcorn into her mouth, and chewed.

"You're all watching something strange," he said as the killer stood over his latest victim. Charlie had seen the old flick before. It was a B-list horror movie with a gratuitous amount of nudity and cheesy dialog, but at least they all died in the end.

"All the channels are playing something like this tonight. Well, all except the Roth channel." Fara said reaching up to turn the TV off. The gothic teenager turned toward him and with black painted fingernails, slowly fed him the popcorn. There were a half dozen silver rings on her fingers. Dark crimson lipstick adorned her luscious lips, black eyeliner framed her blue eyes, and Fara had dyed her hair jet black. She was naked from the waist up, except a thick spiked collar around her throat, and black electrical tape made an X over each nipple. Her pants were black leather torn into shreds and held together with hundreds of staples. She leaned in kissing him with her liquorice flavored lips, and smiled, showing off a pair of long vampiric fangs. Elva, jealous of the attention pounced atop him next.

"I want kisses too, nyan," Elva pawed at him, licking his neck.

She was wearing cat ears and had drawn whiskers on her face with black marker. She too was naked from the waist up save a jeweled golden collar. "Neko-Sex Slave," was emblazoned with diamonds around the throat. Connected to the collar was a short length of golden chain which Charlie grabbed. The kitten was pulled up to his lips again and Elva hungrily attacked them. Her tongue forced its way into his mouth as a spotted blond tail swished back and forth. She purred wiggling her hips making the tail dance.

The two white-haired twins looked like 1950's flappers. Thelma wore a red sequined miniskirt and a necklace of red glass beads. Luise wore a green silk skirt, with high heels, and a green feather hat. They smiled together and kissed him deeply, each taking their turn at his lips.

Sofie, by contrast, wore orange suspenders that just barely covered her dark nipples. They ran down to a pair of tight orange prison shorts. At his gaze, Sofie covered her face and turned away in embarrassment. Across her ass, in black block letters, it said, "Prisoner 69, Punish Often." Even after a month Sofie still wore those cuffs, though now they fit the costume.

They all looked good, and Charlie admired the girls for a few seconds. Finally, he climbed from the pile of women and went into the closet. Since contracting with the twins, he'd decided on the obvious costume. Over his light armor he pulled on a pinstripe vest, and gray slacks. He went over to the mirror to make sure his white tie was straight, then pulled on a dark gray jacket. Next he grabbed the matching fedora from the nightstand, and settled it over his head.

He stroked the brim of the hat and said, "You'll nevah catch me coppah." The final accessory was a cigar, that he tucked into his pocket for later. Thelma and Luise eagerly changed into weapon form, and he stood admiring himself in the mirror with the two tommy guns.

"What are we doing tonight, nyan?" Elva asked in a purring voice.

"I heard there is a special event starting in about three hours, so I wanted to head down early to visit Grace."

Elva beamed, and launched herself from the bed with her tail flailing about. Fara put the popcorn down and slid from the mattress followed by Sofie. Out in the living room, Elva was already preparing the thermos. The warm mulled cider was laced with half a dozen shots of bourbon. She and Grace had become fast friends, and Elva often went down to visit the weapon. Grabbing a thick woolen blanket she headed to the garage. The Mustang was an ebony jewel under the lights. Charlie had repainted it gloss black and paid for a mural of racing horses down the side. Sofie moved to slip past him but he reacted quickly.

"Prisoner 69!" He said sharply grabbing the giant's wrist, and she started. "Get into the passenger seat; I want to keep my eye on you."

"Am I in troúble?" She asked nervously.

"You are indeed. I haven't gotten a kiss from you, yet." He said letting go of her wrist. She leaned down immediately, but he covered her mouth. "I'm afraid it's too late for that. You need to be punished, and I'm thinking twenty hard spanks are in your near future."

Her face flushed as a glimmer of hope passed over her eyes. "I very sorry, zir." Sofie said quickly, but she wasn't, not in the slightest. She turned immediately and presented her ass for dispensation. He smiled and pushed her forward toward the passenger side of the Mustang.

"Not yet prisoner. The punishment will have to wait until we get home."

Sofie couldn't quite hide the look of hidden heat that crossed her face. She opened the door and slid inside. "Please vladelets..."

"We'll see how things go. You'll get spanks off for good behavior."

Charlie said opening the car door. Elva and Fara climbed into the backseat as he set the twins next to him. Slowly he pulled out into the leaf-covered street. The California heat hung in the air even though fall had already begun. In fact, it was warm enough to roll the windows down. Outside the full moon was a bright body shining down upon the earth. He glanced up looking for the Roth ship. Sometimes, at the perfect moment, you could catch the flash of reddish light. Charlie always looked, because he envied them for being in space.

He forced himself back to Earth, and pulled his fedora down a little more. A low mist hung over the road as Charlie drove leisurely away from the house. Elva sat behind him holding the blanket and thermos. Fara was next to her but reached a hand forward and slid it under his shirt.

Her sharp fingernails scratched at his skin as she whispered, "I vant to suck your blood tonight." Fara was such a sadist, and it turned her on more than anything.

"Play your cards right, and anything can happen," The engine revved to solidify his words.

The vampire leaned between the seats and bit his ear, and Elva joined her sister in attacking his lobes. Sofie leaned over as well and started working the buttons on his pants. Her long fingers unzipped his fly, and she reached inside for his growing bulge.

"Trying to earn brownie points already?"

The redhead glanced up at him, searched his face, then closed her mouth slowly over his erection. Charlie moaned as her lips slid all the way down the shaft to his base. It was a good thing the road was mostly empty. His eyes momentarily closed as pleasure slammed into his brain. The Mustang meandered into the oncoming lane before Charlie caught himself. Sofie's long tongue was like a living creature as her head worked up and down. Meanwhile, Elva and Fara were both assaulting his ears. He stopped at a red light four blocks from the competition center and sagged back against the seat.

He moaned and said in a hoarse voice, "One spank off."

Sofie pushed herself faster as saliva slid down his shaft. Elva and Fara continued to lick and bite his ears. Near the sidewalk, there was a surprised gasp. A young man, not more than twenty, was staring into the car. His dark eyes flicked over the two topless women in back, then to Charlie and the redhead. The kid wore the gray military uniform from character creation, and standing beside him in a simple bikini was a busty green-eyed ginger. The weapon blushed, and her many freckles deepened in color. Leaning forward she whispered something into the boy's ear. He jumped, then glanced between her and the Mustang.

"You finally made it, nyan." Elva purred into his ear then nipped at his left lobe.

So she recalled the incident as well. He couldn't help but smile remembering that scene so many months ago. Only then he'd been the one standing on the corner looking into a car full of topless women. Charlie grinned at the kid as the light turned green, and gunned the engine. Tires squealed, and rubber burned as the Mustang shot down the street.

Charlie barely managed to park the car before he came. He sank his fingers into Sofie's hair and pushed her further down his shaft. The prisoner was forced to swallow his essence as Charlie panted for breath. Once he was clean, she carefully zipped him back into his pants.

Charlie cleared his throat and announced, "Two spanks off."

"Only two? Dat vas worth half off at least." Sofie argued already shifting back to her forceful personality.

"I admit, that was amazing, so I'll take five off," he said reaching over to fix the suspender strap over her chest. Sofie appeared mollified as she checked her hair in the mirror and climbed out. The Mustang quieted into silence as the engine shut off. He took the unlit cigar from his jacket and bit down on the end.

Outside, Elva pulled his right arm between her bare breasts. His left draped over Fara's shoulders while Sofie clung to his back. Charlie carried the twin tommy guns, and together they made for the small park outside the entrance.

Grace, as usual, sat alone on the leaf covered bench. Her contract collar was gone, so the only thing between her and the world was a thin bikini. At least, it was still warm tonight. Her face was blank, and her gaze distance as Grace floated through the memories of better days. Charlie paused next to the bench, and the girls let go of him.

"How are you doing, Grace?"

The weapon ignored them and continued to stare into the distance. Elva unfolded the woolen blanket and draped it over her. It was the only thing Charlie could give her. His previous attempts to put coats and scarves on Grace had ended up in them being destroyed. A blanket though wasn't worn, it only covered. Elva knelt before Grace.

"You should really go to the Armory, it's warmer there," Elva said pressing the woman's cool hands to her face. Opening the thermos, Elva poured some of the hot cider into the cup. As she placed it in the weapon's hands, Grace finally looked down. She took a sip at first, before draining the entire cup, and Elva quickly added more.

"Are you trying to get me drunk?" Grace asked sipping the cider more slowly. Alcohol did funny things to the girls. Chiefly, it made them randy as hounds in mating season. It also warmed the stomach and flushed blood to the skin. Grace's cheeks almost immediately took on a pink rosy tinge.

"How else is a man supposed to get a beautiful woman like you to come home with him?" He asked with a smile. Grace sipped again and carefully wiped her lips.

"And what—pray tell—would you do with me?" She asked glancing at him over her cider. Grace scanned the skimpy costumes the three girls wore with disapproval.

"To be honest, I'd chain you to my bed, and spend all night—and each night—turning you into a screaming succubus of carnal desire."

"You are a lascivious devil," Grace said before she hiccuped.

"That's a part of my charm."

"I would heartily disagree. I must tell you—here and now—I'll never contract with you." She said glancing with horror at the nearly naked girls.

Charlie laughed. He hadn't picked out their costumes, but they knew what he liked.

"Your words wound me to the quick, and I feel the heat, so the cider appears to be working."

"I'm sorry for ignoring you. It was rude of me." Grace admitted. Charlie waved a dismissive hand.

"You won't go back to the armory?" Elva asked interrupting the banter.

"No."

"You are as stubborn as Montgomery," Charlie said.

Grace laughed lightly and said, "That's the nicest thing you've said to me. Thank you."

"Do you need anything?"

"No, I'll stay a bit longer."

"Elva is right. There's no point in torturing yourself by sitting out here."

"I'll stay a bit longer," she repeated.

That was the most he could do. The wool blanket would keep her warm, and she had food at the Armory. Charlie nodded and moved away. Elva closed the thermos and caught up slipping under his arm.

"I worry about her. Weapons are programmed to seek a Meister. We need to be used." Elva said in a soft whisper.

"Leave her be,"

"Charlie..." Elva said clutching at his elbow.

"I can't Elva. You heard her; she won't contract with me. Besides, it would be unfair to keep her as a trophy weapon. I'm honest enough to say that I'd never use her. Not with Fara, Sofie, and yourself around."

The three girls hugged him, and their warmth was welcome. Charlie had time to burn before the event, and Grace made it rather clear she wanted to be left alone.

Charlie hadn't walked far when he caught sight of an apparition. A man of about twenty walked carefully through the moonlit parking lot. He wore a gray jacket of the Confederate army which was cut in the fashion for the enlisted man. His dark brown hair was short, and his face was cleanly shaven. However, there was something in the nose that was familiar. The eyes too were fierce as they looked only at Grace. In his arms was a bouquet of red roses, and he stopped a few feet from the blanket covered woman. The young southern soldier coughed gently trying to get the woman's attention, but Grace continued to stare into the distance, oblivious to all.

He took a step closer and asked, "Will you evah forgive me?"

Grace turned, and her eyes snapped to the young man before her. She half stood from the bench and her fingers clutched at her bosom as if she could physically stop her heart from pounding.

"These are for you," the Confederate soldier said holding out the roses.

For a few seconds, she continued to stare at the young man. Then Grace launched herself upward, and the blanket fell away. She swept the flowers aside and wrapped her arms around the young man's neck. The bouquet fell to the flagstones as she started to weep.

"Is it you Monty? Am I dreaming still, or are you real?" She wept burying her head in his shoulder.

"I have returned."

She cried for almost a minute before pulling back and raised her hand. The young man saw it coming and made no move to dodge. The moonlight glinted off her pale skin as she brought it savagely down.

"I hate you," she said slapping him. Her blow struck him to one knee, and blood flowed from the corner of his mouth.

He gathered himself, looked up at Grace, and said, "I deserve that for putting you through so much." Anything he tried to say next was lost as Grace launched herself at him. She pressed her lips to his in a kiss that was as much fury as passion. A clear collar formed around her neck as she took in his red essence. She made sounds, grunting, and moaning as her tongue fought its way deeper and deeper into his mouth.

"I waited, and waited but you didn't return." Grace finally said as she stood, but Monty remained on his knee. He reached up taking her hand and kissed it with his bloody lips.

"With God as my witness, I promise never to leave you again. I beg you; please be my weapon." He said.

"Yes, a thousand times yes." Grace cried and fell into his arms.

Charlie approached the two and said, "I have to warn you, I don't believe in ghosts."

Grace blushed realizing the recent kiss had been seen by others. She hid behind Montgomery still trying to collect herself, and caught sight of the dropped blanket. Then ran to the bench, picked up the discarded cloth, and draped it over herself.

"That is fine, sir. I don't believe in you either." Montgomery said stepping forward. Charlie shook his hand, and it was still as steely firm as ever.

"I'll spare you the slap, but I too have missed you. What took you so long?"

"I spent a month in a purgatory of my own making," Monty answered with a self-deprecating smile. He reached up wiping the blood from his lips.

"Elva, that cider will help I think," Charlie said. Elva bounced forward and unscrewed the thermos. Monty glanced at the half-nude cat slave as she poured a cup of bourbon-laced cider.

"Color me surprised; it's Kentucky Rye, you don't strike me as the type," Monty said taking another sip.

"He kept trying to get me drunk, so I would go home with him." Grace answered in a piqued tone.

"He did, did he?"

"Only with the purest of intentions," Charlie said quickly.

Grace hugged Monty from behind, wrapping her arms around his stomach. "He said he wanted to chain me to his bed and turn me into a sex-crazed harlot."

"Only with the purest of intentions..." he repeated more weakly.

Grace finally relented and said. "I only half jest. He comes by almost daily to visit. Charlie has become something of a nagging nanny, which really was tiresome."

"Traitor. You just squashed your chances at getting accepted into my harem."

"Thank you, Sir. I mean that from the bottom of my heart."

Charlie was not one for soul-searching gazes. He sought a change of subject to more neutral topics. "Tell me more about your trip through purgatory."

"A sad, unfortunate tale. It took a week to arrive by ship, but at least the place was as advertised. A transient hotel for people ascending to digital form. I could barely afford the price of admission, but they took my money and slotted me in at the bottom of the list. I assure you, that it was a long list," Monty said holding out the thermal cup again which Elva quickly refilled.

He drank about half before continuing. "Old people complain a lot, especially those standing at heaven's door. If it wasn't the hot weather, it was the rain, or lack of imported mineral water." Monty sighed and quickly drank the other half of his mug.

"Everyone there was a tech boom baby or a wealthy executive... or the wife of one. However, it was the truly rich that bought premium tickets. They got on the short list, and each one pushed my name lower and lower."

"It wasn't as if I was left in a room to rot, though I sometimes felt as much. Miguel was my ward. A nice boy who was handy at getting hard alcohol. I'd run out of my prescription pills about a week into the sojourn. They didn't give out meds, nothing stronger than aspirin anyway, so alcohol was the only alternative. I'd slip Miguel extra cash to bring me the good stuff."

"Miguel and I spent hours watching the local football team. He was a fan, and I wanted anything to distract myself from the pain." Monty admitted. Grace suddenly clutched at his arm like Monty would blow away in the wind. He reached up patting her hand.

"Two days ago, I was hauled from bed—still half drunk—and tossed into a wheelchair. I was halfway to the Gates of Heaven before I realized what was going on." He said pausing again to pat Grace's hand.

To the woman, he whispered, "It's what we jokingly called the Dive Rooms." Grace's deathlike grip loosened marginally, so Monty continued.

"My ascension to digital avatar came at the cost of another. The wife of an Indian diamond tycoon had passed away minutes before her dive. I suppose the thought of it was too much for her old heart. As you can imagine, they don't put much effort in saving people. Usually, they'd have just moved down the list, but Miguel had bribed the technicians with the money I'd been slipping him.

"It was a good thing too. I do not think I would have lasted another week. Without treatment the cancer was running rampant, eating my body alive." Monty paused again to get his cup refilled. He grinned to himself looking down at the mulled cider. "So there I found myself—blubbering like a child—as they pulled the dive helmet over my head."

"It worked, and that's what matters. How was Paris?" Charlie asked, and Monty laughed.

"That pathetic attempt at historical Noir didn't appeal to me in the slightest. I pleaded with Alex to let me go. Not only did he give me his blessing, but he also returned my money. He said he wouldn't beggar a man to enter heaven."

"Did that also come with a change in appearance."

Monty laughed again and said, "When I logged in and looked at my face it seemed wrong. I didn't feel old anymore, so I took what little credits I had and altered my appearance."

Finally, he turned to Grace. "I looked for you at the Armory all day yesterday, but no one had even heard of you. I finally ran into someone who said they'd seen a statue in a fancy dress near the competition center."

She blushed and pressed her face to his chest. "Monty," she breathed. "Monty, I..."

The man stopped her with a kiss. Her fingers tightened on his gray jacket before Monty picked the woman up off the ground. She clung to his neck as he half turned. "If you'll excuse us, Grace and I need an hour to be properly reacquainted."

"It's good to have you back."

"I do declare; I am glad to *'be'* back."

Monty started away toward a set of apartments with Grace still wrapped in the wool blanket, but paused after twenty steps. He half turned and said in a conspiratorial whisper, "We'd best make it two hours—for lost time."

"Don't be late for the event. It promises to be a good one." Charlie called after the man.

"That was the most romantic thing I've ever seen," Elva said sniffling. After a second she added, "nyan." Her cat whiskers were smudged as she wiped at her tears.

"I'm just glad it wasn't a romantic tragedy," Charlie replied.

"Should have just handcuffed the girl to his bed. That would have shown his love." Remy said from nearby. The short girl came out of the bushes and dusted herself off. Ivy leaves covered her small chest and groin. A wreath of flower blossoms crowned her head, and she held a star-tipped wand in her hand. On her back was a pair of flapping gossamer wings. Her innocent pixie costume was marred slightly by the heavy hardware she was carrying.

"I don't think you quite understand the word," Charlie said moving to the bench.

"I do too. It's when a man and a woman make googly eyes at each other. Then a stork comes and delivers a baby." Remy answered definitively.

"That's not love, or even romantic."

"Those two pretend to be all chaste, but as soon as the door shuts, they'll fuck each other's brains out." Remy countered.

Charlie shook his head and walked with his troop into the competition center. A display over the reception desk showed a countdown. In a little less than two hours, the Halloween event would start. Jen and Tobias were already waiting nearby. A flock of tuxedoed males surrounded Jennifer, who regally sat in a chair while they offered her drinks, fanned her, and massaged her bare shoulders. Tonight, she was dressed as a succubus in a red corset gown. Two horns stuck out from the sides of her head and curled back behind her ears. A red whip hung at her waist.

"I am not happy with you," Jennifer announced as she neared.

"And I haven't even opened my mouth yet," Charlie replied sitting in the second chair. The girls settled themselves about him, while Remy leaped atop a nearby console and kicked her legs.

"Because of you, I haven't logged into Blood and Pride in weeks. My clan barely recognized me when I showed up at the ball tonight."

Charlie laughed and said, "I can see why. Four incredibly handsome men to satisfy your every whim... and desire."

She glared at him again, and he laughed.

"I am glad to see you, Brother," Tobias said turning toward them. The man was wearing his heavy armor covered in Scripture. Gadreel was next to him, and had acquired a pair of miniature angel wings. They flapped and fluttered slightly as she hugged Tobias's arm. Two exquisitely beautiful and frocked nuns knelt next to the Crusader in prayer.

"At least someone is," Charlie said.

"I wonder if we'll fight demons again tonight?"

"I didn't see any news on the Roth Channel, so it could be anything." Jennifer added touching the man's hands at her neck. Sebastian stepped back, and she relaxed in the seat.

"I forgot to mention, Monty is back. He should be joining us."

"Monty?" Tobias asked.

"A friend who was absent due to illness."

"We are a full squad, finally!" Remy cheered from nearby.

"Very true, and after the event, we can register as a clan," Charlie said sitting back. Elva climbed into his lap and started to purr. He reached up scratching her behind the cat ears while the conversation meandered back and forth; mostly about the Roth.

A little after an hour Monty showed up with a fully dressed Grace in tow. Introductions were quickly made. Charlie led his squad into the elevators and they found a relatively quiet place to wait for the Halloween Event.

**[Event Starting]**

# CHAPTER TWENTY-EIGHT
## *Halloween Pt2*

In the darkness, an opaque window appeared, "Please select a weapon." The list that followed consisted of his five contracted girls. Without a clear objective, the event could bring anything, so he selected his most versatile weapon—the M16.

Charlie's vision returned in a wash of sepia tones. It was as if he were looking through the lens of an ancient 16mm camera. Worst of all was the fact he couldn't move a muscle, and there was a moment of intense disorientation from the lack of control. He felt strange, as if his body had been reassembled into an unnatural configuration. Pieces locked together in a disjointed mess. Against one side there was a sensation of body heat which was accompanied by the sound of a beating heart. Charlie's other side felt as if it were freezing cold. His point of view blinked and looked around.

They appeared to be in a long concrete hallway, somewhere deep underground. Ice formed thick crystals along the walls and ceiling. The door nearby had an image of two circles, one dark grey with a smaller blue ring on the lower right side. Next to it were the words, "Svalbard Global Seed Vault." Finally, they looked down, and Charlie saw it was a female dressed in arctic combat clothes. She touched the fur-lined white jacket and slid the zipper up more tightly. Hanging via a fuzzy shoulder strap was a heavily modified M16a4.

"What's going on?" A voice asked. Charlie heard it as one listens to the chest of a lover, and he recognized the speaker.

"Fara," he said. The person jumped slightly and looked around again.

Charlie wanted to laugh as understanding finally dawned. Their positions as Meister and weapon had suddenly flipped. It was no wonder he couldn't move—for tonight he was the M16. Elva had said they couldn't see or hear in weapon form, but the developers had obviously bent the rules a little for Charlie and the other players.

"It seems you get to do all the dirty work this time."

"I don't like this," Fara admitted in a whisper.

"You're always watching the Twilight Zone. This event is something strange and thought-provoking, so it should be right up your alley?"

Fara grabbed his grip, and it felt like someone was shaking his hand. Her pulse was steady, but already climbing with nervous anticipation. Breath exhaled from her in a bloom before she sucked in a biting cold lungful of air. With gloved fingers, she pulled back on the charging handle just enough to verify the chamber was loaded. Then it slid forward hard.

"Maybe when we get home I'll be the one that gets to bite you," Charlie said with a smirking voice.

"Shush."

"I'll bury my face between your legs and make you cry out in orgasmic bliss. Then I'll turn and sink my teeth into your thigh while you writhe in pleasure. It's only fair I take an equal portion." He said in a sly voice.

"I will disassemble you and scatter your pieces across the room."

"Feisty," He cooed. Their banter was cut short by the squalling blare from a nearby speaker. It warbled like an air raid siren before cutting off abruptly.

"Unknown ships attacking the earth. I repeat extra-terrestrial vessels are attacking the island. Gather together and defend the seed vault at all cost. We must save this agricultural stockpile for future generations."

"Well, at least you're defending," Charlie mused more to himself.

"What do I do?" Fara asked, and he laughed.

"You are the Meister; I am the tool. In this form I have no eyes to—" Charlie was interrupted by Fara shaking him violently, and he laughed again.

"If there's no one around, you might try looking outside." He suggested in a voice dripping with irony. Even if Charlie couldn't move, he found this situation highly entertaining. Although, if the Halloween event aimed at scaring him it was doing a poor job.

Fara turned back to the doorway and pushed down on the ice-covered handle. A shower of white crystals fell to the floor as it opened. Inside was a short circular airlock. She crossed to the second door and passed through. Just on the other side, several people turned pointing their guns at her. Grace was immediately recognizable via her complicated hairstyle, though she too wore arctic-camo. The southern belle was also carrying a heavy Kentucky rifle, and sighed audibly after realizing who Fara was. All of them appeared unnerved, so maybe this Halloween Event wasn't for the players. Next to Grace was an unfamiliar woman with short brown hair and carried an MGL 32 grenade launcher. She had thin framed glasses perched on her nose which made her appear bookish.

Sebastian raised his massive Barrett M107, and casually rested it against his shoulder. Like the others, he wore a fur-lined camo outfit. Standing halfway up the ramp was a white-haired woman in heavy armor. Gadreel was half turned toward the entrance and aiming at it with the GAU-19B at her waist. She had no harness for the weapon but carried the cannon with ease.

The new girl—Missy, shook her grenade launcher and said, "For the last time, I will not lick you!"

"That weapon is defective. It should be dismantled and buried where it can't hurt anyone." Fara suggested.

"If it weren't for the threat of painful death, I'd be highly tempted," Missy said letting the weapon fall against her on the sling.

"Toby says the demons will seek to burn our grain silos as they did in Jerusalem."

"They might not know what exactly is here, but they'll come. There is no cover to hide behind along this hallway. Hopefully, there's something resembling a defense perimeter outside." Charlie said to Fara.

"Charlie suggests going outside." Fara related. Everyone seemed to agree, so Fara took the lead. She shouldered the M16 and pushed the huge metal door open.

It was night, but an Aurora Borealis lit up the rocky landscape in shifting green hues. Tonight the weather was calm and clear. Everything would have been picturesque except for the alien apocalypse descending upon earth. Thousands of objects were streaking down into the upper atmosphere and leaving long contrails. There were so many ships it was impossible to take them all in at once. Somewhere in the direction of Russia dozens of ICBM missiles were launching skyward to meet the intruders. Red flashes licked out from the descending fighters, and one sluggish rocket faltered, skewing sideways, and fell back to earth. More were shot down as they converged together in a cluster. Suddenly there was a brief, brilliant flash of light and three massive round mushroom clouds formed in the air. A few unlucky alien ships were vaporized in the nuclear fire. More dropped like dead birds into the arctic ocean.

Before tonight, Charlie couldn't have imagined how America had fallen in days. That had seemed impossible to his patriotic mind, but now he understood. This was how it had been. The Roth had come with an armada vast enough to blanket the world in fighters and dropships. Even the success of Russia's nuclear ICBM's was little more than a token gesture. It made the four vessels Charlie had fought a paltry weekend skirmish. Nearby Missy shuddered at the sight, and her grip tightened on the grenade launcher.

"I'd like to go back inside," she said in a small voice.

"That's sadly not an option," Grace said pointing back. The bunker they stood before was purposefully designed to be seen at a great distance. A reflective installation caught the green aurora light and broadcast it out. The aliens would come at some point, and hiding inside would only bring their doom all the sooner.

High above Russian, Canadian, and American fighter craft were desperately battling the aliens. Lasers and missiles filled the sky in a violent, but brief orgy. From across the water, heavy lift Chinooks approached carrying tanks and anti-aircraft carriages. Smaller blackhawks carried American and Canadian troops. They flew low over the ocean waves attempting to avoid notice, but a dozen alien fighters aimed in their direction. A large dropship also turned toward the island. Barely a mile out from land the sleek black fighters caught up, and four escorting apache helicopters turned to confront the oncoming attackers. Air-to-air sidewinder missiles fired in smoking contrails, while lasers lanced out in return. The red beams sliced apart the Cobra gunships in a sizzling crackle. Most of the fighters dodged the missile attack, but two were caught by the Aim-9 missiles.

Without protection, the troop transports were easy pickings for the two remaining fighters. Most crashed into the waves just short of the airport. Four Blackhawks dropped toward the rocky shore, and men threw themselves down the rappel lines. The more massive Chinooks had to slow first before dropping their heavy payloads. One twin bladed helicopter took a glancing hit. The rear engine caught fire, and it began to corkscrew. The Chinook overshot the airport heading toward the seed vault. Underneath the helicopter, the attached tank flailed on its tow cables. They strained, then snapped apart from the forces, and the M1 Abrams tumbled across the rocky ground toward them. It came to a steel splitting stop just below.

The Chinook spun again, and for a fraction of a second, desperate marines could be seen inside the open loading bay. It twisted overhead, passing them, before slamming into the mountain a hundred meters away. A fireball rose skyward as men and women were tossed free like broken GI Joe's.

Grace gasped, covering her mouth and looked away. Gadreel said a quick prayer for the poor souls, while Sebastian and Missy both turned green around the gills. None of the corpses stood or moved from where they lay. Fara felt a little sick herself but glanced south again. At the small airport, the surviving men gathered, though they had only the equipment they dropped with. Fighters zipped past in a second flyover targeting parked cargo planes and single engine Cessnas. The fuel storage went up in a billow of black smoke, and the few remaining helicopters were cut apart as the crews jumped from them.

The lumbering dropship approached the island under heavy escort. It slowed skewing to the side as it moved over the quiet town of Longyearbyen. Other human players must have spawned there for gunfire erupted from the streets licking across the armored underbelly. In response, drop-pods released like diseased ticks.

"You guys won't win if that ship lands. They'll get to respawn as often as they like."

"How do we stop it?" Fara asked. The others looked at her with querulous expressions.

"The cannon on the tank below might have survived the fall. It's a small chance, but it's better than just watching the aliens land uncontested."

Fara didn't like the idea of moving away from the vault, but she couldn't think of a better plan. At the very least the tank made for better cover than anything near the bunker. Just down the slope, the wreck was visible. It had landed right side up, which was a miracle in its own right.

"Let's check that out," she said leading the way.

The loose stones were treacherous, and before long, she skidded into the impact crater. The others followed her down in a small avalanche.

The treads were a complete write-off, and most of the ablative plates had been torn free. Underneath however, the body seemed relatively intact. The turret had been locked in position, so the cannon's barrel still looked pristine. Fara climbed onto the tank, found the main hatch, and was grateful to discover the inside empty. Grace and Missy both shouldered their weapons and mounted the tan colored vehicle. Sebastian set his rifle on the rocky ground and laid down prone, while Gadreel stood by the edge of the pit.

Fara climbed inside and sat in the first seat. Grace entered next and slid down past the breach face to sit in the loader's chair. Missy wiggled in with some difficulty, and crammed herself into the gunner's seat. There were knobs, switches, and dials everywhere. Next to Fara was a small computer screen and keypad. She flicked the cover off a turn key and activated it. A green light flashed, and power came on in the tank. She had no idea what she was doing, but her hand automatically flicked several more switches. Pumps sprang to life circulating air and diesel into the engine.

While she did this Grace yanked open the breach of the loader. Inside was a safety plug which she pulled free. Then the woman unlocked the first ammo storage and withdrew a large shell. She shoved it inside the weapon, snapped the face closed, and locked it. As if against her own will she raised a hand and slapped Missy on the thigh.

"I do declare, HE rounded loaded... I don't know what HE means, but it's loaded." She shouted with a strange expression on her face.

Fara's hand hovered over a final button, because starting the tank would get the Roth's attention. The thought of bringing the aliens toward them made her mouth dry, but she forced herself to press down, and the engine slowly turned over. As it did the rest of the lights inside went active.

"I have feed," Missy said and grabbed the joystick next to her. Fara placed her eyes against a short periscope. It swiveled as she looked around. The dropship finished disgorging it's payload of soldiers, and turned toward the airfield searching for a flat place to set down. A compass was at the top of the display, and Fara red off the direction.

"Target at 33 degrees," Fara called. Quickly the tank's turret spun facing toward the town. It actuated upwards as Missy started to track the vessel.

"I have good target," Missy called.

"Fire at will," Fara said covering her ears.

The tank belched flame as the cannon fired creating a massive wash of snow and dust. A glowing dot flew almost two kilometers toward the ponderously moving ship, and exploded against the dropship's right side. It wobbled slightly but continued forward minus a considerable chunk of armor. Unfortunately, the attack brought upon the notice of two escorting fighters, who immediately turned in their direction.

"Negative effect!" Missy called.

"Switch to AT rounds," Fara said as Grace unlocked the breech face. She yanked down on the loader, and the spent shell slid free landing with a clang.

Outside the fighters were screaming toward their position. Twin bolts of energy slid along the edge of the pit instantly melting the snow and ice. Gadreel braced herself against the tank and raised her weapon. The Gatling Cannon spun up for a second before a rain of bullets sprayed upward. In the night sky, the hot rounds were easy to track with the naked eye. She raised the spray into the path of an oncoming fighter, which slid into the hail of projectiles, and was torn apart like food in a blender. What was left tumbled from the sky.

Sebastian joined her in trying to ward off the fighters. He raised up to his knees and shouldered the M107. He tracked the second interceptor as it turned away from Gadreel's deadly aim. Slowly it spiraled skyward seeking a height advantage. Then it flipped to aim down upon them, and Sebastian fired almost directly upward. It connected with the fighter's wing tip, snapping it off. Immediately the craft spun crazily as its control thrusters overcompensated. The Roth pilot fought to pull out of its earthward dive, but in a twist of fate, the aircraft slammed into the ground almost directly next to the downed Chinook.

"Fighters clear... for now," Sebastian said.

"AT loaded," Grace called slapping Missy on the thigh again.

Missy pressed her face to the sight feed and minutely inched the turret to the left. The cannon fired again at a dropship that seemed considerably closer. The armor piercing round punched through the middle thruster, and into the ship's internals. Highly flammable space fuel exploded making the massive vessel lurch. However, it didn't go down, as the other five thrusters compensated for the loss. Grace yanked open the breach and reloaded again as the ship tried to gain altitude. Without fighter cover, it was now just as vulnerable to Fara, as the helicopters had been to them.

"Aim at another thruster."

"You're joking right?!" Missy asked looking up at Fara. "I was just trying to hit them," she added.

"Well, hit them again... in another thruster," Fara replied pushing Missy back toward the camera feed. The Roth dropship warbled as it rose skyward. Grace slapped Missy's thigh again. The M1 Abrams turret skewed left and rose as it tracked the dropship. The girl fingered the joystick, sending another AT round skyward which just barely clipped the last engine. Fuel sprayed from the damage before exploding. The ship spun, dancing like a toddler high on sugar. Suddenly it flipped over on its back and came crashing down near the airport. The command deck crumpled in as the remaining thrusters were twisted off.

"Good job!" Fara said thumping Missy on the back.

"The demon craft is down, should we capture it, as Tobias did?" Gadreel called from outside.

"No, the objective was to defend the Seed Vault. We are the only ones defending the entrance, so we'll have to leave the dropship to someone else." Fara said and pulled free of the tank.

Down below the surviving men were converging on the alien wreck. Small lasers could be seen shooting out from damaged parts in the hull. However, It was in town that the fighting was most prevalent. Several thousand Roth tried to pull back to the downed Dropship.

"Load HE, and target the larger groups of Roth," Fara said climbing free. The angel was standing at the edge of the pit looking down toward the airport.

"How is your ammo?" Fara asked Gadreel.

"I have only seconds left," she admitted.

"Return to the bunker; the Roth will advance on us soon."

"I wish to remain with you," Gadreel said.

"Your weapon is already low on ammo, but when the Roth breach the vault, they'll be concentrated in the hallway," Fara said pointing back up the hill. The angel clumsily climbed the slippery shale with her heavy weapon, and disappeared over the edge.

Missy fired toward the town. The glowing shell exploded amid a group of lanky armor, and pieces went flying. Sebastian was like a white colored rock next to the pit. He lay on the ground entirely focused on the approaching enemy. His M107 fired, and a much smaller dot shot into the night toward town. More than a kilometer away a soldier's head vanished, but at this distance, Fara could only see a tiny figure falling to the ground.

"Take out the Captain's if you can. They'll have the biggest weapons."

"Yes, Sir!"

Fara certainly wasn't a sir, but she'd forgive the man. The Roth made two blobs. The majority moved toward the airfield, but several hundred were headed in Fara's direction. Players in the city were just starting to push them from behind.

Both Sebastian and the tank continued to fire on the approaching horde, but most had scattered, making them much more difficult targets. The leading troops were less than six hundred meters away. Fara climbed the steep shale pit and lay down next to an outcropping of rocks. She waited a while longer with the M16 tucked into her shoulder.

*"We are going to die,"* Fara thought. It came to her unbidden, and unwanted making her heart suddenly pound. Fear filled Fara's belly like battery acid, and she fought the strange urge to retch.

"I'm very proud of you," Charlie said hearing her heart thunder.

"What?"

"I said, I am proud of you. Keep up the good work, and I'll make the bite later gentle."

*"Ass,"* she muttered but smiled. Fara was going to suck Charlie's blood tonight. Even if he did bite her back, it would be worth it. Just the thought of seeing his pained expression made her a little horny.

A Roth soldier crested the rocks two hundred meters away, and Sebastian fired. The bullet split its chest open and knocked the alien back down the hill. Six more ran over the crest toward them.

Thankfully the alien weapons did considerably less damage at range. The thick air dispersed the red beams making them virtually useless past two hundred meters. Several such beams slashed into the snow nearby and did little more than melt a puddle. Fara fired once at a soldier who was standing still, and the bullet punched into its thigh knocking the alien over. The tank fired one last shell into a group. Several aliens were blasted into pieces and yellow gore rained down over the snow.

"We'll need to pull back. Grace, move to the vault doors under our cover." Fara yelled. The woman clutched her musket and ran up the pit slope. Missy took a position near Sebastian before spamming grenades at the ridge line.

"Save your grenades for inside, and move once Grace takes up position."

Sebastian was a machine. He ignored the lasers zipping past him as he slid another magazine into the well. Reaching forward he charged the weapon and continued to fire. Dozens of Roth were close enough to shout at, but he mechanically fired on them. Fara joined in by quickly firing bursts from the M16. After reloading her grenades, Missy scrambled past Fara toward the Vault with an expression close to panic on her face.

"Sebastian—"

"I am running low on ammo, so I will stay." He said dropping the next mag and reloaded. His rifle wouldn't be much use in the hallway. It rankled Fara, but she had to move. From up the hill, a musket fired filling the night with smoke. A young alien soldier dropped to the ground kicking as it's right shoulder went missing. Fara discharged her clip then stood and sprinted for the vault doors. Lasers raced after her as she scrambled up the short incline.

Grace was just finishing her reload as Fara reached her. The weapon had found a small depression next to the door, and Fara looked around for the same sort of protection. Ten feet away was a second deeper foxhole, and she dove for it. The musket fired again, before Grace suddenly giggled.

"How dare you make me laugh, Monty. I'm trying to fight." Grace said lowering the musket to reload. Her fingers deftly withdrew powder, patch, and ball like she'd done it a million times before.

Fara took the chance to reload her own weapon. Her heart rate was pounding in her ears as she aimed at the approaching Roth. Fara unleashed a long spray into the rushing troops. Six or seven soldiers slammed into the ground in a shower of yellow blood, and the ones behind slowed to return fire.

"Quiet Monty, the girls are at work," Grace said in a sharp voice. She lifted her musket aiming at a closing enemy. A pulse of three lasers hit her shoulder and neck. The woman remained upright long enough to fire back, and the ball slammed into the creature's stomach doubling it over. Fara reloaded as the other woman slouched. She ran forward hosing the area ahead of her to reach Grace, then grabbed the woman by her collar, and dragged her inside.

Lasers skidded off the concrete and metal doors as it slid closed. Grace was still alive, if only barely. Blood flowed from her wound, but she dutifully continued to reload.

"You should go in further," Grace said weakly. Fara ignored her statement, dragging the woman toward the airlock. As the metal entrance opened, Grace fired. The ball caught the creature in the visor, splitting its head open, and knocking it backward. Fara took the chance to pull her wounded comrade inside the second airlock.

"I can't feel my hands anymore. Is this what's it like to die, Monty?" The woman asked. The musket dragged along behind her, and smiled wanly to something the Monty said.

"I'm sorry for slapping you. I'm so tired—"

The woman relaxed as her eyes closed. Fara turned and pushed the second airlock door closed. She didn't want to see Grace's body harmed more than necessary. Both Gadreel and Missy were already aiming weapons at the door.

She let go of Grace near Gadreel, who stood closest to the airlock with her heavy armor. Missy was further down the hall near the actual vaults. Fara moved to put herself halfway between them. There was no point in retreating any further. If the seed vaults were breached, the objective would be lost, so she knelt reloading with one of the few remaining magazines left. The two others she laid on the floor next to her.

From the airlock, there was a loud banging. Gadreel set her feet and spun her barrels up to speed. A Roth opened the door revealing several squads of soldiers were already inside the bunker. The Gau 19-B fired for a little over a second, and a mere forty-two rounds cut through the metal door, but it was a slaughter. Ten or twelve aliens were sent back to their respawn—if it was still active.

Laser fire finally started punching through the metal airlock in return. Gadreel, empty of rounds spread her arms wide to cover her comrades, while Fara slowly fired her weapon one shot at a time. The door opened, and she put a bullet into the soldier's mask. It's body wedged the airlock open, and Fara dropped the magazine to reload. The next few seconds saw a dozen lasers hitting Gadreel. The Angel withstood the assault until her knees buckled, and she collapsed.

A small carbine laser burned a line across Fara's right thigh. She winced. It wasn't the worst pain she'd experienced, but it was close. Fara unconsciously emptied her mag as another laser hit her stomach, and she fell backward onto the concrete. Struggling against the pain, she grabbed the last magazine laying on the ground and reloaded. She was past aiming now, and just held the trigger down spraying bullets into the doorway.

Suddenly exhausted, Fara slumped backward. The airlock contained more corpses than soldiers, and they struggled over them to get inside. Missy waited until they'd clawed free of the blender, then sent grenades skipping up the hallway and into the new crowd. Fara watched in almost detached interest as yellow blood coated the ice-covered walls. As darkness closed on Fara, she thought she could hear gunfire from outside. For nearly a minute nothing happened. Charlie too floated in the dark void, and wondered how things turned out.

**[Event Complete]**

A door opened before Charlie. He stepped out to see the girls hugging Fara between them, while she feigned annoyance at the praise. Something was in Charlie's hand, and he looked down to discover a Golden Ticket.

**[One Free Ride to Space]**
**[Return here with the ticket in your possession on Saturday the 4th]**
**[A special event will begin at noon, but please arrive early]**

Charlie had to admit, that was an impossible task Fara had completed. With it, she'd earned him a place at another special event. Saturday would be in about five days, and he was going to fuck the hell out of that girl. He tucked the thick foil ticket into his shirt pocket carefully, then bowled into the cluster of weapons. Charlie grabbed Fara by the hips and lifted her up.

"You'll get what you want tonight!" Charlie said spinning her around.

"You'll let me bite you?" She asked, blood already flushing her face.

"Anywhere," Charlie agreed. Fara's eyes crossed and started to glow as her processing center went into overdrive. Drool slipped from the corner of her mouth as the scenarios grew more and more vivid. Charlie laughed at her expression.

Monty caught up along with Jen, Tobias, and Remy holding tickets of their own. Charlie set Fara down and turned to them.

"Why don't we take the time to register as a clan?" He asked.

"Secondhand Whor—" Remy started to say.

"I was thinking, Misfits," Charlie interrupted quickly. He'd tried hard to find a name that suited them. It may not have been perfect, but none could think of one better. He led the way upstairs and approached a console. Then he navigated the menu until Charlie found the option he wanted.

"Create Clan?" The console asked, and he selected, 'Yes.' It required ten thousand credits to register which he undoubtedly had. He entered the name and each member stepped forward to put their hands on the screen.

"Take a picture?" The console asked next. Why not? He selected 'Yes,' again.

They were directed to a photo booth. A kind of small room with a digital camera. Remy pulled three grenades out, and started to juggle them. Tobias knelt next to his Angel while she held his two-handed sword. Monty turned grace around in her southern dress in a slow waltz. Jen had her boy toys hoist her up between them. Charlie slowly walked back into the shot with his arms raised, as if to say, these losers are all mine.

Unfortunately, he wasn't watching where he stepped. His arm caught Remy as she continued to juggle. Her hand slipped, and one of the grenades went sailing into the air. Everyone but Charlie saw it's majestic arc, and oblivious to the destruction about to happen, he smiled into the camera.

There was a brilliant flash and a concussive slap against Charlie's back.

"Thank god that was only a flashbang," Remy said in a grateful sigh. Monty and Jen laughed as they climbed to their feet. Tobias appeared from a nearby respawn tube with a confused look on his face. Gadreel rushed to him and hugged him in apology. Remy sheepishly put her bloody grenades away, and they moved together back to the console to see what had happened.

"Oh my god, you are not using that picture," Jen said.

"I think its perfect," Charlie said seeing the image.

Charlie was in the foreground smiling like a doofus, and framed the picture with his arms. Tobias had been trying to save his Angel from the explosion. She'd been attempting to anoint him as a knight. The result was a two-handed sword cutting off the crusader's head. Monty's hand had slipped at the worst time. Grace's breasts were in full view as he accidentally tore her dress front clean off. Remy was scrambling forward to catch her grenade while panic was written on her face. Jen, still dressed as a succubus, had fallen and was pinned between two of her weapons. Sebastian held her parted knees as her legs wrapped around his waist in a desperate attempt to keep from crashing to the ground. Yohan clung to her neck as her face was pressed into the crotch of his pants.

"Hey!" Remy said pointing to the screen. "It totally looks like Jen's getting spit roasted in the background. She knows just where to put her hands too. That took me forever to learn."

"You are not using that," Jen repeated in a firmer voice. Her cheeks started to turn scarlet from embarrassment.

"I completely agree," Monty insisted.

"I think this is the perfect clan picture. We are the Misfits." He said accepting the clan photo.

# CHAPTER TWENTY-NINE
## *Shuttle Launch*

Five days later, Fara slid out of the Mustang, and her eyes genuinely twinkled as she stepped toward him. Charlie smiled seeing that warmth. Today she wore bright green eyeshadow, and her lipstick tasted of mint chocolate when she bounced up to kiss him. As Fara pressed her body to his, he ran his fingers through her dyed hair and grabbed a handful. She forced a tongue into his mouth, and they fought briefly. The bite marks and scratches were a testament to Fara's savage lovemaking last night, though not all the blood spilled had been his. Elva slipped under his other arm dressed in a new business skirt and matching jacket.

Saturday brought with it a busy Competition Center. Just outside the entrance, he found the 'Misfits' already waiting for him. Jennifer and Tobias were describing their exploits during the Roth Invasion to an enraptured Montgomery. Remy was back to doodling on her grenades.

"I'm glad everyone is here," Charlie said approaching the group.

"You only messaged us three times about it last night," Jennifer replied dryly.

"What can I say, this event smells even more special than usual."

"There are about two hours left, but we might as well go inside," Monty said with an equal level of enthusiasm.

The Competition Center was packed with new and old players. Each one eager to discover what today held, and the air was abuzz with speculation. When Charlie neared a console with his golden ticket, the screen activated.

"Event debriefing begins in 1 hour, please enter lobby one."

They walked as a group to the elevators and went down, but it wasn't the lobby Charlie remembered. This morning it was plain without any couches or consoles. A crowd was gathered, and frankly, most of the players looked like high level gamers. In fact, a few famous clans were in attendance, so the Misfits stood out like a bunch of jokers.

Jen settled against the wall as her hunky harem took up positions nearby. "I have good news, not that you would really care."

"What is it?" Charlie asked.

"Stephan is dead," she said with an expression of smug satisfaction.

"Can't say I'm surprised. The asshole played with his power too much and got burned. Did you get to say anything to him?"

A feral smile spread across her lips as she replied, "I did. I reminded Stephan that making me an enemy had not been wise. He called me a bitch just before he crumbled into dust. Not the most intelligent of final words."

"Are you going back to Blood and Pride now that he's dead?"

"Yes, but I certainly won't be investing as much energy or time. I've grown to enjoy the straightforward nature of Gun Meister. It's refreshing."

"Glad to hear it."

Monty quietly played pinochle with Grace and Elva. Charlie found himself losing hand after hand to Elva's keen ability to track numbers. Together the squad waited for the event to begin.

## [Event Starting]

They were transported to an underground missile silo. Charlie stood at the entrance to a tunnel mouth while electric vehicles zipped past with work crews. Stretching almost two hundred meters above them was a massive missile surrounded in scaffolding. About ten thousand people were crammed close to a podium with a middle aged women, wearing the familiar grey military tunic. She tapped the microphone with a clear lacquered fingernail and a nearby speakers squealed in protest.

"Please wait for the meeting to start." She paused, expecting everyone to settle down for her. "For your convenience, this debriefing will not be muted. However, you will be respectful and remain quiet. This is your only warning. The commander will arrive shortly."

From behind them a bulky suit of armor advanced. It was about eight feet tall and broad around the shoulders. The servos whined as it walked stiffly past the crowd, toward the podium, and mounted the steps. The gray armor turned toward them. There was a loud hiss of escaping air, and it's back opened. Colonel William Blake pulled free like a moth emerging from a cocoon. The female assistant stepped forward with a small officers cap to cover his sweaty hair. He approached the microphone and straightened his military jacket.

"I gotta say, that feels like walking around in a tuna can. Smells like it too." He said taking a drink of water. For a few seconds, he continued to arrange his rumpled uniform before starting.

"Humanity has not been idle since the Roth arrived. What you see behind me is the Mark One Power Armor. Sadly we don't have an endless supply of them, which is why only a few golden tickets were awarded. Ugly as they are the suits will prove necessary in the coming mission. We also finished work on the Titan X," he said and gestured back toward a gassing space rocket. Near the bottom, two red armored dropships clung on either side. Tiny men in coveralls were visible working on the ship with spot welders and tools.

"It looks like a giant cock with leeches stuck to the sides," Remy called. There was a ripple of laughter through the crowd.

"That it does. We haven't the time to make it pretty either. Hell, we barely had the time to make it functional, but the Roth have been a nasty leech attached to mankind's cock for too long. It's about time we burn them off." The old man cleared his throat and squared his shoulders.

"I believe most of you have developed a relatively complete picture of recent events, so I'll skip the lecture." The colonel paused for almost a minute as if he were battling the memories of his past. Finally, he cleared his throat.

"I lied when I said that capturing a dropship was our only small victory. It was dramatic but incorrect. The reason you're all here is because you and your weapons saved something we needed. It may have been a research facility, a stockpile of resources, or the evacuation of key personnel." He said scanning the crowd.

"For years we hunkered underground, waiting, praying, and struggling to survive. The eggheads got to work cracking open the secrets to the cloning bays. The engineers started expanding the underground facilities like the one we are standing in. Many more had the dirty, and heartbreaking job of collecting DNA samples. If the cloning technology proved viable, we might be able to bring them back. Not with memories intact, but they'd be reborn. Which spared the ladies from having to debase themselves to repopulating the world."

"You can imagine their relief," he said glancing back at his attendant. She gave a small smile.

"In the years that followed we created this simulated space. As many of you have guessed, firearms don't transform, and they certainly don't crawl into bed with you in the real world. All of us are standing in a digital reconstruction within this universe. Outside, it's a crumbling ruin, and a statement to mankind's fall from the evolutionary ladder."

"The Roth stayed for six months. Mostly just to hunt down the scattered survivors. After the Roth finished kicking our corpse, they departed the solar system but left some insurance. They built an outpost on Mars and left a single carrier to keep guard. The satellites in orbit were just to watch over what remained of humanity."

"You all witnessed first hand the Roth's return. We fought them that first day, and once again humanity tasted their wrath. This time though, we also watched and took notes."

"The Roth are not omnipotent, nor are they that superior as warriors. On average they are slightly stronger, and a bit tougher to kill, but they have some glaring faults. Their society appears to be built on acquiring glory. They need it like a man needs air. The young Roth are especially susceptible, which is why so many of those vainglorious children rushed into battle."

"We also dissected a few bodies as well. They breathe a combination of nitrogen, carbon dioxide, and inert noble gases. If the Roth had arrived on earth a few millennia ago, they might have found the planet very pleasant."

"After we learned our enemies do in fact bleed, we counter-attacked. Men and women around the world rose up to capture one or more dropships. We would need them if we hoped to ever strike back at the Roth. We had hoped for four vessels, and you delivered six. China—the first to attack—captured two of them. France and London managed one while America captured two."

"You may recognize the ones behind us."

"The dropships have enough fuel to enter and exit the atmosphere, but on their own, they wouldn't be able to get to Mars. Among the things we were able to save, were blueprints for the Titan X missile used to send large loads into space. This, I'm told, would give us the needed escape velocity to reach the red planet."

"After capturing the dropships, we had to wait again. The alien carrier and the hundreds of fighters are still a threat in lunar orbit. They'd simply destroy anything we launched."

"Today, we detected movement. The Roth Carrier is accelerating on a trajectory that takes them toward Jupiter. We believe the Roth have built a fuel refining station in orbit over the gas giant. They need to make a pit stop before heading back to Mars. Fortunately for us, a thousand meters of steel isn't a sports car, and it accelerates like a snail on tar paper. It'll take more than a week for them to reach their destination, which will give us a window to launch our operation."

"Finally, we come to the mission." The colonel said and deliberately took a drink of water. He set the glass down and looked across the crowd with hard eyes.

"Extermination."

"Plain and simple, annihilation. Just as they did to us, we will destroy that outpost by any means. This is the last Roth event, and you will decide it's outcome." The colonel said. A player in the crowd interrupted him with a raised hand. The old man paused and pointed to him.

"Why don't you just slam the ship into the outpost. You want it gone, right?"

"We have no idea what sort of defenses the Roth have on mars. I for one am not willing to risk our one chance on a Hail Mary. It's far better to approach the planet from the blind side."

"The inside of the outpost is a mystery to us, but we assume you will find three things. Obviously, they will have a cloning center. The second will be a power facility, likely located near the center of the dome. The last thing will be the atmospheric generators."

"You will need to destroy two of the three objectives. Without power or clones, the Roth will slowly starve. Destroying the air mixers and reactor will bring a much faster end. It won't matter how many clones are made if the Roth can't breathe. Personally, I rather hope for this outcome. Call me a nasty old man, but I like the idea of them respawning and suffocating in their own poison over and over."

"Speaking of poison brings us full circle to the Mark One Power Armor. I have to warn you. The Powersuits will be your lifeline. Think of them less like armor, and more like a diving suit. It will contain roughly six hours worth of air. If you get shot, that air will dwindle to several minutes, and running into the alien outpost will not save you. Just as they cannot breathe our air, we cannot breathe theirs. There is no oxygen on Mars except what we bring."

"That isn't to say the armor is made of glass. You can take hits, quite a few actually. Just don't stand in front of a captain's laser cannon." He said scanning their faces.

"Any questions so far?"

"Are there going to be kids and stuff?" A woman asked.

"That question came up during our briefings. The Roth, by empirical evidence, don't suffer children kindly. The cloning technology lets them spit out new bodies as young adults. However, you will encounter civilians. I warn you, every Roth drinks and bathes in glory. Turning your back on an unarmed Roth is just as stupid as handing him your weapon."

"Can we capture one?"

"You can try, but we won't let you back on the dropships. Not with a Roth in your company." Blake said with some venom. The old man sucked in a ragged breath and gathered himself. "I apologize. There are few of us left that remember that day forty years ago. I watched the destruction of our world, and for years those memories festered into a pure crystalline form of hate. I could care less what you do to any Roth you find, but it's best to remember we are there to do a job."

"Any more questions?" He asked, but no one spoke.

"After the Roth Carrier departs, we will launch ourselves. It will take us almost twenty-two hours to reach Mars, which is fast, but you're all going to be twiddling your thumbs for a day. The actual mission will start on Sunday at roughly noon. Once there we will attack from three directions. The south side, we believe, has the most defenses. It's where the Roth landing pads are located. The Chinese will attack from the east side, while the French and English attack from the North. Our dropships will come in from the west and drop everyone off five kilometers from the dome."

"Your first job will be to force march to the habitat, breach it, and get inside. From there you must locate one of the objectives and destroy it. I'm sorry, but we don't have maps."

"I also have to state that there will be no respawns. The dropships have cloning bays, but we only managed to make so many suits of power armor. That's another reason why we needed the best." Blake said scanning the faces of the assembled crowd. Charlie felt the old man's eyes pause briefly on him and his small clan. He didn't feel like the best, but they had earned the tickets.

"Get into your squads, and board a dropship. Your digital pattern will be uploaded into memory and your equipment added to storage. Other technicians will go over the workings of the armor. For this mission, you may make any change to your loadout free of charge."

"We launch in two hours."

"For better or worse, victory or defeat this is the last special event. Godspeed, and for all our sakes, good hunting." He said giving them a heartfelt but sloppy salute.

An electric golf cart pulled up, and the old man climbed down from the podium. A technician in the passenger seat ran up the stairs and crawled into the power armor. While this went on, the middle-aged woman moved to the podium.

"Let us make this as simple as possible. Everyone to the right will board Dropship Alpha. The rest of you will head to Beta. Squads should stay together." She said gesturing with her hands.

Charlie along with his squad got into a loose line heading for the left side of the rocket. It was still discharging gasses occasionally as the technicians ran tests. A few players were talking amongst themselves as they climbed the long metal ladder.

"Is it too late to tell them I'm mildly claustrophobic?" A black-haired female said.

"You're gonna miss this because of an upset tummy? I'd log off and wrap a barf bag over my mouth." A second man said.

He agreed. Charlie was excited they were getting Power Armor and going into space. The girl was already starting to look a little green, and the people around her laughed.

Players used welded hand rungs to climb into the dropships ramp. It had been attached to the Titan X missile via the roof. Everything was turned on its side, and the ceiling was the wall. When it was his turn, Charlie grabbed a rung and started to climb. Inside the bay, drop pods lined the lower deck. A very young boy in gray coveralls pointed to an unoccupied pod, and the player in front of him started shaking.

"I don't think I can do this," she said holding a hand over her mouth like she was about to barf.

"Don't worry," the kid said quickly. "You'll be transported to the power armor course, as soon as your inside."

Reluctantly the girl climbed into the tiny cylinder and it snapped closed. Charlie wedged himself into the next pod, and the door slid shut. Almost immediately he was standing on Martian soil. In the distance the Valles Marineris was visible, and it made the Grand Canyon look like a scratch on the earth's surface. Before Charlie was a dark-skinned Filipino woman who stood on Mars in plain coveralls. She had fierce eyes and a serious expression. Next to her was a massive suit of armor. The woman glanced down at a small tablet in her hands.

"NA1339872, also known as Charlie?" The woman asked.

"Yes?"

"It will be my job to instruct you on the proper use of the Mark One Power Armor. Failure to heed my instructions will result in your quick demise." She said moving closer. "This will be your armor during the event, please place your palm on the screen to accept it."

Charlie put his hand on the screen. There was a loud beep, and the girl tucked the tablet into her coveralls.

"Damn, it's huge," he said looking up at the towering gray suit.

Charlie was of average height at five foot seven, and the armor towered over him at eight feet tall. The helmet was half molded into the broad torso, so the suit didn't have a neck. Along with large shoulder pads were a pair of rounded arms. Each leg was wrapped in a band of steel, and the feet looked like ice climber shoes.

"You should have seen the prototypes. They were essentially walking metal coffins with arms and legs. One of the test pilots said he could see the ghosts of his ancestors. We told him it was just his reflection on the visor, but he went a little crazy. Thankfully they pulled him out before he did any real damage." She said turning toward him with a hard look of suspicion.

"You afraid of tight spaces?"

"Not really, but I've never been inside a metal coffin before."

"Come around the back here," she said walking around the side. "Hopefully you'll not have to climb in or out of the suit, but there's a trick to it." A rectangular powerpack dominated the back, not unlike the alien armor. The girl reached under this and flicked a hidden switch. The pack slid up over the head as the waist and legs cracked open down the middle.

"Get naked, trust me, you'll cook yourself alive if you're wearing clothes."

Charlie didn't hesitate in removing his coat, and armor. The woman half turned away as he pulled his shoes and pants off. Wearing only his black boxers, he approached the suit. The legs were split open along with the torso, and he stepped barefoot onto a raised padded platform. Then snaked his arms into the suit's sleeves. At the end, he found a set of brass knuckles, and each of his fingers slipped into one of the rings. Finally, he pushed himself forward into the body. As his head entered the helmet, the suit closed shut behind him. Around his body gel pads filled up ensuring there was as little wasted air space as possible.

The clear visor had an excellent field of view considering the amount of armor surrounding him. Pale green text began scrolling down the length of one side as the system booted up. Then a HUD blossomed across the glass. At the top of his view was a compass and an air meter. As soon as Charlie drew in his first breath, it dropped to 99%. He raised both his hands and the metal arms came into view. Testing the knuckle controls caused the fingers to flex, and the armored gauntlet closed its fist with a whine of servos. As he let go, the thick fingers only relaxed into a half-open position. The girl in her coveralls walked around to his front with the tablet in hand again.

"How does it feel?"

"Like I'm getting a full body hand job," Charlie admitted. The gel pads pressing against his naked skin felt like a slime monster was trying to feel him up. A small fan blew air across his face, which made him want to sneeze.

"Is there any way to scratch my nose?" He asked.

"That feature costs extra," the girl said tapping her control tablet. "Try moving around, let's see if we can get the suit calibrated."

He lifted his right leg, and the armor moved as if he were wearing concrete shoes. There was a slight delay as his legs pushed against the gel pads, and the suit finally recognized what he wanted. It didn't help that they were on Mars, so the gravity was only 1/3rd that of Earth's. He felt like he was standing on stilts and swimming in heavy water. Despite being slow, the suit's powerful actuators pushed him into a leaping bound. Charlie flailed in surprise, and the armor bounced once on the rocky red surface, then slid to a halt.

"Your numbers aren't bad," the girl said in surprise. She tapped at the tablet a few more times. "Keep at it, once you get used to walking around we'll start on some of the suit functions."

He closed his fist and pushed himself off the red loamy martian dirt to his knees. Then he awkwardly shifted his weight and straightened. This time when he moved forward, he pictured himself floating. The armor sailed ahead three or four feet, and he came to a skidding halt. After about ten false starts he ended up skating along in a shower of red dust.

"Good, good. Let's move on. You can practice on the way to Mars."

Charlie came to an awkward stop about twenty feet away.

"The radio is voice activated and will be your chief means of communicating with your squad. We have hopefully fixed the problem with the aliens pinpointing your location. Instead of broadcasting like before, the suit will add a delay to your words. It encrypts and sends out packets in little bursts, so a captain will need to be quite close before he catches your signal."

"As a squad leader, you'll also have access to the command channel. To switch over, turn your head to the right. You should feel a small button with your chin. He did as instructed, and Charlie felt a rounded nub. As he pressed it, his HUD changed slightly; SQD was replaced with CMDNET. The girl reached up pressing a finger to her ear.

"Can you hear me?" She asked over the radio.

"Yes."

"Good, you may be given new mission orders or asked for an update. If you find one of the objectives, you will want to call in for reinforcements. Just remember to switch back to the squad channel after you're done talking."

"If you need out of your suit, just say 'Get me out of this Tin Can,' but I wouldn't advise doing it right now." She said with a smirk.

"I suppose the last thing we need to work on is your weapon loadout.

Do you have any preferences?"

"Any hints to the environment?" Charlie asked in reply.

"Sorry, I'm not in the know."

Charlie was thinking of taking the twin tommy guns. The devs were going to give him free mods so he could kit them out. He could carry two weapons that shared the same magazines. With the power armor on, he could bring as much ammo as he wanted. The only problem would be reloading. Tobias could probably manage any captains they met. Jen, Monty, and Remy all had weapons capable of taking on the armored soldiers. However, the old man had said there would be civilians.

"Can you load in the two Thompson Center Machine Guns with drum mags and laser sights?"

The woman pushed a few buttons on her console, and they appeared in the air, then slowly fell to the ground. He picked both up, and as his fingers closed on the grips, the green lasers activated.

"Targets?" The girl asked.

"Sure."

A group of cardboard silhouettes appeared about ten meters away. Charlie turned and leveled both weapons. The Tommy guns began to chatter, but the noise was muffled through the suit like he had cotton in his ears. The fat rounds shot past the targets before he settled both guns onto the middle one. Even on full auto the suits arms barely moved as the weapons emptied themselves. A ragged hole about the size of a pie tin filled the primary target.

"Reloads please," he said and several drums appeared. Charlie picked up a mag but found the release was a little nub, and his thick fingers struggled to press it in.

"I need oversized controls."

The woman was already prepared for it, and a long mag release appeared on the weapon. He thumbed the release, and the empty drum slid free. Then he pushed the fresh mag in and yanked on the top bolt.

Trying to shoulder the gun was awkward in the armor. Jen was going to have a tough time if she brought her .50 caliber Barrett. There was already a sling on the weapon. He could wrap it around the forearm which would keep it from dropping to the ground when he let go. That way he could reload one gun at a time. The only other thing he needed was a belly pack full of mags.

"Grenades?" The woman asked.

"A little bit of everything, and a couple of pounds of C-4." Another thick belt appeared on his torso. All he had to do was yank a Velcro'd grenade free and throw it.

"Are you satisfied with your loadout?" She asked tapping her tablet again.

More weapons would be pointless. Sofie, while a fantastic gun, wouldn't be much use. Charlie suspected it was going to be cramped, urban fighting. The two machine guns would probably serve him better in close quarters, but should he bring Elva too? The pistol would be a last-ditch weapon.

"Put on my 1911 as well. I probably won't need her, but it's best to be safe." He said at last. Around his leg, a thick thigh holster appeared. He let go of the Tommy gun, drew Elva, and thumbed the safety off. Even without a laser sight, he managed to put a few rounds into the target's head.

"The shuttle is going to launch in about ten minutes. You should be there." The girl reminded him. "If you want to practice more just find an open console and restart the simulation."

"Appreciate the help."

"Good luck," she said ending the training session.

Charlie appeared above ground on a flat scrub filled expanse which reminded him of the Nevada desert. Thousands of people, mostly NPC's, lounged in chairs and drank beer while they waited. Camouflage tents and cameras were set up to catch the event. Charlie didn't find his squad right away, so he parked himself in the company of a few young technicians. He suspected this was in the 'real world' version of the game, or at least one of his clones was sitting here. Something cold touched his arm, and he looked over. A young girl with welding goggles on her head smiled.

"You look like you need a beer," she said. The brown bottle was plain without any markings, but it was covered in condensation. Charlie took it and tried a sip. The world may have ended, but someone still knew how to brew a good beer. It was light, hoppy, and Charlie drank about half before he belched.

A siren sounded as dirt and scrub brush rose into the air. Two halves of a massive hatch slowly split open. The crowd started to cheer. It took about a minute for the steel portal to fully rise, and all the while thousands of people roared. The mob was only about half a mile away, so the sound was almost deafening when it came. The missile slid free in a rush and rose skyward on a curtain of fire. The two dropships to either side used their articulating thrusters to keep the rocket stable. The crowd stood raising their hands to shield from the glaring sun.

Charlie watched it until the contrail disappeared. In other parts of the world, three more rockets launched into space. Each of them on a trajectory for Mars.

# CHAPTER THIRTY

## *Spacebunnies*

Everyone laughed as Remy slammed into the ground. There was a shower of red dust as the two-ton suit skidded to a stop. The young girl cursed over the radio and kicked her armored legs about. Her Power Armor was like a miniature version at only six feet tall.

"Bloody help me already!"

"You aren't going to get help on the mission. Most of us will be busy shooting back at the Roth." Charlie reminded her. He was honestly surprised the girl was having such trouble. Typically she was one of their best players. Tobias bounded over in three leaps, bent slowly, and picked up Remy's suit by her power pack.

"Stop trying to shoot while your moving," Jen suggested. "The weapon recoil is just going to spin you around and push you in a strange direction."

"Our battle sister is correct. The sacred engineers cast cleats upon our feet so that they might grip unstable soil." Tobias said letting Remy go, and she just managed to keep her feet in the dusty red soil.

The simulation was momentarily frozen in time. Clownishly goofy T-Rex dinosaurs, which represented the aliens in this training scenario, surrounded the squad on all sides. Red beams slid through the air like molasses on a cold night.

"Let's try this again," Charlie said activating a floating console. "We need to alternate our strides, especially as we approach the enemy outpost. I want two people on the ground ready to fire while the others move forward."

Charlie and his armored squad reappeared some two miles from a low Martian hill. Almost immediately, lasers began to zip past sporadically as dinosaurs spawned ahead. In the distance, a glowing beacon marked the enemy outpost.

"Jen and Tobias first, then Remy and Monty. I will follow behind and guard our flank."

It was like watching ungainly robots moonwalk. Jen and Tobias had proved the most adept and gliding over the Martian surface. He'd made them the point team precisely because of that. Monty had considerable skill, but he still only possessed that flintlock rifle.

Jen and Tobias jumped clearing a ten-meter crater. As they landed Monty and Remy made several small hops before jumping the same obstacle. Charlie brought up the rear and slowly skipped over the rocky landscape. As they neared the enemy position, goofy T-Rex dinosaurs stood from cover. In their stubby reptilian claws, they held laser carbines.

Their aim was atrocious as they fired from the hip, and lasers cut wildly across the expanse. Jen held a heavy British FAL, which was a semi-automatic rifle chambered in 7.62x51. She paused next to a boulder and raised the weapon to her chest. Attached to the Picatinny rail, was an oversized 4x scope. The air density was less than one percent that of earth, and gravity roughly one third. She purposely aimed low at the knees of the distant T-Rex and fired. Sparkles filled the air as the giant head of the dinosaur disappeared. Together the squad bounded forward again, but Remy was still struggling to keep up. Her short legs and lack of coordination meant Monty had to slow too.

"Slow pushes," Charlie reminded them. "The real Roth aren't pee brained dinosaurs. They may be waiting in the shadow of a crater."

Charlie was grateful they didn't sweat because he would have drowned by now as it filled his suit. His skin felt unnaturally hot, and the gel pads were starting to remind him of slimy tentacles wrapped around his body. They managed to make it two kilometers closer this time, but the further they got the more NPCs spawned.

"I need to log for dinner," Jen said.

"I too must depart," Tobias added.

"Fine, over training won't help us anyway. Have a good night and sleep well." He said turning to his right.

A small blue console had followed him all through simulation. He tapped at the screen with his armored finger, which ended the scenario and Charlie came too in a small ship's berth. The room was a converted equipment storage compartment. Five bunks had been affixed to one side. Across the ceiling and walls were hundreds of rounded metal rings, probably for tying the cargo down. All of the weapons were present in the small room. The only ones missing were Monty and Grace, though the man was a digital ghost now, so it wasn't like he would ever log off. Jen and Tobias were logged out in the two bunks opposite, while Remy was conked out on the birth below him.

They must have been in a digital instance of the dropship, which made sense. There were almost five-thousand armored suits in the lower deck. The players would be crammed like sardines in what little space remained. Instead, his squad had this particular version of the dropship to themselves.

Sofie and Fara were floating in the air a few inches above his face while the others played tag in the zero-g environment. He tried to sit up but found his legs and chest fastened down via a thick Velcro belt. At the sound of tearing the girls turned toward him.

"Enjoying space?" He asked.

"Da," Sofie said while Fara shrugged her shoulders.

"Very much," Thelma and Luise called from across the cabin.

As the last belt came free, he floated upward. Charlie grabbed a hold of Sofie to steady himself except he only ended up dragging her into the center of the room with him. For a few seconds, he flailed in the weightless environment before Sofie pushed him. Charlie just barely managed to catch a handhold as he bounced off the wall.

"Play tag with us?" The twins begged.

"I'll pass for now, but you go ahead. I want to check out the dropship. The last time I was here, it was under hectic circumstances. I'd like to see the ship without aliens shooting at me." He said using the cargo rings to pull himself toward the exit. On the wall next to the door was a familiar square button. He touched it with his hand, and the door slid open.

The hallway was filled with black scorch marks, and a two-handed sword was sticking from the wall halfway down. 'Word of God,' was still printed on the blade. He wondered if Tobias would try and yank his weapon out at some point. Charlie snaked through the upper part of the doorway into the passage. The twins sailed through the door after him, hit the opposite wall, and kicked off toward Charlie. A pair of hands pushed him, and he twisted away from the wall.

"Tag!" The twins called in unison. Without handholds, he ended up floating slowly down the middle of the passage. Charlie quickly discovered that wiggling his hands or kicking his feet didn't do a damn thing. He only ended up spinning in place from the motion. Without something to push against all he could do was slowly drift down the hall. The other girls had stopped just outside of the bunk room.

"Any help?" He asked, and they quickly shook their heads. He was 'It,' and they wouldn't risk getting tagged. Up ahead the twins were still giggling as they disappeared up to the command deck.

As he spun in circles, the two-handed blade came into view. He reached out grabbing the hilt and pulled himself to the wall. Behind him Elva, Fara, and Sofie readied themselves to spring away should he come after them. He turned toward the stairs, placed his feet on the hilt, and kicked off. The switchback approached quickly, and Charlie managed to grab the armored cover. From there he used the railing to guide himself the rest of the way. Behind two of the consoles, white hair was just visible. A pair of twinkling purple eyes appeared over the edge then ducked down.

"Did he see you?" Thelma asked in a whisper.

"I don't think so," Luise whispered back.

"This is fun."

"I know, my heart is going doki-doki," Luise agreed.

The rest of the girls stopped just at the switchback waiting to see what he would do. The command deck was about thirty feet across. Several chairs and consoles were grouped in pairs facing the front. A single massive chair dominated a raised central platform. Above him, the glory of space was visible through a thick set of glass windows. Without Earth's atmosphere to defuse the light every star was like a shining beacon. The twins were still giggling behind the console which brought him back to the present.

He pushed himself forward and across the deck. Instead of going for the twins he kicked off the captain's chair, and back to the stairs. Sofie appeared first, and he caught her shoulders. They ended up spinning together toward the glass windows. She held onto him as they bounced off.

"I vas right about you, Charlie," Sofie said in a throaty purr. "There is something special about you."

"You girls are something else too," he replied.

Sofie's steel colored eyes were full of pent-up lust. She spun him about and snaked her hands under his arms pinning him in a zero-gee-half-nelson. "We have been talking while you trained." She purred into his ear. "You are a vicked man, so we thought it time you are made to squeal."

Her teeth bit down on his ear, and he started to grow hard as the other girls hungrily closed in on him. Elva collided with him next, and her fingers began to work the buttons on his pants. Thelma, Luise, and Fara quickly joined in the small tangle as his zipper slid down. Charlie's trousers were pulled free first. Within a minute he found himself stripped naked and his clothes tossed to the corners of the bridge. The girls undressed next, and more clothes flew away. As a mass of clinging arms and legs, they spun through the air. Charlie awkwardly kissed Sofie as she stroked him to full mast. Lips and tongues caressed his skin, but the girls found it almost impossible to mount him. Sex in space was simpler said than done. Newton's third law made for some tricky coupling.

They bounced against the bridge windows and approached the commander's chair. Charlie was dragged toward it and hands grabbed him. Elva curled a hand around his bicep and held him down. Fara floated to his left side and pinned his thigh to the seat. Sofie wedged herself behind the chair and locked her hands together around his waist.

The twins crawled atop him first. Both were identical except two distinguishing marks. Thelma had a small mole on her right breast. Luise had a rosy red splotch on her vaginal entrance. It was two inches wide, vaguely shaped like a heart, and strangely sensitive to the touch. Thelma eagerly closed on his manhood, and guided her entire body toward it. Each of the girls felt a little different inside, maybe just to spice things up for the Meister. Thelma had soft fleshy speed bumps all the way down her love tunnel, and for a second, her eyes crossed and she moaned as his cock slipped over each one. Meanwhile, Luise turned in midair to faced her batch sister. They clasped hands together as she seated herself atop Charlie's face. He licked up the length of her candy flavored sex to her birthmark, and she shivered in response.

As one, the twins ground their hips back and forth against him. His tongue slid over Luise's birthmark, but it was Thelma that moaned. Charlie licked between the valley of her honeyed lips, and deep into her entrance. She was sweet like candy canes and gingerbread.

"Yes," Thelma whimpered. Both girls picked up speed and Charlie groaned in response. Thelma rocked her hips, and his manhood kept rolling back and forth over her slick speed-bumps. He dug into Luise's waist as she fucked his face faster still.

The batch sisters weren't just close. They shared the same database, reading and writing memories, along with a double dose of sensations. What Thelma felt, Luise did as well which explained why both were starting to shiver and shake. They hugged each other as the inevitable climax approached. Charlie joined them in that, and let out a long low groan as he came. They both slowed and Thelma slid free of Charlie's erection with a sigh of pleasure.

The vacancies were quickly filled. Sofie climbed over the captain's chair and closed her long legs around his neck. Her sex was starting to puddle with leaking lubricant. The twins switched places with Fara and Elva as Charlie closed his mouth over Sofie's sex. The tall redhead leaked like a river, and spread copious amounts of slick lube over his face as she ground against his lips. Her voice was thick as she moaned. Hands pushed his legs apart as two tongues licked up the length of his shaft. Two sets of lips kissed his manhood before one settled over the head of his cock. They slowly slid lower and lower until they touched his base. This time it was Charlie who moaned. Despite having just climaxed, he started to grow hard again. While the lips made work of his shaft; a set of teeth bit at his thigh. That would be Fara, and he relaxed slightly.

"Nyet! Don't stop, suck me harder," Sofie begged. Charlie had paused trying to figure out who was going down on him. That and the intense stimulation slamming into his brains. Sofie pushed herself hard against his face, and he sucked her exposed clitoris into his mouth. Long fingers sank into his hair as her hips shivered. Both he and Sofie moaned in virtual unison. Fara's tongue slid over his inner thigh while her nails scratched his balls. The soft, succulent lips pulled from his cock, and he felt a moment of cold air on his saliva covered shaft. Then the lips were back faster than ever. The mouth quickly slid down his length, and he moaned as they touched the base of his shaft. Teeth bit down hard on his other thigh, and nails raked over his stomach.

Sofie's sex was streaming more and more liquid across his face. In the micro-gravity, they made long stringy ropes between his mouth and her groin. Her hips rocked faster discharging fat blobs of clear lube in the air, and they floated away across the bridge.

"Da, da!"

Charlie agreed with Sofie as the mouth on his manhood sent him to second heaven. Another pair of hands started digging scratches into his stomach and thigh. The giant redhead shivered atop him as her orgasm came, and Charlie was moments behind as the mouth on his cock moved even faster. He moaned into Sofie's milky sex as raw pleasure rocked his world. The lips descended down his shaft, and a throat closed around his head as she swallowed, drinking his essence. Afterward, her tongue slowly licked him clean, and Charlie shuddered from the service.

When Sofie released his head and floated free, he looked down. Fara knelt between his legs with her mouth around his manhood. She was looking up at him with her brilliant blue eyes. Elva knelt next to her and continued to rake her long fingernails over Charlie's thighs as he stared in astonishment.

"Holy shit, Fara. I may not have squealed, but only because my mouth was full." He said to the girl, and her eyes twinkled at the compliment. His manhood popped free of her mouth before she turned and sank her teeth into his thigh.

"Fuck," he cried as she quickly drew blood.

# CHAPTER THIRTY-ONE

## *Attack on Mars*

Together the 'Misfits' stood on the bridge of the dropship. The rusty red marble of Mars drifted lazily across the window, polar caps starkly white against the blood-colored craters and valleys. It floated against a backdrop of scintillating stars and a vast dark void. A few kilometers away two more rocket-ships were visible by their engine flares. Those were the Chinese and European forces, and together they would soon assault the alien base.

"That is a spectacular view," Charlie marveled. He hadn't meant to say it aloud, but there it was.

"I tried to come up here when it was first visible, but the Command Deck was—already occupied," Monty said coughing lightly, and glanced toward Charlie. The rest of the squad followed his gaze.

"You saw that?"

"Thankfully, no. There was enough warning to spare us any—awkwardness." Montgomery said pausing on the final word. Grace hung onto his arm while she fanned her heating face.

"Wait, wait... you're telling me I missed the space orgy?" Remy asked in utter shock.

"No such thing happened," Charlie replied immediately. "The girls were showing me how to play zero-g tag. That's all." He said in a quick matter-of-fact voice—which clearly fooled no one.

"I can't believe I missed my chance to get fucked in zero gravity," Remy exclaimed slapping her forehead. She turned and threw her small frame at the massive ebony champion nearby. "Philip, take me now."

"Ugh, some of us just ate," Jen said refusing to look at the girl.

"Keep thy sin bottled; our holy mission is upon us." Tobias agreed.

"Yes, the time for pleasure has passed. Mars may appear little more than a dot, but we are only an hour away." Monty said.

Remy pouted and tried to coax her weapon down below for a quickie. Philip however, was strangely enchanted by the growing red sphere. The long scar of the Valles Marineris Trench could just be seen at this distance. They all stood—more or less—quietly watching the planet approach. The vessel decoupled with an explosive charge, and the Titan-X Rocket slowly tumbled away. It had done its job getting them here, and hopefully, the dropship would have fuel enough to return home. Less than a hundred meters away another armored ship turned on its axis and slid closer.

The mission had been kept quiet until last night when word had leaked about the assault, and the news was quickly spreading. Thousands of players jealously poured into the Competition Center to find out more. Unfortunately, they'd only be spectators today. The camera feeds back to earth would be delayed by a nine-minute light lag, but the world was watching the event.

The bridge intercom activated and a female voice announced, "Please come to the loading bay, and enter your armor. The event begins in twenty minutes."

"Well shucks, I was rather hoping they would orbit the planet once before landing," Monty said slightly crestfallen. Grace clung to him as he turned and pushed from the bridge window. Charlie followed after with his own girls in tow. He glided down the stairs using the handrail before kicking down the hallway.

The loading deck was filled with half-naked players suiting up. Five open sets of armor stood waiting in the corner of the cargo bay. Behind the towering Mark-One Power Armor was his equipment and the drop pod.

"Good luck," Elva said kissing his cheek, then transformed in a flash of light.

Charlie unlaced his boots and shucked his pants. After pulling his shirt free, Fara took them and clutched his clothes to her chest. Her eyes flicked across his face, and she smiled. Charlie reached forward pulling the girl toward him for a kiss as well. Her lips were soft, and tasted faintly of cherry. "Good luck," she whispered and floated backward. They had certainly come a long way since their first meeting. Thelma and Luise hugged him next before changing into their weapon forms.

Jen's armor was next to his, and she hastily stripped down to her red underwear. While Charlie didn't exactly look, it was impossible not to notice her shapely figure. Mostly naked she stepped onto the raised platform for the feet. The blond wiggled her arms down the sleeves of the suit and pushed her head into the helmet. Her butt went in last, and the Power Armor closed.

"We got twenty minutes. You sure I can't have a quickie?" Remy asked next in line. The short flat-chested female floated naked next to her suit, and Charlie caught sight of her teal pubic hair before quickly glancing away.

"Focus on the event. We'll be returning to the ships, so you'll get a second chance." Charlie said turning to his armor.

He put one foot on the raised pad and thrust his arms inside the sleeves. As his head entered the helm, the suit closed over him. The inside reeked like an unwashed jockstrap, and for a second he held his breath against the foul stench. Thankfully the odor began to fade as bottled air shot up his nose. Slowly the armor powered on and green text crawled down the visor. The HUD appeared, and he straightened in the suit. Jen was shifting her weight back and forth familiarizing herself with the delay lag. He followed her example. Remy finally crawled into her armor, butt naked, and it closed. Tobias and Monty were already inside their suits and gearing up. Each of his squad mates had a small green diamond and a name-tag over their heads. The rest of the bay was filled with armored players testing their gear. Instead of diamonds, green dots floated over their heads marking them as friendly.

"Mount up," he called. They had only minutes left, and there was a noticeable pull of gravity again. Charlie gathered his equipment, and double checked everything. The twins had slings which he wrapped around his forearms. Then he waddled slowly into the cramped space of his pod. It snapped closed leaving him in darkness, save the green HUD.

A square formed in the lower right corner, and Colonel Blake's wrinkled face appeared. "This is a last minute reminder. Your objective is to get inside the dome and destroy the key installations. Killing aliens is only a means to that goal. Don't get bogged down in fighting. Today you are the ones outnumbered, and they will quickly swamp you."

"It's currently day on this side of Mars, and the enemy compound will be five kilometers to the east."

"Squad leaders, should you find the objective call for immediate aid. Your radio broadcast will automatically tell us your location."

The image on the screen flickered a few times, and the old man scrubbed his face before looking into the pickup again. When he spoke, his voice was troubled. "Someone once said mercy is for the weak, but humanity could not be more so. No, that statement is patently false. I believe mercy is a luxury of the strong, and it's something we cannot currently afford."

"Show them our mettle and courage, but above all—show them no quarter. Godspeed, and good hunting." He said before the window closed.

Gravity was unquestionably back as the ship fell through the atmosphere. The engine noise grew so loud that it blotted out everything else. In the center of Charlie's HUD, a circle spun as it counted down from sixty seconds. The massive ship bucked as it continued to descend through the thin atmosphere. As they approached the landing site, pods began firing from the belly of the craft. Charlie was glad for the gel padding as his pod ejected from the ship, and his head slammed against the helmet of his suit. There was a whistling sound as his thin-shelled cocoon plummeted through the Martian air. He hit the ground hard and the sides of the pod exploded away, which left him standing on a roughly circular platform looking out at the rocky terrain.

Charlie was facing south, but honestly, every direction looked the same. It wasn't blood red as it appeared from orbit. Instead, the broken boulder filled landscape took on various shades of brownish rust. The dropship continued on its flight as it disgorged more and more squads.

"Beautiful scenery, but I suspect this would be an unpleasant place to call home," Monty said over the radio. The heavy gray armor raised a gauntlet over his visor, for a better view, and Monty looked like a hunchback gorilla staring into the sunrise. For once Charlie didn't bother gawking. The remarkable fact he was on Mars, was quelled slightly by the bleak, barren landscape. Arizona came to mind as he swept his eyes over the rocky ridges. His team had landed within a hundred meters of each other, and he picked them out quickly among the armored figures skipping across the Martian soil.

Jen was carrying her new British FAL with a short padded stock and a four-times scope. Her chest was festooned with magazine pouches and she carried her 9mm USP on a thick thigh holster along with a string of extra grenades.

Toby's giant sized Power Armor was already standing next to her. A pack loaded down with eight-thousand rounds took up what little space was left on his back. A metal covered linkage wrapped around his waist bringing ammo, and power to the Gau 19B affixed to his chest armor. The auto-cannon was stabilized via the articulating arm and another pair of cleats on his boots. On his thigh was a holstered Desert Eagle and a few extra magazines.

Remy was clinging to her MGL grenade launcher as she struggled not to trip again. The only reason she hadn't brought her new flamethrower was the Martian atmosphere. The lack of oxygen would prevent the mixture from igniting, so she'd settled on carrying a hundred or so 40mm grenades. The girl had also found time to attack the drab gray paint job of her armor with a sharpie. Just under the sunken head was a massive leering smile.

Monty had only his civil war rifle, but he carried it easily. Across his left forearm was a satchel for powder, ball, and primers.

"Jen and Tobias on point, just like we trained."

"Remy—"

"I know, I know—keep up," she interrupted gliding forward.

"I was going to ask you to spare us any of your jokes today," he replied.

"Aww, I found a bunch more too." Remy whined. The short armored figure skidded to a halt. Then after a few second asked in a wheedling voice, "Just one?"

"Only if we get to shoot you—if its bad," Monty said following after.

After they had spread out slightly, Charlie moved. He lifted one leg against the gel pads and pushed forward. The servos whined, and the power armor lurched across the rocky ground in a floating glide. His cleated boot barely sank into the soil before his momentum carried the suit forward again. The only tricky part at this point was avoiding the boulders. Charlie took up the rear position in a loose star formation.

"So a priest, a rabbi, and a minister are all sodomizing a little boy when the priest turns to the—"

"Finish that sentence heathen, and I shall send you straight to hell," Tobias growled over the radio.

"Aww, that was the punchline. Have you heard that joke too?" Remy asked innocently.

Everyone groaned, and Tobias began to spin up the auto-cannon, but he didn't turn on the midget. Not yet at least. Around them, other dark gray armored suits skipped across the broken landscape like dark fleas. A few squads were racing each other to be the first inside and were already a half kilometer ahead from the staggered mass of troops.

"I don't believe for a second we managed to land undetected. Slow, and low—just like we did in training. Jumping to your max height will only silhouette you against the horizon." Charlie warned over the comm.

Time passed quickly as they bounded toward the Martian outpost. Charlie settled into the rhythm of kicking forward as his cleated boots sank into the red soil. Two kilometers shy of their goal the first lasers began licking out. Unlike the goofy dinosaurs in training the Roth could shoot, and their weapons were also far more effective in the thin atmosphere. By now Charlie's squad was some distance from the lead elements. A red beam cut across a standing boulder Charlie landed next too, and the rock exploded from the heat.

"Remy, fire smoke grenades at the first line. Everyone else keep a smoke ready." He said bounding forward and joining his squad. They'd paused at the lip of a depression to examine the Roth forces. Two ragged semi-circles had formed short of the massive crater. The glass dome of the alien structure was just visible.

In the low gravity, Remy overshot the first line of defenders, and the smoke immediately thinned so that everything looked like a morning fog. More and more squads emulated them in blanketing the battlefield with smoke.

"We dance with the devil today," Charlie said jogging forward.

"I much prefer filling them with lead," Tobias replied.

"I danced with a demon once, he was quite good." Jen admitted.

"I'll do more than that if he's hung enough." Remy said firing another string of grenades.

In the thinning fog, long limbed shapes began to resolve themselves. Bullets and lasers filled the air as Charlie ran into the first line of defenders. He pulled the smoke from his vest bandoleer, and the pin automatically flew away. He cocked his arm back and hurled the grenade in a herculean throw. The smoke canister sailed several hundred meters and danced wildly through the air as it activated.

"Bound in formation," Charlie called, but Jen was already engaging visible targets. She held the butt of her weapon against her suit's chest and fired at something just to their left. Charlie stopped next to her and pushed the sniper onward.

"Shoot and scoot," he ordered.

Lasers criss-crossed over the Martian landscape all around them, and it was only thanks to the Heads-Up-Display he kept track of his squad in the chaos. Charlie bounded forward over a group of low boulders. A Roth in green armor was laying against the stones with a hand over its wounded stomach. In its loose grip it held a laser carbine absently while it struggled to plug it's leaking suit. Charlie half skidded to a dusty stop and pointed one of his Tommy guns back at the alien. The weapon—in the near vacuum —was unsatisfying to fire. Through the suit's internals, he could barely hear a soft thump, thump, thump as the machine gun spit death into the creature. Thankfully the rounds had just enough extra velocity to punch through the advanced alien armor.

The Roth jerked and raised its laser, but Charlie gave the alien fifteen or so rounds just to make sure it was dead. Strictly more than necessary, but it was better to be safe than sorry. He turned and took a few gliding steps before bounding after the squad. In the dust, and smoke all he could make out was their green icons. He kept one weapon trained ahead and the other on a swivel. He crested a low ditch, and found three more green suited aliens were standing within the trench. His suit was still in air, and he aimed down with both guns and fired. The bullets tore into the group, and catapulted him across the gap to the other side. A single laser cut over the back of his legs, but he ignored the sensation of heat and continued forward. The Roth were everywhere, and stopping wasn't an option.

"We're almost to the crater, and the smoke is thinning," Jen called over the radio. She and Tobias had paused in a low ditch a hundred meters ahead. The Roth had built their dome inside a giant impact crater. Smoke pooled at the base of the hill, and through the thin mist, he could see a final line of defenders at the top. One or two squads had already tried rushing the mound, and armored suits lay along the sandy slope like forgotten action figures.

"Wait one," he said switching to the command frequency. "My squad has reached the crater, but we need help pushing inside."

A female voice replied almost immediately with, "Roger that, Misfit One. Move to waypoint gamma two-two and assault with the gathered forces." A new icon appeared in his vision about two hundred meters to their north.

"Thanks, ummm... command," he replied and switched back to the squad frequency. "Move north two hundred meters. Squads are gathering for a push."

The squad bounced through the thin smoke until a cluster of eighteen armored golems came into view. They had killed a group of Roth and were using the bodies as meat shields. It was a good idea to use the armored corpses, and Charlie was annoyed he hadn't thought of it.

His squad fell in behind the Spartan shields as they started to charge the hill. Roth stood from the ridgeline to shoot down at their moving formation, but for once the thin atmosphere worked in their favor. Usually, a near miss from the heavy cannon was enough to cook a man alive. In the vacuum, a thick red beam cut across the corpse shields. The alien armor melted but the Mark-One's continued to charge. None stopped moving until they'd reached the crest. A laser carbine slashed a long black scar across Charlie's right arm, but he only noticed it by the slight increase in temperature on his skin.

The entire alien structure came into view. The dome was about twelve kilometers in diameter and made of segmented glass sections. The inside looked like a glowing cityscape within a crystal snow globe. Bright orange spotlights surrounded the circular base. On the south side, a long tunnel pierced through the crater hill to a spaceport, and just visible were a number of spacecraft sitting on the tarmac.

Charlie could also see the fighting in its full glory. Along the crater rim, Roth defenders were struggling to fend off the humans attacking from three sides. To the east Chinese forces painted in red poured over the crater edge.

Tobias stopped next to him. A wild grin was visible on his face through the thickly armored visor. "Hell is not such a bad place to visit. There is beauty to be had, but better still, are the scores of demons to slake the angel's wrath upon." He said through the comm.

The tri-barrels were already spinning up as he turned to face the rest of the ridgeline. The aliens aimed at them from either direction, but Tobias stood his ground. Golden fire leaped from the weapon and churned through the nearest Roth squad. He held the trigger down sweeping the rain over the defender's exposed positions. Jen knelt awkwardly and joined Tobias in firing on the flanked Roth.

With the enemy distracted, player squads took the opportunity to take the hill. Pot marked, and scorched armor rushed the Roth from below. Remy's small suit skipped past Charlie, and into the crater with Monty just behind. Down below more and more human armor was bounding toward the dome. Only Charlie and his team had stopped to shoot back, but thanks to them more humans were breaching the final defenses. A laser beam splashed over Charlie's chest armor reminding him that he was a sitting target.

"Get inside. The Roth will be pulling back, so let's not get shot in the ass."

Charlie rode a dust cloud down into the crater bottom as he followed

Monty's trail. An explosion ahead tore open the side of the dome wall, and the alien atmosphere began to pour out. Remy rushed inside with the others. Charlie took up a position next to the hole, while Monty aimed using a cantilevered rear sight and fired at a distant Roth soldier. Yellow blood sprayed across the soil as the ball tore apart the light alien armor. Three more continued forward, and Charlie leveled both Tommy guns at the oncoming soldiers.

"Say 'ello to my little twins," he laughed while unloading on the squad.

Red dust kicked up from his first few misses, but he tracked the next shots onto his targets. Under cover of Charlie's fire, Jen and Tobias bounded past into the breach. Monty poured powder down the barrel, loaded a ball, and primed the lock. Then he raised the weapon and backed through the hole. Charlie followed in last as other players caught up.

# CHAPTER THIRTY-TWO
## *Roth Outpost*

Charlie turned and gaped at the view from ground level. Yellow and ocher skyscrapers rose more than two hundred stories to the dome above. Pathways criss-crossed between the mega-structures in a complicated spiderweb, and long-limbed figures were visible running along them to other parts of the city. All the doors and windows were taller than human standard, which made Charlie feel a little small. What really struck him— among the many sights—were the thousands of Roth statues. They lined the avenue and covered the buildings like vicious gargoyles.

"Prideful and vain creatures—these demons are," Tobias commented dryly.

"I was going to suggest they have a fondness for art, but by god, I think you are correct. Every one of them is posing with a weapon or trophy in hand." Monty said.

"Jen, pick a direction and lead the way," Charlie said dropping the empty drum mag. He slid a fresh one from his ammo pouch, then switched weapons and reloaded the second. As he did, Jen's armored figure moved to the next intersection. Tobias slowly jogged down the street while keeping the barrels of his weapon spinning. Remy and Monty were next, while Charlie walked along behind everyone.

They made it only two blocks into the city before the Roth counter-attacked. Thirty aliens charged them from a side alley. None had combat armor. Instead, they wore drab brown synthetic coveralls and metal grav boots. He hesitated to shoot them because they were a pathetic mob armed with wrenches and alien screwdrivers, but the colonel's warning had been clear enough. The Roth would gladly pull his entrails out and wear them as a necklace. Charlie leveled the twins and fired into the approaching civilians. The bullets slammed into their unarmored bodies and chewed them apart. Half were already dead by the time the rest of his squad turned toward the enemy. The other half ran. It was the first time he'd seen a Roth not charge to his death, so he let them go. There was probably a million Roth in the city, and Charlie didn't have enough bullets for them all. Ten or twelve bodies littered the road, but he turned to check their surroundings. His eyes never stopped as his attention flicked from one building to the next.

"Keep moving," Charlie ordered scanning for threats.

Twice more waves of civilians charged looking for glory, so Charlie took to carrying Elva in his off-hand. The fat .45 acp round was usually enough to put down the unarmored workers. He was edgy and on high alert, so Charlie barely kept from jumping out of his skin as the radio squelched.

"Misfit One, this is Command," A sultry female voice said into his ear.

Charlie took a second to calm his nerves before replying with, "Go ahead."

"There is a squad pinned down near your location. They are requesting assistance, please head to point Delta." She said as a new icon appeared on his radar. A distance marker indicated they were about four blocks away.

"Roger."

He switched back to the squad frequency. "Jen, get moving south. Command says there's a squad that needs help."

The sound of combat was easy to follow. High pitched lasers mixed sporadically with the rattle of heavy weapons fire. Roth soldiers were nearby, and the squad quickly jogged the four blocks to the corner of a bullet-ridden wall. An alien mob converged on the remains of a human squad. Civilians with improvised weapons were pushing toward a cargo transport. A gray armored suit half stepped out of cover and tossed several grenades across the street. They landed among the Roth dregs and exploded turning the air yellow and sending pieces of Roth flying in all directions. From a block down a heavy Roth captain fired his cannon. He indiscriminately cut through a dozen Roth civilians and sliced into the transport. Smaller soldiers moved in during the lull, and began to circle the beleaguered human group.

Charlie motioned for Tobias. The tank waddled around the corner, and aimed down the street. His cannon whirred to life, and a hail of rounds slammed into the giant red armor. The storm quickly tore apart the captain, and Tobias swept his fire over the crowd. The civilians broke, but the Roth soldiers returned fire. Two pulse beams melted long grooves into his armored suit. Jen half knelt next to the building, took aim with her scoped FAL, and sent a bullet into a soldier's faceplate. Three remaining players came out of cover, and together they pinned the Roth between them. Charlie did little more than fire Elva a few times as his squad massacred the rest. Yellow blood ran down the street from the pile of bodies left behind. The other squad waved their thanks, and quickly departed the scene.

"Do you know who that was?" Remy asked.

"No, they're wearing armor," Charlie admitted.

"They all had emblems on their suits. That was Girls, Inc. They turned me down when I started over. I am going to enjoy needling that bitch of a commander."

"Let's get moving before we end up caught by the Roth," Charlie said turning away from the bloodbath.

He quickly became lost in the mega-city as Jen led them deep into the city center. She was almost too good at her job. They switched back and forth down the city streets, so twenty minutes passed before encountering another mob of Roth workers. Charlie didn't bother shooting them. They rarely attacked anymore, and the few that did were knocked out with an armored fist.

"I wish I'd brought the 'Word of God' with me," Tobias lamented with a pang.

Remy picked up a large alien lug wrench and offered it to the crusader. "Your holy weapon, sir," she crowed over the radio. The giant growled and bounded away from her. She shrugged and tucked the metal club into a slot on her grenade belt.

"Roth soldiers ahead," Jen whispered into her radio. She stood at the corner of another ocher mega-scraper.

"Thank god. They must be protecting something."

The group converged, and Charlie glanced around the corner. Two blocks down was a circular structure which immediately made it unique. Six huge coolant tanks sat behind the building. Surrounding the building was a flat plaza, with little more than statues for cover. Four heavy turrets continuously scanned the approach while a dozen Roth squads hunkered behind armored pillboxes.

"By Custer's beard, we may have found their power facility," Monty exclaimed excitedly.

Charlie had no idea how far into the city they'd come, but the heavy security certainly gave it away. To be honest, he had gotten lost quickly in the maze, so he hoped command could figure out where he was.

"Let me call it in," he said and used his chin to activate the command channel.

"Command."

"Go ahead, Misfit One." A sweet and sultry voice acknowledged.

He drew in a breath and reported. "We located the power facility two blocks north of my position." Charlie's statement was greeted with a long silence.

"Thank you, Misfit one. We have alerted all nearby squads to converge on your location. Secure the immediate area, and wait for reinforcements. Command, out."

He flicked back over to the squad channel. "We wait for backup."

"Out here?" Jen asked. They were exposed from both sides on the street, and vulnerable to anyone coming up from behind.

"Get inside the building. We'll use the first floor to stage from."

Remy happily slapped the door control and bounced inside. Small drab Roth scampered away as they entered the building, and Remy gleefully fired grenades into the fleeing crowd. None made it to the elevators, or the exits. Tobias glided in next, and Charlie followed in after. The first floor was a tribute hall to the Roth conquerors. Every surface was like a book written in an alien script, and Charlie hoped it wasn't a catalog of every atrocity committed during the Earth invasion.

The armored schoolgirl skipped to an almost Earth-like elevator and touched the up arrow. While Remy waited, she withdrew a large block of C4 and added a radio detonator to it. The elevator opened to reveal a single thin Roth worker. He clutched a long knife but balked seeing the miniature Power Armor with the leering face.

"Going up?" Remy asked, but the Roth probably didn't hear the question.

"Be a dear and hold this for me," She said thrusting the C-4 into his four-fingered grasp. With one hand she kept the Roth inside while she pushed several buttons on the control panel. The doors closed on the wide-eyed Roth, and it started upward. Alien characters scrolled over the nearby display screen as Remy withdrew the radio detonator and clicked it. High above there was a loud explosion, and the elevator zipped past crashing into one of the subterranean floors.

A few extra troops trickled in first as small squads, then more and more armor piled into the building. Charlie glanced around the corner once again. The Roth had dug in, and heavy beam emplacements scanned all the approaches. Even with all the players, the problem was crossing that plaza. There was no cover so the Roth would fire on them with impunity.

"This is going to be a meat blender."

"Then make some cover, good sir. Do not let them dictate the battlefield. Alexander the Great was fond of constructing ramparts and stone bridges to bypass the enemy defenses." Monty shook his head as he addressed Charlie.

"We aren't crossing a moat," Charlie said with a sigh.

"I dare say we are. The moat is made of concrete, and the water will be our blood should we cross it."

378

"Well, I forgot my mixer back on Earth."

"Sir, we are standing in all the material we need." The Confederate man said patting the wall.

"Can we demolish the building?" Jen asked.

"I watched the alien invasions, to catch up on recent events. Several groups collapsed buildings atop the Roth squads. Most died in the attempt, but the concept is sound." Monty admitted.

*"It might work,"* Charlie thought, and it was undoubtedly better than charging into the grinder.

He turned to the reinforcements. Squads still couldn't talk to each other, so he was forced to press his suit to theirs to conduct a conversation. Thankfully almost every team had brought along some C-4. He acquired nearly twenty pounds of the stuff, and approached the short armored dwarf with his collection.

"I can't believe I'm going to say this—but do your worst," Charlie said holding out the explosives.

"Uhhgggmpf... I might have just creamed myself a little," Remy admitted over the radio. With twitching armored fingers, she took the bundle.

The troops realized what was going on and quickly vacated the building. Remy whistled an out-of-key tune as she attached two groups of explosives to the bottom floor. The first was to weaken the middle supports, then blow out the side facing the power plant. Out in the street, Remy clicked the first detonator, and something inside the building shook. With a flourish, she clicked the second radio detonator, and the supports all along the north side exploded outward, but the building stood.

"Remy..."

"Wait for it, just wait." She interrupted holding up an armored hand.

Slowly the entire thing started to twist. High above several connecting transit paths snapped off and crashed to the street. Like a tree in a forest, it fell in slow motion, but sadly not atop the power plant. That would have been too good to ask. Instead, it crushed a heavy turret and several pillboxes.

"Good job Remy—" Charlie paused catching sight of the small armored figure. Remy was running metal gauntlets over the crotch of her Mark-One Power Armor.

"I am so jilling off to that later." She murmured over comms. Charlie grabbed the back of her suit and shoved the pervert toward the Roth.

"Squad Forward," he yelled as the assembled troops charged.

Almost a hundred players had gathered, and all of them charged the power plant. Charlie bounded forward toward the ruin of the mega-scraper. He stayed low, picking his way through the fallen structure. Everything was covered in a thick cloud of ocher dust, and alien body parts stuck out of the rubble. Lasers from the enemy positions shot overhead, and gunfire erupted all around him. A heavy beam sliced through the wall Charlie was climbing, which collapsed under his weight. It landed atop him, and he was covered in the stone. He struggled for a few seconds to free himself, but the loose rubble closed around him like quicksand.

"I'm stuck." He said over the radio. Two sets of powered hands grabbed his armor and pulled. Monty and Tobias dragged him a few feet.

"Don't dally, friend. The others are getting ahead of us, and they'll have all the fun." Monty said moving into the next room.

Charlie gained his feet and searched for his weapons. Elva was missing, but he found Thelma next to the pit he'd fallen into. He checked her load, then started after the squad. The green dots of other players were already intermixing with the Roth defenders. Remy's icon was lost within the mess, but the others had stayed near him. He climbed the wall, and punched through to the top of the fallen skyscraper. The rest of his squad climbed through after him. They were in the open now, but the full battle came into view. One of the heavy emplacements fired into a group of charging humans, and their armored suits melted like plastic soldiers under the cruel focus of a magnifying glass. However, there was enough going on that he could risk the jump.

"As Tobias once said, let us descend upon our enemies." Charlie quoted. He charged across the roof in a whine of servos, and leaped into the air. In the low gravity, he flew more than twenty meters, and landed next to a red pillbox. Charlie withdrew a grenade from his chest belt and pushed it into the firing slit. There was an explosive thud followed by some interesting screeching sounds. Walking around the side, he pumped .45 ACP rounds into the lightly armored soldiers as they came out the back. Afterward, he tossed one more grenade inside before moving on.

Monty and Tobias landed nearby, while Jennifer remained at the fallen tower. The heavy tank turned toward a cannon emplacement and fired at its side. His .50 caliber bullets punched into the weaker side-armor and something inside exploded. The concrete bunker blew apart in a green fireball, and pieces rained down on the nearby Roth soldiers.

"Good show!" Monty commended sprinting forward. Charlie did his best to keep up while he reloaded his weapon.

"Watch your left, a Roth squad is coming out of the plant," Jen warned over comms. Three lightly armored Roth came around the corner. Monty didn't slow, and lowered his rifle as his suit carried him into them. The long nine-inch bayonet slammed into the leaders chest. It tried to raise its laser, but Monty pulled his trigger first. A hole appeared in the soldiers back as the ball tore completely through, and the alien flopped to the ground as its spine was destroyed.

The other two skidded to a hasty halt in surprise. Charlie leveled his tommy gun at the second soldier and held down the trigger. A dozen bullets stitched it's front armor, knocking it backward, and making a single ragged hole. The last Roth briefly fired at Charlie. A laser skipped over his chest armor severing the bandolier, and set off a smoke grenade.

A bullet missed Charlie's shoulder by inches and slammed into the Roth's head. The helmet shattered, along with the alien's skull. The laser weapon in its hands dropped to the ground, and Charlie looked back to see Jen laying on the fallen mega-scraper. The ex-vampire had come a long way, and she'd developed into a hell of a sniper. He gave the woman a small wave, then turned back to the alien bodies.

"Where's your commander?" He asked. Normally a heavy traveled with in the squad. His question was answered by a massive form coming around the corner. They were scant feet apart as the Roth aimed it's cannon at Monty. There was no way Thelma could hurt that armor, so Charlie dropped his weapon and started forward. A crystal within the Roth's barrel began glowing red as he reached it. Charlie kicked up with his servo-enhanced legs and a blast of red energy sliced through the glass dome above and continued into space. He was blinded by the light, but managed to get his hands on the heavy weapon. To his chagrin, Charlie discovered the captain's armor was much more advanced. The heavy Roth swung his power suit around and slammed him into the wall, but he hung on.

"Little help?" He asked over the radio. Charlie was pulled away from the wall and dragged across the ground. He tried to dig his feet into the concrete as they wrestled for the cannon. Tobias finally came around the corner, and his barrels were still spinning as he leveled the weapon at the captain.

"Let go, Brother."

Charlie did, and skidded across the dusty ground as the Gau-19b tore apart the red suit. That had been too close for his comfort, but he was glad to be alive. Charlie climbed to his feet slowly, then went over to fetch Thelma. Tobias and Monty were both grinning behind their visors.

"What?" he asked.

"Brother, you went hand-to-hand with a greater demon. That is a feat. I had the guidance of God and a good blade."

"Here, here." Monty agreed.

"It felt more like I was being toyed with, but these suits are pretty strong," Charlie admitted with a returning smile. Several players rushed past them into the facility. He followed them with his eyes. Remy's icon was already inside, so he didn't bother messaging her.

"Jen, are you OK there?"

"I'm just cleaning up the remaining Roth. Do you want me to keep over-watch?" She asked.

"Yes, let us know if they send reinforcements."

The plant itself was a series of six power routing stations surrounding a circular building. Roth workers scattered as they entered the central reactor room. Hexagonal objects came down from the ceiling, and blue electricity crackled between the massive capacitors. Everything was covered with a thin layer of frost except the black rubberized floor, and water vapor immediately crystallized on his visor. The containment cylinder sat in the middle of a recessed pool of blue coolant. Three catwalks crossed over the pond to the pulsing iridium plasma reactor.

Without hesitation he fired at it, unloading Thelma on the containment cylinder, but his weapon's rounds barely managed to scrape the ice off.

"Tobias! We need your firepower in here."

"I am sorry. Gadreel ran dry during the push."

Other players tried firing on the reactor with the same results. Frost and sparks flew off, but the reactor was made of something stronger than steel. Charlie was out of C4, and his grenades were gone.

*"This can not be happening,"* he thought. They were so close to completing the mission.

"Did someone call for firepower?" Monty asked coming into the reactor room.

"Yeah, if you could find someone who can dent this bloody thing, that would be great." Charlie groused.

"Am I the only one that can appreciate how special Grace is?" Monty asked with a weary sigh. "Of course, all of you only see an old rifle, and the has-been carrying her."

As Monty spoke, he unlimbered the weapon and fetched the powder horn dumping a load down the barrel. Then he loaded a second and third charge. As he replaced the horn, he said, "All of you have cartridges. Grace may have her limitations, but she is the only weapon in the game that can vary her projectile velocity. Unlike her real-world equivalents, Grace is made of the finest of steel."

He dragged a patch and Minnie-ball from his forearm satchel and sank the bullet home. Crossing the catwalk, he withdrew a percussion cap with practiced dexterity. He cocked the hammer, replaced the firing cap, and pressed the barrel to the reactor's scratched faceplate. It was like a cannon going off, and in the low gravity, Monty was thrown all the way across the coolant pond.

A .58 caliber hole had drilled straight through the hardened titanium containment shield. Iridium plasma sprayed out both sides and the reactor started shaking. An eerie high pitched alarm sounded signaling the beginning of Ragnarok. Red and orange warning lights appeared around the room, as the hexagons above retracted into the ceiling, but the reactor only pulsed faster. The temperature in the room spiked a hundred degrees, and ice quickly turned to water. Charlie and the others hastily bounded from the chamber. Behind them, something made a loud cracking sound, but no one dared look back.

Part of the titanium wall melted, and glowing green iridium fuel spilled into the coolant. It exploded upward against the ceiling shorting out the surge protectors. A storm of unchecked power blew all six switching stations. Every light, every console, and every turret connected to the power grid within five blocks exploded. The entire alien dome went dark, save a few dim service lights. For a second Charlie couldn't see anything until his HUD switched over to a neon green night-vision mode.

"Misfit One, this is Command, all objectives have been met. Retreat to the dropship rendezvous. I repeat, make haste to the dropships. It's time to come home." The radio message was followed by a mission point popping up on Charlie's HUD.

"Command says we did it. Someone else must have taken out another objective before us. We are out of this shit-hole. Get back to the dropship." Charlie ordered excitedly.

"I am going to take a very long shower in game... and out, after this," Jen grumbled jogging forward through the darkness.

"I'll join," Remy suggested.

"No."

"Think about it. We could be the first girls to do it, on Mars. Now that's an achievement."

"Absolutely not."

"Anyone else?" Remy asked hopefully.

384

Charlie cut over the conversation before it went even more south. "Focus, and keep formation. Just because it's dark doesn't mean there isn't Roth out there. Tobias switch places with Montgomery since your dry." Charlie ordered skipping down the street. He kept his weapon swiveling in case of attack, but his worries were unfounded as they passed through the breached dome wall and out of the crater.

They made good time skating over the Martian surface. In less than an hour the armored beetle-like dropship came into view. The crew hadn't been idle. Surrounding the loading bay was tons of discarded equipment. Deck plating and ship consoles made a loose pile to one side. Hundreds of armored suits lay open in the dusty red soil. A yellow Mark-One Suit came down the ramp carrying another. He dropped the blackened armor to the ground and turned in their direction.

"Go up to the cloning bay and exit your suit, we are dumping everything not nailed down to make it back." The technician said over the radio. Well, that explained the junkyard of parts. Charlie stomped up the deck and got into line as they filed into the airlock. It opened, and he joined the others in the large room. Naked men and women were climbing out of battle-scarred armor.

It took him a second to remember how to exit the suit. "Get me out of this metal coffin," he called, and there was a hiss of escaping air. Cold air licked across his backside, and he pulled himself from the clammy confines. Dozens of black marks covered his armor, and Charlie was surprised by the damage. Each time the airlock opened a metallic smell like dirty pennies flooded the room.

More technicians were waiting to take the armor away. As soon as Charlie was free they pointed to an unused pod and said, "Enter a cloning pod so you can be re-imprinted."

Charlie waited for his squad to enter the pods first, then followed. As the door snapped shut, darkness closed over him, and words floated in the void.

[Event Complete]

# CHAPTER THIRTY-THREE

## *Return Home*

"I want to congratulate all of you. A full debriefing will soon happen, but you've done it. The alien base has been destroyed, and Earth is momentarily safe," Colonel William Blake announced over the intercom. After a few seconds, there was a loud static filled squelch as the channel disconnected. Charlie glanced around the command deck. The engineers had really stripped the ship bare. Alien tubing, ductwork, and exposed cables hung from the ceiling. All the bridge consoles were missing. In their stead was a closed laptop with wires running into the floor.

The trip from Mars had taken almost twenty hours, and Charlie had spent most of that time on the command deck staring at the stars. If this was the last event involving the Roth, it would be his final time in space. Jen and Tobias were both offline getting dinner, and Remy had started a twelve-hour space orgy in one of the storage rooms. He however, wasn't going to waste this opportunity. The dropship was silent except the low thrum of the reactor, and they drifted through space on sheer inertia. Dozens of players pressed against the glass windows for a better view. The small blue gemstone that was Earth hung on the left side of the ship, and for the last hour, it hadn't gotten any larger.

Monty stroked a hand over his short dark beard. "I wonder if they'll send a rocket after us," he mused.

"Probably not enough fuel to land," a girl nearby agreed.

Slowly the Earth disappeared as the ship turned. Sliding across the right window was a half-shadowed moon, and soon the ship's nose was pointed directly at a darkened spot near the north pole. The blasted and cratered face perceptively grew.

"Ahh, now things have become clearer, but that still begs the question. Why are we approaching the moon?" Monty asked in a bemused voice.

Charlie had no answer for that, and no one else ventured to guess. Without Power Armor, they'd still be stuck on the ship waiting for rescue.

The stark landscape quickly filled the bridge windows. Four of the six engines ignited with a low rumble and began to throttle up. The ship slowed but not fast enough for Charlie's peace of mind. The brilliant lunar surface raced to meet them, and just when he thought they'd slam into it, a small crater appeared underneath them. The bottom of which opened in two giant halves revealing a deep shaft. The dropship continued to slow as it descended past two more vertical airlocks. Gray concrete filled the viewport as spotlights illuminated a massive underground cavern blasted from the moon rock. Blinking red strobes directed them down a runway, and the thrusters quieted to a trickle as the dropship moved forward. The vessel turned again before landing roughly on a marked rectangular square. Several more dropships touched down nearby.

"By my whiskers, I hadn't expected this," Monty marveled.

The colossal airlocks closed one at a time, and the flashing strobes turned from red to yellow. Tanks along one wall began spewing oxygen into the space, and after a minute, the lights switched to a dark green. A much smaller circular hatch opened and workers bunny-hopped toward them in the low gravity.

On the bridge, and across the ship, intercoms came to life, "Please exit the ship and head into the base. The commander is eager to speak to you all."

Gravity was back, if only scarcely, as he joined the crowd heading below. They floated down the stairs using the rails as a guide. Half naked players stumbled from the first storage room. Philip came out of the doorway shirtless and carrying a limp girl in his arms. Remy was dressed sloppily in a school uniform. One of her black shoes was missing, and her feet dangled in the air.

"How was it?" Charlie asked.

Remy smiled letting her head roll back against the chest of the large ebony weapon. "The orgy was amazing, but the zero-gee not so much," Remy sighed pleasantly. "Turns out you can't really pound a girl good and hard without gravity." She shrugged her shoulders and shifted in the man's arms.

Philip finally let her go, and she drifted to the deck. Her teal colored hair was a mess, and Remy tried to gather it into a single ponytail. Just as she finished Tobias and Jen came out of the last storage room holding hands.

"I did not see that coming!" Remy shouted pointing at the pair. It was a surprise to Charlie too, but he quickly gathered himself.

"How was your dinner?" He asked them. Jen snatched her hand away and slipped ahead into the cloning chamber. Tobias was left looking after her, and Remy laughed at their antics. Charlie wished the big lug the best because, in his opinion, Jennifer was a girl with baggage.

"We just logged in at the same time," Tobias muttered joining the crowd.

"Mmmmhmmm," Charlie mused.

Remy laughed again and asked, "It's more likely you logged in at the same time—in a locked and private room—then fucked like space bunnies. That sounds far more plausible."

Tobias said nothing as he turned to join them. The girl bounced along with one missing shoe, but that didn't stop her from leering at the giant.

"This is why I say just screw and be happy about it. Why does everyone make sex into a huge event?" Remy asked.

The airlocks were opened, and everyone passed into the lower loading bay and down the ramp. The air smelled like burning wires with a touch of ozone, and Remy sneezed. The hanger was constructed of reinforced cement. Warning lines circled the landing pad and led towards an exit. Another airlock opened, and several pallet loaders drove into the hanger with repair equipment. The other dropships disgorged players in a disorganized mass, and they shuffled into the base. The bleak circular hallway was made of yet more gray concrete, but at least it was brightly lit. A thick black and yellow line had been laid on the ground and led deeper inside. The crowd was guided mostly by locked doors, and inaccessible corridors, so the only way forward was to follow the dashed line. Eventually, they came to a major intersection. Young and very young teens picketed the side branches off with linked arms. Most were between the ages of ten and fifteen years old. Charlie wondered what role these children played in all this, aside from ferrying the players toward their destination.

They came to another portal, and above it was the word, "Astronomy." Inside was a circular room about two hundred meters across, and hanging high above were several laser emitters. The hologram of a solar system floated in the darkness with the Sun at its center. Charlie's squad filed into the room with five thousand other players, and were forced to walk around the podium to find a place to see from. The old man was already standing on the raised dais, and he looked even worse than usual. There were another ten wrinkles on his face, and his hair was completely white, but his back was still straight. Blake was deep in conversation with a much younger girl. He took the datapad from the teen and quickly scanned the report.

"We have all the building supplies we need. Tell them water, and food is infinitely more important than cement. Refuel the dropships and send them back to Earth. We need supplies as soon as possible." He said handing the pad back. The young girl clutched the tablet to her chest, ran down the platform stairs, and through the crowd of people. Several turned watching her bounce away in the skintight gray uniform.

"I'd appreciate it if you didn't eyeball my granddaughter." The Colonel rasped giving the players a long glare. They quickly straightened facing forward. The old man put his hands behind his back and started walking in a slow circle on the platform. Earth was spinning slowly just to his left-hand side, but the moon had been replaced with a pulsing blue icon. Charlie looked for Mars and found it much farther away than he'd expected. The red ball was about a quarter the way around the sun, which meant they'd traveled a hell of a long way in just eighteen hours.

Colonel Blake pressed a finger to a nearby screen, and for a few seconds, silence manifestly reigned. He tapped it again and raised his voice so it would reach everyone.

"Revenge is best served cold, and in this case a very cold, very dark, near vacuum. The outcome I'd secretly prayed for has come to pass, and it warms my old heart."

"I will spare you the unsightly video we are still receiving from the power-suits on Mars. The Roth continue to respawn over and over. There are so many bodies in the cloning bay it might as well be a mass grave. Unfortunately, a few small ships managed to take off from the spaceport, and are headed out of the system. They are going to warn the Roth about the loss, but we can't do anything about that." He complained with some annoyance. The old man glanced off to one side at two tiny red dots just visible at the edge of the system.

"No, no... let's hand out goodies first before I get too deep into things. You're all here to get paid for your hard work, so I'm going to give you a hard choice between two rewards."

"The first is a special contract slot. You can visit the 'Armory' and create a new weapon. You'll be able to decide what gun they are, what they look like, and what underlying personality they are born with."

Almost immediately murmurs started throughout the crowd. He continued before the noise grew too loud. "If that sounds like your game, then jump aboard one of the departing dropships. You'll be given a quick ride home." Blake said pointing toward the door. A large crowd of people left. The gift of making a unique weapon was just too alluring a prize.

"To everyone staying, there is a nasty caveat. Choosing option two means being temporarily barred from logging into Gun Meister." Blake warned in a deadpan voice. The crowd noise surged, and over a thousand more departed. They weren't even interested in hearing the rest. The old man waited again until they had cleared the observatory room, and less than half of the players remained.

"The second option will be more work," he said with a small toothy smile. The old man laughed seeing the expression crossing their faces.

"We at SkyBot Studios would like to invite you to take part in the closed beta of our new game." He declared pausing for dramatic effect.

"Star Nova Online."

Several people started to whisper nearby, "A new game?"

"Holy shit, I heard they were working on something."

"You'll have to sign an NDA, and I'm afraid that's the reason why we can't let you log into Gun Meister. I understand your hesitation, and I can sympathize with the loss of your time invested in the game. In return, you'll bring one weapon into the Beta. Whoever you choose will have their memories uploaded to a 'human' clone. I must warn you, again, that weapons in Star Nova are just that—weapons. They don't bounce, or jiggle, or fuck you. They go boom, that's it.

"Uncontracted weapons in Gun Meister will have the option to transfer into Star Nova after the release. In Star Nova they are considered citizens and no longer beholden to you as a Meister. You can and may lose their loyalty. How you act or speak will affect that. We at SkyBot Studios want to be fair to everyone, but you have worked hard. When you create a character in Star Nova, you'll start with weapons, the armor you currently possess, along with a custom space suit." Most of the crowd glanced to one another with wary expressions. Remy especially was looking sour faced.

While the players talked, the map of the solar system moved. It zoomed in on a pulsing red icon approaching Jupiter. A small vector line appeared, and the Colonel spoke again. "The Roth just lost their outpost on Mars. The carrier is making a U-turn, and will be back in orbit in about seven days. You have the opportunity to make history, and the chance to defend Earth from another Roth attack. How successful you are will decide humanity's starting point in Star Nova. On Halloween, your weapons already took one step in that direction. Everything saved was another resource we begin with."

"Those are the choices. Go back to Earth and enjoy the fruits of your labor, or join us in Star Nova. Any questions?" He asked.

"Do we get to keep our creds?"

"During the beta, yes. You'll be able to buy upgrades for your ship. However, the other playable races have different economies, so everything will be reset after release. Gun Meister and Star Nova will also have divergent worlds." He said pointing to another person in the crowd.

"How long will the beta last?"

"Closed beta will end in seven days. The public beta will last until New Years, so roughly two months. Then we'll reset, and everyone will start fresh. Sorry, you will lose your harem by then, but after the beta, nothing prevents you from having accounts in both games."

There was a long silence.

"It's a tough decision, so I'll give you twenty-four hours to decide. Anyone who hasn't signed up for the beta by this time tomorrow will respawn on Earth." Blake said turning slowly to gauge the crowd. It was a hell of a conundrum and he gave them almost a minute.

"I hate to be inconsiderate, but I have a lot of work ahead of me. The Roth Carrier will be here in seven days, and there is much left to do. Before I go, I just want to say, thank you. You've done humanity proud." He said climbing from the platform stairs. The crowd parted for him, and he disappeared down the corridor. Charlie and the Misfits were left standing in nearly total silence, but it was Remy that broke the spell.

"Pfft, I worked my tail off to get Missy back," Remy grumbled.

"Sinner, you're just worried they will abandon you." Tobias scoffed turning towards the girl.

"I always wanted to go to space," Charlie admitted. He felt bad saying it because they had all worked hard to rank up. He'd just gotten the Twins, and despite everything hadn't used Sofie much in battle. That was shameful of him, but he'd see the girls again if they transferred into Star Nova.

"I must agree, as an amateur astronomer, the allure of space exploration is appealing," Monty said.

"You've only got one weapon. The rest of us have enough contract slots to count as a platinum Meisters', and when we do rank up, that'll be even more pussy." Remy argued in a disgusted voice.

"Jen?" Charlie asked.

"I don't know," she admitted.

"Tobias?"

"I'll go where Jennifer does."

"One lay, and he's already pussy-whipped," Remy whispered from the corner of her mouth. Charlie thumped the girl atop her head. "What?! It's true..."

Charlie knew he would sign-up for the beta just for the chance to get in on the ground floor of a new game. They'd learn the game mechanics before anyone else. He would miss the girls; damn, would he miss them. But...

"I'm going," he announced.

"I'll venture into space with you, friend," Monty agreed stepping next to him.

"Remy?"

"You guys are stupid. I mean come on. How much sex can you get in real life? Never as much as Gun Meister, that's for sure."

"But, you'll come," Charlie said with a knowing smile.

"Why am I friends with you?" She groused.

"Cause we put up with your bullshit."

"Screw you!" She swore storming away. The small girl shoved her way through the crowd toward the exit.

"See you in Star Nova," Charlie called after her. She didn't look back but raised a finger as she stomped down the hall. He turned to Jennifer next. If Tobias was already hip-locked to the sniper, Charlie only needed to convince her.

"I paid for a three-month subscription. It'll be over by New Years, so that'd be a waste." She dithered chewing her lip.

"Oh no, what a waste of money. You'll lose your harem too, and good men are so hard to come by." Charlie teased, and glanced toward the towering giant, who was suspiciously not looking at Jennifer.

"You're such an ass," she pushed him away.

"Monty and I are going. The blue pervert will probably leave too, not that it affects anything. Do what you want Jen." Charlie said giving the woman space.

"If I may be so bold, young lady. Gun Meister is not entirely your game. Call it a gut feeling, but you'll grow sick of it soon enough." Monty ventured coming to his aid.

Charlie never could put a finger on Jennifer, which was why they'd never hit it off. She was a strange mix of sexual innocence and bloodthirsty monster. The woman looked at them both, then up at the ceiling and sighed.

"Fine, I'll go."

"Great! We best go talk to the weapons, and decide which one to bring with us." Charlie said and started down the hallway.

"I will take Gadreel to the heavens," Tobias stated. Of course, the big guy would.

"For me, the deciding factor was being able to bring Grace into Star Nova," Monty said keeping step with Charlie.

"Can't fault you for that," Charlie added.

They moved down the corridor until locating the yellow and black line. Then Charlie just had to follow it to the hanger. Crews were crawling over the six dropships getting them refueled and ready for flight. He stopped a teenage kid racing past him.

"When are they leaving?"

"Twenty minutes, sir."

"Thanks," he said letting go.

Charlie boarded the first dropship and found the girls waiting in a storage room. He paused in the doorway watching them. The twins climbed over the walls using the tie-down rings. Fara and Elva were quietly making plans in the corner while Sofie dozed on a bunk. For a few seconds, he changed his mind. Charlie would return to Earth, and go back to screwing them daily. Remy was right. He'd paid for his harem with too much blood and sweat. Then the moment was gone. Monty pushed into the room after him and went over to Grace.

"Love, I have news."

"My heart is aflutter," Grace said rising to her feet.

"We are going to space."

"I hate to point out the obvious, darling, but we already accomplished that feat."

Montgomery laughed and wrapped an arm around the woman's supple waist. He turned her around in a circle then gestured toward the ceiling. "I meant permanently in space," he chortled in a theatrical voice.

"You're selling the manor? Say it ain't so." Grace gasped.

"We are upgrading, and looking to the stars." Monty agreed.

Charlie looked at the girls. All of them had stopped after hearing the conversation. He pulled his determination up by the boxers and walked toward them. "It's true; unfortunately we can only take one person with us into beta." He said, stopping before the group.

"What about the others?" The twins asked.

"You'll be able to transfer into Star Nova at the beginning of the year, but we're being barred from logging into Gun Meister for the next two months." He said looking at them.

The twins grabbed each of Charlie's arms and clung to him. Amethyst eyes searched his face expectantly. Elva and Fara both straightened while Sofie came out of sleep mode. Her red hair was a bouncing mass as she floated toward Charlie, and long muscled arms wrapped around his neck. He smiled up between her heaving cleavage. Each had grown special to him in their own way, but he had to make a decision.

"I'm taking Elva with me," he said extracting himself from Sofie's grasp. He turned and saw Elva was hugging her batch sister. Charlie approached

Fara first because he felt he owed her the most.

"I know—you don't have to say it. I'm a broken girl." She said, and he cupped her face.

"That was a mistake, and I wouldn't change anything about you. Well, except the biting." Charlie said with a chagrined smile. Fara made a soft sound and he flicked her nose.

"You'll join me in Star Nova?" He asked.

"I make no promises," she said with waterlogged eyes. Her black makeup smeared as she furiously wiped them away, then smiled more naturally.

"That's the Fara I know, and love." He said lowering his hands to the black collar at her throat. She lifted her head proudly, even though her eyes streamed liquid. Charlie pulled yanking the collar, and it broke apart. Fara gasped and fell to the decking as a glow encapsulated her. Gun mods appeared in the air and shattered in a shower of crystal glitter. For a second the teen was naked in the light, then she was wearing a black bikini.

"You vill not escape me so easily," Sofie said, grabbing him from behind. Charlie laughed and turned in her embrace.

"I look forward to seeing you, but I hope you'll join Star Nova for more than just me. Space is amazing, and it's something I've secretly yearned for." He said hugging her around the hips.

"I vaited so long, and just when I find a special man, he leaves. Such is my life." She said in a husky sob. Charlie reached up touching her face, and wiping the tear away from her cheek. Before his resolve failed him, he tore the collar from her neck. Her steel colored eyes closed as she released him, and fell back. There was a quick flash, and she was reset to factory default.

Charlie turned to Thelma and Luise last, who were clutching each other in panic and staring at him. Lips trembled as they pleaded with their eyes. "You two are unique, and I would never dream of breaking you up." He said.

"We really liked you, Charlie."

"Will you join?" He asked and the two looked to one another. They shared a conversation without speaking.

"We might," they replied suggestively.

"I'm going to miss all of you." He said taking one of their collars in each of his hands.

"Ready?" he asked. They whimpered but nodded in unison. Charlie pulled yanking the collars free and stepped back. As he did Elva took his arm.

"Stay aboard the ship. It'll be headed back to earth." Charlie said and wrapped an arm around Elva's waist.

That was a lot harder than he wanted to admit. The girls had quickly grown on him like family, and he sympathized with Elva. The weapon clung to him for support as she wept. She was losing her friends and being dragged into a strange new world, but Elva followed him as he turned away from the uncontracted girls. Tobias and Monty had already collected their weapons and left the dropship. That just left him and Jen in the room. She was on the other side of the compartment locked in a dilemma of her own. He approached interested in what was taking the woman so long.

"What's going on?" He asked.

"I can't decide who to bring," she admitted.

"Ahh, well..." He considered the four handsome men surrounding her. That must have been nice. It wasn't often a woman got to experience a reverse harem, and she even dressed them up as butlers to serve her. In a way, all of them were identical except for hair color and facial features.

"How about this, you take them into one of the extra rooms and have a blast fucking them. Whoever lasts longest comes with you into Star Nova."

"That's awful," Jen gasped.

Charlie shrugged and said, "It's fair, and it gives them something to remember you by."

The four men quickly exchanged looks and said, "We agree to this."

"I am not going to—" Jennifer was interrupted by the weapons taking each of her arms and legs. "Hey, let me go!" She insisted, but they carried her from the room and off the dropship. Charlie followed with a sly smile, as Jen continued to struggle in vain. She looked genuinely annoyed, but couldn't stop the hot flush from her face.

"Consider it a final hoorah!" Charlie called as they dragged her into an empty room.

"I'll get you for this," Jen said as the door slid closed.

"Shall we?" He asked holding out an elbow. Elva smiled slipping a hand into it, and they headed down the hallway. He randomly picked a direction until they came to a green line. The first room was open, and he poked his head inside.

"Excuse me?" He asked seeing a very young girl laying in bed. She had a tablet in hand and was reading, but as he spoke, she sat up blushing. The girl had brown auburn hair, and flannel pajamas on.

"Sir, I'm sorry... I umm."

"What are you doing up here on the Moon?"

"This is the Lunar Naval Academy, and I'm studying to join the Space Defense Force." She said coming to attention in her nightwear. The girl was maybe twelve or thirteen, and Charlie felt a little strange seeing someone so young talk about joining the military.

"I'm looking to sign up for the Beta."

"You can access the admission page from any console," She said. The girl scanned Charlie's face blushing like any teenager, then tried vainly to push her hair into order. Simultaneously she hid behind the tablet in her hands. "You can use mine if you wish." She said pointing to a desk in the corner. Elva stood behind him with a sympathetic smile.

"I'm not intruding?" He asked.

"No—no sir." She stammered taking her tablet and rushing from the room. The girl sprinted down the corridor in her PJ's and vanished into another open door. A high pitched squeal and girlish laughter followed her entry. Damn, the developers did excellent work. That girl had acted precisely like a flustered teenager, and it made him nostalgic. To be that young again...

Charlie entered the room and sat down at the desk. He put a palm on the screen, and it flashed to life with his statistics. Immediately he noticed the number of kills. Wow, the civilian Roth had been like wheat before his scythe, and every one of them had given him another thousand credits in his account.

---

**Player ID - NA1339872**
**Registered Competition Name - Charlie**
**Clan - Misfits**
**Hours played - 332**

**Wins - 56**
**Losses - 20**

**Kills - 188**
**Deaths - 30**
**K/D Ratio - 6.2**

**Battle Rank - Gold Master**
**Player Score - 1984**

**Credits - 260,482c**

"This account has been assigned to join the Star Nova Online_09A3 Closed Beta. Please fill out the following forms, and sign the attached Non-Disclosure-Agreement." It said after a few seconds.

Charlie spent about ten minutes inputting his personal information, including his dive helmet model number. It even asked him if he was claustrophobic, or agoraphobic.

*"Well, I managed to climb into your Power Armor,"* he thought to himself and selected 'No' to both.

"Please select the weapon you'd like converted to Star Nova," it asked next. Charlie had already sent the others home, and the only option was Elva. Afterward, he was forced to read through a rather lengthy NDA and sign it.

"You will receive a download link in your email shortly. Welcome to the fight." The screen said at last. He closed the console and turned around. Elva was sitting on the bed kicking her heels and toying with some of the knick-knacks on the shelf.

"That's it," Charlie said pushing from the desk.

"I'm going to log off and download the Star Nova Client. I'll see you on the other side?" He asked, and she rolled over on the bed.

"Thank you for picking me. I'll miss everyone, but I want to be with you."

"You were always the first and only choice," Charlie admitted.

Elva bit her lip before saying, "I'm excited and nervous."

"I hope everything works," he said joining her on the bed. Charlie reached up and touched his temple with two fingers. Whoever owned this room would just have to live with his body occupying her bed for a while.

"Charlie?" Elva asked eyeing him with her baby blues. He paused with his finger over the logout button.

"Would you like one last, hoorah?" Elva asked reaching down and thumbed the top button of her shirt. Her red bra became visible, and she pushed her chest out seductively. There were seven days before the Roth arrived, and twenty-four hours before the Beta deadline. He technically had time to burn. Charlie closed the system menu, went over to the door, and locked it. By the time he turned around Elva was already naked and waiting.

The End.

Made in the USA
San Bernardino, CA
05 April 2018